I0685091

The Mostest Man

Danielle and Friends
Book One

Written by: Nick J. Mercorella

Creative Consultant: Deb Rhodes
Cover by: Gabrielle Mercorella
Author Photo Credit: Eileen Escarda
Editor: Bridget Hutchinson

ISBN: 978-0692492727
0692492720

Acknowledgments

First, I must thank my sister, Vicky, who was the very first person to read my story and never hesitates to give me her opinion.

Then there is Kathleen Alvarez and Pam Jorgensen. These two ladies are the only ones interested enough to read every draft and encourage me to continue.

Trish Nehren, who reminded me that GRITS had more than one meaning and southern ladies, had a style all their own.

Eric Zygela, who took time out from his busy schedule while traveling around the country with Ringling Brothers Circus to read and comment on my work.

Eileen Escarda, my photographer, who was kind enough to spend an entire weekend morning trying to make me look good.

And, finally, Deb Rhodes, my editor and creative consultant. I will never be able to thank Deb for her input into this work. Her insight and advice turned my bland story into a readable novel. I sometimes feel this is as much her work as mine.

Thanks to all and thanks to those of you who have taken the time to read this book.

To my Texas Annie

I miss you every day

Table of Contents

The Mostest Man

Chapter 1 – First Encounter

"I still don't understand your silly rule about inter-office relationships. We work in different departments. A relationship between us wouldn't affect us at work."

It was the same old argument Andrew had used many times before. I had developed the no office relationship rule when I started my first real job, after college. When I moved over to Strollman, I broke my rule.

Not the best decision I ever *made.*

Jack Reynolds was a salesman at Strollman Bros., and he was the most gorgeous man I had ever seen. On a scale of one to ten, I'd give Jack a twelve. Handsome, polished, classy, sophisticated. Every woman's dream man. Every girl in the office was crazy about him, and he chose me. When he asked me out, I was thrilled. When he asked me to move in with him, I jumped at the chance.

When I finally found out the truth about him, I was devastated. Jack's infidelity left me broken. If it wasn't for my friend Dan Patrick, I don't know where I'd be today.

After that episode, I reinstated my rule about no relationships with someone I worked with. But, in this case, it was more than that. Andrew was a sweet guy, and I always had fun when we dated, but a romantic or intimate relationship with him wasn't going to happen. I just wasn't into him that way. An occasional dinner and a movie were all I would agree to, except when we had one of those charity or corporate banquets to attend. Sometimes he'd be my escort.

It was time to end this particular conversation.

"Andrew, if we don't get going, we'll miss the show."

Andrew knew the argument was over. He frowned and called for the check. There was no parking valet at this particular restaurant, so we had to walk to Andrew's car. In the parking lot, we came upon a confrontation. Four men and a woman were between us and Andrew's car, and they were having a very heated argument. One of the men was screaming at the woman, and another man was holding the man who seemed to be the woman's date. A third man punched the woman's date in the stomach. The woman screamed.

I was stunned, and it seemed so was Andrew. Before either of us could react, I heard a man's voice from behind us.

"Get to the car and lock the doors. If I go down, drive away."

Before I had a chance to turn and see who the voice was connected to, he was passed us and headed for the confrontation. The woman who was with him hurried away.

The stranger walked up to the group and spoke very quietly. Too quietly for me to hear what he was saying. The big man who had been yelling at the woman told him to mind his own business. That was loud enough for everyone to hear.

Again the stranger said something quietly.

Suddenly the big man took a swing at the stranger. After that, everything happened so fast, I wasn't sure if I had seen it correctly.

The stranger ducked under the punch, came up with his right arm across the man's chest, and the man went over backward. He landed on his back with a thud.

The third man, the one who had punched the woman's date, was behind the stranger, and he slid his arms under the stranger's and clasped his fingers behind the stranger's neck. The stranger's arms were pointed straight up in the air.

The man who was holding the woman's date let him go and came over. He was ready to hit the stranger, just as his friend had done to the woman's date. Before he could take a swing, the stranger grabbed the hair of the man who was holding him. He lifted both feet off the ground and brought them down hard. But he didn't land on his feet. He folded his legs and went down to his knees.

Still being held by a hand full of hair, the guy holding the stranger had no choice but to roll over the stranger's back, right into the third man. Both men went down to the ground.

Before the three attackers had a chance to regain their footing, the stranger pushed the couple between two parked cars and stood in front of them. He shed his jacket and took off his tie.

It became apparent very quickly that the stranger knew precisely what he was doing. The three men came at him, and without throwing a punch, he put them on the ground again with a series of twisting, bending and turning motions. All almost too fast to see.

You would think that the three men knew they were outmatched, but they got up and came at the stranger again. This time, he shook his head as if he was sorry for what was going to happen.

One at a time, the stranger had each man bent over the hood of a car, and he punched each of them in the kidney. The big guy, the one who had been screaming at the woman, was tougher, and the stranger had to slam his face onto the hood of the car before he kidney punched him.

That ended the fight just as a Broward County Sheriff's car rolled onto the scene. Three more sheriff's cars arrived in short order, and the five men and one woman were placed in the back of the vehicles.

Before the three attackers were put in the Sheriff's cars, they paramedics looked them over. They were still doubled over from the punch in the kidney. The three of them had abrasions and bruises from their unexpected and quick meeting with the hard ground, and the big guy had a big bruise on the side of his face where it hit the hood of the car, but other than the kidney punch, the stranger hadn't hit them. The stranger, although flushed, didn't seem to have a mark on him. All the paramedics did for him was give him a bottle of water.

"Let's get out of here," Andrew whispered.

But before he could lead me away, a Deputy asked us for statements. Andrew didn't want to get involved, but I told the officer everything I saw. We both gave him our cell phone and work numbers, and we were allowed to leave.

I had lost my desire to see a show, so I asked Andrew to take me home.

I usually permitted Andrew to kiss me goodnight after our dates, but I never responded. He always held me close and tried to get me involved, but he just didn't do it for me. Tonight he seemed to be unusually amorous.

"Seems like that fight has gotten you all pumped up."

Andrew was surprised by my statement.

"It's a shame your testosterone didn't kick in earlier when that man could have used some help."

"It didn't seem he needed any."

"True, but you didn't know that until it was all over."

That was enough for Andrew. He got the hint and said goodnight. Since we had skipped the show, it was only nine o'clock when Andrew left. There was nothing on television that interested me, so I called Dan.

"Hi, Beautiful! What's up."

"Nothing important, Dan. I had dinner with Andrew tonight, and we had the same argument about relationships."

"Even if you didn't work together, Danielle, he's not the man for you. I'd put him closer to Jack's category."

That reminded me of my one experience with love and how devastated I was when it was over. It all started with Dan's suggestion.

"Danielle, there's no chance for you to advance here. The job Strollman has open is just a stepping stone for you. You'll be able to move up there."

I took Dan's advice and made the move.

I had met Dan on my first job out of college. We liked each other, but my rule about inter-office relationships was important to me, so we became friends. Very good friends.

Once I made the move to Strollman, Dan and I weren't working together any longer, and I considered a possible relationship with him, but it didn't happen. The reason it didn't happen was because I met Jack. When I left Jack, it was Dan who got me through the pain. I moved out of Jack's apartment and moved in with Dan. That brought significant changes in my life, and it was Dan who saw me through them. That's when I realized the real value of a true friend. Dan was the foundation I built the rest of my life on.

There was definitely an attraction between us, but I was hurt and vulnerable at the time, and Dan refused to take advantage of the situation. The time with Dan changed me. After living as Dan's roommate for six months, I was no longer a naive South Georgia country girl. With Dan's support and encouragement, I became more aware of myself. I developed faith in myself and my abilities. Never again would I look to a man to determine my worth as I had done with Jack. Thanks to Dan, I realized I was a strong and capable woman, and I would make my own way.

Any man in my future would be a compliment to my life, not the reason for it.

Dan also helped me find a job with Deltron Motors where my career took off.

"How come you're home so early?"

I told Dan about what happened in the restaurant parking lot.

"Now, that's the kind of man you need in your life."

"You're that kind of man, Dan."

"Thanks, beautiful. I appreciate the thought, but we already tried that. I'd rather have you as a lifelong best friend than lose you as an ex-lover."

I knew he was right. After I got over Jack, Dan and I did try for something more, but we both realized we were too intimately connected to make a go of it. Dan was more like an older brother, who watched out for me. We talked for a while, and I got ready for bed. I couldn't get the scene in the parking lot out of my head.

Chivalry is not dead. It seems there are still Knights in Shining Armor roaming the earth.

I couldn't possibly know at the time I would meet this same stranger again, and how he would have a tremendous impact on my life. It started with a simple thing, a silly idea I had after watching a program on television about natural gas.

"Why couldn't we use natural gas for trucks instead of diesel fuel?" I asked innocently.

After the laughter had died down, Gene, our Chief Engineer explained.

"Liquid natural gas doesn't have the power to pull a fully loaded truck, and also the large amount of liquid natural gas, a truck would have to carry on the highway would be dangerous. It's okay for local buses, but not long-haul trucks."

"Couldn't we mix diesel and LNG together? Wouldn't that cut down the pollution and still give the vehicle enough power."

"Anything is possible, Danielle, but it would take a computer to continuously adjust the mixture. With this fuel injector upgrade, I'm working on, I don't have the time to look into it."

I thought that was the end of my silly idea. But, when the Marketing Department canceled the fuel injector upgrade, Gene found himself with a lot of free time. Two months later, he walked into my office and dropped a rectangular, black box on my desk.

"It seems your Diesel/LNG idea does work. This little box could mix a small amount of LNG with diesel to create a cleaner and stronger burn, thereby reducing pollution and increasing fuel mileage. I need permission to test this system on one of our company's trucks."

I took Gene into Charley O'Rielly's office, and after thirty minutes we had approval for a test. The test was a success. It would be a costly conversion, but the long-term savings would be enormous. We put the new system on two other trucks in our fleet and matched their performance with our standard vehicles. The combined results were a fifteen percent reduction in fuel costs and a thirty-five percent reduction in carbon dioxide and sulfur emissions.

We had a winner.

Although all of the credit belonged to the two engineers and the mechanics in the shop, the team would tell everyone who cared to listen, "The entire project was Danielle Palmer's silly little idea."

I loved the attention, but as Director of Special Projects, my real job at Deltron was to convert innovation into profit. First, I had to figure how much the gadget would cost to manufacture and install in our shop. Then there was the cost of financing the project, and where the money would com from. The toughest part was the financing. Although Deltron was a well-respected and stable company, money was tight, and the banks weren't interested in lending us the money we needed to get the project off the ground. Just when I was losing hope of ever getting the financing necessary to get the project rolling, Dan Patrick, called for a lunch date. I accepted immediately, thinking lunch with Dan would get my mind off the financial issue. Knowing my moods as well as he did, Dan asked what was wrong.

"The banks are giving me a difficult time. They keep talking about unproven technology and unknown market share and other banker talk which simply meant they're not interested."

"Danielle, my company has used a capital finance outfit a couple of times for special projects. They specialize in risky ventures, and they might be interested in your problem. Why don't you give them a call?"

Dan gave me a name and phone number and told me to stay positive. Being desperate at this point, I went back to my office and called the number. A sweet young lady listened to my story and agreed to meet me at my office the following day.

Janice Alvarez was a lovely, petite gal, maybe five to ten years younger than me. She was well dressed and very talkative. I tried to explain what we were doing.

"I'm sure this new invention we developed will be a big seller. We have our marketing plan and the startup costs for the project. Everything's been tested, and we're ready to go. I understand the banks' reluctance to lend us the money we need, but I know we have a good product, and all we need is some seed money to get us started."

Janice asked intelligent questions and seemed to understand what it was we were trying to do.

"I'm sure I could work something out. Let me talk to the board. I'll get back to you within twenty-four hours."

True to her word, she called the very next morning and set up a meeting with her board to go over the details. With Janice's help, we got the money. Once we were organized and financed, we got a few small trucking companies interested.

Within months, we had five trucks owned by three different companies on the road with our new invention. We monitored their performance and found during normal operation, the results were as good as our tests. Now, we were going after bigger fish. We started working on a proposal to pitch the idea to Paterson Trucking, a San Antonio, Texas company that ran fifteen thousand short and long-haul trucks throughout the country.

Our idea was to convert fifteen hundred of their vehicles a year in our plant. The ten-year plan would allow Paterson to pay for the new conversions with the savings from the previous conversions. Everything looked rosy. The Paterson proposal was coming along. We had signed two other small companies, and we were looking at another five to ten trucks on the road. Life couldn't have been any better. That is until I ran into Murphy's First Law:

Everything that can go wrong will go wrong, and at the worst possible time.

Just when I needed him the most, my Administrative

Assistant quit without notice. His boyfriend had decided to go to Hollywood and become a movie star, and Chester was going with him. The next morning, I had an important appointment with Janice. We were at the point with the Paterson Trucking proposal where we were discussing what the costs would be for us to increase our facilities to do conversions on one hundred and twenty-five trucks a month.

When Janice walked into my office, she realized I was in a panic. I told her about my predicament. In spite of not having Chester there, the meeting with Janice went reasonably well, and she promised to get back to me. After she left, I went to see my boss, Charlie O'Reilly. I gave him the update on my meeting with Janice and told him about my problem.

"Charlie, you know Chester quit yesterday without notice. "

"I heard, Danielle. Call Human Resources and ask for a list of possible replacements."

"That's what I intended to do, Charlie, but after my meeting with Janice, I have to consider another possibility, and I need your opinion. When Janice saw the turmoil, I was in she asked me what was happening. I told her about Chester quitting without notice and how long it would take to find a replacement and bring them up to speed. Chester's assistant Crystal isn't experienced enough to move up to the position. Janice thinks she may have a solution."

I paused to let Charlie digest what I had said.

"Janice told me she knows an older man, who has been in management most of his adult life and wants to slow down for a while. She suggested he would be a perfect temporary replacement, at least until we get the Paterson Trucking proposal organized. I can't ignore her offer."

Charlie thought about what I told him. I could see he was as undecided as I was.

Janice Alvarez is our financial contact, and, after all, the banks turned us down, she was the one who got us the seed money to get the new product to market. Now, I was asking her to front us additional money for the Paterson deal. As usual, Charlie had an answer.

"That young lady recently gave us a check for a million dollars and now, we're asking for more money. You, at least, have to interview this guy. We don't want to insult her. Make a decision after you talk to him."

Charlie was right. I called Janice, and I set up an interview for Monday morning. At the time, I couldn't possibly imagine where this simple meeting would lead.

Chapter 2 – The Temp

Nicholas Amonti turned out to be a very nice man, probably early forties, very well dressed, wavy light brown hair and deep-set brown eyes. He stood a little over six foot, which was good for me. At five-eight, before I put on my usual three-inch heels, I tended to feel uncomfortable alongside shorter men.

Prejudice, I know, but I am who I am.

He was dressed in a very nice suit, white shirt and tie and polished shoes. He was nice looking in a way. Not what you'd call a head turner, but he had a great personality, and he seemed to be in great shape.

I had a strange feeling that I knew this man, or, at least, I had met him before. As we talked, I tried to recall where I knew him from, but it never came to me. He was polite and respectful, could be funny at times and very perceptive. He did ask for one consideration.

"Ms. Palmer, I know you are out of the office on business trips and all-day meetings. Would it be alright if I didn't come to the office on those days?"

Since he would be working solely for me and his assistant, Crystal could handle things when I was away, and since he was temporary, I didn't think it would be a problem. We talked about duties, hours, salary and such and I decided Nicholas would be good enough to fill in until I had the time to search for a permanent replacement.

Nicholas turned out to be excellent at the job. In addition to being very efficient, he was light-hearted, funny, and inventive. We worked well together, and he was so perceptive we were able to communicate in shorthand code that was a marvel to all the other members of the team.

If I was in a meeting or on the phone, and I needed something, I would scratch a few words on a pad, hand the note to him and he would know exactly what I needed and have it in my hand, opened to the specific page and have the right notes highlighted. We developed an excellent working relationship. We were so busy with the Paterson proposal, and Nicholas worked out so well, I never did conduct a search for a replacement. I didn't know too much about his background, but it didn't seem to matter. I really liked him, not only as an Administrative Assistant but also as a person.

Janice had said he had been in management almost all of his working life, and his knowledge and manner seemed to indicate it was true. He seemed too young to be retired or burned out, but I decided it was none of my business. Nicholas kept the atmosphere in the office loose when things got heavy, and we were up against a deadline. He also managed to contribute some ideas to our ongoing proposals with our potential customers, including one for the Paterson proposal that caught everyone off guard.

"Why don't you consider including an advertising budget in your proposal. Everyone is environmentally conscious these days, and you could capitalize on the idea of the reduction in pollution the system provides. You could tell Paterson you would be willing to co-advertise with them to push the idea of Paterson converting to a Green Fleet."

Charlie liked the idea and directed Nicholas to expand it and help the team include it in the Paterson proposal before we went to San Antonio. Because it was his idea, and no one on the team could explain it any better than he could, Nicholas was added to the team that would go to San Antonio and make the pitch to Paterson.

Two weeks before the San Antonio trip was scheduled, I had to attend a Saturday night charity ball. Charley O'Reilly had gone to the last dinner, and it was my turn. These things were usually dull affairs. We were always seated at a table with people I didn't know, and the conversation always seemed to be forced.

I was with Andrew. He was a reasonably good dancer, and these affairs usually weren't worth wasting a real date on. Even though Andrew kept pushing for more, I managed to keep our relationship simple. Usually with the no inter-office relationship' argument. Halfway through the cocktail hour, Andrew pointed across the hall.

"Isn't that your secretary?"

I looked to where Andrew was pointing, and I saw Nicholas with a group of people across the hall. I was surprised.

These weren't the kind of affairs Administrative Assistants would typically be invited to.

When Nicholas noticed us, he moved toward us with an absolutely gorgeous woman on his arm. In addition to being a truly beautiful woman, I saw she was wearing what must surely be a Stacy Geer Designs gown. Stacy Geer was the hottest designer in South Florida, and her gowns were very expensive. I knew, because I was wearing one myself. It was the only one in my closet, the only one I could afford. It had cost me almost two month's pay. But, when I saw myself in the mirror, I knew it was worth the money.

Every woman looked good in a Stacy Geer gown.

"Good evening Ms. Palmer, may I introduce Ms. Stacy Geer? Stacy, this is Danielle Palmer of Deltron Motors. Ms. Palmer is my boss, and the gentleman is Andrew Lighter of the Deltron Motors Marketing Department."

When Nick was done with the introductions, I had to ask, "Of Stacy Geer Designs?"

"Guilty," was her reply.

It was just fortunate I was wearing one of her gowns, and her comment went right to my head.

"May I say, Ms. Palmer, you are the type of woman I most enjoy designing for. You are stunning."

I definitely had to return the compliment, because it was true. Stacy Geer was stunning. The mutual admiration continued for a while as we complimented each other, and I told her how very much I liked her designs.

"Although, as a working girl, I can't afford many."

"I'm working on a new line a working girl will be able to afford, and it will be out for the fall season."

Andrew and Nicholas seemed amused at the two of us but kept quiet as gentlemen should at times like this. Then, it was time for dinner, and we were seated at different tables. Andrew, who always acted superior to other people, was astonished that my secretary was dating Stacy Geer.

I was a bit surprised myself.

I did manage to get a few glimpses of Nicholas during the evening and noticed he seemed at home with the high rollers at his table. Janice had said he was in management most of his life, and he appeared to fit right in.

But, Nicholas and Stacy Geer? My curiosity was definitely aroused!

Monday morning the office routine moved along until I couldn't control my curiosity any longer. Nicholas shared an alcove with his assistant, Crystal, directly outside my office door. A glass partition separated their alcove from my office, and when I noticed the two of them quietly working at their desks, I ventured out there. Their desks faced each other with an aisle in between. I propped myself on the edge of Nicholas' desk facing Crystal.

"Crystal, what will the break room gossip be about today?"

"Not sure, Ms. Palmer, I haven't talked to any of the other girls yet."

"Well, I've got an interesting tidbit that may get the conversation started."

"What's that, Ms. Palmer?"

"Guess who I ran into at the charity dinner Saturday night?"

"Who?" Crystal asked, seeming interested.

"Our very own Nicholas."

That really got Crystal's attention and a surprised look from Nicholas.

"And, you'll never guess who his date was," I added teasingly. I really had Crystal's interest now, and she looked at me, waiting for me to reveal the answer.

"Hmm," I pouted as I crossed my legs. Nicholas seemed to take notice of that.

"Let me see if I can remember her name… Oh yes, Stacy Geer, wasn't that it Nicholas?"

"THE Stacy Geer?" Crystal asked in total shock.

"The very same."

With awe in her voice and a new found respect for Nicholas, Crystal said, "I've seen her in person Ms. Palmer, she's beautiful."

"Stunning is the word I'd use."

"Okay, okay," Nicholas finally said, "it's not what you're implying. Stacy is just a good friend."

"An extremely good friend, by the looks of it."

"Well, man does not live by Delton Motors alone!"

"Tell us more," I implored.

"There's not much to tell."

"Do you believe that, Crystal?"

"Not at all, Ms. Palmer, he's definitely hiding something."

"Stacy and I go way back to a time before there was a Stacy Geer Designs. Stacy worked for another fashion house at the time. We've known each other a long, long time, and occasionally when she needs an escort for one of these functions, she calls me."

"That's it?" I asked.

"That's it!"

"Bull," Crystal shouted.

"That's all you're going to get," Nicholas said, grinning.

"But you would agree she is a very stunning lady?"

"Yes, Ms. Palmer, Stacy is a stunning woman, and if I recall, she paid you the very same compliment."

"Probably just being nice to a customer."

"Ms. Palmer, Stacy is in the beautiful woman business, and when she says a woman is stunning, she means you were stunning... And, I must say, I completely agree with her assessment."

That comment made me blush.

"Thank you, Nicholas, and next time you see Ms. Geer, please tell her thank you for me. And tell her if I appeared stunning that evening, it was because I was wearing one of her gowns."

"I will tell her, Ms. Palmer."

I trotted back into my office and thought about Nicholas and Stacy Geer. Just from his manner here in the office, I thought he must be a fun date.

I'll bet this man really knows how to treat a lady!

The San Antonio trip was finally scheduled. Bob, my Assistant Director, Gene, Nicholas and I flew to Texas and did what I thought was a complete and thoughtful presentation. We all took turns talking about various portions of the plan, and Tony Paterson seemed to be listening intently. He was really intrigued by Nicholas's idea of joint advertising touting the green fleet of Paterson trucks. His primary concern was the time frame.

"Can you rework the numbers and see if you could reduce the time needed to convert my entire inventory?"

Since he had shown real interest, we decided to stay over in San Antonio and attempt to shorten the conversion time. We agreed to a second meeting the next day and headed for a hotel instead of the airport. Bob was driving the rental, I was riding shotgun, and Nicholas and Gene were in the back seat.

"Gene, how much could we reduce the cost of each unit if we ordered twenty thousand units instead of two thousand?"

We didn't build the units in-house, we farmed out the actual production to a fabrication company, and we did the installations.

"I'm not sure, but probably about fifteen to twenty percent per unit."

"What's going on back there?" I inquired.

"Just running some ideas around. I'll tell you when I've got a better picture of the situation, Ms. Palmer."

Nicholas took out his cell phone and hit a speed dial key.

"I need information about how, when and where Paterson Trucking of San Antonio, Texas services their trucks. As much information as you can get, and I need it now!"

When we got to the hotel, Nicholas made a suggestion.

"Why don't you get a small suite for yourself with a table we could work on, and also order lunch. I think we're going to be very busy."

I did as Nicholas suggested, and we checked in and headed for our rooms. Nicholas was the first to knock on my door. He was talking on his cell as I let him in. He had his laptop open, and he was attempting to listen, read, and greet me all at the same time. I heard him tell whoever was on the other end of the line, "Send everything to my computer and keep digging."

By the time Bob and Eugene got to the room, Nicholas had drawn a rather crude map of the United States on a large scratchpad a Bellman had dropped off. He had put ten circles on it. He was back on his cell and working on his computer and was so engrossed with what he was doing he didn't notice we were all there.

I used the time to order lunch, and around the time it arrived, Nicholas was ready to explain. He looked at the three of us.

15

"We can do this!"

Being the team leader, I figured it was my job to ask, "Do what?"

"Think big. We can we do all fifteen thousand trucks within a year."

"Impossible!" Bob said.

"We don't have the facilities!" Gene told him.

"True," Nicholas answered, "But Paterson does."

"It's crazy, completely off the wall!" I cried.

Nicholas looked directly at me, into my eyes.

"Trust me, Ms. Palmer, this is possible. It will take a lot of work, and you'll have to convince, Paterson, Mr. O'Rielly, and Ms. Alvarez."

"What does Janice have to do with this?"

"This will require a lot of upfront money, both by Paterson and us. You have to get Ms. Alvarez to not only front our end, but she also has to be willing to talk to Paterson about his end. And, we need her agreement to speak to Paterson before we make our pitch to him."

"Slow down," Bob told him, "I'm open to out of the box thinking, but we haven't heard word one about how we're going to do this. From the beginning, if you please."

Nicholas stood up, walked over to the map he had drawn on the easel and started his presentation.

"Paterson Trucking has the best safety record of any trucking company in the industry. The reason is they take excellent care of their vehicles."

Pointing to the ten circles on the map, he continued.

"Every Paterson truck is brought in to one of these ten service centers, once every three months. They have regularly scheduled quarterly, semiannual and annual service programs. For the annual service, the truck is in the service center for forty-eight hours. It's checked out completely, and many components are automatically replaced, worn out or not. Two trained mechanics can install our system in three to four hours, isn't that right, Gene?"

Gene smiled and nodded as he began to understand what Nicholas was proposing.

I won't bore you with the details of what happened in that hotel suite for the next twelve hours, but by two o'clock in the morning, we had a general outline of a proposal to present to Paterson. It most definitely was a team effort. I will say it was a brilliant idea, and it was all started by Nicholas, with some help from someone he called 'T.' If we pulled this off, it would be a deal worth close to fifty million dollars, and my team was solely responsible.

Danielle Palmer, Vice President of Special Projects, sounded really nice!

Later that morning, we presented our proposal to Tony Paterson. We didn't have fancy presentation slides and such, just a bunch of numbers on the large scratchpad we used in the suite, and some spreadsheets on our computers, but it was evident we had impressed the CEO of Paterson Trucking.

"When can you have a formal proposal ready to present to my Board of Directors?"

We were in the door.

And here, we have another simple thing that evolved into so much more. Because of what happened here in San Antonio, I made a decision that would change the direction of my life, forever.

The flight back to Fort Lauderdale was a party. We were all so giddy we had to be admonished a couple of times by the flight attendants to quiet down. Although, as a group, we weren't big drinkers, a stop in the airport bar and a few more on the plane had the four of us in a fantastic mood.

For the next week and a half, we worked on the proposal, getting all the details right. Janice attended some of our sessions to get an idea of what Paterson would require. She seemed to indicate NAS Financial Group might be interested in financing both ends of the project. We finally had it all together. Not too slick. Again, Nicholas's idea.

"Let's not overload them with jazz. Let's just present the numbers in a straightforward and clean presentation."

Friday morning, Crystal dropped the completed proposal on my desk. One by one, as they had a chance to check over their copies, the team members stopped by my office to signal their approval. All I needed was the okay from Charlie, and I was ready to FedEx everything to San Antonio.

Charlie had been in meetings most of the day and didn't get to my office until four thirty. He gave his approval, and I had Crystal send it out.

"Charlie, since I don't expect to get an answer for at least thirty days, it might be a good idea for me to take some vacation time. If Paterson gives us the go ahead, we will be very busy, and vacation time would be out of the question."

Charlie agreed, and I scheduled two weeks off starting a week from Monday.

"Danielle if the Paterson deal is approved, you'll have to increase the size of your staff. I think Nicholas should be included as a team member and not as your Administrative Assistant."

Charlie knew the entire Paterson deal was initiated by Nicholas's idea. I had to agree.

"I'll bring up the idea to Nicholas on Monday."

Charlie looked at me with a very guilty expression.

"Spit it out," I said.

He dropped an invitation to a charity ball on my desk.

"Oh no, you don't. I went last time. It's your turn."

"I promised my grandson I would attend his soccer match tomorrow, and it has been moved from an afternoon game to a night game. You wouldn't want me to disappoint my grandson, would you?"

"That's not fair Charlie. And, besides, it's Friday evening, where do you expect me to find a date by tomorrow night?"

"How about your friend Dan Patrick, or Andrew from Marketing?"

"I've never asked Dan on twenty-four hours' notice, and besides, he's seeing someone special now, and I'd rather not encourage Andrew. Charlie, I don't know anyone I'd call on such short notice."

Before anything else could be said, Nicholas poked his head through my office door.

"Need anything before I take off, Ms. Palmer?"

"No, I'm fine, have a good weekend."

"See you Monday Ms. Palmer, Mr. O'Rielly."

"Nicholas," Charlie called. Nicholas turned back into the office.

"Sir?"

"Do you have any plans for tomorrow night?"

"Nothing planned so far, Sir. Do you need something?"

Charlie smiled at me.

"Ms. Palmer has an important dinner to attend tomorrow night, and she needs an escort."

"Charlie!" I screamed.

"It would be an honor to be Ms. Palmer's escort...if it's all right with you Ms. Palmer?"

Charlie had put me in a box. If I said no, I would be insulting Nicholas, and I didn't want to do that. If I said yes, I was giving in to Charlie and taking his turn for one of these silly dinners.

After glaring at Charlie, I turned my attention to Nicholas.

"Of course, Nicholas. Say seven thirty, my apartment. Do you know where that is?"

"Yes, Ms. Palmer. The same address I send the car service to when you go to the airport."

"Of course. You of all people would know where I live."

"Formal?"

I looked at the invitation.

"I'm afraid so."

"See you at seven thirty, tomorrow."

Chapter 3 – The Date

When I was sure Nicholas was gone, I yelled at Charlie.

"How could you do that?"

"Do what?" he said innocently.

"How could you put him on the spot like that? You didn't leave him any room to say no."

"Say no? Danielle, I don't know any man that would say no to a date with you."

"It's not a date, Charlie. It's more like an obligation."

Charlie just smiled.

"I'm sure that's not how Nicholas feels right now."

I hadn't the faintest idea what Charlie meant, but somehow, he had gotten me to take his place tomorrow night, and Nicholas would be my escort. It could be worse.

At least, I'd be able to confirm my suspicions that Nicholas was a fun date.

Saturday, as always, was chores day. Pick up the dry-cleaning, food shopping. Career girls don't eat out as often as people might think! And, as usual, there weren't enough hours in the day to take care of everything, and suddenly, it was time to get ready for my date. Although, it wasn't really a date, was it?

I thought about Charlie's comment about what Nicholas thought about it, and I did remember thinking Nicholas was probably a fun date. But, it's not as if he had asked me out, and he was my Administrative Assistant. Political Correctness notwithstanding, he actually was my secretary.

But, I found myself taking more time than usual getting ready. I was sorry I had worn my one and only Stacy Geer gown to the last dinner. It wouldn't be right to wear it again, tonight. I tried on a number of dresses before I finally settled on a simple gold gown with a long slit along the left leg. I remembered the attention Nicholas paid to my legs when I was teasing him with Crystal. I fussed with my makeup and hair, and when I decided I couldn't make myself any better, I checked the results in the full-length mirror.

Since my middle-high school days, I have received enough compliments and been flirted with enough times to realize I am attractive to men. I've been told I was a TEN a few of times and once a man said I was off the chart. I'm not the typical blue-eyed blond Hollywood portrays as the ultimate beauty, but I know I can hold my own among most women. I am five foot eight, light auburn hair that I usually wear below my shoulders and brown eyes that can appear hazel in certain light.

I have a trim, proportional body, not overly large in the bust. I get enough looks and whistles in my bikini at the pool or beach to know that I don't have a problem there. Because of my height, I have long, shapely legs, and I'm always in three or four-inch heels to give them definition. I am never without a date if I want one, and I've had enough intimate relationships to satisfy me. I was pleased with the reflection staring back at me. Good enough!

Seven thirty on the dot, the intercom buzzed. Andy, the doorman, announced there was a gentleman in the lobby. I told him to inform the gentleman I was on my way, grabbed my wrap and purse, and headed out the door.

When I reached the lobby, Nicholas was waiting with a single white rose in his hand. He looked great in his tuxedo. As I mentioned, Nicholas is not what I'd consider a head turner, but once you get to know him, his personality, charm, and charisma make him seem better looking. His inner self shines through. He greeted me warmly, commented on how good I looked and handed me the rose.

"I didn't think you were the corsage type."

The single white rose seemed so appropriate to the situation. Offering me his arm, we walked out the door to find a stretch limo waiting for us with the driver holding the door open. Nicholas thanked the driver by name and away we went. I had ridden in limousines many times before, but there was something different about this one. It seemed more personal than the ones you hire. It was as if this one was privately owned.

"Yours?" I asked in jest.

"Belongs to someone I know. They let me use it for important dates."

"Important dates?"

"Yes, Ms. Palmer, extremely important dates."

"Very impressive. Must go over big with all the ladies."

"It does have its advantages," he replied with a smile, "But there aren't that many ladies."

"Nicholas, it won't do for you to call me Ms. Palmer all evening."

I thought it was as good a time as any, so I told Nicholas about Charlie's idea of bringing him onto the team as a full staff member instead of my Administrative Assistant. Nicholas said he appreciated the offer, but he already considered himself a member of the team.

"Ms. Palmer, I took this job because of the limited responsibility I would have, and I like the position I hold. This is only a temporary position, and someday soon, I will have to leave. I don't need the extra money a promotion would bring, and if it is all right with you and Mr. O'Rielly, I'd just like to remain where I am.

"The reason I refer to you as Ms. Palmer instead of Danielle is due to my upbringing. It is a respect thing, and good habits are as difficult to break as bad habits. I will use your given name in the appropriate places this evening, but I prefer to continue to call you Ms. Palmer at all other times. You are my boss, Ma'am, and I do respect you and your position. You don't have to worry about this evening. I promise I won't embarrass you."

Then, he uttered a phrase I would hear over and over again. He looked into my eyes and said very sweetly, "It's covered, Ms. Palmer."

I took his word everything would be okay and relaxed. When we arrived at the hotel ballroom, Nicholas informed Thomas, our driver, "I'll call when we're ready to leave. I don't know how long Ms. Palmer will want to stay."

At the reception desk, Nicholas announced, "Ms. Danielle Palmer, Deltron Motors."

The young lady smiled and informed us we were seated at table number ten with eight other people whose names I didn't recognize. We entered the hall for the cocktail hour and were immediately confronted by a tall, good-looking bear of a man in his fifties. He approached us and appeared ready to take a punch at Nicholas. But when he saw me, he stopped.

"Where have you been hiding her?"

Nicholas smiled.

"Ms. Danielle Palmer, may I introduce Mr. Terrance Daniels of Daniels Industries."

"You are Danielle Palmer?" the man asked, seemingly shocked by the revelation.

Borrowing a phrase from the night I met Stacy Geer, I answered, "Guilty."

"The Danielle Palmer that came up with the Diesel/LNG idea?"

"Guilty again."

Shifting his gaze to Nicholas, he scolded, "You dog, you never mentioned how beautiful she was."

"Watch out for this one, Danielle. He not only wants to steal you away from Deltron Motors but now that he's seen you, I'm sure he has other things on his mind."

"Afraid of some competition, old man?"

"Not from you, Terry. I know all your secrets. After I tell Danielle all about you, you won't have a chance."

"Excuse me, gentlemen I'm standing right here!"

"No Ma'am, excuse us. Neither of us is usually this impolite in front of a lady."

"That's alright Mr. Daniels. This lady doesn't mind two handsome gentlemen fighting for her attention."

A big grin spread across his face as he turned to Nicholas.

"I like her. Beauty, brains, and a great sense about herself. Please, call me Terry, and Nick is right about one thing, I would very much like to talk to you about moving over to Daniels Industries."

"Okay, Terry! But I'm way too involved at Deltron right now to consider leaving. I do appreciate the offer."

"The time will come, Ms. Palmer. Those bozos at Deltron don't know how to treat real talent. Just promise me when the time does come, you'll give me the first chance to make a qualified offer."

"It's Danielle, Terry, and I will promise if the time for a move ever comes, you'll be the first one I call."

That brought a smile. A punch to Nicholas's shoulder and he was gone with, "Don't let this one get away, she's a keeper."

"A keeper?" I asked Nicholas as Terry Daniels walked away.

"Terry's full of bluster Ms. Palmer, but he's a terrific guy, a great boss to work for and I know he'd love to have you work for his company,"

"How do you know him?"

"The same way I know Stacy Geer. We go back to before there was a Daniels Industries. Terry and I met when he operated a small appliance repair shop in Pompano Beach. His company is the result of a great idea and some very hard work. Believe me, he's earned everything he has."

"Any other surprises I should be aware of?"

His answer was the other phrase I would hear over and over again.

"Well, I do know people."

"You know people! What does that mean?"

"Ms. Palmer, I've met a lot of people in my life, some personally and some through business. For many years, I worked in the Hospitality Industry. I managed some top of the line restaurants, and as a result, I got to know a lot of people and a lot of people know me. I know important people, not so important people, big people, small people, good people, and some bad people. It's just a natural fact of living and opening yourself up to relationships. I know people!"

I would have liked a further explanation, but other people came over to talk to us. Some I knew, some Nicholas knew. Everything moved along smoothly, through the cocktail hour and dinner.

Neither of us knew anyone at our table, but Nicholas, being so outgoing and friendly, kept the conversation inclusive. I was still Ms. Palmer when he spoke to me quietly, but I was Danielle when we talked to other people.

When asked what he did, he said, "I'm on the Deltron Motors Special Projects Team."

Which technically was true, never mentioning he was my Administrative Assistant. He never failed to mention I headed the team, and there were the usual comments about having a female boss. Nicholas answered them with comments like, "It's not a problem because this lady knows what she's doing."

Between the appetizer and entrée, the band started playing a very lovely tune. Nicholas asked me if I waltzed. I said yes, and he led me to the dance floor. We did the basic waltz step.

"You dance well, Ms. Palmer."

"Thank you."

"Do you trust me?"

"What do you mean?"

He squeezed my right hand gently and pressed his right hand against my back.

"Forget the music. Listen to the beat and feel my hands."

And we proceeded to swirl across the dance floor like a professional dance team. I felt him directing me with his hands, and I knew exactly what he was doing and where he was going. It wasn't Dancing with the Stars, but it was wonderful! I wasn't dancing, I was floating. It felt so natural. It was fun. It was exciting. And...I liked his touch. The dance ended too soon, and we were back at our table.

"Thank you for the dance, My Lady!"

"My pleasure, Kind Sir. Any other secrets you'd like to share with me?"

"Need more tidbits for the break room gossip pool?"

"I guess I deserved that."

"Not to worry pretty lady, it was kind of fun. But, if you really want something to tell them back at the office, wait until the band plays a Rumba."

"I don't know how to Rumba."

"Ms. Palmer, when you start to swivel those hips on the dance floor, no one will be looking at your feet!"

"I'll make a complete fool of myself. I don't know how to Rumba."

"Nothing to it. Only one thing you have to do, I'll take care of the rest."

"And what is that?"

"All you have to do is trust me!"

We never did get to Rumba that night, but we did dance some more, a lot more. It was the best Corporate/Charity dinner I had ever been to. My other dates at these things were always pleasant and fun, but Nicholas was so outgoing, got so involved with other people it seemed like we were sitting with friends instead of strangers. And, he did appear to know people, a lot of people, including some elegant looking women. I was sorry when it was time to go home.

Thomas waited while Nicholas escorted me to the elevator. Nicholas took my hand and kissed it.

"Thank you for such a lovely evening, My Lady."

"It was all my pleasure, I assure you, Kind Sir."

I had only one thought on the way up to my apartment.

WOW!

Back at the office Monday, it was business as usual. I thanked Nicholas for such a lovely time, and he responded with the appropriate compliments, but no indication he would like a repeat. It was disappointing but understandable. I was his boss, and he did seem to have access to some very charming ladies. Too bad! He actually had turned out to be a great date!

The Paterson proposal was out, and the routine around the office was, …routine. I spent a good deal of time thinking about my upcoming vacation. I was going home to Cauldwell, Georgia. It was not going to be a vacation in the ordinary sense of the term. Cauldwell Industries was in trouble. They were losing customers and had reduced their operation from two full shifts a day to two half shifts in an effort to keep everyone working, at least, part-time. I was hoping to meet with Mary Ann Cauldwell, who had taken over the company when her father passed away. Maybe I could find a way to help them recover their lost business and keep the company from closing.

If the company closed, there would be no employment for the town, and people would move away, and the town would cease to exist. It had happened before in other one employer towns, and I didn't want it to happen to my hometown. So I was headed for a working vacation. Unfortunately, I wasn't sure I was equipped to find a solution. I knew this would require knowledge of bookkeeping and finances, and that wasn't my expertise.

I heard Nicholas tell Crystal, "I'll miss the office routine while Ms. Palmer is on vacation."

I remembered he didn't come into the office when I was out of town. I also knew how quickly he had gathered the information for the second meeting with Paterson in San Antonio.

I was desperate.

"Nicholas, would you be willing to go to Cauldwell with me and look at the situation? I'll pay all of your expenses and pay your salary while we're gone. You're the best numbers person I know. You proved that in San Antonio."

"Ms. Palmer, even if we find the problem, there may not be a solution. Can you deal with that?"

"I'll have to."

"Okay, here's the deal. You can pay my airfare and hotel room, but no salary and I'll cover all my other expenses."

I balked at that, and when he came up with a compromise, I had to agree.

"You can pay me one dollar a day, and throw in all the fish heads I can eat."

"Deal," I told him when I stopped laughing.

We flew to Atlanta Saturday morning, and Nicholas drove the rental car to Cauldwell.

Neither of us realized at the time just how much this trip would change both of our lives.

Chapter 4 – Cauldwell, Georgia

We checked into the Cauldwell Hotel. I introduced Nicholas to Mr. Blumberg, the owner, and Sheriff Travis, who had been in the Army Special Forces before returning to Cauldwell and running for Sheriff. I also brought him to Carl's Place. Carl's was a café/diner during the day and a bar/dance hall at night.

I was born in Cauldwell and lived there until I left for college. I had known the people of Cauldwell all my life. They were good people, and if we couldn't find a solution to the company's problem, they would all have to move away and find other work. Sunday, I brought Nicholas to my niece's house for dinner. Anna Lee was my sister Lindsey's daughter. Anna Lee liked Nicholas immediately, and Nicholas seemed to get along with her son Johnny.

Johnny had always been special to me. He was a very introverted little boy. He stuttered and was laughed at by the other kids in town. His father was gone, and Johnny had turned inward and had become a sorrowful child. Nicholas seemed to ignite the life back into him.

Monday, we went to the factory and talked to Mary Ann Cauldwell. Mary Ann and I had been grammar school and high school classmates, and she was delighted I had taken an interest in her problem. She gladly opened up her books to Nicholas and seemed to have more than a business interest in him.

After a week of checking the numbers and an additional three days of checking out the equipment, Nicholas had an idea as to what needed to be done. Nicholas and I talked every day, had lunch together occasionally and dinner together once or twice. He was good company, but my mind was on Cauldwell, and I wasn't paying attention to anything else, but I did notice Mary Ann was making time for him.

Nicholas with the help of the mysterious 'T' managed to develop a plan that would save the company and the town. Wednesday, Nicholas, Mary Ann and I had lunch at Carl's. Nicholas was ready for his final report.

"As I suggested to Ms. Palmer before we arrived, over the

years, your father never modernized or upgraded the plant and now your competitors are more efficient and can offer better prices and a guaranteed on-time delivery."

That didn't make either of us happy. But Nicholas had more.

"Ladies, I have good news and bad news. The good news is that there is enough business available to keep Cauldwell Industries going for many more years. The bad news is that Cauldwell Industries will not get that business until the plant is modernized. Unfortunately, the cost is prohibitive. It would require an influx of over a million dollars to upgrade the plant and get the business needed to keep the company solvent for the future. The company is so unstable, I'm not sure we could get any bank interested in financing the modernization. The service on a debt that size wouldn't leave the company with any operating capital. It's not hopeless. There are other alternatives than banks. Maybe you can find an investor or other solution."

Billy Hastings, a boy who had pursued me in high school, thought he would give it another try while I was in town. Billy was the school bully, and I wasn't interested in him back then. He had grown up to be the town bully, and I surely wasn't interested in him now. But, he persisted. While I was having lunch at Carl's on Thursday, Billy sat down at my table.

"I don't understand why you're being such an uppity bitch. It's not bad enough you waltzed into town as the big city gal who was going to save us all, but you had to bring your Yankee boyfriend with you. And, since your boyfriend is doing both Mary Ann and Anna Lee, why shouldn't you have some fun too."

I was shocked at Billy's outburst, but I had an answer ready for him.

"A: Nicholas is not my boyfriend, he is an employee. B: he's not 'DOING' my niece. C: if something is going on between Mary Ann and Nicholas, it's none of my business and none of yours either. And D: under no circumstances would I consider going out with you. I had no interest in you when I lived in Cauldwell, and I definitely have no interest in going out with you now."

Billy was not a happy camper when he stormed out of Carl's Place. I had no reason to care if Nicholas and Mary Ann were getting together, but for some reason, I had a strange feeling, just like the night I saw Nicholas with Stacy Geer. I didn't believe what Billy said about Anna Lee, but Nicholas had been spending a lot of his free time with her.

Could he be making a play for my niece?

He was ten or fifteen years older than her. It didn't fit with the Nicholas I knew, but what did I really know about him? He was charming, and a young girl like Anna Lee could mistake that for something more. I had to find out. She was my niece, and I should try to protect her.

I knew Nicholas would be at the plant putting together a proposal to take to the banks and potential investors. I walked over to Anna Lee's house and invited myself in for a cup of coffee. I didn't know how to bring up the subject, so I tried to be subtle.

"Anna Lee, Nicholas is from the big city, he's not a country boy. He's charming and exciting and very polished. He knows a lot of beautiful ladies and..."

I wasn't subtle enough. Anna Lee cut me off.

"Auntie Danielle, Mr. Nick is a perfect gentleman. He wouldn't do anything to hurt me."

"But, he's been spending so much time at your house. Almost every night for supper."

"Auntie Danielle, Mr. Nick has been helping Johnny with his numbers and other school work. Johnny got an 'A' on his math test the other day, the first time ever. He ran home to show me. "See Mommy, I'm not stupid. I'm smart like Mr. Nick said."

"Johnny has been a different boy since he met Mr. Nick. And Mr. Nick told me the clinic in Albany has developed a new procedure for helping kids that stutter, and he could get Johnny enrolled for free. I know about that place, Auntie Danielle. I've taken Johnny there before, but I couldn't afford to pay for the procedure. It's not free, Auntie Danielle, I know Mr. Nick is paying for it, but I want Johnny to be a normal boy, so I pretended I believed him. Did I do wrong, Auntie Danielle?"

What could I say to her?

"Anna Lee, I Mr. Nick is a good man, and he would be hurt if you refused his help."

I told Anna Lee not to worry, but I intended to talk to Nicholas about this. I wanted to know what he has on his mind.

Why would he do this?

"Mr. Nick asked if he could invite you and the Sheriff to supper here tonight."

I hadn't seen Nicholas all day, and I didn't know what was going on, but I had to agree to be there. Later that afternoon when I did see Nicholas at Carl's, he asked me if I could come with him and the Sheriff to Anna Lee's for supper that evening.

"I have some information about Anna Lee's husband she should know about and I'd like you there because she might get emotional."

"Where did you get the information?"

"I told you, Ms. Palmer, I know people."

"What kind of information?"

"You'll have to wait until this evening."

"If it will make her emotional, why would you tell her?"

His answer melted my heart.

"Ms. Palmer, that poor girl is hurting, and it's not right. Her Robbie was a good man, and she should know just how good he was. It may be years before the government declassifies the information and it's not fair for her to wait that long. Anna Lee believes Robbie is a hero because he killed a bunch of people. That's not the truth, and she should know what actually happened."

"If it's still classified how, did you get it?"

"I told you, Ma'am, I know people. You'll have to trust me!"

Trust him or not, Anna Lee was my niece, and I had to be there for her.

When Nicholas and I arrived at Anna Lee's house, the Sheriff was already there talking to Johnny. The men sat at opposite ends of the table, with Anna Lee and me across from each other. Johnny sat next to his mother. Supper was pleasant, the conversation was light. Johnny told us about his math test. He was so proud. After Anna Lee and I cleared the table, Johnny asked Nicholas to help with his homework.

"Johnny, the grownups have some talking to do. I'll check your homework before I leave."

Johnny went into his bedroom, and the four of us were left alone at the table. Nicholas nodded to the Sheriff.

"Miss Anna Lee, Miss Danielle. What Nick is about to tell you is classified Top Secret by the United States Government. If any of this conversation gets out, some people, including Nick, are going to be in big trouble. Do you ladies understand what I just said?"

Anna Lee and I both nodded our heads. Nicholas looked at the three of us individually, then took a deep breath.

"Anna Lee, I know some people in the Navy, and I have had the opportunity to talk to Robbie's Commanding Officer. Like the Sheriff said, this information is secret. The reason it is secret is because the missions Robbie was involved in are still ongoing, and if word leaked out about these missions, many people would be in danger."

He paused to allow us to absorb what he said.

"You know Robbie joined the military for the college benefits. Because of his promise to you he wouldn't hurt anyone, he requested assignment as a medic: the Navy and Marines call them Corpsman.

"After training, he was temporarily assigned to a Marine Rifle Company. The company was standing down after weeks in battle, and Robbie was there just to take care of sprains, bruises, and the kind of things that happen when these men are not in combat. They train hard, and someone is always getting hurt. After that, he would be assigned to a permanent station. He could have been sent anywhere, to a ship, a Naval Hospital, another Marine Corps Company. But, no matter where he was sent, he would always be a medic."

Nick paused to make sure we understood.

"Anna Lee, the military has rules by which they are allowed to conduct operations. They are called Rules of Engagement. Under these rules, Medics, or Corpsmen, are not permitted to fight. They are not authorized to handle weapons. They are not allowed to shoot at anyone. Robbie never used a weapon and never killed anyone."

"Then why did they say he was a hero?"

"Because Anna Lee, he is a hero. He is a hero because he saved lives, not because he took them."

Nick let that sink in before he continued.

"While Robbie was assigned to them, the company was sent out on a mission, a vital mission. Robbie didn't have to go because this wasn't his permanent station, but that would mean the Marines wouldn't have a Corpsman with them.

"Robbie volunteered to go on the mission, and during a firefight one of the Marines was wounded. Robbie crawled out into the line of fire, pulled the man to safety and stopped the bleeding. Robbie was credited with saving the man's life. He also received a minor wound while dragging the man to safety. It wasn't serious, but that's the reason he received his first Purple Heart. Almost immediately, the company was assigned a second mission, and again in the middle of a firefight, Robbie crawled out to pull a man to safety and kept him alive until the helicopters evacuated him. The Marines were so impressed with Robbie's bravery their Captain had him assigned to the company permanently."

Nicholas paused again, while Anna Lee and I poured coffee for all of us.

"Anna Lee, I want you to understand the missions these men were on were designed to save people. These missions are still going on today, that's why they are top secret, and that's why I can't tell you about them, but I can say these missions saved hundreds of civilian lives."

Another pause as Nicholas took a sip of his coffee.

"On Robbie's fifth mission, the Marines got into a ferocious firefight. Because of the earlier success of the missions, they found themselves up against a superior force. The company took six casualties. Five times Robbie crawled out into the line of fire and dragged men back to safety. On his fourth trip, he was wounded again, this time seriously. Ignoring his own wound, he crawled out a fifth time. But, because of his own wound, he did not have the strength to pull the man all the way back to safety.

"Another Marine crawled out and pulled them both back, and although Robbie was too severely injured to tend to the fifth wounded man, he shouted directions to the Marine, who had dragged him back, and between them, they were able to save that man also. Unfortunately, by this time, Robbie had lost so much blood he was beyond help, and he died there."

Nicholas pulled an envelope from his jacket pocket. He looked into Anna Lee's eyes.

"Anna Lee, Robbie was a real hero, the best kind of hero. He never hurt anyone. He never broke faith with you. He is a hero because he risked his life to save others. Not only his teammates, but according to my information, the missions Robbie went on resulted in saving over twelve hundred villagers from being killed, or enslaved."

Nicholas opened the envelope and took out some photographs. He looked into Anna Lee's eyes.

"Anna Lee, you have no husband, and Johnny has no father."

He placed the photos in front of her.

"But these seven women still have husbands, and these eighteen children still have fathers because of Robbie's sacrifice, his bravery, his selflessness. Be proud of your man, Anna Lee."

Anna Lee looked at the photos and then at Nicholas.

"Is it true Mr. Nick? You're not just saying this to make me feel good about Robbie?"

"Every word is the truth, Anna Lee. Someday the missions will be over, and it won't be a secret anymore. Then everyone will know what a great man Robbie was."

There were tears in Anna Lee's eyes, but not the emotional breakdown one might expect. I saw relief in her eyes. She wanted to believe in her man, and Nicholas had allowed her to believe again.

After Nicholas had said goodnight to Johnny, he and the Sheriff left.

Anna Lee asked, "Is it all true, Auntie Danielle?"

"I know Nicholas is a good man, Anna Lee. I can't think of any reason he would lie about this. He said someday everyone would know, so it must be true."

I sat with Anna Lee for about an hour. We talked some, and we were quiet some. I kept thinking about Nicholas.

How much trouble could he get into for telling us this? Why would he put himself in jeopardy like that?

When I left Anna Lee's house, the Sheriff was waiting to walk me back to the hotel.

"It's sweet of you to wait for me, Sheriff, but it's not necessary, I feel perfectly safe in Cauldwell."

"I don't like the way Billy has been carrying on about you and your boyfriend. I'm afraid Billy will do something stupid."

I started to explain Nicholas wasn't my boyfriend, but the Sheriff stopped me.

"I know Nicolas is just an employee of the company you

work for, and he's here to check out Cauldwell Industries."

It seems Nicholas and the Sheriff had talked a lot.

"But, Billy has been spreading a rumor all over town that the two rooms at the hotel were just a ruse, and you two were sharing the same room."

"Billy is a pain in the butt, but not dangerous, Sheriff."

"This is not the same Billy you remember. He's a numbers runner for the mob in Albany. I allow them to run the numbers racket in town in exchange for keeping the drugs and prostitution out. His connection with the Albany mob make him more arrogant than ever, and he feels he can get away with anything. Keeping track of Billy and his cohorts is a full-time job for my deputies and me."

"Can we get into trouble because of what Nicholas had told us?"

"Only Nick could get into trouble, plus the people who told him the story. Nick has active Top Secret clearance with the government."

"Nicholas had mentioned he had never served in the military."

"Nick told me that also, but he had done some work for the government in the past, and it was still considered active. That's how he got the information about Robbie."

The Sheriff made me laugh when he said, "That boy knows people."

I stopped by Carl's to talk to Nicholas, but he wasn't there. I went next door to the hotel and climbed the stairs to the second floor. My room was at the head of the stairs, directly across the hall from the room Nicholas occupied. I thought about knocking on his door but decided I would wait until morning to talk to him. It had been an emotional evening.

I unlocked my door, and suddenly I felt a hand on my arm. It was Billy. He was obviously drunk. He pushed me into my room. It happened so quickly I didn't have a chance to scream.

Billy tried to close the door with his foot, but something was keeping it from closing. He shoved me toward the bed and turned to shut the door. I scrambled to my feet and turned toward the door just in time to see Nicholas grab Billy, twist his arm behind his back, grab a handful of Billy's hair, and walk Billy to the top of the staircase. I thought he was going to throw Billy down the steps, but he stopped with Billy's toes at the very edge of the top step. I could tell Billy was in pain. Nicholas said something into Billy's ear, which I couldn't hear. Billy just stood there for a few seconds, yelped once and screamed.

"Okay, okay, let me go."

Nicholas released his hold. Billy walked halfway down the staircase and turned around.

"This is none of your business."

"When a lady is in danger, it's always a gentleman's business."

"This isn't over," Billy yelled as he continued down the stairs.

"And that goes for you too, Danielle."

"I'd think about that if I were you," Nicholas yelled after Billy, "I can still teach you how to fly."

When he was sure Billy was gone, Nicholas walked over to me.

"Ms. Palmer, I'd be really careful if I were you. That boy is dangerous. Please, don't be alone anywhere in town. Stay out of dark places and have someone walk you to your room until we leave."

"Billy just had too much to drink. Don't worry about him."

Nicholas wasn't convinced.

"Ms. Palmer, believe me, that boy is a danger to you. Please watch yourself."

Nicholas escorted me back to my room and made sure I had double locked the door. I looked through the peephole in the door a while later and saw the door to Nicholas's room was open. It stayed open all night. I stayed in my room and thought about the events of the day.

Who is this man? Who does he know, and how does he know them? How did he handle Billy so easily?

There was a lot more to the man I had known for the past six months. And, was what I didn't know about him all good?

Was he truly the man he appears to be, or is there a side to him that isn't yet visible?

The next day was Friday. We had three more days in

Cauldwell and then back to Florida. I knocked on Nicholas' door, it was still open, and I asked him to join me for breakfast. He agreed to meet me next door at Carl's. While waiting for Nicholas, I sat at the counter and talked to Carl.

"Billy has been spreading rumors all over town about you and Nick. Nobody believes him, but you know how small towns are. Once a rumor gets started, it spreads like wildfire and becomes the truth. Billy is trying to convince people that you aren't here to help them. He's telling anyone who will listen that you have become an important big city gal since you left and were just here to show off your success and your fancy big city boyfriend and to make it worse, he's a Yankee!"

I had noticed the mood of the townspeople turn cool over the past week and a half, but I thought it was because the town was in so much trouble. With everyone working half shifts, life was harsh. Carl had more to tell me.

"My daytime business is off because people don't have as much money to spend, and my nighttime business is off because the dance hall about thirty miles away has a new, fancy sound system. They've taken a good many of my out of town regulars over there."

When Nicholas arrived, we took a table and ordered breakfast. Carl served us and mentioned to Nicholas, "I made the call, and it looks possible."

When Carl left, I asked Nicholas what that was about.

"I know someone in Orlando who is modernizing his club and has a sound and light system he wouldn't need any longer. I thought it might help Carl's Place. All Carl has to do is pay for shipment and installation."

Chapter 5 – Billy Harris

I asked Nicholas if what he told Anna Lee last night was true and how he found out about it. He was vague at first, but I pressed.

"It all true, and I know about it because I have security clearance with the military."

"I'm sure I remember you telling me that you had never been in the service. How do you happen to have Top Secret clearance?"

Nicholas hesitated before answering.

"Ms. Palmer, many years ago, I was asked to do some work for the United States Government. It required top security clearance, and it's still active. It was a long time ago, but I still know people."

I pushed for more information, and I was not pleased with his answer.

"I never talk about that part of my life. Not only because it's still top secret, but because I'm not proud of what I had to do. It's not a pretty story, and no one except the people involved know it. I wish I could forget it."

I decided to let it go. It was obvious Nicholas didn't want to talk about it. I thanked him for being Johnny on the spot with Billy last night.

"What did you whisper to Billy and why did you whisper?"

"A friend of mine is an instructor in hand to hand combat, and he told me if I was ever in a brawl, and I wanted to threaten someone, to do it quietly and make it reasonable. If I had threatened Billy loud enough that you could hear, Billy would be forced to defend his honor or macho in front of you, but because I said it quietly, Billy could back down. Also, it had to be something that Billy was sure I was capable of doing."

"What exactly did you say to him?"

"I told Billy he had a choice. He could walk down the stairs and leave under his own power, or he could fly down the stairs and be carried out feet first."

"Nicholas, I really appreciate what you did last night, but I'm sure I could have talked Billy out of whatever he was planning. I've known him my whole life."

"I'm not so sure, Ms. Palmer. Billy is angry with you for some reason, and I'm sure his intention was to hurt you. Please be very careful while we're still in Cauldwell. I don't think you've seen the last of Billy's anger."

After breakfast, Nicholas went back to the plant, and I went to see how Anna Lee was doing. Nicholas and I didn't see each other again all day. That night I stopped in Carl's and saw Nicholas talking to the Sheriff. I didn't want to disturb them, so I spoke with Carl for a while and then said goodnight to the people in the kitchen. Instead of going back to the front of the hall, I went out the kitchen door, which led to the alley between Carl's and the hotel. It was dark in the alley and realizing I had made a mistake, I attempted to double back to the kitchen door. Before I got there, Billy grabbed me and pushed me against the wall.

I could smell the liquor on him, and it was apparent he was not in a good mood. With the music blaring inside Carl's, I knew screaming would be useless. For the first time in my life, I was genuinely afraid for my safety. Billy leaned against me. I could hardly understand his garbled words, but from the tone of his voice, I knew I was in trouble. Suddenly, Billy was gone, and Nicholas was standing in front of me.

"Danielle, get back inside!"

I didn't hesitate. I had to step over Billy, who was lying on the ground in pain. I ran out to the street but worried about Nicholas, I didn't go inside Carl's. I watched from the corner as Nicholas knelt down beside Billy. His left knee was on the ground, but his right knee was on Billy's groin. Nicholas was whispering to Billy, and I moved closer to hear what he was saying.

"I know who you are connected with, Billy. But you don't know who I am connected with. Tomorrow, Billy, my friends in New York are going to talk to your people in Albany. You are going to get a message from your friends in Albany. They are going to tell you Ms. Palmer is under their protection and off limits. I suggest you listen to them, Billy because if a second message is necessary, it won't be so pleasant, and it will come directly from my people!"

Nicholas shifted his weight, and I heard Billy howl in pain.

"Do we understand each other?"

Billy didn't answer. Nicholas lifted his knee off Billy's groin and then dropped it down back to the same spot. This time, Billy let out a loud pathetic cry.

"Yeah, Okay, okay!" Billy screamed.

Nicholas rolled Billy over onto his stomach and gave him a vicious punch to the kidney. Billy screamed in pain again and lay there, unable to move. Nicholas rose to his feet and headed for the street, leaving Billy on the ground. He spotted me standing halfway down the alley, came over, grabbed me roughly by the arm, and dragged me to the street corner. There, he pushed me back against the building wall, looked directly into my eyes and yelled at me.

"I warned you to be careful. That boy is bad news!"

I was still frightened by my encounter with Billy, and now I was being scolded. I knew I was wrong, but I shouted back at Nicholas.

"Who made you my keeper? I'll be the keeper of my own virtue, thank you."

Nicholas was shocked at my outburst. He didn't change his tone, but he did lower his voice.

"Ms. Palmer, I don't care who you decide to sleep with, but as long as you're with me, I'll try making sure it's your decision. If you want to have a tryst with Billy, that's none of my business. But this boy is bad news. He's pissed at you. He doesn't only want to rape you, he wants to hurt you. Hurt you badly. And that Ms. Palmer I will not allow."

Nicholas finally let go of my arm and continued in a gentler voice.

"Ms. Palmer, I am the keeper of no one's virtue except my own, but as long as I'm here, I cannot allow anyone to hurt you physically. If that is a problem for you, I will be happy to leave Cauldwell tomorrow morning."

With that, Nicholas walked away from me and went into Carl's.

It took a few minutes for me to gather myself and realize what a fool Nicholas must think I am. The man just saved me from Billy's rage. Rape and a beating were not impossible with the mood Billy was in. I went into Carl's looking for Nicholas. He was sitting at a table with the Sheriff. They seemed to be engrossed in an important conversation. I wondered if it was about what had happened in the alley.

I sat at the bar and waited. When the Sheriff got up from the table, either to make his rounds or check on Billy, Nicholas was alone, nursing a beer. I went over and asked if he'd mind if I joined him. He smiled as if nothing had happened between us.

"Of course not Ms. Palmer."

"Nicholas, I'm sorry. I was frightened, and I wasn't thinking right. Thank you for saving me a second time. I promise to be more careful."

"Not a problem, Ms. Palmer."

"Nicholas, what you said to Billy tonight. Do you really know those kinds of people that well?"

"Ms. Palmer, when I was in the restaurant business in New York, I met all sorts of people. I made a lot of friends, all kinds of friends."

He was smiling at me. Not laughing, but a genuine, sincere smile.

"Does this mean I won't be leaving Cauldwell tomorrow?"

I made a decision that didn't seem like much at the time but was the most monumental decision I have ever made.

"Yes Nicholas, you're leaving Cauldwell tomorrow. We're both leaving. We'll spend tomorrow night in Atlanta and fly back to Fort Lauderdale as planned on Sunday. I'll get us two rooms at the Doubletree for tomorrow night."

"If that's what you want, Ms. Palmer. What time do you want to leave?"

"I'd like to be out of here by ten AM if that's okay with you."

He said it was okay, and after he finished his beer he walked me to my room and said goodnight. It was a long night. The same thought came back to me over and over.

Who is this man? How much more is there to him?

After six months in the office, I thought I knew him. But, then there was seeing him with Stacy Geer. How comfortable he was when he escorted me to the charity dinner. What a great dancer he was. What important people he knew. Top Secret

Security clearance. Government work. Protector of women. Friend to troubled boys. And, what about the friends that were going to talk to Billy's friends.

Does that mean what it sounds like?

Morning came, and there was a knock at my door. Nicholas was in a cheerful mood.

"Good morning, Ms. Palmer! The bellman has the keys to the car. Call him when you're packed, and he'll put your suitcases in the trunk. I'm going to say goodbye to Anna Lee, Johnny, the Sheriff and Carl, and I'll meet you back here at ten, ...okay?"

Of course, it was okay, and at ten o'clock I called the bellman and went downstairs to say goodbye to Mr. Blumberg.

"Miss Danielle," he gushed, "Mr. Nick has gone to Carl's."

"I know. He's gone there to say goodbye."

"But, Miss Danielle, Billy, and his boys are there waiting for him. They said they were going to give him his comeuppance!"

I dropped everything and ran out the door, straight into the Sheriff who was headed for the alley next to Carl's. I told him what Mr. Blumberg had said. The sheriff already knew about it.

"Nick stopped by my office to say you were leaving, and I told him about the rumor."

"You have to stop it!"

"Why?"

"Because he could get hurt!"

"Who are you worried about, Miss Danielle, Nick or Billy?"

"Nicholas of course."

"That man can take care of himself. He was trained by the best," the Sheriff responded.

"What does that mean?"

"Miss Danielle, listen to me. Nick can take care of Billy and his friends, and it would help me to keep them under control after they've been embarrassed in front of the townspeople.

Come with me, I'm on my way over there to keep an eye on things. I have two deputies at the front door in case it gets out of hand."

He walked me to the alley, and we entered Carl's through the kitchen door, the same door I had used last night when Billy

42

was waiting for me. He insisted we stay in the kitchen out of the way and just watch.

Nicholas was standing with his back to the bar. Billy and his friends, Bobby Joe and Tommy Lee, were in front of him. Nicholas was talking to them in what appeared to be a calm manner. Suddenly Billy took a swing at Nicholas.

Nicholas ducked under the punch and managed to reverse positions, and now Billy and his boys were between Nicholas and the bar. Nicholas started backing away from them, but they stalked him.

"Smart move," the Sheriff said.

"Why doesn't he run?"

"He's heading for the pool tables. Watch!"

The Sheriff was right. Nicholas kept backing away until he was in the aisle between the two pool tables. He backed halfway down the aisle and stopped.

"See that? The pool tables protect his flanks. The boys have to stay in front of him now. They can't get behind him or alongside him."

Tommy Lee was the first to make a move. He came at Nicholas, fists cocked and ready to swing. Nicholas stepped aside, grabbed Tommy Lee's arm and pulled him forward. When Tommy Lee was passed him, Nicholas pushed him in the back and sent him flying into the tall bar table against the far wall. Tommy Lee bounced off the table and fell face first onto the bar stool. The stool broke, and Tommy Lee and the remains of the stool wound up on the floor. Bobby Joe was next, and mainly with the same move, Nicholas sent Bobby Joe to the far wall where he landed on top of Tommy Lee.

I was amazed at the way Nicholas moved, the way he handled those two men so easily. With Billy the previous two nights, Billy was alone and intoxicated. Nicholas caught him by surprise. It didn't take much to subdue him. I had no idea Nicholas was so capable. For some strange reason, I felt as if I had witnessed this scene before but while I was trying to remember where and when, I heard Carl yell, "Behind you!"

I looked back to where Nicholas was standing. Billy had picked up a pool cue and was swinging it at Nicholas's head. With his back still to Billy, Nicholas crouched down and raised his hands to protect his head. The butt end of the pool cue hit Nicholas right in the palm of his hand. His fingers closed around the stick, and he pulled it out of Billy's hand.

Nicholas stood up, faced Billy, and snapped the pool cue in half over his knee. The broken ends of the pool cue were extremely sharp, and for a moment, I thought Nicholas was going to stab Billy with them. But instead, he placed both halves in one hand and tossed them onto the pool table next to Billy. He then took two steps toward Billy and said something to him. I couldn't hear what he said, but Billy turned white. That was enough for the Sheriff. He told me to stay in the kitchen, and he and his two deputies gathered up Billy, Tommy Lee, Bobby Joe and handcuffed them. Nicholas looked at the Sheriff.

"No problem here Sheriff. The boys and I were just getting some exercise."

Sheriff Travis looked around.

"Someone will have to pay for the damage."

"I'll take care of it," Nicholas answered, and walked over to the bar. He took some money out of his pocket and handed it to Carl.

"That's way too much."

"Use what's left over for the sound system."

"It's still too much."

"Carl, please take it as a thank you for your hospitality during the past two weeks."

Carl finally backed down, thanked Nicholas, and put the money away. Nicholas turned to the Sheriff, who had moved over to the bar, with Billy in handcuffs.

"Okay, Sheriff? No problem?"

"Okay, but I think I'll keep these three on ice until you and Miss Danielle leave."

Nicholas turned to leave, but Billy, feeling safe in the Sheriff's custody, shouted at him.

"Yeah, get the fuck out of town and take that slut with you."

Nicholas stopped, spun around, and stepped toward Billy. I thought he was going to pummel him. Apparently, so did Billy, because he tried to hide behind the Sheriff, but could only back up against him.

"Did I hear you say slut, Billy. Your problem is the only women that will have anything to do with you are sluts and tramps. An elegant lady like Ms. Palmer wouldn't give you the time of day. That's why you found it necessary to attempt to force yourself on her. That didn't work either, so now you call her a slut. The truth is, all of the men in this town who requested favors from Ms. Palmer were disappointed. But only a slug like you would try to take her by force. Let me try to explain the facts of life to you. You see Billy, a fine lady like Ms. Palmer is very fussy as to who she will grant the honor of sampling her charms, a privilege I'm sad to say has never been extended in my direction."

Nicholas took a breath, shook his head, and brought his face to within an inch of Billy's.

"I gave you some advice last night, Billy. I strongly suggest you follow it. Ms. Palmer will most likely visit this town again, and I probably won't be with her. So, I'm counting on you to ensure her safety while she's here."

The look on Nicholas's face was menacing.

"What that means, Billy is if anything bad happens to that fine lady while she's here in Cauldwell, I'll be looking for you to answer for it. And, I'll find you no matter what rock you try to hide under. Your friends in Albany will not be able to help you. I'll finish what I started last night, Billy, and then no woman, decent or slut will have to fear you ever again."

Nicholas backed away from Billy and glanced at the Sheriff.

"Sorry about that Sheriff."

The Sheriff just nodded, and Nicholas turned toward the door again. But, as he turned, he noticed the people standing and staring at him. Most of the town was there, either in Carl's or standing outside trying to see what Billy and his boys were going to do to Nicholas.

Nicholas looked them over, from one side of the hall to the other. He started to say something to them, changed his mind and turned toward the door again. He took two steps and stopped, turning back toward the crowd.

"I've met a lot of people in my life. But, never have I encountered a group of ungrateful, stupid, gossip spreading idiots as I have seen here in this town. What is wrong with you people? This beautiful lady, one of your own, born and raised right here in Cauldwell, from a fine family, gives up the comforts

45

of her life to come here and attempt to save her hometown from oblivion, and you treat her as an outsider. You not only allow this bottom feeder to spread rumors about her, but you compound his sin by repeating them. Does no one here have any decency? Is there no man here who is man enough to defend this lady?"

Then Nicholas spotted the Minister and aimed his wrath at him.

"Preacher, you told me this was a good Christian town. Well, Preacher, if this is your idea of a good Christian town, then I suggest you are one lousy Preacher. Maybe you should go back to school and learn what the word Christian means. I haven't met many here."

No one was looking at Nicholas now. Everyone had their eyes turned down to the floor. Besides the Sheriff, Carl and the deputies, everyone was hit hard by Nicholas's words. But, he wasn't finished.

"I've heard of ignorant, southern rednecks, and you people are the definition of the term. I hope the factory does close, and all of you people have to move away to find other jobs, and this town ceases to exist because it's not worth the Georgia clay it stands on."

Another Knight in Shining Armor. The second one I've run into in the last eight months. But this one was my Knight come to defend my honor!

Once again, he apologized to the Sheriff and turned toward the door. Anna Lee, who had been standing just inside the doorway the entire time, stepped out to block his path. She looked up at him.

"Mr. Nick...Mr. Nick, I..."

And then this young, beautiful, reserved girl. The same girl I saw blush when she was caught holding hands with her own husband in public, got up on her toes, threw her arms around Nicholas's neck and planted a killer kiss on his lips that I was certain was going to set him on fire.

Nicholas caught completely off guard, quickly regained his composure. Now, most men I think would have swooped this beautiful creature up in his arms and held her tightly as he enjoyed the sensuousness of this young woman.

46

But, Nicholas, bent slightly at the waist so he could keep their bodies apart, placed one hand on the bar for support and held the other hand at his side and just let Anna Lee do what she felt she had to do.

When she finally backed away, blushing a bright cherry color, she said sheepishly, "I'm sorry Mr. Nick," and lowered her head.

Nicholas lifted her chin with his hand so he could look into her eyes. He smiled at her sincerely.

"Miss Anna Lee, I swear Ma'am you could melt the heart of a cold stone statue. I surely do appreciate the gesture, Ma'am. It means a lot to an older gentleman like me."

He turned around again and found Bobbie Joe, who was being held by one of the deputies.

"Bobby Joe, rumor has it you're kind of sweet on this beautiful young lady. Well, forget it, boy. This woman has had a real man in her life. She wouldn't be interested in the likes of you. No, Bobby Joe, you're one of Billy's boys, and when you get to be his age, you're going to be just like him. Only sluts and tramps will have anything to do with you. You'll find fine ladies like Miss Anna Lee want real men, not punks like you."

Turning back to Anna Lee, he said, "Miss Anna Lee, it has been a privilege and an honor to have made your acquaintance. You take care now and take good care of that fine boy of yours. He has the makings of a great man, just like his daddy."

With that final word, Nicholas walked out the door. I was still caught in the kitchen. How was I going to get back to the hotel without Nicholas seeing me? I don't know why I didn't want him to know I was there and had witnessed everything, but at the time, it seemed important he didn't know. I headed up the alley and peeked around the corner.

The Sheriff was talking to Nicholas. Sheriff Travis was positioned at the curb, so Nicholas's back was toward me, and I could hurry passed and into the hotel's front door.

A couple of minutes later, Nicholas walked into the hotel as if nothing had happened. I was standing at the reception desk, and when I looked in his direction, he asked, "All set?"

"Ready," I answered, not sure if I was.

Was I really prepared for this trip?

Chapter 6 - Drive to Atlanta

Nicholas held the door for me as I slid into the passenger side of the rental. I had my seatbelt fastened before he walked around the car and popped into the driver's seat. He started the engine and off we went, neither of us commenting on the fact that practically the entire town was out on the street watching us leave, but we were both aware of it. I sat very quietly on my side of the front seat, trying to understand what had just happened and why it had such a profound effect on me.

About twenty miles out of town, we had to stop for gas. While he filled the tank, I went to the store to get us some drinks and snacks for the trip. My cell phone chirped. It was Anna Lee. She sounded out of breath.

"Auntie Danielle, you should have heard him. He was wonderful. I can't tell you everything he said, but ..."

"I was there Anna Lee, at Carl's. I was in the kitchen. I saw and heard everything."

"Oh Auntie Danielle, wasn't he wonderful?"

"Yes, Anna Lee."

"Did I do wrong, Auntie Danielle, I didn't intend to do that, but I couldn't think of the proper words to tell him how I felt."

"No, Anna Lee, you didn't do wrong. I'm sure he understood what you were trying to say. I'm sure he appreciated the gesture as much as he said he did."

"Auntie Danielle, you knew my Robbie, and you heard what Mr. Nick said about him. You know my daddy, and my granddaddy was your daddy."

"Yes, Anna Lee," I said, wondering where she was heading.

"I've had good men in my life, Auntie Danielle, great men."

There was silence between us for a moment, and then she changed my entire world.

"Auntie Danielle, that man you are with is the mostest man I have ever met in my entire life, and you have to tell him that."

The mostest man she has ever met in her entire life, and...she was right.

He was the mostest man I had ever met in my life also, but how do you tell him that? How do you put those feelings into words? Maybe that's how Anna Lee felt at Carl's. Words weren't enough!

I told Anna Lee I would find a way to let him know, promised to call her next week, paid for our drinks and went back to the car. The door was held open for me as usual, and after I was settled, he got in his side, and we were on our way to Atlanta. Anna Lee's words kept swirling around in my head.

The mostest man I have ever met in my entire life.

I thought about my relationship with this man, from the moment he first walked into my office right through this morning. He wasn't one man, he was many men. There were so many facets to this man I didn't think I would ever see them all. My concentration was broken by the sound of his voice.

"Are you okay, Ms. Palmer?"

"I'm fine, just going over everything one last time."

"Ms. Palmer, don't let the situation in Cauldwell upset you. They know the factory will probably close, and they'll have to move, and everything they know and have known all their lives will change. They're not bad people, just frightened Ma'am."

After dressing down the entire town, now he's making excuses for them.

Why? Just to make me feel better!

"Don't give up. I know people. I may be able to find someone who will be willing to take a chance on Cauldwell. It's not a dead issue yet. When we get back to Fort Lauderdale, I'll make some calls. I can't promise anything, but there's still hope."

That put my brain on overload. After everything that happened in Cauldwell. After everything that happened this morning, first he defends them, and now he's trying to save them.

No Danielle! It's not them, it's you. He's doing this for you!

I had to settle myself down. I thought about how we had met, and the eight months I had known him. I thought about my life before we met. I thought all the way back to my childhood and the reasons we had come to Georgia.

The car was heading for the Interstate Highway that would take us to Atlanta. I closed my eyes and brought it all back. I don't know how long I sat like that, but an idea began to form.

When I opened my eyes, we were on the Interstate. We passed a sign, 'Rest Area 2 miles'. No food court or gas station, just one of those places that have toilets, a Visitor's Center, and vending machines. I asked Nicholas to stop. Having made a decision, I felt better. I asked Nicholas to retrieve one of my suitcases from the trunk of the car, and I rolled it into the restroom. I'm sure he had no idea what I was doing, but he never questioned me or complained. It must have been twenty or thirty minutes before I exited the restroom.

If you don't know me well, you won't understand just how crazy and off the wall my plan was. I am primarily a reserved, proper lady. I'm not shy about coyly letting a man know I might be interested in dating him, but, I'm not forward, and definitely not flashy. I like to dress up and make myself as pretty as possible, hence, the two months' pay for a Stacy Geer gown, but in a conservative way. This was not me! This was outrageous conduct. But, I didn't want there to be any doubt as to what I had in mind.

After my breakup with Jack, my kid sister Colleen had bought an outfit for me. She called it my vamp outfit, and it was that. It was something I would never wear in public, and I was even embarrassed when I tried it on in my apartment. Colleen insisted I keep it and suggested I put it in my suitcase.

"On one of your business trips, you may run into a situation that calls for something extra."

I didn't want to hurt her feelings, so this outfit had traveled all over the country but had never left my suitcase.

It was time. This was the situation.

This vamp outfit consisted of black lace panties and a matching demi bra. A hot pink skirt that was so short, it barely covered the essentials. A beige silk blouse with buttons that stopped just above the top of the bra and a pair of high heel strapped sandals.

I let my hair down, brushed it out, redid my makeup, put on my vamp outfit, and checked myself out in the mirror. You really don't get a real reflection in those metal mirrors they have inside road restrooms, but even so, I thought the lady staring back at me looked pretty hot.

As I exited the restroom, I looked for Nicholas. He was in the car, sitting in the driver's seat, watching the restroom door.

When he spotted me, he got out of the car, moved over to the sidewalk, and watched me as I strutted toward him. And, I mean I strutted over to him. He never took his eyes off me as I made my way down the walk and over to the car. When I was within a few feet of him, he opened the car door and stood aside so I could enter.

As I slid into the passenger's seat, I was sure all of my womanly charms were readily available for his enjoyment, and I glanced up at him to gauge his reaction. He was not looking at me. His eyes were pointed straight ahead. So typical of him. Not wanting me to feel uncomfortable by leering at me.

But my friend, I'm not going to give you a choice today.

Nicholas put the suitcase away, got in the left seat, and while he was fastening his seat belt and getting ready to start the car, I said in my most casual tone, "Well?"

"Excuse me, Ma'am?"

"Don't I, at least, rate a comment?"

Nicholas turned to look at me. He has a habit of always looking directly into your eyes when he speaks to you. He never looks down, up or to the side. His eyes are directly on yours as if he's trying to read the reaction to what he's telling you. But not this time. I saw his eyes move from my head to my toes and back very slowly as if he was trying to categorize every feature. He looked very thoughtful before he spoke.

"Ms. Palmer, when I was in high school, there was a sign above the blackboard in shop class. It read; 'Please engage brain before starting mouth.' I am trying to do that now, Ma'am, but I am having difficulty finding the correct words. Seeing you like this brings only one thought to mind."

"And what might that be?"

"Well," he hesitated, "No disrespect meant Ms. Palmer, but the only thing that comes to mind is **VA VA VOOM**."

He said it so loud, and with such energy, I was shocked at first, and then I giggled.

"That will do Nicholas. That will do very nicely. Thank you!"

"Yes Ma'am," was his only reply, as he turned straight and prepared to start the car.

"Aren't you curious as to why I'm dressed this way?"

"Well Ma'am, I expect you feel so bad about the situation in

Cauldwell, you just wanted to feel better, and dressing up helps."

About what I should have expected from him. So, now to the direct approach. Remember, this is not the Danielle Grace Palmer we all know. This is a gal on a mission to tell a man ...what?

Well, as the saying goes, in for a penny!

As Nicholas was backing out of the parking spot and headed out toward the highway, I took a deep breath.

"Nicholas, let me tell you what I have in mind. My plan is to drive to Atlanta, cancel one of the hotel rooms, have dinner, have a few drinks, maybe one or two more than usual, and then, you and I spend the night together."

Before he could answer, I added, "But, there are rules Nicholas."

"Rules, Ma'am?"

"Yes, Nicholas, rules. Rule number one, it starts when we get to Atlanta. Rule number two, it ends when we get out of bed tomorrow morning. And, then Nicholas, you will forget it ever happened, because as far as we are concerned, it never did!"

We were almost on the highway by the time I had finished my little speech. Nicholas pulled over to the shoulder of the road, put the car in park, and turned to look at me, this time directly into my eyes.

"Ms. Palmer, any man who would turn down such an offer from you, would be considered a complete fool, and my daddy didn't raise any fools. But, before I agree, I need to ask you a question.

"Okay, Nicholas. What's the question?"

Ms. Palmer, I need to know WHY?"

"Why?"

"Ms. Palmer, I like you, I think we are more than boss and employee. I believe we are friends."

"We are friends, Nicholas."

"Yes, Ma'am. And I really like being your friend. I like the relationship we have. I'm afraid if the reason you propose this is because you feel bad about what happened in Cauldwell or as a way to say thank you for anything I've done, I'm afraid later on you may regret this and maybe even resent the fact I took advantage of the situation. And that Ms. Palmer would undoubtedly affect our friendship. As much as a night with you appeals to me, it's not worth losing you as a friend. So, Ms. Palmer, I need to know why!"

Is it possible that one word could make you fall head over heels in love with someone? If it is, then Nicholas had said that word!

How do I answer that? How could I possibly put into words what I was feeling? How could I make him understand when I didn't understand myself? It was nothing he had done and everything he had done, everything he was. I tried to recall every minute I had known this man. I tried to find the perfect answer to his question. In the end, it came down to one thing ...Anna Lee. I looked into those deep-set brown eyes of his.

"Nicholas, when you were getting gas, Anna Lee called me."

A worried look from Nicholas and I knew he was afraid Anna Lee had told me what had happened at Carl's this morning.

"Miss Anna Lee is a very fine lady, Ma'am, what did she have to say?"

"We couldn't talk long. She just wanted to tell me something she wanted me to pass on to you."

I kept my eyes focused on him in hopes he could see the sincerity of my words.

"Ann Lee wants you to know you are the mostest man she has ever met in her entire life."

That brought out one of his great smiles.

"That's a very nice thing for her to say."

"I agree with her, Nicholas. You are the mostest man I have ever met in my entire life also. It's not anything specific you've done or said it's who you are! You are truly one of a kind, Nicholas. The most honorable, caring, responsible, open, loving, and sincerest man I've ever had the good fortune to meet."

I paused, searching for the right words. I decided the truth would be best.

"Nicholas, I want to know what it is like to be intimate with such a man!"

He looked into my eyes for a very long time, and then he looked down. I could feel the wheels turning as he tried to make sense of what I had just said. His eyes came back up to meet mine, and I could hear the sincerity in his words.

"Ms. Palmer, I must admit the thought of spending a night with you has crossed my mind on more than one occasion. But, there are three things I must say first."

I waited, wondering what he was thinking.

"First, if it takes a few drinks more than normal than I feel your reasons aren't quite what you say."

"Oh, Nicholas! That was such a stupid thing for me to say. I didn't mean it at all. Nicholas, I have never tried to seduce a man before and I ...I didn't know how to go about it. I don't need alcohol. Not a few more or any drinks at all. I want to know you intimately, Nicholas, and cold sober is the way I want this to happen."

That brought a smile to his face.

"Second, your rules are all wrong."

"What's wrong with my rules?"

"They don't leave time Ma'am."

"Time for what?"

"The before and after. The before and after are at least as important as, maybe more important than the actual ...doing!"

Before and after. What man cares about a before and after? The before is usually just a necessity to get you into bed, and the after is mostly non-existent.

What have I let myself in for?

"What would your rules be?"

He sounded serious again.

"Ms. Palmer, I can't promise you I will ever forget this happened. I have a feeling I will never be able to forget this weekend. But, I do promise, you will never see or hear any indication from me anything happened between us. I promise you, as a gentleman to a lady, you or anyone else will never know I have any recollection of this weekend. And Ms. Palmer, a gentleman never breaks a promise to a lady."

"I trust you Nicholas."

"My rules would be, rule number one: it starts right now. Rule number two: it ends when we walk off the plane in Fort Lauderdale. And then, Ms. Palmer, I promise you, you will never see any indication from me that anything happened between us."

"A gentleman's promise to a lady?"

54

"A gentleman's promise to a lady!"

"Okay, Nicholas, your rules!"

At that, Nicholas turned in his seat, put the car in gear, and drove onto the Interstate.

"You said there were three things."

"Yes, Ma'am. Nicholas is my Deltron Motors name, my friends call me Nick."

"Okay, Nick. What now?"

A quick glance in my direction and a smile.

"Now Danielle, you trust me!"

It wasn't a question, it was a statement, and I did. It was the very first time he had called me Danielle, except for when he shouted for me to get back inside last night.

And this time, I liked the sound.

Once he had gotten the car up to speed and set the cruise control, he reached for his Bluetooth earpiece, put it on, took out his cell phone, and punched a speed dial number. When the party on the other end answered, he started a very unusual conversation.

"I need accommodations in Atlanta, Georgia, tonight, just the one night."

I don't know what the person on the other end of the phone was saying, but Nick's end of the conversation was a series of yes, and no's. He ended the conversation with, "Thanks, Sweetie, get back to me."

When he put down the phone, I reminded him, "We already have reservations at the Doubletree."

His answer was one of the two lines I had heard many times before and would hear many times again.

"It's covered."

"Don't like the Doubletree?"

"That's where we stay on company business. Tonight is special, requires something special."

"I am completely in your hands," I said teasingly, "And I guess Sweetie's also. Girlfriend?"

"If I had a girlfriend, Danielle, this wouldn't be happening."

Why was it so easy for me to believe that statement?

"Sweetie's name is Pam Dugan. She is the Director of Corporate Travel for a major company in Fort Lauderdale, and she is superb at getting last minute reservations and special requests. When we get back to the office, I'll give her number to Crystal for the phone log. I'll give Pam your name, and if you ever need anything last minute or special, she's your gal."

"She seems to know exactly what you want. You must know her well."

"I'd say I know her well, Pam is my late wife's daughter."

Oops. That brought ten minutes of silence between us.

Nick's cell phone broke the mood. He answered and pulled over to the shoulder of the highway. He cleared the GPS and inserted a new address. Then he asked Sweetie to cancel our reservations at the Doubletree and check our flight reservations to Fort Lauderdale tomorrow. After disconnecting the call, he sent a short text message and pulled back on the highway. We were back up to speed, and the cruise control was engaged. I decided it was time to really get to know this man.

"Tell me about her."

"Who?"

"Your late wife."

Nick glanced at me, smiled, and then we began a very intimate conversation about both of our lives, loves, triumphs, and failures. We stopped for lunch and continued our talk, all the way to Atlanta.

I was interested in the man and his feelings, not his career or worldly accomplishments, but the inner man. He seemed to want the same from me and managed to pull out feelings I usually kept to myself.

We hadn't made love or had sex or shared a bed yet, but talking to him like this felt so intimate. Isn't this what I had told him I wanted?

Yes, it was exactly what I wanted, and I felt so close to him, I didn't want the trip to end.

Chapter 7 – Our Stories

Nick told me he had been married twice.

"First time to my childhood sweetheart. We produced two beautiful children who I am very proud of and very close to. We were young when we married, and as we matured, we grew in opposite directions.

"In our fifth year of marriage, we separated. I'm old school Italian, and divorce was not an option. Even though she started to date, we still attempted to find something to hold on to. When I'd pick up or drop off the kids, we'd talk, and sometimes we'd wind up in bed together. One night I realized she was sleeping with both this other guy and me, hedging her bet, so to speak. That was the end. We divorced, and she remarried.

"It took me many years to fall in love again. This time, it was love at first sight. I was living in New York at the time, and she lived in Texas. I met her on a business trip, and we started a long distance relationship that lasted a year. We would send cards and letters to each other, and since we always knew when we would see each other again, I started signing the cards 'Till Then,' which I eventually shortened to 'TT.' Joan had three girls of her own. When I moved to Texas, and we married, the girls became part of my family. Pam is her oldest. Five years after we were married, cancer took her away from me, and I've never found another love."

I responded to his openness by telling him what it was like to grow up in Cauldwell. I talked about my birth parents, and how they had been killed in an auto accident when I was ten and my sister, Colleen was eight.

"We were lucky. An older couple who had known my parents officially adopted us, and our name was changed to Palmer. At that age, I don't know what I would have done if it wasn't for Mommy and Daddy Palmer. They were so loving and caring. After a while, we evolved into a real family. As if we were born to them.

"The Palmers had an older daughter, Lindsey. She was fifteen years older than I was and she became a big sister, advisor, and protector to Colleen and me. Anna Lee is Lindsey's daughter. I was devastated when Daddy Palmer was killed by a drunk driver. I was in college, and the utter despair I felt was compounded when Mommy Palmer died six months later."

I had never been this open with anyone, not even Colleen, my closest confidant. He asked probing questions, proof he was paying real attention to what I was saying, and not just pretending he was interested as so many men do on dates.

"How did you wind up in Fort Lauderdale?"

"Being a GRITS, I was expected to attend the University of Georgia, but I knew that Colleen was only two years behind me, and it would be difficult for Daddy Palmer to send both of us to college. So, when I was offered a volleyball scholarship at Florida State, I became a Seminole instead of a Bulldog."

Nick chuckled. "Grits?"

"G.R.I.T.S... Girls Raised In The South."

That brought out one of his great smiles.

"By the time I graduated, my parents were gone, Colleen and Anna Lee were in Athens at the University, and Lindsey and her husband had moved to Montana. There isn't a lot of work for a college girl in Cauldwell, so when I was offered a job in Tallahassee, I took it. A promotion meant a move to Fort Lauderdale."

Since Nick had been so open with me, I decided I wanted to be as open with him.

"Do you remember the man who picks me up for lunch occasionally?"

"Yes, I do. Dan, Dan Patrick isn't it?"

"Yes. Dan is my very best friend in the whole world. We met when I transferred to Fort Lauderdale. We hit it off immediately, but because I had been warned about inter-office relationships, we became friends and never officially dated. Dan suggested that my career would be at a dead end with the company we worked for, and he knew of a position open at Strollman Brothers that he thought would be perfect for me. When I moved over to Strollman, I thought that maybe now Dan and I could get together, but it never happened. It didn't happen because I met Jack Reynolds. Jack was a salesman for Strollman. He was the most beautiful man I had ever met."

I brought up an image of Jack and wondered how I could have been so foolish to be taken in by his looks.

"Not only was he handsome, but he was charming and worldly and charismatic. I fell under his spell immediately. But, so did every other girl in the office and every girl who met him."

I thought about how far I wanted to go with this and decided to tell Nick the entire story.

"Out of all the girls Jack had after him, he picked me. When he asked me to move in with him, I jumped at the chance. It was amazing for a while, and then things changed. Jack became demanding and controlling and very jealous. He only allowed me to dress up when he was with me. At all other times, he wanted me to dress down and not look so nice.

"He began to come home to the apartment late and didn't want to talk about why or where he was, or who he was with. All he ever said was, it was business. He didn't like my relationship with Dan, and Dan didn't like Jack at all. When Lindsey and Colleen came to visit, they both took a dislike to Jack. Lindsey tried to talk me into moving out. I was becoming uneasy with our relationship, but when I was in his arms, and he kissed me, everything changed. All my misgivings disappeared. When I was in Jack's arms, I just melted, and all was right with the world. He was magnificent at that!"

I glanced at Nick to see if he was actually paying attention. He seemed to be interested, so I told him the rest.

"I didn't see Jack much at work. He'd come in early, and after the sales meeting, he'd be out with his customers. One day, I was preparing a proposal for Mr. Strollman. I was supposed to go to dinner with him and a new client. I was making copies of the proposal for us when I had a problem with the copy machine, and the black carbon got all over my skirt. I couldn't brush it out. Mr. Strollman suggested I go home and change and meet him at the restaurant.

"When I got to the apartment, it was quiet. Jack knew about my dinner engagement with Mr. Strollman and he told me he was having dinner with a client, so I didn't think it unusual that no one was home. When I walked into the bedroom to change my skirt, I found Jack and one of the girls from the office naked in bed together. It didn't take any imagination to figure out what they had been doing."

I glanced at Nick again in an attempt to determine if I was going too far. He was looking at me. He couldn't look in my direction too long, we were traveling at high speed on the interstate, but I was sure I saw sympathy in his eyes.

"How did you ever get over that?" he asked in a very sympathetic voice.

I took another minute to decide if I wanted to tell him everything. I decided to be completely open with him. I didn't know why, but I trusted that he would understand.

"I ran out of the house and found myself in a neighborhood diner. I called Dan. He could hardly understand me, I was crying and sobbing so much, but he knew I was in trouble and did manage to find out where I was. He came right over and managed to calm me down. He took me home with him and spent the entire night talking to me. The next day, he went with me to pick up my things from Jack's apartment. I was sure he was going to beat Jack, but I managed to stop him. I lived with Dan for six months. I couldn't face Jack and the other people at Strollman, so I quit my job there. Everyone felt sorry for me, but Jack bragged about it. He was proud of the fact that he had used my gullibility to his advantage."

Again I glanced at Nick. He still seemed to be paying attention, so I continued.

"The time I spent as Dan's roommate changed me. Dan helped me find an apartment and the job with Deltron. My career took off from there. I was more in tune with myself and decided that no man would ever define who I was. I knew who I was, and I was sure that any man who had my attention would be lucky. I grew from a simple country girl into a stable, self-assured woman. It was Dan Patrick who was responsible."

"Did you and Dan ever get together?"

"Once I was on my own and surer of myself, Dan and I did try for a more meaningful relationship. We were exclusive, even lovers for a while, but something was missing. Finally, one Sunday morning, after we had spent the night together, I asked him what was wrong. Dan told me he loved me, and he was pretty sure I felt the same way, but we weren't **in love** with each other.

"What we had was more than friendship, but he was pretty sure it's not what either of us was willing to settle for. When I thought about that statement, I knew he was right. We still see each other and date occasionally, but we both know what we have is not true love."

I thought about what I wanted to say next. This would be difficult for Nick to understand.

"I know it sounds foolish to believe that former lovers can be friends, but the truth is, Dan Patrick will always be my best friend."

Nick's answer surprised me.

"It's not foolish at all, Danielle. I know it's possible because I experienced something like that myself."

Now, he hesitated, and I was sure it was his turn to decide how far he wanted to go.

"Remember Stacy Geer?

"How could I forget her? She's beautiful and talented."

"After Joan died, I didn't know what to do with myself. I went back to New York and got a job managing a restaurant, but it wasn't the same. A man I used to work for moved to Florida and opened a Wholesale Lobster Plant and asked me to come down and help him operate the place. I made the move and felt no better than I did in New York. I met Stacy at a party. She wasn't 'THE Stacy Geer' at the time. She worked as a designer for another fashion house. The sparks flew immediately. We never talked about a relationship or being exclusive, it just sort of happened. We spent every weekend together. We went to parties together. We were a couple."

He paused as he changed lanes to pass a slow-moving truck.

"It was a little over a year into our relationship. We had a great weekend. Friday night we went to the theater. Saturday we went to dinner and then dancing. Sunday we had brunch at our favorite place. I stayed at Stacy's place all weekend. I had to be at the plant at four o'clock Monday morning for a delivery, so after brunch, I went home to get some sleep. The following Friday, I was talking to one of our suppliers on the phone, and he asked for our shipper's phone number. As I pulled their business card from my wallet, the tickets from the play Stacy and I attended the previous Friday night fell out of my wallet. After I hung up the phone, I stared at the tickets for a long time. I realized I had not given Stacy a thought since I left her Sunday afternoon.

"With Joan, she was never out of my mind. If I wasn't talking to her, I was talking about her. If I passed a new restaurant, I'd wonder if she'd like to try it. She was always in my thoughts. With Stacy, it was great when we were together, but when we weren't, it was as if she didn't exist."

Nick paused again when we ran up on another slow-moving truck and had to wait for traffic to clear before we could pass. But once up to speed, he continued.

"That night we had dinner at her place. We were going to stay in and watch a movie. Stacy sensed my mood and asked what was wrong. When I told her, she laughed. She said she hadn't given me much thought all week either. I asked her if that didn't seem odd. We never did watch the movie. We talked about it all night. The decision was that we liked each other, but were not in love with each other. We decided to end the exclusive part of our relationship, and eventually, the sex stopped, and we became friends.

"The first time I ran into Stacy at a party when she was with another guy, I thought I'd be jealous. But, I felt no different than when I run into Marc or Tony or Terry with a woman. He was just my friend's date."

Nick glanced in my direction for just a second.

"I can understand the relationship you have with Dan because I consider Stacy, my best friend. I can tell her anything, my innermost secrets and I'm sure they will be safe with her. I can confide in her, and I respect her advice. It's unusual, I admit, but it can happen."

He does understand.

And to a certain degree, he even helped me understand my relationship with Dan in a way I had never thought of before. We continued to talk. I told him more about my college days and my early work history. We talked about my move up the corporate ladder at Deltron. Nick asked if I remembered Terry Daniels.

"Terry was right. You'll never get the recognition you deserve at Deltron, and after the Paterson deal is signed, you should think about making a move."

"Mr. Daniels was only being polite."

Nick response surprised me.

"In spite of the fact he wanted to put the make on you, he

meant what he said about moving to Daniels Industries. Other CEOs know about you and would be more than happy to give you a job in middle management."

"And just how do you know that?"

With a big grin, he replied, "I know people."

I told him about some of the men I had dated. I mentioned how much I missed Colleen and Lindsey.

We talked about Anna Lee, and I again asked how he knew what he knew. He responded that it was a long story, and no one who wasn't involved knew about it. I asked him to tell me what he could. Nick hesitated.

"Danielle, I've already told you I don't like to talk about that time in my life, but if you must know, I'll tell you the sanitized version."

He hesitated again and getting no reaction from me, continued.

"You remember I said I know people?"

"Yes, I seem to remember that phrase being mentioned."

That brought out a smile, but not a real smile.

"Well, back in my restaurant days, I knew both people in the government and some bad people that didn't like the government people at all. The government had a major problem to solve. I can't tell you the details, but it was crucial. The bad people were in a position to assist in resolving the problem for the government.

"The government people, knowing I was very close to the other people, asked me to be a go-between and try to get the other people to help solve the problem. To properly understand how important the problem was, I had to know certain top-secret government information. So, I was given top secret clearance. For some unknown reason, it's never been deactivated. I negotiated between the two parties and got an agreement. The problem was solved, and everyone was happy, and I still have top secret clearance."

"But, what has that got to do with the Navy and the Marines?"

"That part is simple. Because of the people I was dealing with, the government people decided I should know how to protect myself, so they arranged to have me take hand-to-hand combat and small arms training at the Navy Seal Training Center. Because I was a civilian training with the Seals, the Naval Officer who was running the training was curious. I couldn't tell him the reason I was there, but we became friends. When Anna Lee told me about Robbie, I called my friend, and he put me in touch with Robbie's commanding officer."

"That's why Sheriff Travis said you were trained by the best and could take care of yourself. That's how you handled Billy and his boys so easily."

"Excuse me?" Nick said, not in a friendly tone, "Billy ...and his boys?"

Oops, damn. I did intend to tell him, but not like this.

"Yes, I was there," I said carefully. "I was at Carl's this morning. The Sheriff and I were in the kitchen. He wanted me out of the way, and he was there in case things got out of hand. I heard and saw everything."

"And that's why I'm the mostest man you've ever met?" he said in an even less friendly tone.

"No," I said quickly, "No, no, no. I didn't want to tell you because I knew that's what you would think. That's not the reason!"

He wasn't happy. This wasn't going to be easy.

"Nicholas...Nick," I tried in my most sincere voice, "You made a promise, to me, a promise from a gentleman to a lady. You made me trust you. Now you have to trust me."

"Yes Ma'am," he said, not very convincingly.

"Nick," I pleaded, "I make a promise to you, right now, from a lady to a gentleman. Please trust what I tell you. I promise I will never lie to you, deceive you, or keep anything from you, ever again. I promise you this Nick, and a lady never breaks a promise to a gentleman."

"Not fair using my own words against me."

"Please listen," I pleaded, "I can't say this morning didn't affect me. I can't say what happened at Carl's didn't help me make the decision I made today. But, Nick, it's not the only reason. There are so many reasons. I can't tell you all of them because I'm not sure myself what they all are. Yes, it was the way you defended me this morning, and the way you handled Anna Lee's kiss, and the way you protected me from Billy. All of those things had a part in my decision, but they aren't the only reasons."

I was trying to find the right words.

"Nick, I've respected you from the day we met. I've admired the way you handled yourself in the office. I felt jealous when I saw you with Stacy Geer. I loved the way you treated me when you escorted me to the charity dinner. I love the way you dance. I was disappointed you didn't ask me out on your own. I asked you to come with me to Cauldwell because I knew you could find a solution if there was one, and I could trust you to be a gentleman while we were there. There are so many reasons why I think you are the mostest man I have ever met. What you did for Anna Lee, what you did for Johnny, and this morning was just the icing on the cake, but, it's not the cake, Nick ...you are."

"Danielle, I'm just a man, I'm nothing special. I just happened to be in a position to do certain things that seemed to impress you. There's nothing special about any of it."

"That's what you don't understand. It's not the things you did that impressed me. It's the man who cared enough to do those things. Sure, circumstances put you in a position to do what you did, but not every man ...not any man I know would have responded the way you did. It's everything about you. It's the man behind the deeds I want to be intimate with. And we have been for the past hours. I have never opened myself up to anyone as I have to you today. We have been intimate and please don't let it stop now!"

"Danielle, you really don't know anything about me. I'm not who you think I am. Even our meeting wasn't exactly on the level. My taking a job at Deltron was not an accident. I like you, Danielle. I really like you. I think you are the finest lady I have ever met. I meant what I said earlier. I don't want to ruin the friendship we have. I need to know nothing that happens this weekend will jeopardize that."

"I promise you, from a lady to a gentleman, my reasons are what I have tried to explain to you."

He glanced at me quickly, We were doing seventy miles an hour, so a long look was out of the question, and I didn't get a chance to see his eyes.

Then he smiled.

"Tell me more about Colleen and Lindsey."

It was all right. I could feel it. He was not going to change our plans. I almost jumped out of my seat, but instead, the intimacy continued. I was with a very caring, sincere, and sensitive man. The rest of the ride was even better.

I couldn't imagine what lay ahead for me in Atlanta.

Chapter 8 – Atlanta

Talk stopped when we got to Atlanta. We followed the GPS instructions, and around four o'clock in the afternoon, we stopped in front of the Grand Hyatt Hotel.

"Kind of ritzy?"

"Nothing but the best for My Lady."

"But Nick," I started to say, but he cut me off.

"It's covered," and that was the end of the discussion.

Nick seemed to know everyone there. He addressed everyone by name and shook their hand, the valet, the bellman, the doorman, but he didn't tip anyone. On the way to the desk to check in, I asked, "Been here before?"

"Nope, first time."

"But, you know everyone's name."

"Name tags."

"You read name tags?"

"A very great man once told me it's important to use people's names whenever possible, people in the service industries, most of all. I try to follow that advice."

"But, you don't tip anyone. Isn't that, even more, important?"

"It's covered," he said with a smile.

When we got to the front desk, I took notice of the clerk. She did have a name tag, and Nick addressed her by name.

"Afternoon Charlotte, reservation for Amonti."

Without looking at the computer, Charlotte answered, "One moment, sir."

She picked up the phone and announced, "Mr. Amonti has arrived."

The manager walked out of his office and came over to us with the biggest smile you can imagine.

"Good afternoon, Mr. Amonti. We are so pleased to have you with us today. Everything has been arranged as you requested."

He handed two key cards to the bellman and instructed, "Penthouse Suite."

No ID asked for, no credit card, Nick didn't sign the Guest Folio.

On the way up in the elevator, I looked at Nick. Seeing the expression on my face, he smiled.

"Nothing but the best for My Lady."

The suite was gorgeous. Huge living room. The dining room table sat twelve. French doors opened onto a patio that overlooked Atlanta, a mini kitchen, wet bar and two bedrooms.

Nick directed the bellman to put my luggage in the larger of the bedrooms and Nick's luggage in the other bedroom. I waited for the bellman to leave before I questioned that, and while I waited, I checked out the suite. There were two dozen beautiful white roses on a glass table with a card. I went over to look at the card, hoping to get some idea as to why we were being treated like royalty. The card was blank on one side and on the other side was just one word, in bold letters;

BEFORE

Again, a handshake and a thank you by name to the bellman, but no tip. Nick moved into the living room and sat on the arm of the couch. I showed him the card from the roses and gave him an inquisitive look.

"Text message."

I remembered him sending a short text after Sweetie called back with our reservations.

That brought a smile to my face.

"Nick, this has to cost a fortune."

"Not as much as you might think."

"Really, could you explain that?"

"Danielle, a couple of things you have to understand. First, I'm not going to miss any lunches next week to pay for this. It must be obvious I don't live on my Deltron Motors paycheck. I'm okay financially. Please trust me on this!"

I started to say something, but he interrupted.

"Second, not everything is what it seems. Pam does a lot of business with the Hyatt chain, and she gets perks. She's more than happy to pass them along to the family, and I'm family. This place doesn't cost nearly as much as you might think."

Again, I started to say something, and again he interrupted.

"Danielle, money is just a tool. Its importance is not how you spend it, but how you invest it. Please, if you want me to enjoy this weekend, forget all about money and let us enjoy our time together."

"And just what are you investing in today, Mr. Amonti?"

"A perfect weekend for the two of us."

"Fair enough, no more talk about what things cost, but why two bedrooms, and why is your stuff in one and mine in the other?"

Now, his face took on a serious look.

"Danielle, I meant what I said before. As much as this means to me, it's your call. We have a little over an hour to get ready, and then we're going to have a nice relaxing dinner at a very nice restaurant. And then, if you want to, we can share one bedroom. But, I want you to know that if anything changes, your bedroom door has a lock, and you can sleep soundly tonight knowing you won't be disturbed."

I could hardly believe what I was hearing. After all of this, he was still letting me off the hook if I changed my mind. Well, I was not going to change my mind, and I was not about to let him off the hook either. I stood directly in front of him.

"Did you enjoy the drive today?"

"Yes, it was most pleasant."

"And intimate?"

"Very intimate."

"And lunch?"

"Extremely pleasant and very intimate."

I moved my hand behind my back and undid the button and zipper on my skirt.

"Doesn't that, this beautiful suite and the beautiful roses count as before," I said as I slid my skirt over my hips and let it drop to the floor.

No answer.

I continued as I unbuttoned my blouse and let it slip to the floor.

"Dinner can be part of the after. Now, I think it's time for ...the doing!"

Still, no answer. He sat there for a moment looking at me in my lacy bra and panties. Without a word, he got up, looked around the room, and turned away from me, moving toward his bedroom.

Damn! You've gone too far; He must think you are a slut, just like Billy said.

But, he didn't go to his bedroom. He walked over to the desk, picked up the phone, and pressed a key.

"Concierge please!"

A few seconds later, "Rodney, this is Mr. Amonti in the Penthouse Suite. You're holding a dinner reservation for me at six. Would you please change that to eight, and notify the car service?"

Another few seconds pause as he listened.

"No, don't notify me. If you can't change the reservations there, make one where you can. I'll pick up the information on the way out, later. I trust your judgment. Thank you."

Two Hours? What were we going to do for over two hours! What have I gotten myself into?

Nick hung up the phone and walked over to me. He picked me up gently in his arms and carried me into my bedroom. He placed me back on my feet at the side of the bed, tore the bed covers off the bed and just left them laying there on the floor. There was nothing left on the king-size bed except the sheet and pillows.

He picked me up in his arms again and lowered me gently onto the bed. He stood up and gazed at me for a few seconds. Then he moved to the foot of the bed, placed two fingers of each hand behind my knee, with his thumbs on the side of my knee, and proceeded to slide his fingers down the back of my calf to the strap of my shoe. I felt the sensation run throughout my entire body. He removed my shoe and tossed it over his shoulder. I heard it hit the wall and then the floor: Clunk ... Clunk.

He wasn't even in bed with me yet, and already I was losing control. I had to say something. Finally, as he started the same procedure on my other knee, I managed to squeak out, "Be careful, you'll break my shoes!"

"I'll buy you a new pair."

When I heard the second clunk, clunk I managed, "They're very expensive."

"It's covered."

My eyes were closed tight. I didn't dare look at him. I felt rather than heard him move to the other side of the bed and undress. Then the bed moved as he crawled in beside me. For a while, nothing happened. Eyes still closed, I could feel him looking at me. Then I felt his fingers on my wrist. As they moved to my elbow and then my shoulder, it felt, not like someone's fingers, but more like a cool breeze caressing me. But, it couldn't be a cool breeze, because inside I was on fire.

The fingers explored every part of my body, as the fire inside me raged. His fingers were replaced by his lips, and the fire grew hotter until I couldn't stand it anymore. Then he was over me. Eyes still closed, I could feel him, not his body so much, but his presence. We were hardly touching, but I knew he was there ready to enter me.

A condom! Is he wearing a condom?

He knew somehow, I was hesitating, and I felt he was ready to move back to the other side of the bed. I opened my eyes and looked directly into his. There was a question there, and I answered it quickly.

"YES! Most definitely YES!"

And I exploded the very second he entered me. He was so tender, so gentle. I was naked, my bra and panties gone. I don't know how. Did I take them off? Did he remove them? The most likely scenario I could think of at the moment was they disintegrated from the fire that was burning inside me. He brought me to the peak of passion again and again, and after each explosion, he gently brought me back down. The physical sensations were erotic, but even more, the emotional feelings were unlike anything I had ever experienced. This was not sex as I knew it. What was this? Could this be …?

I didn't want it to stop ever, but my body could take only so much, my heart was pounding. I couldn't catch my breath. And just like at the beginning, he seemed to sense where I was and then he was beside me, on his back. I felt his hand slide across the bed sheet until it touched mine. Just a gentle touch, pinky to pinky, as if he didn't want to lose the connection we had. Neither did I, and I wrapped my pinky around his to let him know. I had to say something. I had to let him know what he had done to me. I tried to slow my beating heart and catch my breath. I was both physically and emotionally drained. When I had enough breath to say something, the only thing that came out of my mouth was, "WOW!!!"

I could hear his breathing as labored as mine, and I swear I could hear his heart beating, but he did manage to say, "In spades, My Lady, in spades!"

I hadn't the faintest idea of what that meant, but it had to be good. It had to be a compliment of some kind. No one could make me feel this way and not feel something special himself. I don't know how long we lay there, side by side, with our pinkies touching. I suddenly realized I was naked.

It was a shock. It's not that I haven't been naked in front of a man before. It was alright to be naked before sex, and during sex, but not after sex. I had always had the need to cover myself after it was over. Pull the sheet over me? That was impossible; it was in a ball on the floor. Put on my blouse? On the floor in the living room. I broke contact and went into the bathroom. On the way out, I grabbed a bath towel to wrap around myself. I stopped and thought about what had just happened.

I am thirty-five years old. The very first time I had sex was in college. I am not very loose with my virtue, but I have had a few lovers in the fifteen-odd years since then. I do have a few idiosyncrasies about sex. And, the first one is: I have never had sex with a man unless he was wearing a condom. I have had to insist with some men, I carry them with me, so there was no excuse. And, one time I walked out on a man because he was adamant about not wearing one. I have never used any other form of birth control, and my romantic encounters were usually with men who I never could think of as celibate. It was self-protection on my part. Even Jack and Dan always wore one. When I found out that Jack was screwing other women while we were living together, I was glad he had always used one. And here I had allowed this man to enter my body, and I was sure he hadn't put one on. As I came out of the bathroom, I saw him lying in bed.

I don't want any rules with this man.

I threw the towel on the sink, crawled back into bed, and

reconnected our pinkies. Another first for me. We lay there side by side. It was nice.

Then, suddenly he was on me. Not gentle and tender, but demanding, dominating. Not a word was spoken, but I felt his demands. Open your eyes I felt him say and I did. I looked into his eyes and read the desire, the need, and I submitted. I gave him everything he asked for.

No, it was never a request, it was a command, and I said yes, yes, yes. He took everything I had and demanded more. I couldn't count how many times he brought me to orgasm, and this time, he didn't bring me down gently. But again, he knew when I could not submit any longer. When I felt as if my chest would explode from the wild beating of my heart, it was over, and he was beside me, sliding his hand toward mine, reconnecting our pinkies.

This time, I knew exactly what to say. Something I had heard just hours earlier. When I had enough breath back in my lungs to get the words out, I turned my head toward him and shouted, "VA VA VOOM!"

He turned on his side to look at me, a big smile on his face.

"The gentleman appreciates the comment, My Lady."

I turned on my side to face him. Our eyes were locked on each other.

What have you done to me?

How can this one man be so tender and loving and so demanding and dominating? He is not one man; he is every man I could ever hope to be with. My thoughts were all over the place, but my eyes never left his, nor his mine. He could read me so well. I never had to tell him where I was, he knew.

But, Danielle, after tomorrow, it never happened. That was your idea.

Well, if it was my idea, I could change my mind. If I made up the rules, I could change them.

But, what if he liked the rules? What if he doesn't want to change them? Impossible! There had to be feeling there. He couldn't make me feel this way and not feel the same, could he? Take what you can now and worry about later, later!

That brought a delicious thought to mind.

Take what you can now. I wonder how he would like to be

dominated.

The thought circled around in my head. I reached out and pushed his shoulder, putting him on his back. I rolled onto him, and ...I took him!

I gave it all back. I demanded. I ordered. I made him submit, and he did. Without complaint, without resistance, I got everything I demanded, and this time, when I felt my heart ready to explode, I demanded, even more, I wanted everything.

"Now," I demanded, "NOW, NOW, NOW!"

And he gave me everything.

Another first for me. Since no man had ever entered me naked, no man had ever come in me. I never thought about it before. I had no reason to think about it. But, now it had happened, and it was wonderful. This man had given part of himself to me. I know it happens all the time between men and women, but never to me. I felt he was part of me now, and I was part of him.

I stayed on top of him and rested my head on his chest. I wanted to stay close to him. I wanted the connection to be real. I felt so different than I had ever felt before, like something had been awakened in me. I lifted my head and looked at him. It was impossible to see his eyes from this angle, but I had to tell him how I was feeling right at the moment. I had taken the time to relax, and as sincerely as I could I whispered, "Thank you, Kind Sir!"

I waited for his reply. I knew he was thinking of something special to say to me. He seemed to always have the perfect response. I finally felt his chest expand as he gathered his breath, and in a smooth, confident voice he said," We live to serve Ma'am!"

We live to serve ...

Is that what he said? We live to serve!

I got up on my knees and looked at him. He had this stupid grin on his face. I started pounding on his chest with my fists.

"We live to serve, you bastard. You were servicing me?"

The grin stayed, and he managed to grab my arms and pin them to my sides. He wrapped his arms around me in a bear hug.

"I may be a bastard, but you still love me, don't ya!"

"Not even your mother could love you!"

At this point, he rolled us over to my side of the bed, him over me, me over him and back over to his side. But, he went too far, and when we reached the edge of the bed, I was hanging over, and he almost dropped me on the floor. But he managed to roll us back the other way again, and when I was back over the bed, he let me go, and I rolled away from him.

I gathered myself and prepared for another attack on him, only to see he was laughing. Not just laughing, but a way down deep belly laugh.

"What the hell is so funny, you idiot."

He waved his hands across the air as if he was unfolding a banner and said between laughs, "Breaking News! Female corporate executive and male secretary found naked and dead in Atlanta hotel suite. Coroner's initial report indicates it appears the couple was locked in a romantic embrace when they rolled off the edge of the bed, both victims striking their heads on the oak nightstand. Cause of death has been listed as blunt force trauma."

And after a few seconds, he added, "Details at eleven."

I just stared at him.

"You're an idiot."

He still had that silly grin on his face, and he nodded in agreement.

He must be going crazy.

Then, I giggled. It was so stupid, the giggle turned into a laugh. Suddenly I was laughing so hard I thought I was going to pee myself. I jumped out of bed and ran to the bathroom.

From the bedroom, I could hear he had stopped laughing. But then he started again as if he just realized how funny it was. Another first for me. Sex was serious business. I had never felt the desire to laugh when I was in bed with a man. It felt so good. I could almost forgive that, "We live to serve," comment.

I came out of the bathroom, still naked to find him on his way out of the bedroom. I appreciated the rear end view.

"Oh no, you don't! Come back here and take your punishment."

He turned to face me. He had gathered up his clothes and was holding them against his chest. His pants legs were hanging down and managed to cover his manhood, or we might still be in that bedroom.

"Danielle," he crooned, "You can't really be angry with me. You know I didn't mean it. It was just a little joke to break the mood we were in. Otherwise, we'd never get to dinner. And I really think we both could use some sustenance about now."

"Dinner isn't until eight o'clock."

He pointed to the alarm clock on the nightstand. It was digital, and the numbers read seven forty-seven.

"Is that right?"

"Afraid so, My Lady. Now we'll have to rush."

It couldn't have been much later than four thirty when he carried me into the bedroom. Was it possible we were at it for over three hours? It felt like we had just gotten started.

He turned to go.

"Wait!"

He turned back to me.

"What do I wear?"

He looked at me with that wicked grin he uses when he's thinking something mischievous.

"Ma'am, if I had my druthers."

Did he actually say druthers?

"You'd wear that spiffy outfit you had on this afternoon."

That's a positive sign.

"But, the restaurant we are going to is very upscale, and you might feel a bit uncomfortable dressed like that."

And he walked out of the room.

"Wait!"

This time, just his head came around the door frame.

"That tells me what not to wear. That doesn't tell me what I should wear."

He came back into the room, looked me straight in the eye.

"Danielle, you don't need **me** to tell you how to dress. You're always appropriately elegant!"

And, this time, he was gone.

Appropriately elegant?

I had packed for Cauldwell, not an upscale restaurant in Atlanta. And, I didn't have a lot of time to get ready. I heard him talking on the phone, and then he yelled to me from the living room.

"I just bought us an extra half hour."

I shouted my thanks back out to him and jumped in the shower. Luckily I always packed a girls' best friend, a simple black dress, and pumps. It would have to do.

At eight twenty, I walked into the living room, as put together as was possible under the circumstances. Nick was nowhere in sight, but the patio door was open. I stepped onto the patio and spotted Nick sitting and staring out over the city. He didn't seem to be looking at anything, just staring and he appeared to be troubled. I placed a hand on his shoulder, and he jumped to his feet. He looked at me and smiled

"As I mentioned earlier, My Lady, appropriately elegant."

He offered me his arm, and we proceeded to the elevator. Down in the lobby, he stopped to talk to the concierge for a moment, and out the door we went. Waiting for us was a stretch limo, and this time, it was the kind you hire for special occasions. The driver's name was Thomas, a coincidence, and after a drive of five short blocks, we were in front of the restaurant.

Both Nick and I laughed at the ridiculousness of hiring a limousine for a five-block drive, and when we exited the car, he asked if I would mind walking back to the hotel. Of course, I told him I didn't mind, wondering if his suggestion was to save the cost of the rented limo, or for romantic reasons. My question was immediately answered. Nick asked Thomas what he did with the limo when he was done for the night.

"If I get in before midnight, I bring it back to the garage. After midnight, I bring it home and then to the garage in the morning."

"Sign us out at two-thirty AM. Go home and spend some time with your wife."

Thomas thanked Nick, handed him a business card. Nick promised to call Thomas the next time we were in Atlanta. The restaurant was very classy. After being seated and ordering drinks, Nick asked if I was hungry.

"Famished."

"What are you in the mood for?"

"After this afternoon, red meat!"

"Good, steak it is," he said, pleased.

The ribeye was perfect. I am fussy about few things, but the way my steak is cooked is something I am very fussy about. As seldom as I allow myself the luxury of red meat, I want it just so. The waiter was very patient, Dexter was his name. He listened patiently as I ordered.

"Caesar salad, easy on the garlic but lots of cheese. A baked potato with extra sour cream and chives and creamed spinach."

Nick ordered Bananas Foster for dessert, coffee for him and a cappuccino for me. He also ordered five different wines, none of which were in stock. He finally told Dexter, "Ask the sommelier to suggest something appropriate."

The wine was excellent and fit the meal well. I asked Nick about his knowledge of wines, thinking his time managing restaurants would make him an expert.

"I know what I like. I have a list of wines I enjoy, and when I dine out, I ask for them. If none of them are available, like tonight, I ask the wine expert to suggest something. If I like it, I add it to my list."

I told him that sounded like a reasonable way to select wine, and we both giggled. We were both in a very, very good mood. After dinner, on the walk back to the hotel, Nick asked, "Do you mind making a stop? Pam said there is a very nice piano bar in the neighborhood, and I'd like to check it out."

"Of course, I don't mind."

He could take me to a coal pit tonight, and I wouldn't mind.

Chapter 9 - The Keynote

The bar was on a side street between the hotel and the restaurant. It wasn't really out of the way. It was called the Keynote, and there were two seats at the piano when we entered. The piano player/singer was between songs, just tinkling the keys. Nick introduced us, with his customary handshake. The man's name was Roger, and he seemed very pleasant and easy going. Roger asked Nick if he wanted him to play anything special.

"Do you have anything in your repertoire as pretty as this lady?"

Roger looked at me.

"Nick, I don't think there has ever been anything written that is as pretty as your lady!"

That made me blush like a school girl.

"That's enough you two. The gentleman has already made his bones tonight!"

Roger and Nick both laughed.

"Made his bones? My, my Ms. Palmer, the type of people you must hang out with!"

Nick told Roger, "Do your best."

He took my hand and led me onto the dance floor. Roger played the Theme from Love Story and Nick, and I didn't dance, we just swayed wrapped in each other's arms.

It was perfect!

When we got back to the piano, Roger was sifting through piles of music sheets.

"Looking for something special?"

"There's a couple due here soon. They got engaged here ten years ago and come here every anniversary since their wedding. I always play something special for them. After nine years, I'm running out of ideas."

Nick offered some suggestions, and Roger said he had used them all. Then Nick suggested one that Roger didn't know. As the two of them talked about it, I excused myself and headed for the little girl's room. When I got back to the piano, Nick was sitting next to Roger. He was playing notes with one finger, and Roger was writing on a piece of paper that looked like a music sheet. When they were done, Nick suggested, "Give it to me, and I'll cheat it up for you."

Nick started making marks on the sheet Roger gave him when a new couple arrived. Roger introduced them as Mike and Agnes and told us this was the couple that celebrated their anniversary here at the Keynote.

Agnes asked, "Do you have something special for us tonight?"

"Nick and I were just working on it."

Nick suggested, "You sing while I play. I'll run over the verse and chorus once so you can get the flavor, and then you come in, verse and chorus, verse and chorus. I'll spread the last three bars out."

Roger looked dubious at first, but after looking at the cheat sheet Nick had prepared, he agreed. Nick looked to Mike and Agnes, "Do you waltz?"

They both nodded their heads and headed for the dance floor. Nick sat at the keyboard. Roger announced Mike and Agnes were celebrating their ninth wedding anniversary, and Nick started to play.

It was a beautiful waltz, and Nick was playing not with one finger, but as an accomplished musician. Agnes and Mike whirled around the dance floor and then Roger started singing:

The song was about a couple who danced all night at their wedding. Their love was so strong, there was no need for words. She had stars in her eyes and angles were singing to her. When dawn came, they were still dancing. Their love was so strong, they knew it would last forever. The song ended as Roger sang, "My darling, I ....love ....you ....so!"

When they got back to the piano, Agnes had tears in her eyes. She threw her arms around Roger's neck and gave him a kiss. Roger said it was Nick's idea, and Nick got the same treatment. It really was beautiful and touching.

Roger turned to Nick.

"I guess I owe you: pick it!"

Nick gave me his wicked smile.

"Rumba!"

He took my hand and led me back to the dance floor.

"Not here please, Nick. I've never done this before."

"Remember the waltz? Feel the beat, feel my hands, shake those beautiful hips of yours, and...trust me!"

This was going to happen. I couldn't stop it. Just before Roger started playing, Nick showed me the basic step. One, two, three, slide together.

We began slowly in place, and when I got the rhythm, Nick said, "Now, Danielle, let's dance!"

And we danced. Just like the waltz at the charity dinner, he was so easy to follow. He transmitted his every move. Again, I wasn't dancing, I was floating. The rest of the night was as perfect as it could be.

We danced a waltz, a foxtrot, we swayed a couple of times with our arms wrapped around each other. It was turning out to be the best date I had ever had. Then someone asked Roger to pick it up and suggested a boogie. That made me smile.

"I haven't boogied since high school, and this is one dance you don't have to teach me."

"Unfortunately, Danielle, that's one dance I don't know."

"Harold, your waiter, boogies," Roger suggested. Nick called Harold over to the piano.

"My lady needs a boogie partner, would you mind?"

I tried to tell Nick it was alright, I didn't have to boogie, but before I got the words out, Harold was leading me onto the dance floor.

Harold, and I boogied. It was a blast. I really hadn't done that since high school, and Harold was superb. It brought back memories of how much fun it was to grow up in Cauldwell. I glanced at Nick to judge his reaction, and he was smiling.

When it was over, Harold escorted me back to the piano and thanked me for the dance.

"It's been a while since I had such a good boogie partner."

I turned to Nick, and his face was lit up with an expression I had not seen on him before.

"Ms. Palmer, I am impressed! You can move."

"Thank you Kind Sir, and thank you for allowing me to dance with Harold."

"Allow you to dance? You don't need my permission, Danielle."

"I didn't mean I needed your permission, but most men would be annoyed if their date danced with someone else."

"You hang out with the wrong people. Too many corporate types."

"What does that mean?"

"Corporate types. "You know, the kind of guys who are trying to climb the corporate ladder to success. By their very nature, they're self-centered and selfish. Otherwise, they'd have no chance. You need to hang out with regular people."

"Like you?"

"For instance!"

"And it's okay if I'm on a date with you, and I dance with other men?"

"As long as you don't insult me."

"How could I insult you?"

Nick turned to Roger, "The Drifters, 1960 or thereabouts. 'Don't forget who's taking you home'?"

Roger nodded, and Nick took me by the hand and led me to the dance floor once again.

"You didn't answer my question."

"Just wait one minute."

Nick wrapped his arms around me, placed my head on his shoulder, and began to sing to me.

He's not perfect. There is something he can't do well. He can't carry a tune.

But, I listened to his attempt, because I knew there was a message there. After his feeble attempt to sing, 'Save the last dance for me,' he said, "Danielle, why did I bring you here tonight?"

"To have some fun, I guess."

"Then, why would I want to prevent you from having a good time?"

"But, I'm your date!"

"Yes, Danielle. "You're my date, I don't own you. As long as you don't insult me, you can have as much fun as you possibly can."

"And how could I insult you?"

"I'm your date. You have a responsibility to me as I have a responsibility to you. You dance, thank the gentleman, and come back to me. You don't go off with him, you don't go sit with him, and you don't go home with him. You came with me, you go home with me. You have no rings on your left hand. If you meet someone you like, and you want to get to know him better, you make arrangements to meet him at another time, because I'm your date, and you are going to stay with me and leave with me. As long as we follow those rules, I have no problem with you having fun, even if it means you're having fun with someone else. Remember, any fun you have tonight is the result of my bringing you here. So, technically, I'm responsible for all the fun you have tonight. Okay?"

"And what if I was wearing a ring?"

"Same rules apply. Except, if you have no ring and a guy makes a pass at you, you have the option of making arrangements to meet him at another time or not. And, if you are wearing a ring, you probably don't want to dance with the man anyway, because he's insulted you."

"And how did he insult me?"

"Because Danielle, when a man makes a pass at a lady who's obviously wearing a wedding ring or even an engagement ring, what he is actually saying to her is she appears to be the kind of woman who would cheat on her man."

"You have it all worked out, don't you?"

"Just common sense. I'm sure you've never given it a thought, but I know you follow the rules because you are a lady. No matter how dull a date may be, I'm sure you respect the fact you are someone's date and act accordingly. That's how a lady acts."

Nick looked into my eyes.

"Danielle, I am really enjoying myself tonight. I want you to have a great time. I want you to remember this date fondly. If dancing the boogie with Harold makes you happy, why should I resent that? Whenever you think about tonight, you'll remember who brought you, and who you went home with, so have fun! Deal?"

"Deal!"

The rest of the night was even better. I only danced with one other man that night. Maybe he was right. Maybe I should expand my horizons and get away from the corporate types. Although, with the way this day was going, I may not need to worry about any other man ever again.

Easy, Danielle. Don't read more into this than it is. He may be the mostest man you've ever met, but that doesn't mean he wants this to go past this weekend.

We stayed until closing. Just before last call, Roger asked Nick if he wanted to jam. Nick looked at me, and I sang, "You can dance with the gal who …"

Nick laughed, kissed me gently on the cheek, and sat down next to Roger at the piano. Roger told Nick it was his choice, and Nick started playing the Bumble Boogie. I was mesmerized by his fingers flying over the keyboard. He may not be able to dance to a boogie beat, but he definitely knew how to play it.

Roger took over and embellished the song as he did what Nick later told me where 'riffs' and the sound coming out of the piano was fantastic.

While Roger was playing, Nick leaned over to me and whispered, "It's his piano, should I let him win?"

I don't know why I said it. It wasn't important, really, but he was my date.

"Kick his ass!"

And he did. I couldn't believe the music that was coming out of one piano.

I don't know how long they kept at it, but it was apparent they were having fun and getting tired, and with a look between them, they finished in a flurry. Nick and Roger gave each other a high five.

"God that was fun. I can't remember the last time I did that!"

Yesterday I thought this man was wonderful. How do I find a word to describe what I feel today? He looked at me, obviously pleased with himself. I smiled.

"I forgive you."

"For what My Lady?"

"For not being able to sing worth a damn."

That brought a broader grin and then a genuine laugh.

"I'll work on it."

"Don't, you have to have at least one flaw."

Then Roger announced, "Last dance, your choice Nick."

"Loveliest night of the year," Nick said, as he took my hand and led me back to the dance floor.

It was a waltz, Roger sang, and the words were so appropriate.

It was the loveliest night of my life. And I was definitely ...in love!

We thanked Roger, and Nick shook his hand as he had when we first arrived, but I noticed something.

When Nick went to shake Roger's hand, there were a couple of bills folded up in his palm. At least one of them was a hundred-dollar bill. When he took his hand back, it was empty.

That's why he didn't tip. He did, but he palmed the money. I call it his magic handshake. He could make money disappear.

Chapter 10 – The Other Room

The walk back to the hotel was much too short, even considering what I anticipated would happen when we got back to the suite. I held onto his arm with both hands as if I was afraid if I let him go for a second, he would disappear.

When we were inside the suite, I hustled into my room, and Nick disappeared into his. I knew I didn't have anything to wear that night. I had brought everyday pajamas with me to Cauldwell. Nothing that was suitable for this night. I came back out into the living room, tiptoed over to his bedroom, and when I heard the shower, I darted into his room. His shirt was flung over the back of a chair. I grabbed it and ran back to my room.

Showered, hair brushed, make-up retouched, and wearing his shirt, that luckily had long enough front and rear tails to cover my butt, I walked back into the living room. Nick was sitting quietly in an armchair, staring out the patio doors. The same stare I had seen earlier.

As light-hearted as he had been all evening, now he seemed genuinely troubled. As I approached him, he caught my reflection in the glass doors and rose. Turning toward me, he smiled.

"As I said earlier, Danielle, appropriately elegant!"

I didn't say anything. I took him by the hand and began to lead him to my bedroom. He pulled back. I turned and looked into his eyes.

"Let's use the other bedroom tonight."

"The housekeepers made up the bed. They even managed to cover up the burn marks on the mattress."

That brought a smile. Nick looked down at the floor for a few seconds, then lifted his eyes to mine.

"We had sex in that room."

"And if I recall, it went pretty well!"

"I agree!"

Then in a whisper that was almost inaudible, "But tonight, Danielle, I want to make love to you."

"What's the difference?"

That brought another smile, a sincere smile.

"I'll answer that question tomorrow if you still need an answer."

I got my answer that night. I never did have to ask.

It definitely was different. We did have intercourse, of a sort, but it wasn't sex. He was most definitely with me, but there was almost no movement. Where this afternoon had been filled with so much emotion, I could hardly feel my body, I was aware of my body reacting to him, and his was reacting to mine. This was all emotion. It was if we were communicating with each other, but neither of us said a word. I could almost feel what was in his heart, what was on his mind. It seemed as if he was telling me he was in love with me.

"I've been in love with you for months. I desperately want you to love me, but it's impossible. There is too much between us for us to ever be together."

I answered him in the same fashion. I did love him, I did. And that's what I attempted to tell him.

"Yes Nick, I do love you, I most definitely do love you."

I don't remember too much after that, but the next morning, I realized there had been another first for me that night.

When I had been with other men, and we were finished with the sex part, and I was ready for sleep, I curled up by myself on the very edge of the bed. If the man I was with moved over close to me, I didn't complain, but I was uncomfortable.

When I first opened my eyes Sunday morning, I found myself curled up next to Nick, with my head resting on his shoulder and my arm across his chest. He had his arm wrapped around my shoulder. I had to lift my head to look at his face. He was looking down at me, smiling.

"Good morning, lovely lady."

It all came back to me in a rush. I wondered how long I had been wrapped around him like that.

"Did you manage to get any sleep?"

"Enough. Hungry?"

"Famished."

"I'll give you thirty minutes to wake up. Bacon and eggs

okay?"

"Perfect."

I jumped out of bed, picked up Nick's shirt and dashed for my bedroom. Just about thirty minutes later, I heard conversation coming from the living room. I put on a pair of panties and again donned Nick's shirt, and when I heard the suite door close, I came out to the living room for breakfast. Nick was sitting on the couch with a table filled with breakfast goodies spread out in front of him. I joined him on the sofa, and we ate in silence. After we had satisfied our appetites, Nick poured us each a second cup of coffee.

"What would you like to do now?"

I crawled onto his lap.

"Talk!"

"Okay. You start."

"Well, for starters, don't give up your day job, you'll never make it as a singer."

"And after all those years and all the money spent on vocal lessons."

"It's just as well. I was beginning to think you weren't human."

"That special?"

"That special!"

"Good, I knew I'd have to be very special to impress you."

And, we talked, intimately, just as we did on the drive to Atlanta. I was cuddled up on his lap, with his arms wrapped around me, and I was as content as I had ever been. I told him I was glad he had asked me WHY, back on the interstate.

"That one-word question turned a one-night stand into the best day I've ever had. You really are the mostest man I have ever met."

"Danielle, I'm just a man who was so happy to be with you I had to make everything as perfect as I possibly could. I want you to remember this weekend fondly, and not regret a moment."

"It was all so perfect that it would be impossible to pick out one particular thing to dwell on. Do you have a favorite part of the day?"

He answered without hesitation.

"That's easy, Danielle when you fell asleep."

I jumped off his lap, knelt on the couch, and looked at him in astonishment.

"If you're going to give me one of those "we live to serve" comments, you're in for big trouble, mister."

"I don't understand."

"I say you have given me the best day of my entire life, everything was so beautiful that I can't pick out anything that stands out, it was all so perfect. And you tell me the best part for you is when I fell asleep after you made love to me."

Nick shook his head.

"Danielle, it wasn't after we made love, it was while we were making love."

"Don't you dare say that. Don't you dare say I fell asleep on you while you were making love to me!"

"I promise, I won't tell anyone, but it's true."

I knelt there looking at his face. This wasn't one of his jokes, he was serious.

"Danielle, do you remember yesterday afternoon in your bedroom?"

"Of course, I remember."

"What happened after the first time?"

"What do you mean, what happened?"

"What happened? What did you say, what did I say, and what did we do?"

"I said Wow, and you said in spades, whatever that means, and then you touched my hand."

"Spades is double! When in spades is used in that way, it means whatever you said goes double for me."

"Oh," I said, somewhat mollified.

"And what happened after the second time?"

"I said Va Va Voom, and you told me you appreciated the comment, then you touched my hand again."

"And after the third time?"

"What is this? Twenty questions? You made that stupid comment, and then you almost dropped me on the floor. It would have served you right if I had cracked my head open!"

"Just one more question. What happened after we made love last night?"

What happened after we made love? We...I...he... I couldn't remember. I racked my brain. He said he loved me. He said he had loved me for months. Actually, he didn't say anything. I felt that's what he wanted to say. I told him I loved him. At least, that's what I was thinking. And I couldn't remember anything after that.

I was back in his lap. I held his face in my hands and looked into his eyes.

"Oh, Nick! I am so sorry. How could I have done that to you? Please forgive me!"

He put a finger to my lips to quiet me.

"Don't be sorry. It was wonderful."

I stared at him.

"Danielle, when I realized you were asleep, I rolled over on my back. You immediately reached out, searching, and when your hand felt me, you slid over to me, cuddled up to me, put your head on my shoulder, wrapped your arm around my chest and sighed. And then, you slept the sleep of angels. You were so peaceful, so content, I swear I thought you were going to purr. I looked at you and thought, "Did I do this to her? Did I make her feel this comfortable?" You made me feel as if you didn't have a care in the world and you felt perfectly safe because you were in my arms."

He hesitated for a few seconds.

"How much happier can a man be than to have a woman like you feel safe and content in his arms. There is nothing better in the entire world. Danielle, you are such an exceptional lady, the thought of spending a day like yesterday with you was so far out of my reach it was never a consideration, then to have it end with you cuddled in my arms like that was ..."

He never got to finish his thought. The kiss that interrupted him was long and passionate. And, I am happy to report, led us back into my bedroom. It was the gentle and tender kind, and we didn't stay in there for three hours. I wanted to do something for him, and at the Keynote last night, I had heard the Mets were in town to play the Braves. I knew, coming from New York, he was a Mets' fan, so I suggested the ball game.

90

"Ballgame? Since when did you become a baseball fan?"

"I want to do something nice, just for you."

"This is pretty nice,"

"Pervert."

"So, I'm a pervert, perverts need love too!"

"In that case, I'll wear the same outfit I wore in the car yesterday."

That got me a shocked look and some questions.

"When was the last time you were in a ballpark?"

"Been a few years."

"Remember what a ballpark looks like?"

"Green grass, some dirt, three bases, pitcher's mound ..."

"No, I mean the stands, where the people sit."

"And your point?"

He got up on his knees behind me and looked down at my naked breasts.

"The people behind you sit behind you and above you."

And then he sat on the floor, looked up at me.

"And the people in front of you sit in front of you and below you."

I giggled at what he was telling me.

"You *are* a pervert,"

"So sue me! I'm only a man, Danielle, but probably a perverted man. And so are most of the men we will see at the ballpark."

"And, they'll know you're with the hottest chick in Atlanta."

"That would be true Ma'am."

"And I promise you they will surely know who has dibs on the last dance."

That brought a big genuine smile.

He complained when I used his own words against him, but I knew he loved knowing I was paying attention. It took some convincing, but Nick finally agreed to the ballgame, and, even more, convincing before he agreed to my vamp outfit.

The ballgame was everything I expected. Nick managed to get the car rental company to pick up the rental and Thomas drove us to the game and then to the airport. I got whistles and catcalls from all the men, and I hung on to Nick's arm as if my very life depended on him. There was never any doubt in anyone's mind who was taking me home, and I hoped Nick was enjoying the attention he was getting!

Only one guy got out of line, and I thought Nick was going to do something, but a strange thing happened. As if they knew something special was going on between Nick and me, some of the other men around him shut the guy up. The Mets lost, but Nick didn't care. We went straight to the airport from the ballpark, and I didn't have a chance to change, which didn't seem to bother Nick at all.

The flight back to Fort Lauderdale was uneventful. Sweetie had upgraded us to First Class and when we got to the baggage claim the other Thomas and another man were waiting for us. They helped us with the luggage, and when we got outside, I noticed my bags went into the limo, and Nick's went into an SUV parked directly behind. Nick put me in the limo, and I overheard him whisper to Thomas.

"You're carrying very precious cargo tonight, Thomas, take special care of the lady."

It was a very long and lonely night. I hadn't been this lonely since I first left Cauldwell for college. I couldn't wait for tomorrow morning, so I could see Nick at the office.

Monday morning finally came, and I spent extra time getting ready for work. I got into the office a little before nine, and, as usual, Nick and Crystal were already there.

As I passed through their alcove, Nick asked, "How was your vacation, Ms. Palmer?"

And then, that bastard, that cretin, that miserable excuse for a man did something that cut me right to the bone …

92

Chapter 11 – After the After

He kept his promise!

Not a word, not a look, not even a sneak peek when he thought I wasn't looking. It was as if it had never happened. He was Nicholas, and I was Ms. Palmer, and everything was exactly as it was before we left for Georgia. The office routine went back to being routine. He was the same Nicholas, funny, lighthearted, efficient. And I was in hell! How could anyone make me feel the way I felt in Atlanta and not have any feelings himself? Wednesday of the second week we were back, Charlie came to my office and dropped another charity ball invitation on my desk.

"Oh no you don't, I went last time."

"But it's your turn."

"But, I went for you last time."

"Right, that was my turn, and now it's your turn."

"Charlie!"

"Danielle, you haven't been yourself since you got back from vacation. Do this, it will do you good to get out."

"I don't have a date."

"Ask Nicholas, I'm sure he'll be happy to take you."

"I doubt that very much."

"Why, I thought you two had a good time at the last affair?"

"That was then, and this is now."

"Do you want me to ask him for you?"

"No! I'll ask him myself, thank you, but if he says no, I'm not going."

Maybe this is my chance to find out what Nick really feels. Maybe this is a good thing. But, how it would hurt if he said no! Gathering up all the fortitude I could muster, I called Nicholas into my office.

"Charlie stuck me with another charity dinner this Saturday night. Would you be available to escort me?"

I held my breath and waited for his answer. It only took a second.

"It would be an honor to escort you, Ms. Palmer. "Formal?"

"Yes," I said, relieved.

"Seven thirty, your apartment?"

"That would be fine, thank you, Nicholas."

"My pleasure Ms. Palmer."

The next three days were awful. Suddenly Saturday couldn't come quickly enough. I bought a new gown just for this night, a white strapless gown with a slit along the left leg. Not a Stacy Geer gown, way out of my price range, but something I was sure would please Nick. Saturday finally came. No chores were accomplished that day. I spent the entire day prepping for that night.

Seven thirty on the dot, Andy announced a gentleman was in the lobby. I gathered myself together and headed for the elevator. When I emerged in the lobby, Nicholas was there in his tux with a single white rose in his hand. He commented how beautiful I looked.

"I hope Stacy doesn't see you looking that good in someone else's gown!"

Of course, that went right to my head, and I could hardly get the words out to thank him. Nicholas offered me his arm and led me outside. Thomas was waiting for us.

"Very nice to see you again, Ms. Palmer."

I thanked Thomas as Nicholas slid in beside me. There was hardly any conversation on the way to the hotel. Once there, Nicholas was as charming as usual. During the cocktail hour, he introduced me to some people he knew. I introduced him to some people I knew. Again, we didn't know anyone at our table, but Nicholas managed to include everyone in the conversation as if we had been friends for years. Nicholas and I danced once to a beautiful waltz when we first sat down to dinner, but he never asked me again. A gentleman, whom I had dated months ago, came over and asked me to dance. I glanced at Nicholas. He didn't seem to mind, so I accepted. When we reached the dance floor, I realized the man was intoxicated. He wasn't really drunk, but he was buzzed.

He made a pass at me, and I very politely turned him down, but he wasn't going to take no for an answer. He pulled me closer to him and started running his hands over parts of my body that weren't his right to explore. I attempted to break free from his hold, but he had me in a very firm grip. I struggled until I heard Nick say, "Mind if I cut in?"

The man told him, "Buzz off, Pal!"

Nick grabbed the man's hand, and suddenly the man let me go. He was obviously in pain. When the man let go of me, Nick released the man's fingers, moved me a few feet away and finished the dance with me.

"Are you okay?"

"Only my damaged pride."

We went back to the table and the remainder of the evening continued without any additional fuss. Nicholas didn't ask me to dance, and I turned down every invitation I received after that. After dessert, Nicholas excused himself and went to the men's room. He returned about ten minutes later with blood on his shirt and tuxedo.

"What happened?"

"Some drunk slipped on the wet tile floor in the men's room and hit his head on the counter. I checked him to see if he has been severely hurt and then informed management. They're calling the paramedics."

Everyone at the table was curious about what happened, and Nicholas gave some additional details. Unfortunately, that seemed as if it was going to be the highlight of my evening. Other than that, the evening was pleasant. On the drive back to my apartment, Nicholas was quiet. He escorted me to the elevator, thanked me for a lovely evening, and said good night. It wasn't at all what I had hoped. I was convinced Atlanta was nothing more than a good time. There was no love there. It was what I had told him in the car in Georgia. I wanted to be intimate with him, and we were, and that was that!

Monday morning, two Detectives from the Broward County Sheriff's Department came to the office and asked to speak to me. The receptionist showed them into my office.

"Ms. Palmer, could you tell us about the incident at the banquet Saturday night?"

I told them what little I knew.

"My date left the table to go to the men's room, and when he returned, he had blood on his shirt and tuxedo. He told me someone had slipped in the men's room, and he helped him."

"Can you tell us how to get in touch with your date?"

"Certainly Detective, he's right outside my office."

I asked Nicholas to step into my office. The Detectives were very interested in what Nicholas had to say.

"I walked into the men's room and found a man lying face down on the floor. There was blood on the counter. It looked as if he slipped on the wet tile floor and hit his head on the counter as he fell. I turned him over to check his condition. He had blood all over his face. I wiped some of it away with paper towels and realized his nose was broken. I notified a waiter, and when the Banquet Manager came into the room, I washed my hands and returned to the table."

The Detectives had a different version.

"Mr. Amonti, the victim in the men's room, told us he was in the foyer kissing a woman, and the woman's date caught them. He said the date pulled him into the men's room and smashed his face on the counter. The date told the victim that the woman was spoken for. You wouldn't know anything about that would you?"

Nicholas smiled at the two Detectives.

"Why would I know anything about that, Detective? My date was sitting at our table when I went to the men's room."

"It's a shame there's no one here to verify that," the Detective said.

Still smiling, Nicholas answered, "Detective, Ms. Sidney Alders runs these charity events. You can get her contact information from the ballroom. I'm sure she has the names and contact information of the eight people seated at our table, all strangers to Ms. Palmer and myself. They will be able to verify Ms. Palmer was at the table the entire time."

Turning to me the Detective said, "You knew the victim and had a confrontation with him earlier in the evening, isn't that true?"

"I'm sorry, Detective, I don't know who you're talking about."

"According to witnesses, you were dancing with the victim, and your date came over and rather roughly pulled you away from him."

"I didn't realize that was the man who was hurt in the men's room. Yes, I did dance with a man who was very crude and rude. Nicholas rescued me and finished the dance. It was nothing."

"Right …But, you do know the man you danced with."

"Yes, Detective, slightly. His name is Timothy …something. We met some months ago at a charity event just like Saturday night, and I dated him once."

Turning back to Nicholas, the Detective asked, "What is the relationship between you two?"

"Ms. Palmer is Director of Special Projects, and I am her Administrative Assistant."

The two Detectives looked at each other. Nicholas almost laughed as he told them, "Yes, Detective. I am Ms. Palmer's secretary! There is nothing personal between us."

"Right …And you just happened to be her date at a fancy ball?"

"Ms. Palmer received the invitation very late last week and didn't have time to arrange for a proper escort. She was kind enough to extend an invitation to me."

Nicholas looked at me and then back at the Detectives.

"I can think of no man who would refuse such an invitation from this lady."

The Detectives said they would be in touch and left.

"Nicholas, is there going to be trouble over this?"

"Ms. Palmer, you were sitting at the table with eight other people at the time of the incident. How can there be trouble?"

"Are you in trouble?"

"No, Ms. Palmer. The man was obviously drunk. They can't take anything he said seriously."

Nicholas wouldn't say anything else about it, but I couldn't help wondering whose version was accurate. Wednesday, Gene, Nicholas and I went to lunch together. We were working on a proposal for Florida East Coast Railroad. If we could get the black box to work on an engine that large, we could get every railroad in the country. We were talking about the progress Gene was making with adapting the black box to such a large engine when a man stopped at our table. It was one of the Detectives that had talked to Nicholas and me on Monday.

"Pardon the interruption, but if you have a minute, I have

additional information about the incident on Saturday."

Nicholas invited the Detective to join us and brought Gene up to speed on what the Detective was talking about.

"First, Ms. Alders did give us the names of the people at your table. We interviewed two couples so far, and they both agree Ms. Palmer was sitting at the table the entire time."

"Well, there goes your theory about my stopping the man from kissing her in the restroom foyer."

"Right! ...But that doesn't mean that it didn't happen. It could have been another woman."

"Why would that concern me?"

"I don't know, but it doesn't matter."

Both Nicholas and I looked at the Detective for an explanation.

"The victim stopped in my office and changed his statement. He was very adamant about recanting the statement he gave us Saturday night and Sunday at the hospital. Now, he insists it's just as you reported. He was intoxicated, slipped on a wet floor and hit his head on the counter. You, Mr. Amonti, were kind enough to help him."

"And you were kind enough to come here to tell us this?"

"No, Mr. Amonti. There are a few things that still bother me about this entire affair."

"Such as?"

"Do you happen to know Ed Healy?"

"I know a Sgt. Healy of the Broward County Sheriff's Department."

"May I ask what your relationship is to Sgt. Healy?"

"We go to the same gym."

"Is that what you call it, a gym?"

It's a private facility, Detective. It's run by a local security agency that I happen to be familiar with."

"Right! ... Ex-Navy Seals and retired police officers."

"That's true, Detective. I have a very sedentary job, and the gym keeps me in shape."

"Right!"

"Is that a problem, Detective?"

"No, but there are still some things that are troublesome. The victim seemed frightened when he gave us his revised statement this morning. I tried to get him to tell me why he was changing his story, and he was very evasive."

"Probably afraid of the consequences of filing a false police report."

"Right! ...There are a few other things that bother me. For instance, Sgt. Healy stopped by my office and vaguely suggested that my career would not be enhanced if I continued this investigation. Don't you find that strange?"

"Not at all Detective. Sgt. Healy is a good man and probably doesn't want you to waste valuable time running down dead-end alleys."

"Right! ...Also, we always do a background check on possible suspects. Yours is fascinating. For instance, about eight months ago, you were involved in a confrontation in the parking lot of De Georgio's Restaurant."

"That's true, Detective but I was absolved of any blame concerning that incident."

"Yes, I saw that. Mostly because of the statements of two eyewitnesses."

The Detective took a notepad out of his pocket and leafed through the pages.

"A Mister Andrew Lighter and a Ms. Danielle Palmer, to be exact."

Nicholas looked surprised. I was in shock.

That stranger was Nicholas?

Nicholas turned to look at me. Before he had a chance to say anything, the Detective added, "Interesting that Ms. Palmer would be you alibi in two such incidents."

Nicholas turned his attention back to the Detective.

"I wasn't aware that Mr. Lighter and Ms. Palmer were the witnesses to that incident."

"Right ..."

"Detective, I was not acquainted with Mr. Amonti at the time. I was leaving the restaurant with my date, and when we reached the parking lot, we saw three men harassing a young couple. A stranger intervened and stopped them. It was too dark to see who the stranger was, and until this very minute, I was unaware that it was Nicholas."

"Right ..."

The Detective turned more pages in his notepad.

"We also have a report from New York City. It seems that you were under surveillance for consorting with two known Organized Crime suspects."

"Not true, Detective. The two men in question were frequent customers at a restaurant I operated, and the restaurant was under surveillance, not me. When it was discovered that the men in question were not conducting any illegal activities there, the matter was dropped."

"Right ...but only because the United States Justice Department asked the NYPD to drop the case."

Nicholas just shrugged his shoulders. The detective had more.

"One more interesting note. When we checked the Federal Data Base, your name came up with a Red Flag. So, did the two men under surveillance from New York."

"A Red Flag?"

"Yes, all files relating to Nicholas Amonti, Angelo Chassy, and Carlos Vito have been sealed. They are listed 'Secret,' and you need Department of Justice clearance to view them."

Again, Nicholas just shrugged his shoulders.

"I have no idea as to why, Detective. I can't imagine why there would be any files concerning me with the Justice Department."

"Right ..."

The Detective rechecked his notes.

"A United States Attorney by the name of John Casivetis called me about an hour after I made the inquiry. He asked what my interest was in you, Mr. Amonti. When I told him about the incident in the men's room, he informed me that it was a local matter, and the federal government had no interest, but he suggested in very strong terms that I should not inquire into your background. Don't you find that strange?"

Once again, Nicholas shrugged his shoulders.

"As I said, Detective, I have no idea why the Federal

Government would have any interest in me."

"Right ..."

The Detective paused as he looked Nicholas straight in the eye.

"I haven't told you the strangest thing of all, Mr. Amonti. About thirty minutes after I hung up on Mr. Casivetis, he called back. He wasn't in his office. I could hear traffic noises in the background. He must have left the building and called me on his cell phone. He said he wanted to give me a heads up."

The Detective paused, seeming to judge Nicholas' reaction.

"He told me, again, in strong language not to pursue anything in your past, Mr. Amonti and then he said something else ..."

We waited for the Detective to finish. He seemed unsure if he should tell us the rest.

"Mr. Casivetis said, "Nick Amonti is one of the good guys." And then he hung up."

The Detective was still looking directly into Nicholas' eyes.

"Is it true, Mr. Amonti? Are you one of the good guys?"

"Nicholas kept his eyes directly on the Detective.

"I'd like to think so, Detective."

After what seemed like an eternity, with both men taking measure of the other the Detective said.

"Right ...Well, you'll be happy to know that the incident has been changed from a possible assault to an accident. The case is closed."

"Thank you for letting us know Detective."

"Just one more question, if you don't mind ..."

We waited for his question. It took a moment.

Looking directly at Nicholas again, the Detective asked, "Who are you Mr. Amonti?"

Nicholas smiled.

"I told you on Monday, Detective, I'm Ms. Danielle Palmer's Administrative Assistant."

"Right! ..."

The Detective excused himself and left. Gene wanted to know what that was all about, and Nicholas told him that the

Detective realized his victim wasn't completely honest and decided to stop wasting time on a crime that didn't exist. Nicholas turned to me.

"I had no idea you and Andrew were the witnesses that night."

"I didn't know either. Andrew and I had dinner at that restaurant and were going to a movie when we came upon the scene in the parking lot. I didn't realize that it was you who came to the rescue of that young couple. It was too dark to see faces. We just told the police what we saw."

"Thank you for that, Ms. Palmer. Your statement saved me a big hassle with the police that night."

The conversation returned to Florida East Coast Railroad, and after lunch, we returned to the office. Around four-thirty that afternoon, Nicholas stopped in my office.

"Gene sent this report for you to look over. The prospects look good."

"Thank you. Nicholas, please notify everyone that I want to have a full team meeting tomorrow. "

Nicholas said he would take care of it. I watched Nicholas walk out of my office. Way down deep in my heart, I knew I was in love with him. But, there were parts of his life that were very secret, and by his own admission, those parts were not pretty.

Could I deal with that?

Not that it mattered, I also knew he wasn't in love with me. But, more than anything I wanted the answer to that last question the detective asked.

"Who are you Mr. Amonti?"

The following day was the team meeting I had asked Nicholas to schedule. We all met as a group occasionally to make sure we were all on the same page, to discuss any problems that arose or throw out new ideas. Our meetings were usually set for eleven in the morning, so everyone had a chance to clear their desk of anything that needed immediate attention. We held these meetings in the conference room, and around ten-fifteen, I stopped in the break room for a cup of coffee.

The break room in our office is rather large and set up in two sections. There's a service area: vending machines, cabinets, a small sink, refrigerator and a counter with a coffee pot and a microwave. The seating area is separate. The two sections are separated by a seven-foot-high partition. To get to the tables in the seating area, you must go through the openings at the end of the partitions. The way it is set up, when you walk into the service area, you cannot see into the seating area or be seen from there.

Naturally, the coffee pot was empty, and I set about making a fresh pot. I could hear the secretaries and clerks on the other side of the partition, but I couldn't see them. As usual, the conversation was about men.

Maybe it was because of my age, or maybe it was because I was brought up in a small conservative Georgia town, but I never did understand how young girls could talk so freely about their sex lives. One of the girls was complaining, "My boyfriend is so naïve I had to teach him how to make love properly."

Another girl said, "My current boyfriend is the greatest lover I've ever known."

I heard Nicholas ask her, "At twenty-two, how many lovers have you had?"

That brought loud laughter from the group. I wasn't surprised that Nicholas was there, he often hung out with the other Administrative Assistants. He was one of them!

Ladies, I could tell you a story about a great lover that would curl your hair, and he's sitting right there with you.

Then, as if she read my mind, one of the girls asked Nicholas about his conquests. He tried to beg off, saying he had been married twice, and that didn't count. They weren't going to let him get away with that.

"You told us, between your two marriages, you've only been married ten years. That leaves a lot of time for other women, and we've all heard about Stacy Geer. Give!"

"Okay," he finally gave in.

This ought to be good.

Chapter 12 – The Lie

"There was a time in my life when I managed the hottest restaurant in New York City. All of the celebrities wanted to be seen there. We made the social pages of the newspapers at least twice a week. This was the type of place that, if you wanted to eat there, you had to make reservations two to three weeks in advance. But, if you knew the manager, **me**, you could get a table the same day, and if you knew him really well, you could be seated without a reservation. Of course, everybody wanted to know me, and I got to know some pretty important and influential people. Some of those people operated other restaurants and clubs. I could not only get you a table at my restaurant but also at most of the other hot spots in the city. I could also get you into the hottest clubs without waiting in line."

One of the girls commented, "Sounds like a tough job!" Nicholas chuckled.

"It was pretty heady stuff, and, of course, some of the people who wanted to be my friend were beautiful, sexy, and sensual women. All ages, all sizes. But, I had already learned I didn't like one night stands, and I really didn't enjoy going to bed with strangers. It was more exciting if we had a relationship. I don't mean we had to be madly in love. Just that we knew each other and were more than passing acquaintances. I had to like the women I slept with. A beautiful face or a sexy body wasn't enough. Maybe it was because I had access to so many beautiful women, but I was fussy."

Just another conquest. He had to have a relationship with me, had to like me, but didn't have to love me.

One of the girls said, "There had to be some special women, or, at least, one."

Another girl chimed in, "Was it, Stacy Geer?"

"Stacy is a good friend. We had a thing a while back. There were a lot of sparks, but it never caught on fire."

I had heard enough. I picked up my coffee and was headed for the door when I heard one of the girls ask, "Anyone else?"

Nicholas didn't answer right away. Then, my knees buckled,

my heart pounded, I became so weak, I thought I would fall over as I heard him say in a very wistful voice, "There was this one weekend …in Atlanta."

After a pause, he continued.

"She was beautiful, she was sexy, she was sensual, and she was talented and intelligent, and funny. She knew who she was, and she liked herself. And I was madly in love with her."

He paused again.

"When I was younger, I thought there was one true love out there, and if you found her, you were lucky, and if you didn't, you'd never be truly happy. But I've been married twice, and I've loved them both sincerely and honestly, but differently. And I felt truly loved by both of my wives.

"But never had I met a woman like this. We talked intimately for hours. The sex was more than physical. We danced, we laughed. I teased her, she teased me. I even sang to her. She is loving and caring. She is tender and submissive. She is gentle and demanding. She is every woman I had ever hoped to be with."

I thought I heard him sigh before he continued.

"There is no such thing as a perfect mate. We all settle for less than we want. We look for the closest thing to perfection we can find, and make allowances for the imperfections that we all have. But, not this time. This was truly a lady, a warm, sultry, stable, charming, elegant lady. And I was totally in love with her. And, I think she was in love with me."

"What happened?" came a chorus from the girls. He continued, and I could hear the sadness in his voice.

"Sunday night, I put her in a limousine, watched her drive off, and I never saw her again."

"But if you loved her and she loved you..."

"Just couldn't be. Too many things stood between us that couldn't be fixed."

"That's crazy! If you love each other, anything can be fixed."

"Not true, ladies. Only in fairy tales does love conquer all, in real life, many things can't be overcome. Nobody lives happily ever after. For instance, I am quite a bit older than the lady, and that can't be changed."

I heard a chair scrape against the floor.

"Breaks over ladies, time to get back to work."

I ran out of there as fast as my weak legs would carry me. Back in my office, I had to sit down.

He had to be talking about you. He does love you. Whatever he thinks is important enough to keep us apart, you have to find out what it is and get him to understand that it doesn't matter to you. Find a way to fix this!

He said he was quite a bit older. Five years, maybe as much as ten, I can deal with that. What else could it possibly be?

You've got to find a way to talk to him, you just have to!

I got myself together as much as possible and went to the conference room. I was the last one to arrive, which was very unusual. Nicholas, efficient as ever, had everything laid out for the meeting, and the boys were already discussing how far the engineering department had gone with our next project: Florida East Coast Railroad.

My mind was only half on the meeting. The other half was on Nicholas. I glanced at him occasionally, trying not to be noticeable. It seemed to be business as usual for him, but I did believe I saw sadness in his eyes.

Or is that what I want to see.

What if he knew I was there? What if he said all that to make me feel good? Impossible! No one could have seen me enter the break room. He meant what I heard, I know he did. I couldn't have mistaken those feelings I received from him in his bedroom, Saturday night.

Concentrate, Danielle! You have a meeting to run.

Charlie was looking at me, and I thought he was going to ask me if I was all right when the intercom buzzed. It was a standing rule only the most critical calls got put through while we were in a team meeting.

"Yes, Crystal."

"I thought you'd want to take this call, Ms. Palmer, it's Mr. Paterson."

I grabbed the phone and had to steady my nerves before I could talk to him. He was very pleasant and upbeat.

"I'm going to present your proposal to my Board of Directors on Tuesday morning at eleven o'clock. Could you be here to answer any question they might have?"

Of course, I agreed.

"I'd also like to go over the proposal with you one more time before the board meeting, so could you be at my office Tuesday morning at nine o'clock?"

And, of course, I agreed to that.

I hung up the phone and looked at each member of the team. I was thinking of how I could get Nicholas to make the trip with me. I couldn't ask Charlie to send him without asking Bob or one of the engineers to go also.

But, I knew Nicholas was never in the office when I wasn't, so all I had to do was to get Nicholas to agree. It would be so much easier to talk to him away from the office. We would leave Monday and come back Wednesday. That would mean three days and two nights, even better than Atlanta. But, that was four days away. There was no way I could wait that long.

The team was waiting for me to tell them what Paterson had said.

"Paterson is presenting our proposal to his Board of Directors on Tuesday, and he wants me there in case there are questions. He also wants to go over the proposal with me before the meeting."

Then, I looked at their faces and ... I lied. I lied to all of them.

"The only time Paterson can see me before the board meeting is tomorrow morning at nine."

Bob said that would mean two trips to San Antonio. Charlie told him, "For a deal worth close to fifty million dollars, we can afford to go twice."

I had a better idea.

"Charlie, you know my sister lives in San Antonio. I don't have to come home for the weekend. I can make the meeting tomorrow morning and spend the weekend with Colleen, Bob, and my nephews. All the company would have to pay for is my room Monday night and a couple of days on the rental car."

Charlie agreed that it was a plan, and the meeting changed from Florida East Coast Railroad to Paterson Trucking in a hurry.

My mind wasn't on the proposal. I was trying to think of a way to tell Nicholas what my plan was and hoped he would agree to it. I couldn't ask him to step out of the office, which would seem peculiar. But, I had to let him know. Nicholas and I had a unique way of communicating at these meetings. I'd scribble a few words on a pad and Nicholas would understand what I needed. That was my answer, but what do I say. My notes are always in shorthand code that Nicholas manages to decipher.

What I wanted to tell him is I want Atlanta all over again. I want to be intimate with him. I want him to dance with me. I even want him to sing to me. Only, this time, let's spend a week, not a weekend. I can't let him know I'm crazy in love with him, or he might not agree. What do I say, and how do I say it, so no one else catches wise?

The answer came in a flash, and I scribbled a note and held it up as I usually do. Nicholas took it out of my hand and headed for the door. I knew he'd think I was asking him to make travel, hotel, and car rental reservations for San Antonio. He looked at the note as he walked away. He paused, looked confused.

Please, please don't blow it. He should understand. He shouldn't be confused. The note was self-explanatory.

Rules

1 starts when we board plane FLL
#2 ends when we leave plane FLL
Details you & Sweetie

Deal?

He reread the note, turned back toward me and looked directly into my eyes.

"Ms. Palmer, who is Pam Dugan?"

YES, YES, YES! He got it!

"She is a lady who is excellent at getting last minute plane and hotel reservations. Under the circumstances, I think we should use her this time. Crystal has her number in the phone log."

He got the message, but did he agree? I couldn't be sure. He could have made arrangements for me and told me after the meeting he wasn't interested. The agony kept getting worse.

Twenty minutes later, the intercom buzzed again. It was Nicholas this time.

108

"Sorry to interrupt, Ms. Palmer, but Ms. Dugan said the Doubletree is booked. She wants to know if the Hyatt would be Okay."

"The Hyatt will do just fine," I answered. And inside I was doing cartwheels!

Nicholas came back into the conference room just as the meeting broke up. Everyone had left except Charlie. Nicholas placed my briefcase on the table.

"I put your airline ticket, hotel reservation information, car rental information, and a copy of the proposal inside. I included the address of the hotel, the Hyatt River Walk, and of Paterson's office. The rental will have a GPS so you can find your way around. The car service will pick you up at your apartment at four this afternoon for the trip to the airport. You won't have much time to pack if you don't leave now."

Then he went to his office. Charlie asked me if everything was alright.

"You've been acting funky ever since you got back from Georgia. And today you seemed distracted."

"Charlie, everything is great. Just nerves about waiting for Paterson's decision."

"Danielle, you know I'm here for you. Anything!"

"Yes Charlie, I know. You've always been there for me!"

I didn't get a chance to talk to Nicholas before I left for my apartment. The last time I saw him, he was talking to Charlie, hopefully asking if he could leave early. I packed as quickly as I could, taking as many pretty things as possible. This was not a working vacation in Cauldwell. This was a weeklong love fest with him. I made sure I included some sexy nighties, and I threw in Nick's shirt which I had worn in Atlanta and failed to return to him.

Four o'clock on the dot, the doorman let me know the car service was waiting. It wasn't Thomas, but the standard car service the company used. At the airport, I checked my bags and ran to the gate as quickly as possible, hoping to catch Nick before we boarded the plane and tell him about my lie to the team.

First Class boarded. Of course, Sweetie had gotten me a first class ticket, and no Nick. I waited until they announced final boarding call and still no Nick. I finally had to board. I was in seat 1A, and 1B was empty. Just before the cabin door closed, a last-minute passenger rushed aboard. He was a young man, about twenty-five or so, and he sat in seat 1B.

What does this mean? Did he just miss the flight? Was this young man a last minute standby passenger, assigned to this seat because Nick didn't get to the gate on time? Or wasn't he coming? I never did get a chance to talk to Nick before I left the office.

Door closed cell phones off, no chance to get in touch. The flight to Dallas was horrible. The young man attempted to start a conversation, but I wasn't in a conversational mood. I had to fight to keep the tears away. I had a short layover in Dallas, and before boarding my flight to San Antonio, I called Nick's cell. Voicemail.

At baggage claim in San Antonio, I was surprised to see a man with a placard which had the name D Palmer written on it. I introduced myself, and the man said he was from the car rental company, and my rental was right outside the terminal. I didn't have to take the bus to the rental car lot. Arrangements had been made to have the car waiting at the terminal.

At the hotel, I tried to read name tags and refer to everyone by name. It seemed like a good habit to get into, and it wasn't difficult. But, I didn't try the Magic Handshake. At the front desk, I announced, "Reservation for Palmer!"

The manager came out of his office, and I got the same treatment Nick had received in Atlanta. I wasn't asked for a credit card or identification, and I didn't have to sign in. I was shown to the Penthouse Suite and had the bellman put my luggage in the larger bedroom. I tried Nick's cell again. Voicemail!

My next call was to Colleen. I told her I was in San Antonio, and I had a lot of free time. Colleen was my confidant, and over the weeks since our return from Georgia, I had given her a rundown of my weekend with Nick. Her very first question tonight was, "Is he with you?"

That started the tears flowing. Colleen and I talked for a while, and I told her I'd be over tomorrow and spend the weekend with her. What I really wanted to do was fly back to Fort Lauderdale, track down Nick and find out why he wasn't here with me. I was trying to decide if that's what I should do when the phone rang.

It was him!

In his most business-like voice, he said, "Ms. Palmer, if you come down to the lobby, I'd like to take you for a stroll along the River Walk, and maybe get some dinner."

I put my shoes on and ran out of the suite. I was still in the clothes I wore on the flight, but I didn't care. The elevator seemed to take forever to arrive. Finally, I walked into the lobby and spotted Nick. I ran to him and threw my arms around his neck. He gave me a gentle kiss and held me tight.

"I thought you weren't coming."

"How could any man possibly turn down such a beautifully worded invitation?"

That made me giggle.

"I couldn't get out of the office in time to make your flight. Pam had to rebook me."

I didn't care. He was here now, and all was right with the world. We strolled along the River Walk for a while and found a nice cozy restaurant for dinner. When we returned to the suite, we got ready for bed in my room.

I had a choice of lovely things for that night, but I decided to wear his shirt. The one I wore in Atlanta and never gave back to him. He liked that! The night was magic. I don't remember many details, but I will never forget the feelings. Again, as it was the first time, not many words passed between us, but none were necessary. When I opened my eyes the next morning, I was cuddled against him, with my head on his shoulder and my arm across his chest.

Chapter 13 – San Antonio

Since we had gone to bed pretty early, it was early morning when we awoke. Nick ordered breakfast, and while we were waiting, I told him about my lie to the team.

"If Paterson calls the office, or they call him looking for me, I'll be in big trouble."

Nick picked up his cell phone and hit a speed dial key.

"I need a favor. I need you to reach out to someone who knows Tony Paterson of Paterson Trucking in San Antonio, Texas. Have them tell Mr. Paterson Ms. Danielle Palmer has an appointment with him on Tuesday. Explain for family reasons, Ms. Palmer had to be in San Antonio today, and she told her office she was meeting with him this morning, also. Ask him if he would be kind enough to cover for her if necessary. Thanks! Let me know."

"Just that easy?" I asked.

"We'll see," he replied.

Twenty minutes later, while breakfast was being wheeled into the room, Nick's cell rang.

"Right, I forgot about that."

Nick gave me a smile.

"It's covered!"

My eyes opened wide as I looked at him. I didn't have a chance to say anything before he laughed.

"I keep telling you, I know people!"

We lounged around the suite for a while. I called Colleen to tell her Nick was here, and I was bringing him with me this afternoon. We strolled along the River Walk again, and after we had stopped for lunch, we drove to Colleen's house.

Her two boys were home, and Nick made friends with them immediately, just as he had done with Johnny. And, while he was dealing with them, I told Colleen what I had heard him say in the break room, yesterday. I begged her to help me find out why he felt we couldn't be together and find a way to fix it. Her advice was simple.

"Tell him openly just how you feel. Make him explain what his objections are."

Colleen spent a lot of time with Nick that day while my nephews entertained me. When my brother-in-law Bob came home, the two men grabbed a couple of beers and went out to the patio while Bob started the grill. They seemed to be getting along just fine. Colleen and I puttered around in the kitchen until the steaks were done, and then we all sat down for dinner.

Naturally, Colleen, Bob, and even the boys had questions for Nick, and although he didn't evade anything, you could tell some things were being left out of his answers. Colleen, who always kept in touch with Anna Lee, had questions about our trip to Cauldwell, and how Nick had managed to beat up on Billy and his two cohorts. Nick just laughed.

"I got lucky."

He wouldn't go any further. They wanted us to stay overnight, but Nick said we couldn't let that big, beautiful suite go to waste, and he promised we would be back tomorrow. On the drive back to the hotel, after what was an incredible day, I asked him why he didn't want to stay.

"That's their love nest."

"Some love nest, with two pre-teen boys running around."

"That doesn't seem to deter them."

"Explain that comment."

"You're probably too close to it because you knew them since they were dating, but they are as much in love today as they were then."

"And you know that how?"

"All you have to do is observe. Watch the way they look at each other. Listen to the way they talk to each other. Hear how they speak about each other. Bob never passes Colleen with touching her. Nothing you might notice if you weren't paying attention, just a brush against her arm or their fingers touching. It's so obvious if you look for it."

"And you look for it."

"I like to be around people like that. It makes me feel good that there are married couples that are still in real love, and not just in married love. Remember Mike and Agnes from the Keynote? You commented on how much they still seemed to be in love after nine years. You noticed because you didn't know them. With Colleen and Bob, you take it for granted. You accept the fact that your sister is happy and don't look for the reason. The reason is they're still crazy about each other."

"You're probably right. I've never heard her complain about him, ever!"

"Maybe that's why you like being around them so much."

The remainder of the ride was quiet. I mulled over what Nick had said, and I had to agree with his conclusions. I had never known a man could be so sensitive.

The mostest man I have ever met gets mostier every day!

Back in the suite, I was hoping to use his bedroom tonight. While I was changing in the bathroom, Nick was waiting in my room.

"You sister is beautiful. It's amazing two such gorgeous women could come from the same family."

Knowing how Nick liked to tease me, I thought it would be a good time to tease him a little.

I shouted through the bathroom door, "Watch yourself, mister. I saw you trying to get into her panties all afternoon."

After a moment's silence, I heard, "Sorry about that Danielle, I didn't think I was that obvious."

"Is that so," I yelled at him, "One more comment like that, and these panties of mine are going to stay right where they are tonight."

Another moment of silence.

"Danielle, there are a lot of things you don't know about me."

Where is this going?

"Such as?"

"Well, for one thing, when I was a kid, I was interested in magic. Sleight of hand stuff. I got pretty good at it. In fact, you might say I developed magic fingers."

Almost ready to emerge in my sexiest nightie, I yelled back, "And what has that got to do with this discussion?"

"Well, I could get those panties off of you, and you wouldn't even know they were missing."

"Is that so," I shouted at him as I burst through the door.

There he was, standing next to the bed, twirling a pair of ladies panties around his finger, and with a big grin on his face, he said, "Just ask your sister."

I knew they were my panties that he had taken from my suitcase, but the fact I was going to tease him, and he turned it around on me, infuriated me.

I ran over to him and started pounding on his chest with my fists.

"You bastard," I yelled.

He grabbed my arms, wrapped me in the bear hug he had used in Atlanta, and still with that silly grin on his face, said, "But you still love me, don't ya?"

I stopped squirming and looked into his eyes.

Now or never.

"That's not the first time you've asked me that question," I said softly.

He laughed.

"You're not going to bring up the 'we live to serve' comment, are you?"

As sincerely as I could, I said, "No Nick, I didn't mean then. I meant later in your bedroom. You asked me if I could love you, and I said yes, most definitely yes!"

He let me go. Backed away a few steps, and looked at me. The nightie I was wearing was very revealing. He went to my suitcase and picked up my robe. I objected.

"What's this?"

"Danielle, we have to talk, and I can't afford to be distracted."

That comment has to be a good sign, doesn't it?

I allowed him to put the robe on me and lead me into the living room. I curled up on the couch, and he sat at the other end. He was having trouble getting his thoughts together.

"Nick, let me go first, please?"

He nodded. I looked directly into his eyes, just like he does when he talks to me.

"In Georgia, we made some promises to each other. I promised never to lie to you, deceive you, or keep anything from you, remember?"

Again a nod.

"You never made that promise to me, but I'm asking for it now. You don't have to say it, but please know I expect it from you."

I rushed on before he could answer.

"On the side of the road in Georgia, I said you were the mostest man I had ever met. Everything that has happened since that moment has made that belief stronger. I know it doesn't sound possible, but the truth is I am totally in love with you, and I'm sure you know it, I told you so that night."

He tried to say something, but I pushed on.

"That night, you told me you loved me. It's true, I know it's true."

Now I was rushing to get the words out.

"Since we got back from Atlanta, I've been waiting for a sign you meant what you said that night. But, there was nothing. After I heard what you said in the break room yesterday morning, I knew you were just keeping the promise you made to me. Believe me please, I wasn't eavesdropping, I just happened to be there."

I had to finish quickly before I lost my nerve.

"I love you; you love me. That much is sure. So, why can't we be together?"

"Danielle," he started to say. I interrupted him.

"Start by telling me the truth. Begin by telling me you love me, ... or, say you don't!"

Looking into his eyes, I knew this was a man in pain.

"Danielle, the truth is, I am crazy in love with you. And, I believe you are in love with me."

"There's nothing else to say," I insisted.

"There's a lot more to say. Danielle! Do you honestly believe I would give you up if I thought there was a chance for us?"

"We have every chance, better than most because our love is real, it's true."

"Yes Danielle!" But love does not conquer all like it says in the fairy tales."

I couldn't answer him. He took a breath and again looked into my eyes.

"As much as we love each other, some things will be a wedge between us and eventually drive us apart. Things that are not under our control. Things that cannot be changed."

"Like what?"

He resigned himself to the fact I was not going to let this go until I had an answer.

"Like the fact that I'm fifteen years older than you are."

It can't be. Five, maybe even ten years, but he can't be fifty!

"Impossible!"

"Birth Certificates don't lie, Danielle, my son is only five years younger than you are."

"But, why should that matter?" I pleaded. "There are a lot of May – December marriages that work. You not only don't look your age, but you also don't act that old, and I'll bet that you don't feel that old."

"That may be true today, but in fifteen years, you'll be fifty, in the prime of your life and I'll be sixty-five. And, when you're sixty, I'll be seventy-five. I will definitely feel my age then. Also, I have no wish to make you a young widow, it's no fun, I know!"

"Okay, it's a problem, but we can work on it, we can deal with it, we can find a way around it."

"The fact is I will always be fifteen years older than you are."

I had no answer. Nick had more.

"How would you feel if we went to one of those charity dinners and you heard someone say, 'There's Amonti and his trophy wife'?"

"That only happens to beautiful young girls who marry old rich guys,"

"Exactly."

"So, you're rich too."

He nodded.

"How rich? Millions?"

He nodded again.

"You must have realized I had money?"

"Yes, I just never thought about it in terms of dollars. I assumed you told me the truth when you said you wouldn't miss any lunches because of our date, and I assumed you were well off. How many millions?"

"More than I can spend in a lifetime."

"I forgive you for being rich."

"That brings up another problem. I know people!"

"So you keep telling me."

"I do. I know a lot of people and a lot of people know me."

"Are you telling me you'd be ashamed to be associated with a working girl because of all the important people you know?"

His tone changed.

"Danielle, that's not fair, and it's not like you."

"I'm sorry," I said, and I meant it.

"What it means is being associated with me will have an effect on your career."

"How?"

He was quick to answer.

"How would you feel if you landed a great job and later found out the only reason they gave you that job was because you were my wife. Or, you landed a great project like the Paterson deal and heard that it was your association with me that was responsible. Or worse, what if you lost out on a great job, or lost a big deal because of me? It could happen."

"You're rich, I don't have to work," I said sarcastically.

"Not true. Danielle, I am in love with you, the whole person. And your career is part of who you are. I know you're not in it for the title and the corner office that goes with it. You need the challenge that the career offers you. You wouldn't be happy being a rich man's stay at home, do nothing wife. If being with me caused you to lose your career, you would eventually resent me for it. Even though you know Deltron will never let a woman get too far ahead in the company, you stay there because the job keeps you on your toes. You enjoy what you do, and any man that takes that away from you is a fool looking for a troubled relationship."

We talked for over four hours without settling anything. We were both adamant about our positions: his being a relationship with him would hurt me, and mine being now that I know him, life without him would be unbearable. I didn't have any answers. I needed to buy time.

"You can't do this to me without giving me some time to think. It's unfair for you to decide for both of us and not let me have a say. I need time to come up with logical arguments."

I knew it was the only thing that would get through to him. He agreed.

"I'll go back to Florida, and you can stay here, visit your sister, and deal with Paterson, and we'll talk when you get back to Fort Lauderdale."

"NO...NO...NO! You have to stay with me this week. If I can't change your mind, this week will be all I have to remember!"

I pleaded with him to give me this week. Finally, he agreed, but I didn't just want to spend the week with him. I wanted the week I had thought about since I first decided to lie to the team. I told him what I meant.

"If we are through after this week, it has to be a special time, just like Atlanta."

He asked me what I wanted him to do.

"Just treat me the way you feel about me. You love me, and I love you. Treat me like a lover, as you would have if this discussion never happened. Don't hold back because you think it will be worse for us if we have a great week together. Promise me this, and I will promise you after the meeting with Paterson on Tuesday, we will talk again and come to some conclusion. No tears, no hysterics, honest discussion."

He promised, and I made him say the words.

"A promise from a gentleman to a lady."

And I promised too.

And again, he kept his promise. Everything was wonderful, except he never did invite me into his bedroom. We used it twice, but both times I had to ask. He never suggested it. But each time we were in there, it was just like the night in Atlanta.

Tuesday morning, I attended both meetings. The meeting with the board went so well I was sure we would have a deal. They promised an answer within thirty days.

Nick and I had lunch together, and I was so up from my meeting he never mentioned our deal about discussing our relationship. He allowed me to enjoy the moment. But, at dinner that evening, we did talk. He was still sure a romantic

119

relationship with him would be bad for my career and hurt me in other ways, and there was the unfixable problem of the difference in our ages.

"Nick, I appreciate the fact that you kept your promise, but you kept it so well I couldn't concentrate on the negative side of your argument. Please give me more time. I couldn't think about it when we were sharing so much. Back in Fort Lauderdale, when we're not romantically involved, I'll give it serious thought, and if we could meet privately just one more time, I'm sure we could come to an agreement."

"How much time?"

"A month."

"It's early June. How about July Fourth weekend? Would that be enough time?"

I agreed, and that night I asked Nick if we could use his bedroom. Unless I could find a way to change his mind, it might be our last night together. He agreed, and it was as wonderful as ever.

The flight home was uneventful, and Thomas met us at the airport and drove me home. There I probably spent the worst night of my entire life.

Thursday morning, I arrived at the office intending to be very professional with Nicholas. I would show him I could keep a promise also. But, Nicholas wasn't in the office. I asked Crystal if she knew why, and she informed me before I left for San Antonio, Nicholas had asked Mr. O'Rielly for two extra days off. I stopped in Charlie's office to get the answer..

"Nicholas informed me while you were in San Antonio, he was going to be with his family, and if he could have Thursday and Friday off also, it would mean he could spend an extra four days with them. He said he had been working with Crystal, and she was more than qualified to fill in during his absence."

I wouldn't see Nick until Monday. Maybe that was good. It would give me time to think without him being so close to me.

I gave the team the update on the Paterson deal and told them how good I felt about it. Thursday night I called Colleen and told her of my predicament. Nick and I had kept it mostly to ourselves when we were with them. Colleen and Bob really liked Nick and thought we made a good couple, and in spite of his age, she promised to help me figure a way to change his mind.

Friday afternoon, Charlie stopped in my office.

"Nicholas called. He's not coming back to work. Some kind of family problem."

"Quit without notice?"

"No! Nicholas told me after his time off when you were in Cauldwell that he might have to leave soon. He also said Crystal would make an excellent Administrative Assistant if given a chance. He's been teaching Crystal how to do his job since he started here."

This did not come as a surprise to Charlie, but it was a shock to me. What should I do? I had his cell number. Should I call him and tell him this was cheating? Or was this the smart thing to do? Without Nick around five days a week, I might be able to concentrate on how to convince him he was wrong.

But, what if this was his way of dealing with the situation? What if he doesn't intend to see me again? What if he just disappeared and I never get a chance to convince him we can make it? Do I really have a date with him over July Fourth weekend? We never made plans just that we would meet over that weekend. I expected to get the details of our meeting from him at the office. Would I ever see him again?

Would he do this to me? Would he make the decision for both of us? I had to believe the man I loved couldn't do that. I know he loves me, he couldn't hurt me like that.

I have to put my trust in his love! I have to!

Chapter 14 - Houston

Monday, I received an e-mail from Nick. The subject line read: 'July 4th Weekend.' I opened it up and found three attachments. The first was an airline reservation for a first-class flight to Houston, Texas on June thirtieth with an open return. The second was a hotel reservation at the Houston Hyatt Hotel in my name for the same date. And the third was a reservation for a car service to pick me up at the Houston Airport, take me to the hotel, and then take me from the hotel to a restaurant. In the body of the message were just two letters in bold type:

TT

I knew what TT meant: 'Till Then,' and it gave me hope.

I called my sister Colleen every night. I also called my older sister Lindsey a couple of times, but after hearing how old Nick was, and that he was rich, she didn't think I should pursue him and wasn't any help at all. My niece, Anna Lee, on the other hand, was so happy Nick, and I had made a connection, but sad at the fact it might be temporary.

"Even a short time with such a man was wonderful."

She should know, her time with her husband Robbie was very short.

One of the times I talked to Lindsey, she asked, "If he's so rich, why was he working as your assistant?"

I didn't have a clue. I did remember he had mentioned our meeting wasn't honest, or something. I thought about calling Janice Alvarez and asking her how she knew Nick and what she knew about him. I could also call Terry Daniels, and possibly Stacy Geer.

No, I know this man. I don't care about his past.

I love the man he is today. I can't be wrong about him. But I can't think of any compelling arguments to fight him with.

The first week, Colleen tried to help me think of a way to change Nick's mind. But as time went on, she started asking me questions that startled me at first, until I realized they were meant to make me think.

She would ask me questions like, "Have you thought about what it would be like to be married to a rich man: the responsibility that goes with that?"

And, "Do you know where his money comes from. Does it have anything to do with the people he told Billy about?"

Then later it was, "How would you feel if you lost a good job or a big deal just because you were married to him?" or, "How would you feel if you were considered a trophy wife?"

Every night I talked to my kid sister, and most nights to her husband also. Both of them liked Nick and sincerely tried to help.

I wondered how Nick was doing. Was he going through the same agony I was or was he so convinced it wouldn't work, he wasn't thinking about it at all? It must have been on his mind since Atlanta. Why else would he tell Charlie he was thinking of leaving?

After three weeks of utter misery, not only for me but for my sister and her husband, it was time. I was to fly out to Houston on June thirtieth. The return was open, so I made plans to be away from the office for a week.

If everything went as badly as I expected, I would go to San Antonio and stay with Colleen.

How would I deal with that?

I remembered how I felt after my breakup with Jack. I was just a silly girl then. I wasn't really in love with Jack, I was just infatuated with his good looks and his charm. I realized that after I got myself together. This would be nothing like that. I was truly in love with Nicholas Amonti. This was no schoolgirl crush. This was real.

If everything went as badly as I expected, I would be crushed.

The flight was uneventful. The limo from the airport was no problem. I knew what time the dinner reservation was, and I asked the limo driver to pick me up so I could arrive at the restaurant twenty minutes early. At the hotel, I received the same royal treatment I had received in San Antonio. I took my time getting ready. I wore the same little black dress I had worn in Atlanta, hoping it would bring me good luck. As the limo moved toward the restaurant, I wanted to bolt. I didn't want to go there. As long as I didn't see him, he couldn't say no, and I still had hope.

But I knew it was inevitable. I arrived twenty minutes early as I had planned. I found a dark corner outside the restaurant and hid, waiting to see Nick as he arrived, and maybe judge his mood. The time came and went. No Nick. Five minutes late, ten minutes. Nick was never late. Was it possible he couldn't face me? The plan was made over three weeks ago, did he get cold feet?

No, not my Nick! But, he was not MY Nick!

What could have happened? Maybe he got to the restaurant before me, or I missed his arrival? I had to know. I walked into the restaurant and asked the maitre'd if Mr. Amonti had arrived. He indicated that Nick was seated and offered to bring me to his table. I asked him to allow me to go over alone. Nick was sitting with his back to the door. He later told me he didn't want to jump every time the door opened, thinking it might be me. I walked to his table and stood just off his right shoulder.

"Excuse me Kind Sir, the maitre'd said they are overbooked tonight, and he has no table for me. Since you're alone, would you mind sharing your table?"

Nick got to his feet and smiled.

"How could any gentleman refuse such an elegant lady?"

We sat down across from each other. Nick asked, "Stood up?"

"No, sir. My gentleman would never do such a thing to a lady."

That brought another smile, but not his usual carefree smile. He looked at me as if he wanted to devour me, but his usual manner wasn't evident.

"Something to drink?"

"Whatever you're in the mood for."

Nick summoned the waiter, Clarence, and ordered two margaritas. We sat in complete silence while we waited for the drinks.

When they arrived, I asked, "What shall we drink to?"

"How about we drink to the rules?" he said sadly.

"I was hoping there wouldn't be any rules tonight."

He wasn't looking into my eyes as he always did. His eyes were turned down looking at his hands.

"We've always had rules, Danielle."

"Okay," I offered, trying to sound upbeat.

"How about this. Rule Number One, it starts as soon as we take the first sip of our drinks?"

"Sounds good. And Rule Number Two?"

"Does there have to be a Rule Number Two?".

"Can't have a Rule Number One without a Rule Number Two."

"Why don't you tell me what Rule Number Two is," I said, almost in tears.

Nick still wouldn't look at me. He studied his hands for a long time. Finally, he reached for his glass. I picked up my margarita with shaky hands and spilled part of it on the tablecloth. I could see his hands were also shaking. Lifting his glass, he finally looked into my eyes. I saw pain, disappointment, hurt.

"Rule Number Two, it ends, …"

I was screaming with my eyes:

"No, please don't say it. Please…please. I love you so much, don't send me away!"

Suddenly, the hurt in his eyes turned to confusion. I wasn't sure what was happening. He studied me for a very long moment and then he said, "Never."

I wanted to die. I wanted to hide. I wanted to beg him yo reconsider

What did he say?

"How about it never ends!"

I was stunned. Before he had a chance to change his mind, I clinked my glass against his and shouted, "**DEAL**!"

Nick finally smiled.

"Deal!"

I didn't know what to do. I didn't know what to say. He said it never ends. That's not what he was going to say, I know it wasn't. What changed his mind?

Without another word, he took out his cell phone and pressed a speed dial key.

I remembered his call to Sweetie during our drive to Atlanta.

"We already have a beautiful suite at the Hyatt."

He put his finger to his lips to silence me. The party on the other end answered.

"Colleen, it's Nick."

I stared at him. He just turned me from a miserable wreck into the happiest woman in the universe, and the first thing he does is call my kid sister?

Maybe I'd better check her panties!

"Yes, Colleen, she's here. Yes, she's alright. Yes, Colleen."

When she took a breath, he managed to continue.

"Colleen, I need a favor. I have a problem. I just asked Danielle to marry me!"

I could hear her squeal all the way on my side of the table.

"That's the problem. I'm not sure. Maybe you can find out for me?"

He handed me the phone. Tentatively I asked, "Colleen?"

"Tell me you said yes!" she screamed at me, "If you don't, I'll never speak to you again!"

"Of course, I said yes, most definitely yes!"

And another squeal. She wanted details, she wanted to cry, she wanted to jump through the phone and hug me.

Nick took the phone back and got Colleen to quiet down.

"Colleen, Danielle and I have a lot to talk about tonight. I promise she'll call you in the morning. Tell Bob to get the grill ready, we'll be there for dinner tomorrow."

After a pause

"Yes Colleen, we're both okay. First thing in the morning, but Colleen, it won't be too early."

After another pause.

"Colleen...thanks, thanks for everything, and tell Bob thanks also. Tell him, last night was a big help."

With that, the phone was put away. Nick called the waiter and ordered two bottles of Taittinger, Blanc d Blanc champagne. He took a business card from his wallet, wrote something on the back.

"Two bottles? If it is your intention to get me drunk so you can have your way with me, I assure you, Sir, alcohol will not be necessary."

Nick pointed across the dining room.

"See that young couple over there?"

I nodded.

"Well, about ten minutes before you walked in, that young man got down on his knee and proposed to that young lady. Judging by her reaction, I assumed she didn't expect it. Then he placed a ring on her finger, and they kissed to polite applause from the other diners."

Nick showed what he had written on the business card.

> This beautiful lady just agreed to be my wife.
> So please enjoy this bottle of wine,
> From one lucky bastard to another!

When Clarence returned with the two bottles of champagne, Nick instructed him where to bring the second bottle. We watched as Clarence explained who the wine was from and gave the young man the card. A big smile followed. The young man handed the card to his lady, looked at us, and nodded his appreciation. The young woman, after reading the card, blew Nick a kiss. Nick caught the kiss and smacked it against his cheek, which made the girl smile all the more.

Nick's attention returned to me.

"Before you ask: yes, I'm hungry, and I'm in the mood for red meat."

Nick smiled and called Clarence back to our table.

"Caesar Salad, easy on the garlic and heavy on the cheese. Two rib eye steaks, for the lady, charred first, and then a warm pink center. Medium rare for me. Baked potato with extra sour cream and chives, creamed spinach and Bananas Foster for dessert. Also later, coffee for me and a cappuccino for my lady, with just a hint of nutmeg."

Nick had just ordered the exact meal we had in Atlanta. He remembered every detail. Just how I liked my steak cooked. The extra chives and sour cream, the way I liked the salad, right down to the touch of nutmeg in my cappuccino. He had remembered every detail.

Clarence told us creamed spinach wasn't on the menu

tonight. Nick took Clarence's hand into both of his and looked him in the eye.

"Clarence, tonight is a very, very special night and everything must be perfect. Not near perfect! Absolutely perfect! I'm sure Chef has a can of spinach in the kitchen, and he could whip up a cream sauce in no time. If Chef gives you any trouble, talk to Seamus. He'll talk to Chef for you!"

Clarence left us and headed for the kitchen. After glancing into his hand, he changed direction and went directly to the maitre'd. After a brief conversation, they both headed for the kitchen.

"How much?"

"How much what?"

"How much did it cost you to get me creamed spinach, tonight?"

"Well, you seemed to enjoy it in Atlanta."

"How much?"

"A hundred."

"It had better be good. Who is Seamus?"

"Seamus is a waiter who worked for me during my restaurant days in New York. He owns this place now."

Dinner was wonderful. The restaurant had the first bottle of wine on Nick's list, and it was magnificent. We talked, but not about us.

While Clarence was preparing the Bananas Foster, Nick excused himself and went over to speak to the young couple he had sent the wine to. Their conversation was very animated and seemed to please the young lady very much. When he returned to our table, he told me what they had talked about.

"I invited them to our wedding and asked that we receive an invitation to theirs."

"Are you planning to get married in Houston?"

"No, I thought you might want Fort Lauderdale, San Antonio, or maybe even Cauldwell, but I never considered Houston."

"How is that young couple going to afford a trip to Fort Lauderdale for a weekend to attend our wedding?"

He was about to answer when I put up my hand.

"Don't tell me! It's covered!"

Nick smiled.

"Now you're getting the idea."

After dinner, Nick wanted to introduce me to the young couple. We made our way over to their table, and I met Judy and Rick. They were a lovely young couple, and Nick reminded them they were coming to our wedding. When it was time to go, Nick, always the gentleman, bent down to kiss Judy's hand.

I heard him say to her, "What a beautiful ring."

Then he suddenly stood up and looked at me.

"A ring, Danielle, it's not official without a ring."

I started to tell him it was alright, we could worry about that later, but he got down on his knee in front of me, took my hand.

"Danielle Grace Palmer, would you do me the honor of becoming my wife?"

I looked into those beautiful brown eyes and almost cried.

"Yes, Nick. Most definitely yes!"

Then he slipped a ring on my finger, and it was official. He stood up and kissed me to applause from the other diners.

On the way out of the restaurant, he introduced me to Seamus. He told Seamus the young couple's entire tab was on him. Seamus said he would see to everything. We said goodnight and headed out the door.

Outside, about ten couples were waiting for the valet to get their cars. Nick said tonight wasn't a night for waiting in line and pushed to the front of the line. But, we didn't stop there. We walked directly to the curb, where Nick's rental was waiting with the valet holding the door open for me. And we were off.

I was admiring the beautiful ring on my finger in the dim light of the dashboard. I knew Nick had come to the restaurant to tell me he didn't believe it would work out between us. I was sure because of the way he wouldn't look at me. But, if that was true, how did he happen to have this ring in his pocket?

Was he hoping I would say something to change his mind?

I suddenly noticed we had been driving for quite a while, and we were on a highway. I didn't remember a highway on the way to the restaurant, and it seemed to be taking too long to get back to the hotel.

"Do you know where you're going? I don't remember it taking this long from the Hyatt."

"We're not going to the Hyatt."

"But, all my clothes are there."

"We'll pick them up in the morning."

"Am I allowed to know where we are going?"

"Galveston."

"And what's in Galveston?".

"Option Six."

"And what is Option Six?"

"It's definitely not options one through five," he said with a smile.

"I'm confused."

"I'll tell you all about it, but not tonight. Tonight is about the future, Okay?"

I knew that was all I was going to get out of him. Nick loved to surprise me, and I knew whatever option six meant, it would be good. I used the opportunity to ask him why he had changed his mind tonight.

"I know you. Your entire manner earlier said we weren't going to be together after tonight. And, then suddenly, you asked me to marry you."

"Danielle, there are a lot of things I want to tell you tonight, and something I want to show you. I will answer all of your questions, but not here in the car. I promise, when we get to Galveston, everything will become clear. But, if you think about it, you already know the answer."

That would have to do. In the time I've known Nick, I learned he does everything in his own time, with his own plan. He can't be pushed, so I just enjoyed the ride, and thought about our future together. I would find out about option six and everything else when he was ready to tell me.

But, since he said Rule Number Two was this would never end, and I was wearing his ring, I was content to sit in the car next to him and dream about never ends.

I did find out about option six later that night. And, a couple of days later, I found out about all the other options, from Stacy. I also found out a lot more about the man I had agreed to marry.

Chapter 15 - Options

When we got back to Fort Lauderdale, I called Stacy. I had a lot to thank her for. She asked if I would meet her for lunch that afternoon and I couldn't say no. During lunch, Stacy told me Nick had talked to her about the impossible situation between him and me.

"I was there when Janice came up with the idea of Nick taking a temporary job as your Administrative Assistant. I saw him a couple of weeks later and asked how it worked out. He said that you weren't right for the position he had in mind. When I asked him why he was still working for you, he told me he was enjoying not having all the responsibility on his shoulders. I didn't give it much thought."

Stacy laughed.

"When he introduced us at the charity ball, I knew the reason. On the way home that night, I told him that he was in love with you. He didn't admit it, but he didn't deny it. I also told him that you weren't in love with him, but there was interest. Nick said it was an impossible situation, and I let it drop."

Stacy said after Nick told her what happened in San Antonio, and he planned to see me once more in Houston, she knew he was suffering.

"Nick was so obviously in love with you, and he was so sure a relationship with him would hurt you, it was out of the question. I tried to give him reasons to take a chance and tried to persuade him not to make a final decision until he saw you again and heard what you had to say. The morning he left for Houston, he stopped by to pick up some things he had asked me to do for him, and I made a final pitch."

Stacy stopped until the waiter had served us.

"I asked Nick if he regretted the five years he was married to Joan. He replied it had been the best five years of his life, and he could never have any regrets, even though it should have lasted longer.

"Then I asked him if he would trade those five years for twenty years with someone who he didn't love the way he loved

Joan. He told me he wouldn't give up those five years for anything.

"I asked if he knew in advance what it would be like, and it would only last five years, would he still have married her. He said he would have married her if he knew it would only last a year.

"I asked him if it was fair to deny Danielle the same thing. No matter how long it lasted, didn't she have the right to be with the man she loved so completely and who apparently loved her the same way? He said he wasn't rich when he married Joan, and his money couldn't hurt her like it could hurt you."

It was evident Stacy loved Nick, and she approved of Nick and me together. I wanted to know more.

"Do you know about the options?"

Stacy smiled.

"Nick didn't become rich by letting things just happen. Everything important had to have a plan, and since nothing in his life was as important as you, this plan had to be perfect.

"Wednesday night when he returned from San Antonio, Nick wrote out on a piece of paper every possible scenario for your meeting in Houston and made plans to implement each of them. He came up with six options.

1. Neither of you shows up at the restaurant.

2. Danielle shows up, Nick doesn't.

3. Nick shows up, Danielle doesn't.

4. Both show up, and Danielle agrees that Nick was right, it was impossible.

5. Both show up, and Danielle wants to move ahead, and Nick has to say no.

6. Both show up, and both decide to go ahead."

Stacy gave me a minute to understand. Then she explained further.

"Numbers one and two weren't going to happen. Nick would never leave you there alone waiting for him. Three was possible, but not likely. Nick didn't think you'd do that to him either. Four was the one he thought would be easiest for him. Five he didn't want to deal with, but he thought it most likely.

"Six is the one he wanted, but felt it was the impossible

option."

Another pause, waiting to see if I was following.

"After listing the six options, he figured what he would do in each case. For options four and five, he didn't know what you would want to do after the decision was settled. Would you want to leave immediately? Stay for dinner? Stay the night? Stay the entire weekend? Would you want to go to your sister? Would you need your sister to come to you? Nick had made arrangements for every contingency of each option from three through six.

"One and two he completely discarded. He had flight schedules available, and he could get you back to Fort Lauderdale at any time. He had limos waiting to take you to San Antonio and Colleen from San Antonio to Houston. He was prepared for whatever happened."

"Sounds complicated."

Stacy smiled.

"Nick thought it was too important to be left to chance. He was not about to tell you there was no chance, and then walk away. He had to be sure you'd be okay."

I knew Stacy was right. That would be what Nick thought. She finished her story.

"Option Six was the one he wanted, but he knew it was impossible. But being who he is, he planned for it. And as things turned out, I'm sure he was happy he had. Since it was the option he hoped for, he spent a good deal of time working and reworking the plan. That diamond on your finger and the look on your face lead me to believe Option Six is the one you wanted also."

My smile should have been answer enough.

"The only real choice was between five and six. I never even considered Options Three or Four. If Nick had gone with Option Five, I don't know what kind of shape I'd be in today. I know I'd be completely devastated."

"Danielle, Nick is a good man. I know that he is in love with you. If he didn't find a reason to move forward, he'd be just as devastated."

I thanked Stacy for everything she had done and for helping to convince Nick to take a chance. She said she only did what she

133

thought was right for Nick.

"But, I'm not the only one who had a hand in changing his mind. Your sister had a lot of input into his thinking. When I talked to her about your dress size, I realized she was on your side from the beginning. While you were calling your sister, every night asking for suggestions on how to convince Nick you two could make it, Nick was doing the same thing. Those questions Colleen was asking you were the questions Nick was asking her. Both Colleen and Bob thought you and Nick belonged together, so they were both trying to help."

The waiter came over and asked if we needed anything. When he was gone, Stacy told me the rest.

"The last time Nick talked to your sister was Thursday night. After talking to Colleen and telling her he had no solution and was going to tell you so, he told her about his options and asked her if she would stand by in case you needed her. Your brother-in-law also said something that night that had a big influence on Nick."

"Do you know what Bob said to Nick?"

"According to Nick, Bob said he's known you since the first month Colleen, and he were dating. He had always wondered why a gal like you never got married and never seemed to be in love. Bob thought maybe your career got in the way, or maybe you were too fussy about men. Maybe it was the situation with a guy named Jack. Or, maybe it was because of how your mother had died. Bob said you had always believed she died of a broken heart, and maybe you feel love hurts too much. He told Nick he believed you never have been open to love. Maybe you didn't even realize it, but you close yourself off to love.

"Nick told Bob he might be right, but now you know how beautiful love can be you should be open to it in the future. Nick said Bob's answer was, "Maybe, but maybe now that she's found it and lost it, she might feel she was right all along. That love hurts too much, and she closes herself off completely."

Stacy smiled.

"Nick bought the ring hoping you would say something to change his mind. He told me if he didn't give it to you he was going to have it framed and hung in his office to remind him of the one he let get away."

I looked at the ring on my finger. It was obviously very

expensive.

Would he really keep it as a reminder? Probably!

I again thanked Stacy for all her help and everything else. I knew that we would be friends. Stacy was Nick's best friend, and I was sure we would be close. I did eventually find out why Stacy loved Nick, and it just made me love him more. I realized there was so much more to Nick Amonti then I knew.

Stacy said Option Six was the one Nick wanted, and he wanted to make it perfect. And it was.

Nick had reservations at a lovely, old hotel, with a suite facing the Gulf of Mexico. It wasn't the type of suite we had at the Hyatt. This one had the bedroom and living room combined, but it was lovely and quaint. After we arrived in the suite, he took me over to the closet and showed me two skirts, shorts, slacks, a sundress, four different tops, and shoes, including sandals, heels, and flats.

"You have your choice to wear back to the Hyatt tomorrow, so it doesn't appear you've stayed out all night."

"How do you know they'll fit?"

"If they don't, you'll have to blame Colleen. She gave Stacy your sizes."

Between that comment and the phone call in the restaurant, I began to smell a conspiracy. Then, he brought me over to the bed and laid out there was the most gorgeous nightgown and negligee I had ever seen. It was a beautiful golden color with an embossed pattern that looked like little flames. And, it was a Stacy Geer Designs Original.

He ushered me into the bathroom to change, and he turned on the fireplace. It was too warm for a fire, but he cranked the AC up. The fireplace was gas fired and didn't throw out too much heat, but it was very romantic. When I had changed into my Stacy Geer Designs Original, I came back into the bedroom and curled up next to him on the couch. The only light in the room was from the fire.

"I have so much to tell you, Danielle, but it isn't yet time. I want us to take a nap because I want you wide awake when I start my story. And, there's something I wish to show you.

"I will admit I intended to tell you we had no future together when you arrived at the restaurant, but while I was waiting for you, I thought about something Stacy had said to me just before I left for Houston.

"Your brother-in-law, Bob, also said something the previous night that made me think I might be wrong. Maybe there was a chance for us!"

Nick looked at me tenderly.

"While I was waiting for you, I kept thinking about what Stacy and Bob had said. Then, when we were making the rules, I finally looked into your eyes, and when I saw the love there, I couldn't say there wasn't a chance. You should have known, Danielle, it's your eyes, it's always been your eyes."

Nick looked deep into my eyes.

"I decided I would try to protect you from the hurts that will come from marrying me, and the ones I can't protect you from I would find a way to make up to you. I can promise you, Danielle, there will be insults and slights, and it will hurt, but I intend to make you so happy you will be able to deal with them. But, right now, it's time for bed. We have to get up at zero-dark-thirty, and we need some sleep."

"What does that mean?"

"You won't like it."

We didn't have sex, but I did cuddle up to him with my head on his shoulder and his arm around me. I realized what he had said Sunday morning in Atlanta was true. I felt safe and secure in Nick's arms. So secure, despite the excitement, I managed to fall asleep. It was a beautiful sleep until the ringing started. It wouldn't stop. I couldn't make it go away. Nick untangled himself from me and answered the phone. He said thank you, leaned over and kissed me gently. I didn't want to get up. I wanted him to come back to bed and cuddle with me.

"It's time to tell the tale," he announced.

Against my protest, he made me get out of bed. It was still dark outside. He pointed me in the direction of the bathroom.

"Get that cute little butt of yours in gear."

"It's a good thing you said little butt," I teased.

I was so happy, I would have giggled at anything he said that morning. When I came out of the bathroom, he was wearing one of those terry cloth robes you find in hotel rooms, and he was holding one for me. I was disappointed he wanted to cover up

136

that beautiful nightgown, but, he ignored my protest. He put the robe on me and slipped white sweat socks on my feet.

"Very sexy," I told him.

He said it would be a bit chilly and led me out to the patio. Outside were a double-wide lounge and a small table with coffee service set up. Nick sat me on one side of the lounge, facing the hotel and he sat on the other side, facing the beach.

He poured us each a cup of steaming hot coffee and began to tell me everything.

"Danielle, I told you I did something for the government years ago. I don't like to talk about it because it wasn't pretty. I'm not ashamed of what I did, it was necessary, and the result required the actions we took, but I'm not proud of what I had to do. But, the personal benefit to me was very rewarding."

He looked to see if I was paying attention.

"First, because I got the bad people to agree, the government is happy with me. Second, to get the bad people to agree, I got the government to back off on prosecuting them for past crimes. That made them happy, and I am in solid with them too. You'll meet them, they'll be at our wedding."

"Should I be happy about that?"

"You'll like them, they're really nice people. And if you didn't know about their past, you'd never guess. Two other benefits were my training with the Seals and the government people I got to know. That's how I found out about Robbie.

"The other thing that happened is there was a lot of money floating around, and the government let me have some of it. Thirty million dollars to be exact. I gathered my kids together and offered them a deal. They each put up ten thousand dollars to buy ten percent of a company I was forming, and I put up fifty thousand dollars for the other half. I loaned the company twenty-five million dollars, and we invested the money."

He waited for me to understand.

"My kids are pretty sharp, and we did pretty well. We all work for the company, but we don't take any of the profit. We each draw a salary and reinvest the profits. Over the years, our salaries have advanced way past what we need, so we each use the extra money for personal investments. I'm happy to say we're all doing quite well. Do you remember when we were in San

Antonio I said our meeting wasn't an accident?"

"Yes Nick, I remember, and I wondered what you meant."

"Over the years, the company has grown, and I only have so many family members. We had to go outside the family to fill key positions. But, because we were a family oriented company, the people we hired had to be more than capable. They had to have a particular personality to fit in.

"I was scouting for a department vice president for my company, and your name had come up a number of times as a rising star. I decided to check you out. But, I didn't want to do it as a job interview. I wanted to know not only how you worked, but how you related to your co-workers. It was just a coincidence Janice heard about your Administrative Assistant leaving without notice, and she suggested I could fill in for a week or two and really get to know you. And that's why we met."

"If that's why we met, why didn't you talk to me about the job? Didn't you think I was good enough?"

"I knew you would be perfect, but once I got to know you, I realized you wouldn't be happy with the job I had in mind for you. It was tedious, repetitive work, and not the innovative and exciting type of thing you were doing at Deltron. I realized you needed a position that offered you a challenge, and not just pushing numbers around."

"If you knew you weren't going to offer me the job, why did you stay with Deltron for six months?"

"At first, I was having fun. It was good to be in a position where I didn't have to make decisions all of the time. The part about my being in management almost all of my working life is true. I enjoyed working with you and the team. They were all good people, and I looked forward to coming to work every day. My business was in good hands, and all I had to do was check in on it occasionally. Eventually, I realized it wasn't the job I was coming to work for, it was to be near you. I was falling in love with you.

"After Atlanta, I knew I had to break it off, so I told Charlie O'Reilly I was planning to leave, and I would make sure Crystal could take over when the time came."

He paused and looked directly into my eyes.

"The only reason I agreed to go to San Antonio is because I

desperately wanted that week with you, even though I knew it was a mistake. Can you forgive me for the deception?"

I looked at the ring on my finger and just smiled. That brought a smile from him and more explanations.

"Remember on the way to Atlanta I told you one of the reasons my first marriage failed was that I quit my job and went into business for myself?"

"Yes Nick, I recall every detail from that trip."

"Well, my very first business was Nick Amonti Services. My logo was two concentric circles with the words 'efficient', 'dependable,' 'economical,' spaced between the two circles. In the center of the inner circle was the company name, but I couldn't put the entire name there, so I used the initials."

I thought about that. Nick Amonti Services, initials. N. A. S, … NAS.

I wasn't thinking on the same line Nick was, so it took a minute for me to catch on.

"NAS!" I stammered, "You're NAS Financial Group?"

"Fifty percent," he replied, "The kids own the other fifty."

Now, so many things became clear. Why I would be a trophy wife. Why people might think my career was the result of being with Nick. Why he was so worried about me getting hurt.

"Oh Nick," I cried, "Is this what you're so worried about?"

"Don't take it lightly, Danielle. Being rich, very rich, does have some drawbacks. It's better than not being rich, but responsibilities and problems come along with the money."

"Problems that we will face together?"

"Yes Danielle, definitely together."

"Danielle, I'm fifty years old. I've lived a long time. I can't possibly tell you about every part of my past life in so short a time. You will hear things from time to time that I may not have told you. Please understand I am not hiding anything from you. I will tell you anything you want to know, except what I did for the government. That period of my life is a closed book, and I will never open it. Okay?"

"Tell me this, do you love me?"

"I honestly believe I love you more than any woman has ever been loved."

"Do you know how much I love you?"

Nick looked directly into my eyes again.

"Danielle, I asked you to marry me because I never have in my life felt love like I feel from you!"

"Nick, I know you are a gentleman, my gentleman. I know you will never lie to me, deceive me, or hurt me. I know that for a fact. Whatever happens, I know you will be at my side to help me, save me, protect me. And you will always have the last dance with me."

"There's so much more, so much more," he said.

"We have a lifetime to get to it."

"One thing, it's difficult getting used to the fact that you're rich. It's not automatic, and it doesn't happen overnight, but it has nothing to do with our love. It's just a fact of life."

"I don't care. I forgive you for being rich."

"Don't misunderstand, I'm not unhappy I'm rich. I like it!"

"Then I'll learn to like it too."

Nick smiled.

"It has its good points and bad points, but the good points outnumber the bad points by a bunch. Let me see if I can put it in perspective. We live in Fort Lauderdale. If I felt romantic, I could take you for a drive to Naples, Florida, watch a beautiful sunset, have dinner at an elegant restaurant, and make love to you in a nice hotel room with a view of the Gulf."

"Sounds fantastic."

"But, we're rich. Instead, I can take you to Naples, Italy on a private jet, watch the same sunset six hours earlier, have dinner on the patio of a beautiful villa in the hills, and make love in our own private bedroom."

"That sounds fantastic, too."

"But, there are drawbacks."

"Such as?"

"Danielle," he said very seriously, "Every member of my family, and now that includes you, is a prime subject for kidnapping, blackmail, and extortion. That is something you must be aware of at all times."

"I never thought of that."

"I have a security team that keeps an eye on things."

"Does that mean I will have a bodyguard?"

"Not in the ordinary sense. Under everyday circumstances, no. But, there will be times: if you decided to go shopping on Black Friday, or wanted to go to the Super Bowl, for instance, you will have personal security with you."

"Not the kind of things I would likely want to do."

Nick was serious.

"You have to take this seriously. No more walking out the side door of Carl's into a dark alley at night."

That got my attention as I remembered Nick pulling Billy off me that night.

"You will have to meet with my security people and receive instructions on how to be aware of your surroundings, what to avoid and how to protect yourself. They will teach you basic self-defense."

"So I can take care of Billy without your help."

"Not quite, but enough to give yourself a chance to run away until help arrives."

"If I won't have a bodyguard, where will the help come from?"

"You will have a special cell phone with a Panic Button and some pieces of jewelry if pressed in a certain way will send out a signal through the phone to tell the team you are in trouble and where you are. They have good relationships with every police department in South Florida and can have a police car to your location within minutes. When you're out of town, they will contact a local security agency to keep an eye out for your signal."

"They're going to know where I am at all times?"

"No, Danielle! You're not being monitored. The signal has to be activated by you for them to know your whereabouts, and in most cases, you won't even need to wear the special jewelry. They'll instruct you on in what circumstances it would be necessary. The important thing, is you are always aware of where you are and who you are with. That means 24/7. My guys will teach you all you have to know to stay safe."

Nick laid back on the lounge and signaled me to join him. It was cozy, side by side, terrycloth robes or not. I looked out to the Gulf. It was pitch black. Nick pointed in that direction.

"Danielle, you and I are going to head toward the horizon out there. But, we're never going to get there, because it will always be out of our reach, right out there in front of us. But I promise you it is going to be one hell of a ride."

He kissed me gently.

"I'm a romantic. The thought of standing on some beach with my arms around you watching a beautiful sunset really turns me on."

"I'll keep that in mind."

"But, the trouble with a sunset is it signals the end of the day. All the things you planned and didn't get around to will have to be put off to another day or forgotten.

He pointed out to the blackness again.

But, a sunrise is different."

As I followed to where he was pointing, the sky turned a lighter hue, and now I could actually see the horizon.

"A sunrise signals the beginning of a new day with all the wonderful possibilities that lie ahead!"

As he was talking, a small crescent of the sun appeared above the horizon, and the sky caught on fire. The clouds turned from white to brilliant reds and yellows and oranges. It was breathtaking. I had lived on the east coast of South Florida for almost ten years and had never seen a sunrise over the ocean.

As the sun rose higher and higher in the sky, Nick looked into my eyes.

"Danielle, today is our sunrise. Today is the beginning of a new life for us. Today is the day all those wonderful possibilities open up to us."

I watched as the sun rose. It wasn't the sun you see high in the sky. This was close. This was on fire. You could see the little fires burning on its surface.

It was a beautiful golden …almost the color of my …I pulled the robe away, and it was the exact color of my nightgown, and the embossed print was exactly like the fires burning on the surface of the sun.

What could I say? What could I do? I did the only thing a girl could do in that situation. I undid the belt on my robe and on his robe, and I DID HIM right there on the patio. And it was glorious!

Chapter 16 - Joan

I was asleep on his chest, and that incessant ringing started again and wouldn't go away. Nick untangled himself from me and picked up the phone.

"Breakfast in thirty," he announced.

"No, no, no," I pleaded.

But, this was a man with a plan, and there was no deterring him. I waited in the bathroom until the waiter left, and then I returned to the bedroom/living room in my Sunrise Nightie.

"I wonder how much sleep Stacy lost getting the color and pattern right."

"From the perfect match, I'd say quite a lot."

"May I assume you have the entire day planned," I asked, knowing the answer.

"Nothing that can't be changed if it doesn't please you. First thing, you have a phone call to make. I made a promise, remember?"

"And a gentleman always keeps his promise to a lady."

He smiled.

"And, did the gentleman promise that particular lady to call her just as soon as he proposed to me?"

"You forget, Danielle, it was not my original intention to propose. The lady in question was waiting to hear if her loving sister needed her!"

"I do have more questions about that," I continued to tease.

"A gentleman never tells. If you need details, they'll have to come from the lady in question!"

Breakfast was fun, as we continued to quibble back and forth about nonsense. It was very relaxing. There were a few serious moments

"I know you're rich, and I know it doesn't matter, but would you tell me how much this beautiful nightgown cost?"

"Cost? I'm sorry Danielle, I thought I told you. That and the clothes in the closet were a gift to you from Stacy."

"I hardly know the woman, why would she give me such gifts?"

"Stacy is a good friend, probably my best friend. Her exact words when I asked her how much I owed her were, "Any woman who can make you love her that much has to be something special, and if you decide to go ahead with this, I want her to know I'm on her side.""

After breakfast and my call to Colleen, Nick said we had to go. I looked at the bed and then at him longingly.

"In broad daylight?" he said, feigning shock.

"What's the problem? Are you a vampire? A little sunshine going to burn you to a crisp?"

With a gleam in his eye and a great big smile on his face, he answered, "I'll have you know Madam, I've been made love to during a sunrise!"

There was no response to that, and I gave in and headed for the bathroom to get ready. I picked the sexiest outfit that was in the closet, and my black dress, nightgown and everything else went into the suitcase Nick had brought it all here in.

What will my future be like with this man?

On the way back to the Hyatt to get my things, Nick got serious.

"Danielle, before we go to your sister's, I'd like to make one other stop. I'd like to stop and visit Joan."

"Of course, I can wait in the car, or you can drop me at a coffee shop."

"I want you to come with me. I don't want to make you uncomfortable, but there's something I want to explain to you."

Uncomfortable doesn't begin to describe it, but if this is what he needs!

"If that's what you want Nick. I won't be uncomfortable. I know you loved her, still love her, and I'm not taking her place. What we have is different. I have no problem with that."

A gentle smile and that conversation was over. The rest of the ride was nice, with us still teasing each other. I'm not really the teasing type, but with Nick, it seemed to come so easily. I never felt this free with a man before. I could say anything to him, and it would be okay. He'd still know that I loved him.

When we got to the Hyatt, we split up.

"Pack your things and have the bellman put them in the car. Meet me in the flower shop."

Since I hadn't really unpacked, just took out the black dress I wore to the restaurant that was now packed in the suitcase from Galveston, it didn't take long.

When I got down to the flower shop, Nick had completed his business. He handed me a single rose, this time, it was yellow.

"To signify our first sunrise together."

I took a pin from the counter and put the rose behind my ear. That got me a disapproving look.

"Problem?".

"You're spoken for. I believe that should go on the other side."

I smiled with embarrassment and quickly moved the rose to the left side.

Then he showed me two dozen white roses we were taking with us. The card read:

Colleen, thanks for putting up with us for the past month.

We were also taking two dozen yellow roses with us. This card read:

Joan, I have someone to love again.　TT

The third order was to be shipped. Seven dozen red roses, one dozen each in a separate vase, with instructions to place one dozen in her office and one dozen in each room in her house, so no matter where she is, she'll be reminded of what she had done. And this card surprised me. Even after our discussion on the patio last night, it never dawned on me. For these, the card read:

Janice, thanks for the intro.　Love, Dad.

Of course: Janice was his daughter.

I forgave myself for not making the connection last night, my mind was otherwise occupied.

The drive to see Joan was quiet. Colleen's flowers were resting on the back seat of the car, but I carried Joan's roses on my lap, all the way. Joan was resting in a private cemetery located on her daughter's property in the hill country of Texas. Nick had to use a code to get past the gate and onto the property. We drove up a winding driveway past a house, a two-story garage, some other buildings and stopped at a bend in the driveway. From there, we walked up a small hill to the cemetery. As I left the car, I noticed there was a woman on the porch of the house watching us.

We sat on a marble bench that was placed at the foot of Joan's grave. The headstone was engraved: Joan Kennedy Amonti. Nick sat silent for a couple of minutes, then turned to me and took my hand.

"After Joan died, I was miserable. I was sure my life was over. I didn't think I would ever fall in love again. It took too long, and only with the help of my family and friends did I finally open myself up to the possibility of life again.

"You are that life. You are my love, and I will not be able to rest if you do the same thing I had done. Danielle, we both know, with the difference in our ages, I'm probably going to leave you sooner than either of us would like. I intend to make you so happy you will mourn losing me. That's okay, but you have to limit that time. I want our life to be so full of good memories every time you think of me it makes you smile. But, you have to promise me here, and now, you will be open to love again, that you will accept it if it comes, that you won't bury yourself like I did for too many years."

"You want me to rush right out and marry someone?"

"No! I just want you to accept the fact that I'm gone. I don't expect you to go looking for love, just that you're open to it if it comes along. You'll never find anyone else like me. I didn't find anyone like Joan. You're different. The way I love you is different. The way you love me is different. Love can happen more than once. Just promise me you will accept it if it comes along, and not use our love as an excuse for being unhappy for the rest of your life."

Nick pointed to the headstone.

"I loved Joan. She will always be a part of me, but she is my past. You are my present and my future. I have never loved anyone the way I love you. I intend to dedicate my life to your happiness. But, when I'm gone you have to move forward."

What could I say? This is one of the primary reasons he was going to discontinue our relationship. He was afraid when he was gone I would spend my time mourning what I had lost. And the problem was I knew when the time came, I would do just that.

And he knew it too. That's why he needed a promise. A lady's promise to a gentleman. Could I make such a commitment? If I did, I'd have to believe I would keep it. Or, at least, try to keep it.

"Nick, I will never make a promise to you I'm not sure I could keep. And, I'm not sure I could keep this one. I am so in love with you if and when I lose you, for whatever reason, I know I will be devastated. I can only promise I'll try. I'll be aware of your wishes, and I'll try. That's the best I can do!"

"A promise from a lady to a gentleman?"

"A promise from a lady to a gentleman.

"I guess I'll have to settle for that right now. I'll find a way to remind you when the time comes."

I thought that was the reason we were here, but there was more.

"Danielle, I am very close to Joan's girls. They will be in our life. We will occasionally visit this property. The family gathers here sometimes for holidays and such. I don't want you to be uncomfortable here. In a very short time, you will be my wife. You will be my life. Nothing here will ever get between us."

I told him I understood, and I wouldn't be uncomfortable. That seemed to satisfy him. With that, we rose from the bench, Nick placed the flowers against the headstone and very quietly whispered, "TT Baby!"

On the way down the hill, I noticed the lady was still watching us from the porch. Nick noticed her for the first time.

"Might as well start getting to know the brood."

Nick led me over to the porch.

"Danielle, meet Sweetie. Pam, this is Danielle Palmer."

"The lady who makes all those beautiful arrangements. Thanks, Ms. Dugan."

Pam acknowledged my thanks and looked at Nick, very seriously.

"Grandpa, why did you take her up to see Mom?"

Nick just smiled.

"Grandpa," she said more urgently.

Nick continued to smile.

"**Grandpa**," she screamed at him, "Don't do this to me!"

This time, Nick nodded, which sent Sweetie into a frenzy of excitement, capped off with a big hug and kiss for 'Grandpa.'

When she regained control of herself, she let him go and looked me over.

"Wow, Grandpa, you sure can pick em! Let me get you something to drink, and you can tell me all about it."

"Can't, we have an appointment in San Antonio."

"You can't do this. You can't spring this kind of news on me and run away."

She turned to me and said pleadingly, "Ms. Palmer, tell him he can't do that!"

"It's Danielle, and he's not going to do that. We can spare some time."

Nick looked at me, still with a big grin on his face.

"Ready for an interrogation?"

"As long as the Fifth Amendment is still in force in Texas."

Pam looked at me, and then to Nick.

"I like her already."

That made me happy. It was apparent Nick had a great relationship with Pam, and I didn't want to come between that. It was nice to know she was pleased he had someone special in his life. I hoped the other four were just as pleased. We stayed for about an hour. Nick explained that yes, this was the lady Pam had made accommodations for in Atlanta, San Antonio and Houston. He revealed we had known each other for a little over six months, and no we hadn't set a date, he had only proposed last night.

"In Houston or Galveston?" she inquired.

"Details at eleven," Nick said, and when both he and I laughed, we got a strange look from Pam.

"I can see where this relationship is headed!"

I showed Pam the ring, and Nick elicited a promise from her she would not say anything to anyone for at least a week. He had a plan to make the announcement, and he didn't want to spoil the surprise.

Pam promised, but that didn't satisfy Nick. He made her promise over and over again.

"Don't tell anyone, not even your daughter."

Chapter 17 - A New Life

We finally left and headed for San Antonio. When we were back in the car, the first word out of my mouth was, "GRANDPA?"

Nick laughed.

"When I married Joan, Pam's daughter was very young, and since Joan was Grandma, I became Grandpa. Pam and her daughter have called me that ever since."

He also told me the first time he met Joan's other granddaughter, she inquired, "Are you Grandma's Yankee friend?" Which I thought was hilarious.

On the way to San Antonio, Nick said we really had to discuss a date.

"I know women like to take their time and plan every last detail, and you'll probably want to get Colleen involved, but for me, the sooner, the better. You're not getting any younger," he announced.

My answer was straightforward and honest.

"Find us a Justice of the Peace, and I'll marry you right now."

"Oh no, you don't. This is going to be the biggest blowout wedding imaginable."

"And why is that?"

"Because I'm marrying the greatest gal in the world, and everyone is going to know how lucky I am."

We settled on a Sunday morning in August and agreed that Fort Lauderdale would be the right place. He asked me how much I intended to involve Colleen in the preparations.

"I wished she lived closer because I want her to be my Matron-of-Honor and I want her involved totally."

"Not a problem. She could fly to Florida as often as necessary and could stay at your apartment or the Hyatt. Since school was out, she could bring the boys with her, and Bob could come over whenever he was free."

"That will be outrageously expensive."

"We're rich, remember. It's really not a problem, plus there are other alternatives available."

"You're rich!"

That earned me a very stern look.

"We're rich, Danielle, Get used to the idea!"

That was going to take some getting used to. I didn't know how rich he/we, were but owning fifty percent of NAS Financial Group probably meant pretty rich. He started with thirty million dollars. He surely must have doubled or even tripled that by now.

The remainder of the trip we discussed some details. My head was swirling. Yesterday I thought my life was over. Now I'm talking about my wedding to the mostest man I had ever met.

We pulled into Colleen's driveway. Nick unbuckled his seatbelt and was halfway out the door when he turned back to me. He expression was solemn when he spoke.

"Danielle, now that we're engaged to be married, do you think I should give Colleen her panties back?"

Before I digested what he had said, he was out of the car, and his door was closed. By the time he walked around the car to open my door, I was laughing so hard I couldn't say anything to him.

Colleen came running down the driveway, threw her arms around Nick's neck and gave him a big kiss. He spun her around a couple of times and when they finally separated he said to no one in particular, "Is this one of the perks you get when you marry a Palmer girl?"

Bob answered, "It does have its compensations, but don't let it become a habit."

We were all laughing as we headed into the house. Colleen brought us into the kitchen, took two beers from the fridge, and handed them to Nick and Bob. With a point of her finger, she directed them to the patio.

"Bossy, aren't they," Nick observed.

"Get used to it my friend," Bob replied.

Both men headed out to the patio while Colleen demanded every detail of last night's adventure. But, I did notice when Bob reached for his beer from Colleen, his fingers did just manage to brush her arm before he grabbed the bottle. The signs are there if you look for them, Nick had said.

150

After Colleen exhausted me with questions and we had called Lindsey and Anna Lee to share the news, we sat down to dinner. Nick told Bob and Colleen about our plans for an early wedding and how he hoped Colleen would be able to come to Florida to help. He explained the cost wouldn't be a problem, and Pam could make all the arrangement as necessary.

Nick also thanked them both for disrupting their life for the past month and dealing with the two of us. And he told Bob their talk Thursday night was a big reason we were sitting here today.

Of course, they protested it was no problem, but I could see they were happy they had played such an important part. Bob really appreciated Nick's comment about Thursday night's conversation.

We stayed the night, and Sunday morning Nick said if we were getting married in a month, we had better get back home and start making arrangements. We left amid hugs, kisses, and good wishes and headed for the airport. Nick had made some phone calls while we were at Colleen's on Saturday, and I assumed, at least, one was to Sweetie to make arrangements to get us back to Fort Lauderdale.

Little did I know just what those arrangements included!

When we arrived at the airport, we didn't go to the terminal. We drove to the Executive section, and Nick stopped the car next to a big plane that had the letters NAS stenciled on the tail. One of the pilots greeted Nick and said we were ready to go. The car rental company had sent an agent to retrieve the vehicle, and up the stairway, we went. Inside, the cabin was not set up like a commercial airliner. It was more like a living room. It was impressive.

"Company plane?".

"Actually, I own it, and the company leases it from me when they need it. Easier on the bookkeeping that way."

"Would you like to watch the takeoff from up front."

"I prefer to stay with you."

After thinking about it, he said no problem he'd be up front too. When we got to the flight deck, both pilots were seated at the controls. Nick introduced me to Jerry and John and told them we were to be married. Nick received congratulations, and I received wishes of good luck and happiness.

"Ms. Palmer will be riding the jump seat, and I'll handle the take-off from the left seat."

Jerry didn't seem too pleased.

"Boss, why don't you handle the right seat and let me handle the take-off today?"

Nick was adamant.

"I said I'll fly left seat today. Show Ms. Palmer how the safety harness is buckled."

I became aware that the atmosphere on the flight deck was tense. Nick took his place in the left seat, and Jerry showed me how the four-point safety belt worked.

Nick asked John if everything was ready, and when John replied that the engine start checklist had been completed, Nick said, "Wind them up!"

Jerry, who was now standing behind me, reminded Nick he had to check with the man on the ground to make sure the engines were clear. Nick fumbled with the microphone, and with John's help found the right button.

"Engines clear for start?"

After a pause, "Clear left, start one."

After another pause, "Clear right, start two."

When the engines were finally started, Nick pushed the throttles forward, but the plane didn't move.

"Boss, the chocks!"

Nick fumbled with the microphone again,

"Brakes on, pull the chocks."

Now I was getting worried. Would this man, who I knew loves me, put my life in danger just to show off to me? It didn't fit the man I knew.

But, just how well do I know him?

When the plane started to move, Nick attempted to steer it with the odd-looking steering wheel in front of him, but it didn't turn, it kept going straight ahead.

"Boss, the tiller on the left bulkhead."

Suddenly, John jammed on the brake, and the plane came to a sudden stop, almost knocking Jerry off his feet. The plane started bouncing up and down. Jerry was trying to say something, but the sudden jolt stopped him. That's when I lost it.

"Let me out!"

I started pulling on the belts that had me strapped to the seat.

"Let me off this thing," I screamed, finally finding the buckle that was holding me pinned to the jump seat.

Nick yelled at John, "Your airplane."

John repeated the phrase. Jerry had regained his balance.

"It's okay, Ms. Palmer, Mr. A is a qualified pilot."

Nick tried to turn around to face me, but with the jump seat out, it was difficult in the tight space on the flight deck. Nick told Jerry to help me get out of the seat belts and tried to placate me.

"It's alright Danielle, it was just a joke. I am a qualified pilot."

I was not placated.

"Honest Ma'am, the boss knows what he's doing, it's just a joke we pull on newbies."

Nick, trying to look at me, pleaded, "Jerry will fly the plane. We'll sit in the cabin. It will be okay,"

I was on my feet now. I looked at the three of them. As loud as I could, I screamed at them.

"A joke? You think this is a joke? You frighten me like that, and you think it's a joke?"

It was obvious Nick was extremely upset.

"I'm sorry Danielle."

I leaned over and got as close to Nick's face as I possibly could. With my face no more than three inches from his, I let him have it.

"If you think that was funny Mister, then you'll believe that this is hilarious."

And, with my hot breath blowing in his face I whispered, "GOTCHA!"

If I had a camera and took a picture of Nick's face at that moment, it would have won a prize. Then I sat back in the jump seat.

"Now that you boys have had your fun, can we get this show on the road? I have a wedding to plan!"

Except for the sound of the engines, there was complete

silence on the flight deck. After a short pause, I asked Jerry to show me how to use the four-point belt again. He was the first one to regain his composure.

"Well played, Ms. Palmer!"

Nick immediately growled.

"Don't you dare encourage her!"

"Yes, sir, sorry, sir."

Nick then faced forward and said to John, "My airplane."

Which John repeated, and the plane started moving again. As we were moving away from the hanger, John leaned over to change the radio frequency, glanced in my direction, and gave me thumbs up.

Nick growled again.

"I saw that!"

"Sorry boss!"

I knew I had won over Jerry and John. We would be friends. After all of Nick's teasing, this was too good to let go. While he was moving us toward the runway, I gave him one more shot.

"Ah, what's the matter? Are you angry because your little joke was turned around on you?"

Nick didn't answer right away. As we were approaching the runway, he relented.

"Okay, one for the lady's team."

"One? I got you, I got Jerry, and I got John. Don't you dare give me this one for the ladies team."

Just as we were turning onto the runway, Nick looked over his shoulder at me.

"Okay, three for the lady, but I hope the lady realizes … this means war!"

And with a big smile on my face, I told him, "Bring it on tiger!"

And then in my sweetest voice, I added, "But you still love me, don't ya?"

Nick turned his head to the left, away from me so I couldn't see his face, but he couldn't hide the great big grin he was sporting.

I heard him say, "Take off power!"

John repeated the command as both of them reached for the throttles, and we were heading down the runway.

Nick said, "You ready to fly, Danielle?"

A strange voice said, "V-ONE."

I said, "Yes, Nick, I'm ready to fly!"

The same strange voice said, "VR."

"Then let's fly … Rotate."

Nick pulled back on the wheel, which I later learned was called a yoke, I lost sight of the runway as the nose of the plane came up, and I could feel the lift as NAS ONE took flight.

And my man was in control!

After we had reached cruising altitude, Jerry sat back in the left seat, and Nick and I went aft to the cabin. Nick explained to stay current with his certification he was required to do so many takeoffs and landings every ninety days, so, he did it whenever he could.

He showed me around the cabin. He explained the aircraft was called a BBJ, which stood for Boeing Business Jet, and it was based on the plane I flew to Houston. It was very spacious for just two people and had a small bedroom and shower in the back for when they had to make overnight flights and be ready for a meeting in the morning. It was really nice flying back to Fort Lauderdale like this.

Beats the hell out of commercial aviation.

Nick retook the controls for the landing, and when we left the terminal at Fort Lauderdale Executive Airport, there was only one car. Thomas greeted me as he had done the last time, and Nick informed him of our pending union. That seemed to please Thomas. And, I knew I had another friend. Nick also told me Thomas was a member of our security team.

Nick spent the night at my apartment, another first for me. No man had ever shared my bed before. All of my romantic encounters had been at his place or in a hotel, never at my place.

I didn't have to report to work on Monday, and we spent the day talking about the wedding.

"The BBJ will be available to ferry Colleen, Bob, and the boys back and forth and if necessary, we can also use my son's 'G.'"

We settled on a church not too far from where I lived. We

talked about living accommodations after the wedding, and we both agreed my apartment would be sufficient, at least at first. Nick had a small house in Tamarac his sister lived in, and he sometimes used. His apartment downtown was too small for the two of us.

The more I got to know about this man, the more I realized the money didn't affect him. Sure, he spent what he wanted, but he didn't drive the most expensive car, his apartment was small and compact. The house he owned probably wasn't worth more than two hundred thousand dollars. He led a comfortable but not flashy life. That suited me. His airplane was his only extravagance.

Tuesday, I was back in the office. Nothing significant had happened while I was away. Nick and I had decided to make our announcement at a small party the following week. But, I had to tell Charlie and Dan.

Charlie had watched out for me since I first came to work at Deltron. He was a good deal past retirement age, and I sometimes wondered if he kept working just to keep an eye on me. His wife Myrtle had talked about retirement a couple of times in front of me, and Charlie just said, "Soon."

I asked Charlie if he and Myrtle would come to dinner at my apartment that night. I said it was important, and after checking with his wife, he agreed. Nick wasn't there.

I told Charlie and Myrtle, "I met a man, an exceptional man, and I intend to marry him within a month."

They were both sure I was rushing into a situation that I should be taking more time with. I explained.

"I've known him for quite a while and only recently did we realize we were in love."

I finally got them around to my side, and they seemed pleased I had finally found that special someone. That was until Charlie found out who that special someone was. I had made arrangements to call Nick when we got to this point, and he arrived ten minutes later. Myrtle and I talked in the dining room while Nick and Charlie went into the living room.

I don't know what they said to each other, but Charlie came away realizing it was a done deal and grudgingly wished us luck. Charlie promised not to tell anyone until we were ready to make the announcement.

Wednesday I was in touch with Florida East Coast Railroad. They were interested in hearing more about our system, but not ready to talk commitment. I met with them on Thursday, and they said when we were prepared to demonstrate the system on a large engine, they would let us use one of their older locomotives. Perfect.

Friday Paterson called. It was a go! I was elated and ran to Charlie's office to give him the good news. He took me into the CEO's office and let me make the announcement. That resulted in a meeting of all the executives. They decided this news required a special announcement, and the PR department would set up something. They asked that I keep the news secret until they have a chance to put something together.

It was a glorious weekend. Nick and I worked on wedding plans, and I talked about how nice it would be to be Vice President of Special Projects. Nick cautioned me not to get my hopes up.

"Deltron Motors doesn't like to promote females to the executive level."

"With the Paterson deal, they don't have any choice."

"They'll probably make you Vice President of the Broom Closet, or some other position that won't let you shine so that they don't have to promote you any higher."

I was so up that nothing he said bothered me. Monday morning, I was called into an executive meeting. All the Senior VPs were there. The CEO made the announcement.

"The PR Department has come up with a plan to announce the Paterson deal on Thursday at a news conference right here at the company headquarters. Danielle, your team, will get all the credit and as the leader of the team you are being promoted to Vice President of Human Resources."

I was stunned. So was Charlie. I left the meeting without any comment. Charlie remained for a while, and I could hear a loud, heated argument coming from the CEO's office. I called Nick and told him he had been right. He was very sympathetic.

"What do you intend to do?"

"Are you willing to marry an unemployed girl?"

"Of course I am, but remember what I had told you. You won't be happy without that challenge."

"What challenge will there be in Human Resources? It's just like you said, a dead end promotion."

"There are alternatives."

"Do you really believe that?"

"Danielle, I can give you phone numbers to a dozen corporations that would be willing to talk to you about a junior executive position.

"And at least six of them will offer you a contract before you leave their office."

"You know it can't be on your coat tails."

"I only know three of the people I'm talking about. I told you before, you have a reputation in the South Florida corporate world. Put it to use."

After hanging up on Nick, I sat at my computer and wrote out my resignation. I signed it and put it in an unsealed envelope. I walked into Charlie's office and handed it to him. He never looked at it. The only question he asked me was, "Are you sure?"

"Yes!" is all I said.

Then he showed me another unsealed envelope. It was his request for immediate retirement.

Chapter 18 – The Next Phase

Before I left Charlie's office, I asked if he could get Deltron to release me immediately.

"I gave them thirty days' notice, but I have wedding plans to make."

Charlie said he'd do what he could.

Back in my office, I called Nick again.

"Who do I call first?"

"As I recall, you made a promise to Terry Daniels he would be your first call."

"He didn't mean it."

"Danielle, He did mean it, but I wouldn't jump at his offer. Before you commit to anyone, talk to Peterson Enterprises. Bill runs the kind of organization that would fit you to a tee. He has a great eye for talent, and when he hires them, he lets them do their thing and shine."

Somewhat bolstered by Nick's enthusiasm, I called the office of Daniels Industries. I was connected with Terry's secretary. I asked for an appointment to see Mr. Daniels about possible employment. She was very pleasant and polite and gave me an appointment for two weeks from tomorrow. Disappointed, I was ready to thank her and hang up, but I decided to take Nick at his word and asked the girl if she would do me a favor.

"If at all possible, Ms. Palmer."

"Please, the next time you talk to Mr. Daniels, just mention I called."

"I can do that for you."

I was looking up the number for Peterson Enterprises when my phone rang.

"Danielle," a big booming voice shouted, "Is it true? Are you finally ready to leave those bozos and come to work for a real company?"

That brought a smile to my face.

"The idea has occurred to me, Terry, and I did say you'd be

the first call I made."

"Danielle," he said very apologetically, "I am really tied up for the remainder of the day. Can you wait until nine o'clock tomorrow morning?"

"That would be perfect, Terry. Nine o'clock it is."

After a few pleasantries, we disconnected, and I was already feeling better. I made the call to Bill Peterson and was put right through to him.

"This is Danielle Palmer; would it be possible for us to meet?"

Before I had a chance to finish my statement, he said, "I don't have any diesel trucks here, Ms. Palmer."

How does he know I work with diesel trucks? Could Nick be right about my reputation?

"That's not what I'm calling about Mr. Peterson. It's a personal matter, not connected with Deltron Motors."

"How's nine tomorrow morning?"

"I'm sorry, Mr. Peterson, I'm tied up until at least eleven tomorrow."

"I've got some time at one PM," he replied.

"That would be perfect, thank you."

Again, after some pleasantries, the call ended. I quit while I was ahead. With two hits in a row, I didn't want to take the chance of a turndown. That night, Nick and I talked almost exclusively about my decision to leave Deltron and my two appointments for the following day.

"Deltron Motors will skyrocket because of the Paterson deal, and you should be there to rise with the company. But the current senior management is too conservative and bringing women into the top ranks of management is too chancy for them. Your career is over if you stay with them."

As to my two appointments tomorrow Nick had definite opinions.

"Terry Daniels is a solid businessman. I helped him get started. It was one of the first jump start projects NAS took on. You will do well over there. The only problem, like most large corporations, there is a corporate bureaucracy that sometimes slows things down. I'm sure Terry would give you your own department, based on your work at Deltron, but everything you did would have to pass through four or five other departments before it could be implemented.

"Peterson, on the other hand, hires talent. Bill is excellent at spotting it, and he leaves his people alone. Sure, you'll have to justify what you are doing, but he'll give you a budget and let you go do what you do. If you succeed, you'll be rewarded. If you fail, you'll have to explain what went wrong, and if the explanation is plausible, you move on."

The next day I was pumped. My meeting with Terry was exciting. He offered me the entire candy store if I would sign with him. His offer was great, my own team, just like at Deltron, but I would start as a VP. My second appointment was even better. I never did get to tell Bill Peterson why I wanted to meet with him only that it wasn't about diesel trucks.

Bill was a tall, older good-looking man and had a charming manner. Instead of sitting at his desk, we moved over to a small seating area in the corner of his office.

"What can I do for you, Ms. Palmer?"

"I resigned my position at Deltron Motors, and I'm looking for a job."

Bill looked at me for a long moment, excused himself, and went over to his desk and picked up the phone.

"Holly, tell Jimmy I want him in my office immediately. And tell Timothy I want to see him also."

He came back over to the seating area and asked me if I had officially resigned from Deltron.

"It was official as of noon yesterday."

He smiled. There was a knock at the door, and a younger man poked his head in.

"You wanted to see me, Bill?"

"Yes, Jimmy, come in. Have a seat."

The young man moved toward the seating area and was preparing to sit down.

"Jimmy, remember that problem we were talking about yesterday?"

"The Innovation Concepts thing?"

"That's the one. I think we may have solved it. Jimmy, meet

Ms. Danielle Palmer!"

Jimmy hadn't completely sat down at this point, but he jumped back up, came over to me, and shook my hand.

"Ms. Palmer!" A pleasure to meet you. Please tell me you're thinking about accepting our offer?"

Before I had a chance to answer, Bill said he hadn't made me an offer yet. That settled Jimmy down a bit, and he asked Bill what he was waiting for.

"Ms. Palmer just got here, and we haven't had a chance to talk yet."

The conversation turned very businesslike. It was interrupted by the entrance of Timothy, who I was told was the head of the Human Resources Department.

Bill and Jimmy double-teamed me and told me about their idea for a new department and how I would be the perfect person to lead it. My reputation for innovation and ingenuity was just what they were sure that they needed. I was flattered and elated of course. It sounded too good to be true. When they were finished with their pitch, Bill asked me who else I was considering talking to. I mentioned my only other contact so far had been Terrance Daniels of Daniels Industries. That changed the mood in the room. Jimmy, looked deflated.

"Ms. Palmer, we can't possibly match Daniels' offer. We are a much smaller company, and we don't have his resources. But, I can promise, you will be happier here at Peterson. Bill is a great boss to work for, and he gives his people room to experiment. You won't have ten layers of supervision over you."

"First, the name is Danielle. And, more important is the fact that money is not my primary concern. A good friend of mine, you may know him, suggested I start my job search here. He seems to think I would be happy here."

"May I ask who this friend is?"

"Yes, his name is Nick Amonti of the NAS Financial Group."

"I've met him. But I can't say I know him. We both belong to a club that he founded some years ago. His reputation is that he got lucky, won a lottery or something, and turned that windfall into a fortune with some risky investments."

I smiled inwardly.

If they only knew where that money came from, and the basis for those risky investments.

"Tim, what can we offer, Ms. Palmer?"

"Danielle," I said again.

Timothy laid out a pretty standard executive employment package, salary, benefits, perks, use of company facilities, etc. It wasn't the deal Terry had offered me, but it was much better than the deal I had at Deltron, and even if I weren't about to marry a wealthy man, I could live very comfortably with his offer and even afford a few Stacy Geer Designs gowns.

"Gentlemen, I've had the freedom at Deltron to do some pretty crazy things. Luckily most of them worked out. I was happy at Deltron, and if some things were different, I wouldn't consider leaving. What I'm hoping for is to find an environment that is open enough to allow some out of the box thinking, without looking over my shoulder, worried that my position is in jeopardy because I screwed up once."

"Then this is the place for you. I already said Bill was a good guy to work for. The reason is he allows his people the freedom to follow their ideas. If it works out, you receive the reward. If it doesn't, then you'll have to explain why. If the reasons are technical, or beyond your control, then we move on. If you screwed up simply because you screwed up, you'll have to be more careful next time."

Bill took over.

"Danielle, I think I have a pretty good eye for talent. Mostly it's because I do my homework. When you have talented people working for you, you let them do what they do."

I thanked everyone and prepared to leave. I promised them I would let them know, either way, about my decision within a week. Bill escorted me to the elevator. On the way, we detoured to a vacant office. It was large and well furnished. After we looked the office over, he closed the door and pointed to the blank nameplate on the wall.

"Danielle Palmer, Vice President of Innovation Concepts, would look pretty good there."

I couldn't wait to get back to my apartment to tell Nick. When I arrived, he was at the dining room table working on his laptop. The moment he saw me, he jumped up, grabbed me in a bear hug and swung me around.

"What's this."

"I can tell by the look on your face you've had a good day, My Lady."

"Not a good day, a fantastic day."

We settled down on the couch in the living room, and I told him everything. I explained both offers and said he was right all along. I was known outside Deltron Motors, and my reputation was pretty good. Nick asked who I was going to see next.

"I'm pretty sold on Peterson Enterprises. I not sure I want to talk to anyone else. I don't want to spend the few weeks before our wedding going on job interviews. Help me decide."

Nick was reluctant.

"Danielle, we could delay the wedding if necessary until you have this matter settled. I don't want you sidetracked while preparing for our special day, either."

"Oh no, you don't. You're not putting this off for a second. You're going to be mine, on schedule."

"I'm already yours," he said sweetly.

A gentle kiss followed, and then he insisted we continue talking. I wanted his advice. Actually, I wanted him to verify that I was making the right decision.

"This is your career. You are the one who has to show up for work every day. You have to have confidence in your own decision. I know Terry very well, and I know that he runs a good outfit. His employees seemed content. Bill Peterson, I have met a few times, but I don't really know him. His company has a reputation for innovation, and the credit for their successes seemed to go mainly to his employees."

I made my decision. Peterson, it was. I told Nick, called Terry and let him know. He sounded very disappointed but said he honestly felt I would flourish at Peterson.

"I hate to lose the opportunity for you to be on my team, but you might have felt closed in here."

He wished me good luck and asked that I keep in touch. My next call was to Bill Peterson.

He was elated at my decision and asked if I could come to his office tomorrow at ten to sign the contract. I said that would be okay. Nick had a serious look.

"You have a problem, Danielle."

"What kind of problem?"

"I was thinking about Delton's announcement on Thursday. Resigning before the announcement, and Charlie's retirement would make them look bad. I believe they need to make some kind of move to save face, and they may decide to promote your assistant Bob to VP of Special Projects."

"That's great! Bob definitely deserves the promotion and he would be a great team leader."

Nick agreed but said Bob wouldn't take the position. When I asked why he felt that way, he said something that made my heart melt.

"Danielle, they all love you over there. You are their leader, and they respect and admire you. When they find out what Deltron offered you, they're all going to be pissed. Bob is most likely to tell them to shove it."

"I can't let him do that."

"Agreed. You have to talk to him before they do. Tell him you know you will be happy at Peterson. Tell him you need to know the work you started at Deltron will go on. Convince him to take the position if they offer it to him."

I called Bob at the office and asked him to have a drink with me after work. We agreed on a place, and I left Nick for the meeting. It took a lot of convincing.

Bob was not happy when he learned I had resigned, and angry when I told him about Deltron's offer. He was pleased to hear about my new position with Peterson, but he worried I would be starting a new position without my team. In the end, I did manage to convince him it would make me feel better if all the work we had done at Deltron didn't go to a stranger and I would be happier knowing the team would survive with a great leader at the helm. And, Paterson Trucking would not be happy we were both leaving and might cancel the deal.

"It would serve Deltron right if they did," Bob said.

"But that wouldn't help either of us."

In the end, he relented and promised if they made the offer, he would accept, but only if I got credit for the LNG concept and the Paterson deal. He asked me if I was going to steal any of his people.

"Only Crystal, if she'll come with me."

"That girl will go to the end of the earth with you. She admires you so much!"

Wednesday morning, I got ready for my appointment with Peterson and asked Nick to come with me. He said it wouldn't be proper for him to be there. I said he could wait for me in the outer office and then we could go out and celebrate. He finally agreed. When I walked into Bill's office, I was surprised to see Terry Daniels there.

"I thought I'd come over and give you one more chance to change your mind and come to work for a real company."

Bill, Jimmy, and Tim didn't seem to mind, and they appeared to be enjoying their victory over Terry. I mentioned that my advisor was in the outer office and asked if it would be alright if he attended the meeting.

"Attorney?"

"No, just a friend whose opinion I respect."

Bill called his secretary and asked her to send the gentleman that had arrived with Ms. Palmer into his office. When Nick stepped into Bill's office, Terry flipped out.

"You! You're the one who touted her to come here? You're a traitor, Amonti! I thought we were friends."

"Be honest, Terry. You know this is the place for her. You would bog her down in so much red tape she'd never get anything done."

"You're probably right, but I'm still pissed at you."

After the back and forth banter subsided, and Nick was introduced to Jimmy and Tim, we got down to business. Tim asked me if I wanted my lawyer to look over the contract. I glanced at Nick. He shook his head, and I signed on the dotted line. There were discussions about putting my team together and various technical matters, but all went exceptionally well. Finally, Jimmy asked me when I could start. I hesitated before I answered.

"I was hoping you would allow me to start the third week of September."

"That long

"I'm sorry, Bill. I should have brought this up before."

166

"If the reason is good enough, I guess we can deal with it."

I looked at Nick, and before I could think up a good enough reason, Nick announced.

"The reason is I intend to take this lady on the greatest honeymoon a girl has ever had!"

Terry looked stunned.

"You agreed to marry this bugger?"

"Afraid so!"

Terry looked at Nick for a long moment.

"Amonti, you have got to be the luckiest son of a bitch that ever walked the earth!"

"You won't get any argument from me," Nick replied.

After the surprise had worn off, Nick received congratulations, and I got good wishes, and it was agreed I would start the third Monday in September.

Bill suggested, "Why don't you come in next week get your office organized and get to know the people you'll be working with?"

That sounded like a good idea, and I readily agreed. Nick suggested he take us all to lunch. Bill and Terry agreed, but Jimmy and Tim begged off.

Terry asked if he could kiss the bride, and of course, I agreed. When I went over to him and offered him my check, he pulled me to him, wrapped his arms around me and gave me a kiss on the mouth. But, it was a gentle kiss, a respectful kiss, if you can understand what I mean. Before he let me go, he whispered in my ear, so only I could hear.

"I have never met a better man. Take good care of him."

In return, he got a smile and a nod from me, and he seemed to accept that, and I knew I had another new friend.

Before we left, Bill brought us to the office he had shown me yesterday, and my name and title were on the nameplate.

Chapter 19 – The Bragger's Club

Lunch was pleasant. Wedding plans, how Nick and I met, plans for my department and other things were discussed. The men talked about the Bragger's Club lunch scheduled for tomorrow. Terry had an idea.

"I think you should join, Danielle. It's a monthly luncheon club for executives from the South Florida area. It's basically a social event, but we use the luncheon to learn about new and up and coming companies and people."

Bill added, "It's beneficial. It keeps us up to date on what's happening in the South Florida corporate world. It's where I learned about you and your abilities."

While Terry and Bill were telling me about the club, I could see the wheels turning in Nick's head. He was acting just like he did in the back seat of the car after the team was leaving the first Paterson meeting. Something was cooking in that brain, and I knew I would soon find out what it was. Terry noticed it too.

"I know that look Amonti, what's going on?"

Nick glanced at the two men, and then at me.

"She's beautiful, isn't she?"

That got nods of approval from Terry and Bill and a blush from me.

"And young," Nick continued.

Terry looked thoughtfully at Nick. "Where are you going with this?"

"When a beautiful, young woman marries a rich, old guy, what is the first thing we think?"

"Not in this case," Terry replied, "Everyone who knows you knows you've always preferred talented, intelligent women, and this one may be the most talented."

"But not everyone knows that. But what if there was a way to let at least the corporate community know what Danielle has accomplished? What if there was a way to make Danielle's accomplishments shine before she is connected with me?"

Nick outlined his plan, and both Bill and Terry agreed. I

wasn't at all sure it was necessary, but I was outvoted. So, we all agreed that the plan would be implemented tomorrow at the Bragger's Club lunch.

Over the years, the Bragger's Club has grown to include representatives of most of the major corporations in the area, and some of the smaller companies. Its primary purpose is to give these executives a chance to swap stories, gossip, and ideas. According to Nick, this is where he first heard about me.

"Your name is known to most members of the club, and although none of Deltron's executives were members, your accomplishments were known because of other companies you have dealt with while at Deltron."

The reason it was called the Bragger's Club was that at the end of every luncheon, members would get up and tell of their accomplishments. They could brag about the big deal they had just signed, or the new technology they had developed, or the first-class executive they have stolen from another company. Terry and Bill both were members, Terry from the very beginning, and they both told me it was a lot of fun in addition to being very informative.

Although Nick had founded the club, the co-chairpersons were Terry Daniels and Stacy Geer, two people Nick had known before NAS was established. And, tomorrow at the July meeting, I would be invited to join.

That afternoon, I called Charlie.

"Charlie, you don't have to worry about me. I just signed on with Peterson Enterprises. It's a great opportunity, and I'm starting as a vice president."

"I'm happy for you Danielle. I knew you'd find something quickly. Will you be here tomorrow afternoon for the Paterson announcement? It's scheduled for four o'clock outside on the steps in front of company headquarters. If you attended and don't tell the real reason you're leaving, Deltron will agree to release you directly after the press conference."

"I'll be there Charlie. I wouldn't miss it."

"Danielle, Bob has been offered VP of Special Projects. He accepted, and that would also be announced at the press conference. Bob accepted the offer only if you were given full credit for the entire Diesel/LNG System and the Paterson deal. It will be announced that you were leaving Deltron for personal reasons and that Deltron was very sorry to lose you."

The timing was perfect. Thursday, I arrived at the Hyatt, where the Bragger's Club met. Nick would be there, but we would not acknowledge each other. I was surprised by the number of women in attendance. This was no male chauvinist society.

After everyone had arrived and was seated, Terry announced that Ms. Danielle Palmer had been invited to join the club. I received a nice hand as I stood and accepted the invitation. As a new member, a short resume of my accomplishments was read by Stacy. Everything was there, from the first job I had after college to the fact that it was my idea, and I was the one who spearheaded the Diesel/LNG System. It sounded impressive, even to me.

After lunch, the bragging began. The people I was seated with told me July was a slow month, and this wouldn't take too long. The last person was telling us about the big deal he had just closed, worth over two million dollars, shutting out his competitor completely.

When the applause stopped, Terry said, "I think our newest member, Danielle Palmer, has something to brag about."

I stood, and a microphone was passed to me.

"Actually, Terry, I have three announcements to make. First, Paterson Trucking of San Antonio has signed an agreement with Deltron Motors to refit fifteen thousand trucks to the new Diesel/LNG system over the next twelve months. The deal will be worth forty-seven million dollars to Deltron."

The applause was deafening. When it quieted down, I went on.

"Next, I have word from Florida East Coast Railroad that they are willing to allow Deltron Motors to install the system on two of their diesel/electric locomotives with a plan to refit their entire fleet if the numbers are as good as we claim. And," I continued, "CSX Railroad is interested in talking to us about a trial installation on their fleet."

This time, not only applause but a chorus of, "Way to go," and "you go girl," from some of the women in attendance.

It took a while for the buzz to quiet down, and Terry finally had to ask for order.

"I believe the lady said three announcements."

When quiet was restored, I concluded.

"For reasons, I will not discuss here, I have resigned my position with Deltron Motors."

That brought complete quiet.

After a minute, Terry said, "Can anyone top that?"

More applause.

As it was finally dying down, Bill Peterson stood up, and a microphone was passed to him.

He waited for quiet, then looked directly at me.

"Very impressive Ms. Palmer."

More applause. Bill held up his hand for quiet.

"But I can top it."

A murmur ran around the room. Bill smiled.

"As most of you know, we have been looking for the right person to fill a new position at Peterson Enterprises for many months. Many of you people here have given me some great suggestions, and I thank you for that. The person we were looking for had to be very, very special. They had to be inventive, well organized, a great leader and innovative. Well, the search is over."

After a dramatic pause:

"It gives me great pleasure to announce that the Vice President of Innovation Concepts at Peterson Enterprises will be … Ms. Danielle Palmer."

Another round of loud and enthusiastic applause along with a chorus of, "Way to go, Bill," and "You dog."

When things quieted down, Terry made some announcements and gave out the schedule for the next meeting. The meeting broke up, and I was inundated with congratulations for what I had accomplished at Deltron and a number of CEO's complaining it wasn't fair for me to sign on with Peterson without giving them a chance to make a pitch. Terry came to my rescue.

"If I couldn't entice Danielle to my company, you guys wouldn't have a chance anyway."

Since Nick and I weren't going to leave together, Stacy offered me a ride to the Deltron press conference. We had time, so we stopped for a cup of coffee.

"Well, so much for a trophy wife, that should tell them who you are."

"That really bothers him, doesn't it?"

"Danielle, Nick thinks you are the greatest thing to come along since sliced bread. He is amazed that you love him. He is prepared to dedicate his life to your happiness and ensuring that no one can hurt you. Yes, if you heard someone refer to you like that, and it hurt you, it would kill him."

"Why do you love him so much?" I asked. That got me a strange look, so I added, "I know it's not romantic love, but it's clear that you love him."

"I am what I am today because of that man. It's a long story, and I'd be glad to tell you, but we don't have the time now. He really is something special, Danielle, and I am rooting for the two of you to be as happy together as he deserves. Be good to him."

"Terry Daniels said the same thing to me yesterday morning: 'Be good to him.'"

"Terry may be the only one who loves your man more than I do. He's a big buffoon, but he has a heart of gold."

Suddenly, Stacy took out her cell phone and dialed a number. When the party answered I heard her say, "Terry, do you have plans for tonight? Good! You're taking me to dinner. Pick me up at seven-thirty. Got a pencil?"

She gave him an address and hung up. I looked at her, surprise in my eyes.

"I said he has a heart of gold. Maybe it's time I did some prospecting."

We had to leave for the press conference, but Stacy promised she would tell me the whole story of her and Nick before the wedding.

Standing on the steps of the Deltron Office Building, the CEO was making the announcement. Charlie, Bob, Eugene, Arthur and I were standing behind him. He praised the entire team for our brilliant work and turned the microphone over to Charlie for Q&A.

The questions were standard stuff. He was asked who had thought of the idea, and Charlie gave me full credit. They asked how it worked, and Charlie turned the microphone over to Gene. It went on and on. Then I was asked why I was leaving Deltron.

Nick had told me not to avoid the question, but to smile and spar with the reporters. He said I should look happy and let them think all is well between Deltron and me. The story will eventually come out, but not from me. I stepped to the microphone.

"That's very personal."

They persisted.

"I think the definition of personal is, relating to someone's private life."

"At least, give us a hint," one reporter begged.

"If I give you a hint, you'll probably make something up that's not true. And if the hint is too good and you figure it out, then it won't be personal anymore."

Charlie stepped up and tried to change the subject. I said to him, loud enough for the microphone to pick it up, "That's okay Charlie. It's fun sparring with them."

That got the subject changed. I spotted Nick in the back of the crowd that had gathered to see what the excitement was about, and he was doubled over with laughter.

Colleen and Bob were in town, and Nick had brought them to the press conference. Afterward, we all went out to dinner, and all had a good laugh at the way I had dealt with the media. Colleen and I talked about the plans for the wedding and Nick, and Bob talked about Bob's schedule and how many days he could sneak away from work and come to Fort Lauderdale. He was here for the weekend and would be back next weekend for the announcement party.

So far, the only ones who knew about Nick and I were, Colleen and Bob, my sister Lindsey, who was not very happy about it, Charlie and Myrtle O'Reilly, and Charlie was not too happy either, but I did have an ally in Myrtle. Anna Lee, Stacy, Terry, Pam, Janice and Dan, and both Janice and Dan had their misgivings. In fact, neither of them were happy about our relationship.

I got to my office at Peterson Enterprises early on Monday. Crystal wouldn't start at Peterson until a week before I returned from my honeymoon, so I was assigned a temp assistant. Sara was a sweet gal and very helpful.

Around eleven thirty, Sara announced a Mr. Andrew Lighter

was asking for me. I told Sara to send him in.

"Hi, beautiful! Thought I'd stop by, congratulate you on your new job and take you to lunch to celebrate."

"Thanks, Andrew, I appreciate the offer, but I'm already committed for lunch today."

Andrew gave me a pouty face.

"How about tomorrow or Wednesday? You have to let me help you celebrate your new position."

"Sure, tomorrow would be great. Say around noon."

Andrew agreed and wanted to give me a kiss for luck. I walked around my desk and offered him my check. Before I realized what was happening, I was in his arms, and he was kissing me just like he did after our dates. I didn't respond, as was usually the case, but he had his arm around my waist, and I was being held extremely close.

When we broke apart, I was ready to tell him he had taken too much liberty, but I noticed Nick was standing in the office doorway, watching us.

I pulled away from Andrew and said, "Hi, Nicholas. You remember Andrew from Marketing."

Nick nodded but didn't say anything.

Andrew asked, "Here to get your old job back with Ms. Palmer?"

Before Nick had a chance to answer, I said, "Nicholas is my lunch date today."

Andrew made some polite comments and left after reminding me of our lunch date tomorrow.

Nick was not in a good mood. I never figured him for the jealous type, but something was bothering him. I tried to get him to open up at lunch, but all he would talk about was the important meeting he had tomorrow night.

When Nick dropped me back at the office, his mood hadn't changed. I brooded about it all day, and when Nick showed up at my apartment later that evening, I was determined to find out what was bothering him.

"What's eating you? You were rude to Andrew, you were moody at lunch, and you're still in a mood. What happened to open and honest? No holding anything back?"

174

"You're right Danielle. No holding anything back."

This wasn't going to be pleasant.

"Tell me exactly what I walked in on this morning."

I wasn't shocked at the question. I did get a jealousy vibe from him this morning, but I didn't expect this.

"It was nothing. An old friend dropped by to congratulate me and take me to lunch."

"Is that how you greet all your old friends?"

"Nick Amonti are you telling me you're jealous?"

Nick took his time before he answered.

"Danielle, you are a beautiful and exciting woman. I will never be jealous if a man makes a pass at you. But it does upset me when you allow a man to believe he has a chance with you."

"Don't you think I know that? What do you think was going on this morning?"

"I have no idea! ...why don't you tell me?"

"It just happened before I realized what he was doing. I didn't kiss him back."

"But, you didn't stop it. You didn't scold him for taking such liberty. And you didn't inform him that you are in a relationship."

"You didn't complain when your friend Terry Daniels kissed me."

"Terry did not kiss you passionately. He did not hold you tightly against him. That was a friendly kiss. Terry's way of showing you he approved. And, it never would have happened if I wasn't in the room with the two of you. You're not naïve, Danielle, don't you dare try to tell me you don't know the difference."

"It was just a kiss. It didn't mean anything, and it couldn't lead to anything. Sara was right on the other side of the open door."

"Sara was not at her desk when I arrived. How do you think I got into your office without being announced?"

"I still don't understand what you're so upset about. It was nothing."

"Wasn't it?"

"Yes, Andrew is just an old friend."

"An old friend you dated many times. An old friend who you refused to be intimate with because you both worked in the same office. An old friend I'm sure got sweet goodnight kisses which encouraged him to take that liberty this morning. An old friend who no longer works with you."

Nick paused. I wanted to answer him, but I didn't know what to say. I was angry at his accusations, but I didn't want to make him any more upset than he was already.

"You no longer work with him. Your objection to an intimate relationship with him is gone. Did he stop at your office just to congratulate you, or to find out if now that you don't work together, might there be something more? Is that how an old friend congratulates a former co-worker or was there more meaning to that kiss and embrace?"

"You're way off base here. Even if that's what he had in mind, it takes two, and I'm not interested."

"Then why didn't you tell him that? Why didn't you introduce me as your fiancé? Why did you refer to me as Nicholas? Why did you allow him to believe I was there for a job interview?"

"It didn't seem important."

"You're wrong. It is important. There is no doubt in my mind, and I'm sure no doubt in yours, what his intentions are. Instead of closing the door on him and letting him know you are in a meaningful relationship, you opened the door wider for him and invited him to pursue you."

I was really angry now. Nick was blowing this all out of proportion. It was just a simple kiss, it didn't mean anything.

"Working together wasn't the only reason I wasn't intimate with Andrew. I didn't feel that way about him then, and I certainly don't now."

"Does he know that? His actions this morning didn't seem to indicate that attitude. Did you bother to tell him that when you were dating him or did you give him the no co-worker excuse?

"Nick, you don't understand…"

"No Danielle, you don't understand."

Chapter 20 – The Argument

Nick had an answer for everything, and that just made me angrier.

"Danielle, you have been an unattached woman for most of your adult life. You are a beautiful, sensual woman. Many men have hit on you. The ones you didn't want attention from you managed to shut down. The ones you did want attention from you found a way of letting them know that their advances might be accepted. Now that you are spoken for, you must shut down every man who hits on you, no exceptions."

"Don't you trust me? Don't you think I know that? Do you really believe I would encourage another man?"

"You did this morning!"

Now I was furious. The one thing I had never expected from Nick was jealousy.

"I can't believe you're saying this to me. I can't believe you're jealous of Andrew."

"I'm not jealous, Danielle. I'm just telling you how things are. You are in a position you have never been in before. You never had to think about men pursuing you. You were free to make choices you are no longer free to make. All I'm saying is you cannot open the door, even a little."

"Are you telling me I can't have men friends?"

"No, that's not what I'm saying at all. You do have men friends. Bob, Gene, and Artie from Deltron. Dan Patrick. Terry Daniels will be a good friend to you, and I'm sure once you get to know him, Bill Peterson will be more of a friend than a boss.

"You can have all the friends you want, but you have to be sure that friendship is all they want from you. You have to set boundaries, and the friends you want must respect those boundaries. The men I mentioned know you. They respect you, and they will respect your boundaries."

I had never seen such a serious look on Nick's face before.

"Andrew could have been a friend if you had shut him down immediately. But you have given Andrew the green light to pursue you. You have opened the door for him, and you will find that he is already making plans to make himself at home. You will have a difficult time moving him out and closing that door on him now. A very difficult time."

I was not angry any longer. I was long past anger now.

Before I realized what I was saying, I shouted, "So, what now? Are you going to smash his face into a counter too?"

Immediately I wanted to take it back, but there was nothing I could say that would undo that statement. The expression on Nick's face was something I had never seen before and never wanted to see again. I had hurt him. Hurt him deeply. He looked at me for a long time. Then he grabbed his jacket and headed for the door. I tried to stop him.

"Nick, please, I …"

He turned back toward me.

"You have nothing to fear, Ms. Palmer. Andrew Lighter is in no danger from me. That only happens to men who molest you without your permission!"

And he was gone.

All night I had mixed thoughts floating around my head. I was still angry with Nick for his accusation, but I felt so guilty about what I said to him.

Would he ever forgive me?

I tried calling him in the morning. Voicemail. I knew he had a hectic day, preparing for the meeting tonight.

I was torn between not interfering with what he had to do and trying to apologize for the remark I made. I had to convince him he was wrong. Around eleven, Andrew called.

"Hi, beautiful. Listen, I'm stuck here at the office. Can we do dinner instead of lunch?"

I wanted to talk to Andrew and tell him I was engaged, and I knew Nick would be busy with his meeting tonight, so I agreed.

"Great, I'll pick you up at your apartment at seven. It will be just like old times."

It wasn't going to be like old times, but he hung up before I had a chance to say anything.

Andrew picked me up right on time and took me to La Chez, the fanciest restaurant in Fort Lauderdale. I knew you had to make reservations weeks in advance. I asked him how he had managed to get a reservation the same day.

"I bring some clients here to impress them. I have a deal with the maitre'd. For a hundred bucks, he gets me in any night I want."

"Are you trying to impress me tonight?"

"You know it."

That answer got my guard up. After the conversation with Nick last night, I didn't know what to think. We talked about my new job until dinner was served and then Andrew made his pitch.

"Now that we're not working together we can have a real relationship."

"I don't understand."

"Danielle, we had a pretty good thing going there for a while, but you made it clear that it wouldn't go any further because we worked together. We're not working together now. That obstacle is gone, we can pick up where we left off."

"Andrew, I'm in a serious relationship."

"Really, you could have fooled me."

"What does that mean?"

"A woman in a serious relationship doesn't act the way you did yesterday morning."

"What are you talking about?"

"Danielle, you folded right into my arms, and you kissed me the way you used to when we were dating. That's not how someone in a serious relationship acts. You can't possibly be sure about this guy, or you wouldn't have allowed that to happen."

"You caught me by surprise. I wasn't prepared for what you did."

"Maybe you were surprised, but you didn't pull away, you responded to me, and you didn't complain."

Andrew, I'm engaged to be married."

He looked at my left hand.

"Engagements usually require a ring."

"We're keeping it secret for a while."

"Your idea or his? People who want to keep their

179

engagement secret usually don't really want to be engaged."

"It's just until Friday. Nick is going to make the announcement at a party. He wants it to be a surprise."

"Nick…You can't mean Nicholas, your secretary?"

"He's not a secretary. He's much more than that."

"I don't care what he is, you never gave us a chance. That no office relationships nonsense stopped us from what I'm sure could be a meaningful relationship."

"It's too late, I'm in love."

"After yesterday morning, are you sure … I'm not?"

I had no answers for him. Could Nick be right? Did I give Andrew the impression I was available and attracted to him? What Andrew said next completely floored me.

"Danielle, technically you're not engaged until you make the announcement and accept his ring. Give us a chance before you do that. Spend the next three evenings with me and let's see if we can recapture what we had. We can take a couple of days off and go to the Haven Rest Resort. If it wasn't for that rule of yours, I'm sure we would have spent some weekends there. I'm sure our relationship would have gone further than it did."

"Andrew, I'm in love with a wonderful man. I'm engaged to be married to him. I have accepted his ring. Accept that or we can't be friends."

"I wonder what he thinks about what he walked in on. I'm sure he must have mentioned it to you, and I'm pretty sure he wasn't happy about it. And, if you're so much in love with him, why are you having dinner with me tonight. I'll bet he doesn't know, … does he?"

What was I doing here having dinner with him?

I excused myself and went to the ladies' room. I thought about what Andrew had said tonight and what Nick had said last night.

Could Nick be right?

Instead of going back to the table, I left the restaurant and took a cab home. Twenty minutes after I got to my apartment Andrew called. He was angry. I didn't care.

"I told you I was engaged to be married. You attitude tonight, and your actions yesterday indicate you have no respect

180

for me or my decision."

I let him rant for a minute.

"You are also wrong about what we had. It is true that I would never have an intimate relationship with a co-worker, but that's not the only reason we never got to that point. The truth is, whether you choose to believe it or not, I never felt that way about you. You were a fun date, and that was all it ever was."

"You're just saying that because you know I'm right. You're afraid to let your guard down because you realize you really don't love this guy. You know that if you spend time with me, you'll have more doubts about him and what you're planning."

For the first time since Nick walked into my office yesterday morning, I was sure of my answer.

"If it helps you to believe that, fine, believe it. I'll send you an invitation to the wedding. Goodbye, Andrew."

Now I have to deal with Nick.

Nick wasn't in his office Wednesday morning. I talked to Janice. Her attitude had definitely changed toward me since Nick told her about our engagement. She finally said Nick's meeting ran very late last night, and he took the morning off. I called Sara and told her I wouldn't be in until later in the day. I had to get this straight with Nick before I did anything else.

The doorman at his apartment waved me through because he knew that Nick and I were engaged. When Nick opened his door, he was surprised to see me.

"To what do I owe the pleasure of your company this morning?"

"You know very well why I'm here."

He opened the door and allowed me to enter.

"Coffee?"

I nodded.

"Nick, I'm sorry for that stupid remark I made Monday night. It was uncalled for, and it was cruel. I was angry. You must know I didn't mean it."

He didn't say anything until he had poured us both a cup of coffee. We sat at the kitchen table opposite each other.

"But, you do believe it's true."

I tried to think of an answer to that, but I couldn't come up with anything. I wasn't sure.

"It not true, Danielle. At least, not entirely accurate. I'm not a violent man. After I did that thing for the government and trained with the Seals, I realized two things. First, I can kill a man in less than ten seconds with no other weapon than my hands. The second thing I realized is that I must keep myself under control at all times. Because of that training, I don't have the luxury of losing my temper."

I didn't know what to say. I didn't know what to think. But he wasn't finished.

"I would never hurt you, and I would never hurt a man because he wants you. You are a desirable woman, and many men will want a relationship with you. But, I will never hesitate to use my training to protect you and my family."

I still didn't know what to say to him.

"Everything that man told the police is true, except for two key points. The woman he was kissing in the foyer wasn't you, and it wasn't consensual. When I walked into the foyer, the man had this woman up against the wall, and he was kissing her. His hands were all over her. She was trying to get away, but he had his body pressed tight against her, and she was trapped. She was about your height, had brown hair, and she was wearing a white gown. In his drunken state, he probably had mistaken her for you."

I just looked across the table unable to speak.

"I pulled him off her, and she managed to run away. She was obviously relieved to be away from him. I dragged him into the men's room intending to talk to him and try to get him sobered up. But, he got mouthy, said some things. I lost my temper. Not a good thing for me to do. He changed his story later because some people I know convinced him that his future health would depend on what he told the police. I'm sorry I did that, and I'm sorry you had to be involved in it."

I still didn't know what to say.

"That Friday night with Billy in Cauldwell could have been a lot worse. But I had already talked to some people, and I knew they would give him a message. Billy will not ignore that message. You will be safe from him in the future, but unfortunately, he hadn't gotten the message before our little confrontation Saturday morning at Carl's. But he has it now, and you will not have to fear Billy Hastings ever again."

Nick looked down at his hands and then back to me.

"Danielle, I told you I know people. Some of the people I know are not very nice, but I can depend on them. I am not one of them, but I have been associated with them. I have done them a few favors, and they have done some for me."

"Please, believe me, I will never hurt you, nor will I ever hurt anyone who wants to embrace you or kiss you or even sleep with you. I don't own you. That will always be your decision. If a man makes a pass at you, that is **your** problem, and **you** will have to deal with it. If you allow that man to believe he has a chance with you, that is **our** problem, and **we** will have to deal with it.

"But, when a man feels he can take what he wants from you against your wishes, that is my problem, and I will deal with it. And it won't be pretty. And I won't apologize!"

We were both quiet for a while. I wanted to take back what I said Monday night, and I wanted to forget about his confession. Yet, I didn't want to forget.

I didn't want to forget that this man would do whatever was necessary to protect me.

I knew he meant what he said. I believed him, and I had to tell him so.

"Nick, I know you love me and will never hurt me, and I know you would only use violence to protect me. I do believe that. But you have to believe I will never be unfaithful to you. I will never deceive you or forsake you. You are the only man I want in my life and the only man who will ever be in my life."

"I do believe that. I think I know you well enough to know that if you ever find someone who offers you more than I do, you will tell me before you accept his offer. But, infidelity is not an action, Danielle. It's a concept. Remember the conversation we had at the Keynote? If a man makes a pass at a woman who is unattached, she has the choice of accepting his advances or turning him down. When a man makes a pass at a woman who he knows is in a relationship, he is insulting her. You seemed to understand that."

I just nodded. I did know what he meant about being insulting. It was true.

"When a woman who is in a relationship allows any man to

183

believe there might be a chance, she is insulting the relationship and the man she is involved with. I'll tell you again. I have no problem when men hit on you. I trust you, and I know you can deal with it. But when a man feels he has a chance because you didn't shut him down immediately, you have a problem. Once you open that door, it is difficult to close it. It is not only that you will never be with another man, but that every man you come in contact with knows that."

"And you think I encouraged Andrew?"

"Maybe not intentionally encouraged, but you opened the door for Andrew, and I'm willing to bet at lunch yesterday he gave you an indication that he wants to rekindle your relationship. It would have been easier for you if you left the door closed. Why didn't you? And, are you really frightened that I would hurt him?"

"No...no, no, no!   I swear to you that never entered my mind. I was caught off guard. I didn't expect what he did, and I was stunned for a moment. If you weren't there, I would have told him he was way off base, I promise you."

I had to tell Nick everything. I knew he would be upset, but I didn't want to keep anything from him. I wanted the open and honest relationship we had talked about. After his confession, it was obvious that's what I could expect from him.

"I didn't have lunch with Andrew. He called and said he was busy at the office, and we had dinner last night instead."

Nick didn't react at all. I told Nick everything Andrew had said to me last evening at dinner.

"I'm sorry Nick, I was so sure you were wrong. I thought you were jealous. You're right. I am used to being unattached, and I wasn't prepared for what happened."

After listening to my story, Nick asked what my answer was.

"I didn't know what to say to him. He was so sure of himself. I went to the lady's room to collect myself. I hadn't believed what you told me Monday night, and I was shocked by Andrew's comments. Instead of going back to the table, I took a cab home. I left him there."

"Tough to close the door once it's opened, isn't it?"

I could only nod.

"You do know it's not over, don't you?"

"He called me when I got home and said he was sure I still had a thing for him and walking out only proved it. He told me I was afraid to be around him because I knew I'd want to get back with him."

"And you said?"

"I told him I was in love with a wonderful man and he could believe whatever he wanted to. I said I'd send him an invitation to the wedding."

Nick smiled for the first time since this conversation started.

"It still may not be over, but I think you made a good start. I'll talk to him if you want, but I believe it would be much better and final if you dealt with this yourself. You don't want it to sound like it's coming from a jealous lover. Just be sure you're never alone with him."

Nick had more to say.

"Danielle, we talked about this in San Antonio. It will not be easy being married to me. You are a beautiful, sensual woman. Some men will see you as a trophy wife. They will not see the honest love we share. Some of them will believe you might be available for a little discreet adventure. You will have to be more aware of this than the average married woman. I can guarantee it you will be a target."

Again, I could only nod. Everything Nick said made sense.

I allowed Andrew to think I was available because I knew I wasn't interested, but I wasn't thinking about what signals I was sending out. I could deal with that. I could be more careful. It didn't sound complicated.

Nick looked at the clock and said he had to get to the bank to sign the papers for the deal he made last night. I asked him how it went.

"It was tough, but we finally got the banks to put up the money. NAS has to guarantee the loans, but that leaves our cash free to invest in other projects."

Nick's attitude seemed to indicate that our argument was over, but I had to ask.

"Nick are we Okay?"

"Danielle, as long as we love each other, we will always be okay. Let this week be a lesson to both of us. There is nothing we can't get past as long as we are willing to talk about it reasonably, openly, honestly. No anger, no spiteful, angry words, no recriminations.

"I wasn't angry about what happened in your office on Monday, but I was upset about your attitude. You didn't see it as a problem, and I did. Now, it's settled and in the past. If you hear from Andrew again, you'll have to deal with it, but never hesitate to talk to me about it or anything else. We are a couple. Rule Number One: If it affects one of us, it affects both of us. Rule Number Two: We work on it together and fix it. Deal?"

"Deal," I answered.

Chapter 21 – The Announcement

Nick said he had to meet Janice at the bank to sign the loan guarantee. He asked me if I had time to drive him there.

I agreed, and after he showered and dressed, we left.

On the way to the bank, Nick asked, "Danielle, will you tell me about your relationship with Dan Patrick?"

Is he jealous of Dan, now?

"I told you all about it on the way to Atlanta. We were friends. When I walked out on Jack, Dan was there for me. He helped me through it. I believe I'm a stronger person because of Dan. We had a thing for a while, but it never bloomed. We're friends. He's probably the best friend I've ever had, besides Colleen. Please, Nick, don't be jealous of Dan."

Nick gave me a very strange look.

"Danielle, I am jealous of no man. If I lose you, it will be my own fault. If another man makes you happier than I can, I have only myself to blame. The reason I asked is I feel he doesn't like me."

Before I could answer, Nick said, "I talked to Stacy the other day. You know the relationship between her and me. You know what it used to be and what it is now. Stacy likes you. She thinks you will be good for me. She feels you two can be good friends."

"I agree with her. I believe we can be very good friends."

"Do you know why Dan doesn't like me? Is he jealous of me? If he's your best friend, then he and I have to get along. Why is there a problem?"

I didn't have to think of an answer. I already knew what the problem was.

"Nick, I promise you Dan is not in love with me, and he's not jealous of you. But, he is concerned. His fears are exactly what you told me yours were in San Antonio. He thinks the difference in our ages and your wealth and power will hurt me, professionally and personally. Once he sees how happy I am with you, he will come around. I know he will. He's only concerned for my happiness."

That seemed to satisfy Nick, and I left him at the bank.

Nick most definitely is my knight in shining armor, even if his armor does have some tarnish on it.

We had invited everyone from my team at Deltron, Nick's family, Bill Peterson, Stacy and Terry and my sister and brother-in-law to a dinner party at the Hyatt to make the announcement. I also invited Dan Patrick and his new girlfriend. Since Colleen and Bob, and most of Nick's kids lived out of town, we had made arrangements for everyone to stay at the Hyatt for the weekend and rented a small banquet hall for the dinner. Everyone thought the announcement was about my new job with Peterson Enterprises. Only a few people knew the real reason.

Nick had arranged three round tables of ten seats each in a semi-circle. He seated the Deltron team on one side, the NAS people on the other and in the center, he had our friends, my family, Nick and me. I sat next to Colleen and Nick sat on the opposite side of the table, next to Stacy. He had place cards on the tables because he wanted everyone in a particular spot. When everyone was seated, I rose and began to speak to the gathering.

"Thank you all for coming. Tonight, is a very special night for me, and I wanted to have the people partly responsible here to help me celebrate. But before I give you the news, I think we should get to know each other. Nicholas, since you seem to know everyone here, would you make the introductions?"

I sat down, and Nick stood up.

"It will be my pleasure, Ms. Palmer."

Nick moved over to Charlie.

"First, let me introduce Mr. Charles O'Reilly and his wife, Myrtle. Mr. O'Rielly is Senior Vice President of Design for Deltron Motors. Next to them are Bob and June Roebling, Bob was Assistant Director of Special Projects at Deltron Motors and as of yesterday was promoted to Vice President of Special Projects. Next, we have Eugene Harrison and his wife Emily and Arthur Billingsly and his wife, Tara. Gene and Arty are engineers at Deltron and are the gentlemen who turned Ms. Palmer's idea into reality. And finally, we have Ms. Palmers Administrative Assistant Crystal and her beau Jason."

As Nick walked over to the NAS table, he said, "As some of you know, I was Ms. Palmer's Administrative Assistant until about a month ago. At that time, it became necessary for me to return to my own family's business."

That brought some odd looks from the NAS table.

"And now," he said as he reached his son, "I would like to introduce you to the NAS Financial Group Executive Board, starting with the founder and CEO, Nick Amonti, that's me!"

As he pointed to himself as chief executive officer of NAS Financial Group, murmurs started around the Deltron table. Touching his son on the shoulder, he went on.

"Here we have the COO of NAS, my son Nick Amonti Jr. and his wife, Karen. Next, our VP of Customer Relations and our Senior Negotiator, my daughter Janice Alvarez and her husband, 'T.' Then we have our VP of Corporate Travel and Mortgage Underwriter, my daughter Pam Dugan and her date, Marc Antonelli. Here we have our VP of Real Estate Holdings, my daughter Kristine Dugan and her Life Partner Janet. And finally, our VP of Finance and Corporate Policy, my daughter Katherine Tyler and her husband, Roger."

Moving to the center table, he introduced the other guests.

"And now, some good friends of Ms. Palmer's. First, Ms. Stacy Geer of Stacy Geer Designs. Mr. Terry Daniels of Daniels Industries. Mr. Bill Peterson of Peterson Enterprises, and his wife, Allison. And some of you already know Ms. Palmer's sister Colleen, and her husband Bob, and Ms. Palmer's good friend Dan Patrick, and his lady Cindy. Terry, Stacy and Bill are all members of the Bragger's Club, to which Ms. Palmer was inducted into last week."

Nick walked to the center of the semi-circle, where he could be seen by everyone. He looked around at all the faces.

"There seems to be some confusion among you. Please allow me to explain."

Nick proceeded to tell everyone how and why he had come to work for Deltron, why he had decided not to offer me the position and why he had stayed so long. He left out the part about falling in love with me.

"All yours Ms. Palmer," he said and took his seat.

I rose and moved to where Nick had just been standing.

I told everyone about what Deltron had offered me for bringing in the Paterson deal. I explained how I had to beg Bob to accept the position of VP. And, I told them in great detail about the meeting of the Bragger's Club.

I included the ovation I received and the numerous complaints I got from the CEO's that I should have contacted them before accepting Bill's offer. Everyone seemed to be satisfied with our explanations.

Although I really hated to do it, I had taken off my engagement ring the day we returned to Fort Lauderdale. The dinner proceeded uneventfully and just before dessert, Nick rose and stood in the center of the circle. He asked for quiet.

"There are a few things I have to say. First, to my family, my NAS partners. Thanks for putting up with my absence for the past six months and for my grumpiness the last two. I knew you guys could handle the business without me, and I hope you've gotten used to not having me around. I intend to be around less and less.

"'T,' thanks for all your help on the Cauldwell Project and Paterson Trucking proposal. Janice and Pam, thanks for keeping my secret.

"To my friends at Delton. Mr. O'Rielly thanks for allowing Ms. Palmer to hire me. My time at Delton was very rewarding in many ways. Bob and Gene, thanks for allowing me to share that all night session in San Antonio. Bob, I know you just made a tough decision. Ms. Palmer felt guilty about leaving the team and knowing the team will go on with great leadership made it easier for her. Crystal, thanks for working so hard to ensure my leaving would not hurt the team."

As Nick was talking, the waiters brought out champagne and filled everyone's glass. Nick asked me to join him. We each picked up a glass of champagne.

"Ms. Palmer, it has been a joy working for you. And, thanks to the fact that NAS Financial Group is financing both ends of the Paterson Trucking deal, you have ensured that my grandchildren will be in cookies and milk for a very, very long time. So, I thank you, my children thank you and my grandchildren thank you!"

Nick raised his glass.

"To Ms. Danielle Palmer. For her work at Deltron Motors and her future success at Peterson Enterprises."

Everyone toasted me. As the waiters refreshed the champagne glasses, I put my hands behind my back and slipped on my ring.

Nick raised his glass again, and this time he looked into my eyes.

"And to you, Danielle …for making my life complete by agreeing to become my wife!"

A sip of champagne and a gentle kiss. I brought my left hand up and wiggled my fingers.

The room went still. You could hear the proverbial pin drop. It seemed to last forever until Nick's son finally broke the silence when he shouted, **"WAY TO GO, POP!"**

And everyone realized it must be true! The Deltron people were in shock. The NAS guys seemed happy. The center table just smiled.

Nick and I had to split up for a while as we went around receiving congratulations and good wishes and answering questions. When the shock wore off, the Deltron people were pleased. We met again at the center table, and Nick said it was time. The two of us walked over to Charlie. Nick quieted everyone down with a look. Standing, with me at his side, he looked down at Charlie.

"Mr. O'Rielly, everyone on the Special Projects team knows you are the closest person to Danielle since she lost Daddy Palmer. I know that it is too late to ask your permission to marry this beautiful lady, Sir, but in the tradition of my people, I do ask for your blessing."

Charlie didn't say anything. Myrtle admonished, "Charlie!"

I begged, "Please Charlie!"

Charlie looked up at me.

"Of course, you have my blessing, Danielle. I wish you all the happiness you can hold."

Then he looked at Nick.

"Take good care of her. I hope you realize what a gem you have here."

Nick's reply was short and direct.

"I do know Sir, and I will take excellent care of her."

Then Nick turned to me.

"Your turn."

I stepped around Nick, so I was standing in front of Charlie.

I looked into his eyes and said as sincerely as I could, "Charlie, you are the closest person to me since Daddy Palmer died. Would you do me the honor of walking me down the aisle and giving me away to this man?"

There were tears in Charlie's eyes. He couldn't answer at first. Then he said in a choking voice, "It is you who honors me, Danielle; I could never refuse you that."

And I threw my arms around his neck and hugged him until my arms hurt.

After that, the three tables started to mingle. Janice, who was familiar with the Deltron team, acted as the cruise director, getting everyone to know everyone else. All seemed to be getting along, and from time to time I was asked how and when by both sides. Nick thanked Pam for keeping our secret, and the party continued late into the night.

There was a piano in the room, and Terry started playing. Some couples took the opportunity to dance. I made a comment to Nick that Terry was pretty good.

"Remember back at the Keynote when I said I hadn't done that in a long time?"

"Of course, I remember. I will never forget one detail of that day."

"Before NAS and Daniels Industries the two of us would meet at this music store in Pompano Beach on Sundays and jam for hours. The owner didn't mind because it brought people into the shop."

Nick and I were sitting with Stacy, and I asked how dinner went. She smiled.

"I found a few nuggets, enough that I may have to continue with my prospecting."

I smiled. Nick hadn't the faintest idea of what we were talking about.

"Ready for that story now?"

Nick looked at Stacy.

"What story?"

"The girl has a right to know what kind of man she's going to spend her life with."

"That's private, Stacy."

"It's my story too, and I can tell her if I want to."

Nick got up from the table.

"I'm outta here," he said, shook his head, and walked over to join Terry at the piano.

"What was that about?"

"You'll understand when you hear what I have to say. He likes to pretend it never happened."

Chapter 22 – More About My Man

Stacy began her story.

"Nick and I had been dating for a while. I was a designer at a fashion house, and I was miserable. It was more important to them to make clothes that made a statement instead of what women looked good in, but it was a job in the industry I loved.

"One Friday night at dinner, Nick wanted to discuss our relationship. It was a serious discussion. We both decided that as much as we liked each other, even loved each other, we weren't in the 'till death do us part' kind of love. So, we became friends. Unusual friends, I admit, almost best friends. And because we had already experienced the intimate part of a relationship, we managed to be friends and not feel the need for sex. We both dated other people, and whenever we needed to talk, or had someplace to go and needed a date, we were always available to each other."

Stacy glanced over at Nick and Terry at the piano before continuing.

"Then, suddenly, Nick was out of reach for over eight months. When I finally got in touch with him again, he had a ton of money. At first, he wouldn't tell me where he got it, I still don't know all the details, but he said it was legitimate, and he was going to start a company and invest in small businesses.

"I jokingly said, "How about your old friend Stacy, got a couple hundred thousand to invest in her fashions?" He didn't blink. He said if I wanted to do this, it would have to be done right. The following week, he showed up at my apartment with a lawyer. He had some papers for me to sign. At the time, I had no idea what signing those papers would mean and how much they would change my life forever, but I trusted him completely."

"Nick made me open a corporation, Stacy Geer Designs. Then he had me sell him fifty percent of the company, for five hundred thousand dollars. Imagine, he paid me half a million dollars for half of a company that was only a piece of paper. And I had to sign a partnership agreement. The deal was as a fifty percent partner, I had to invest the five hundred thousand into the company, and as a fifty percent partner, he would invest the same amount. Now, we were partners in a corporation, that was still only a piece of paper, but it had a million dollars in the bank."

Stacy paused to gather her thoughts.

"Nick helped me find a loft and set it up with the tools we needed. Then he told me to start interviewing designers who thought like me. Fire the ones that didn't and keep looking for people that understood my concept. It took a while, and I went through a lot of people, but we eventually had twenty people that I felt comfortable with, mostly young women, but a few young men. When I was satisfied with my staff, he gathered them together and gave them a lecture.

"He told them women were God's most beautiful creations and Stacy Geer Designs was going to dedicate itself to making women look as beautiful as possible. That meant when they came to work, they must be as beautiful as they could make themselves. He insisted the first thing we did was design a line of clothes for the staff to wear to work. He said if they felt beautiful their work would be beautiful. These were all young kids, and they took to his idea immediately."

Colleen stopped by the table and asked if we wanted another glass of champagne. We both said yes. While we waited for Colleen to return, Stacy continued.

"The first two lines we produced for sale were nearing completion. We had designed evening wear: gowns and cocktail dresses, and office wear. I talked to Nick about a show: that's how you sell your line, but he had a different idea. He invited the buyers, fashion editors, and critics to dinner. He asked them to bring a guest.

"There were going to be fifty people there, half men, half women. He told me we were going to ask some of the female guests to wear one of my gowns to the dinner and swear them to secrecy. That was a lot of work. We had to get these women in for fittings, and they weren't all beautiful women. They weren't all thin women. But, we managed to pull it off. Then Nick made arrangements for these women to get their hair and makeup done the day of the dinner by people he picked out himself.

"The night of the dinner, I was a wreck. This is not how you sold clothes. After everyone had arrived and cocktail time was over, the guests were seated in the dining room. Nick walked out on stage and introduced himself as the MC for the evening. He told everyone to enjoy dinner, which, thanks to Nick, was not standard banquet fare, and he would be back from time to time to talk about Stacy Geer Designs. Before he left the stage, he made an offhand comment that he had never seen such a collection of beautiful women in one place."

Colleen came back with a bottle of champagne and three flutes. She decided to join us, and Stacy gave her a quick recap of her story.

"Nick came out again just before the entrée was served and told the group that the reason Stacy Geer Designs existed was to make everyday women look and feel beautiful, and beautiful women look and feel like angels. Before dessert, he came out again. This time, he said we had no runway, and there were no models backstage to show the line. He told them to fully appreciate Stacy Geer Designs they had to be seen on real women, not models. Then he told them some of the ladies in attendance tonight were wearing Stacy Geer Designs. He asked the audience to look around and pick out those women.

"After a very long pause, he asked if the ladies wearing a Stacy Geer Designs gown tonight would stand up. Every woman stood up. We had dressed them all, all twenty-five women.

"Nick said, "You know these ladies. They are your spouses, girlfriends, associates, and competitors. You see these women all the time. Please, pick out one or two women that you know well and tell me if they have ever looked more beautiful than they do tonight."

"After a long pause he said, "Ladies and gentlemen, I give you Stacy Geer Designs.""

Stacy stopped and look into space, recalling the moment.

"The applause was real. It wasn't polite or faked, it was real. After it had quieted down, Nick told them we had another surprise.

"We have also invited this evening some other people you know. In another hall here in the hotel, having their own party are your secretaries, editors, clerks, and interns. During dessert, they will be circulating around this hall wearing Stacy Geer Designs Office Collection. Please take notice of them, and then ask yourself the same question I asked earlier."

"Although I hadn't made an appearance in the main hall, I

was circulating through the other room, trying to get a feel for what the girls thought of what they were wearing. All the comments were positive. One girl after returning from the main hall said, "I circled my bosses table three times, and he didn't recognize me. On my third trip, I stopped right in front of him and said, "Can't you, at least, say hello." His wife recognized me and said, "If you show up to work looking like that, you're fired.""

Now, Stacy had tears in her eyes and finished her story in a choked-up voice.

"The final time Nick went out on stage, he just looked out over the tables. Everyone quieted down to hear what he was going to say next. It seemed like he waited forever, and then very formally announced, "Ladies and gentlemen … Ms. Stacy Geer."

Nick walked off the stage and gave me a kiss. I entered the stage to a standing ovation. I didn't think it was ever going to stop, with cheers and bravos. We sold every dress in both lines and Stacy Geer Designs was born."

Stacy had to stop to collect herself.

"Three weeks later a well-known Hollywood actress, some friend of Nick's from his New York restaurant days, wore one of my gowns to an awards ceremony. The TV personality who was doing the Red-Carpet interviews was really impressed with the way she looked. Almost at a loss for words, she finally said, "You are stunning tonight!" To which she got polite thank you.

"Of course, the interviewer asked, "What are you wearing?"

"Stacy Geer."

"The TV gal said, "I don't think I've ever heard of her."

"And the actress replied, "You will, honey, you will."

"Six months later, I was the hottest designer around."

Stacy was staring at the far wall as if recalling every detail. After coming back, she said, "On the second anniversary of our partnership, Nick walked into my office and handed me a check made out to him for one million dollars. He asked me to sign it.

"Although Nick kept the books and wrote all the checks, he insisted I sign them. He had never asked me to sign a check that large, and it was made out to him, but I trusted him so completely I signed it. He put the check in his pocket and handed me an envelope. It was his stock certificates, his fifty percent of the company.

"I asked him what this was all about, and he said I had just bought his share of Stacy Geer Designs. We argued over it. I told him it wasn't fair.

"He said it was in the partnership agreement that any time after the second anniversary of the agreement I could buy back his shares. I said could, not must and the agreement stated it had to be at fifty percent of the company's current value.

"It's difficult to argue with that man, even when you have no doubt you are right. He told me Stacy Geer Designs was the result of my talent, my hard work, my initiative and it has to belong to only me. He said I was Stacy Geer Designs, and he was so happy he could be a small part of making it happen.

"I told him his share at this point was worth well over two million dollars. He said to consider it an interest-free loan from one friend to another. He told me to buy him dinner that night and to keep making women look beautiful for him, and we'd be square."

At this point, both Colleen and I had the waterworks going. Colleen squeezed my hand as Stacy finished her story.

"I don't know all of the details, but I think Nick's other four friends will tell you pretty much the same story.

Three of them managed to get Nick to keep some of the stock in their companies, but just like me, he wouldn't keep any of Terry's stock. Marc Antonelli, Tony Marchetti, and Harry Combs convinced him to keep ten to fifteen percent of their companies, and they're still partners."

Stacy looked toward the piano. She was staring at Nick.

"Danielle, that's the man you intend to marry. There is nothing we wouldn't do for him. That's why, if you'll allow me, I would like to design your wedding dress."

I was stunned.

"Stacy," I stammered, "A Stacy Geer Designs Wedding Dress, how could I possibly say no? I would be delighted."

"I want to do all the dresses, Nick's girls, your sisters, your niece, and that young lady, Judy from Houston."

"Oh, Stacy, that's too much."

"I should say he can afford it. But, they'll be a gift from me to you. Call it long overdue interest on a loan. He won't turn it down if you tell him to let me do this for you."

"Okay Stacy," is all I could say.

Then we went over to the piano. I leaned over Nick's shoulder and asked him to dance with me. Nick got up, and Stacy sat down next to Terry.

Terry asked, "What will it be?"

"Something we don't have to move to," I told him.

"It's like that, is it?" Terry said, smiling.

I gave him a smile in return and led Nick away. As soon as we were in each other's arms, Nick said, "It's not like she tells it."

"No?".

"Stacy Geer Designs is all her, from the beginning. I just helped her to realize her potential."

"I know Nick,"

He started to say more, but I stopped him.

"Shut up and dance with me."

I placed my head on his shoulder, swayed to the music, and entirely emptied every thought from my head.

The party lasted late, and Stacy, Terry, Nick and I stopped in the hotel bar for a drink before heading off for some sleep. We were sitting at a table, nursing our drinks, and the guys were teasing us. Finally, Stacy had enough.

"That's enough you two. Stop it, or I'll call Don Chassy and have him cap both of you."

That got my attention.

"Who's Don Chassy?"

Stacy looked at Nick, teasingly.

"Oh, we haven't told the little lady about your Mafia friends?"

"Who's Don Chassy?" I asked again.

Nick smiled.

"He doesn't do that anymore."

"He'd do it if I asked him, and probably wouldn't charge me either."

Terry looked at Nick.

"He just might do it for her."

"Who's Don Chassy?" I asked a third time.

"Don Chassy is one of the people that didn't like the government people." Nick finally answered.

"Oh."

"You'll meet them at the wedding."

Terry looked shocked.

"You're going to invite them to the wedding? Both of them?"

"How could I not?"

Stacy laughed.

"I hope it's a huge hall. You'll have to keep a lot of distance between those two."

"If there weren't so many of them, I'd seat them at the same table. But, I'll probably just put them side by side."

"Why would you do that?" Terry asked.

"Maybe the joyous event will soften the old buzzards up."

Stacy looked at me.

"The eternal optimist, your man is. He's been trying to fix this for years and years."

I was puzzled.

"What am I missing here?"

Terry answered.

"Don Chassy and Nick's other friend, Don Vito, have been feuding for almost twenty-five years, and ever since Nick met them, he's been trying to fix it."

I looked at Nick.

"It's complicated. These two men are responsible for the position I'm in today. And now, they're kind of responsible for you and me."

"That's an odd way of putting it," Terry said.

"Think about it. "No Don Chassy, no Don Vito, no NAS. No NAS, no reason for me to meet Danielle."

"That's really left-field thinking," Stacy offered. "You were trying to get the feud ended before the government thing."

"I can't help it. In spite of what they used to be, they're really nice people. Don Vito is married to Don Chassy's sister. Brother and sister haven't spoken in over twenty years. And one of Don Vito's grandsons is in love with one of Don Chassy's granddaughters. They can't do anything about it."

"How can you fix it when neither one of them can remember what the feud is all about?" Terry asked.

"You're not serious?" I said.

Nick gave me an insincere smile.

"I'm afraid Terry is right. Neither one can remember what started it, but they are too stubborn to back down. They both demand an apology from the other, but neither can remember what for."

"Why is this so important to you?"

"I can't answer that, Danielle. It's just I would give anything to end this feud before they die. And that's not too far away."

That's my man, I thought as we headed upstairs to our room. Worried that two stubborn old mobsters make up before they die. And, it really seems to matter to him.

The following week flew by. I stopped into Deltron to say goodbye to everyone. The girls were thrilled when they realized I was the girl Nick had told them about in Atlanta. All the girls loved him. One of them asked me a question that had never crossed my mind.

It turned out to be one of the four problems I had to face before my wedding.

I asked Charlie and Bob to come to the apartment for dinner that same night. I explained why, and both were dubious about my plan, but they both agreed. I didn't get a chance to tell Nick we were having company for dinner, so he was a bit surprised when he got to the apartment, and they were there.

He took it in stride and as always was a congenial host. Just before the roast was ready, I joined the men in the living room where they were enjoying a glass of wine and talking. I broke into their conversation.

"Nick, I have something to talk to you about!"

Nick looked at me in surprise, and then he looked at Charlie and Bob.

"Is this your backup?"

"Sort of."

Nick looked at me for a long moment.

"The answer is no!"

That made me angry.

"How can you give me an answer when you don't know what the question is?"

"I know you, Danielle, the answer is no!"

Charlie tried to come to my aid.

"Nick, listen to her, it makes sense."

"No, it doesn't Charlie. It's bad karma."

I was furious now.

"What's bad karma?"

"Danielle, there will be no prenup!"

I looked at Charlie and Bob, thinking one of them told him what I was thinking. They both shrugged their shoulders and shook their heads.

"You don't even know what I want."

"I know you, Danielle, I know exactly what you want."

Most of the time I am so happy he reads me so well, but sometimes it infuriates me, and this was one of those times.

"You're so damn stubborn. Why won't you at least listen to what I have to say?"

"Because I know what you're going to suggest. You want a prenup that states if we ever break up, you walk away with exactly what you came into the relationship with."

"What's wrong with that?"

"It's not what's in the prenup, Danielle. It's the idea that we would consider such an agreement necessary. It's a bad omen."

"But," I started to say... Nick cut me off.

"Listen to me Danielle, when you walk into that church, you better be sure of what you're doing, because this is to the death."

"I know that."

"Then why would we ever consider such a document. A prenup is a document that says; "I love you today, but maybe tomorrow I won't, or maybe I'll find someone else I love more than you." It's a bad omen."

Very softly he said, "Danielle, if you ever feel you're no longer in love with me, I'll give you a divorce, and you can have everything. Do you really think I would keep you trapped to me if you didn't love me, or let you leave with nothing?"

"I don't want anything but you."

"Good, it's settled then, we don't need a prenup!"

"You are the most infuriating man."

Nick came to me and wrapped me in his now familiar bear hug.

"But you still love me, don't ya!"

I wriggled and tried to free myself until he kissed me, and then I melted. And the discussion was over. I managed to cool down, and dinner with good friends was delightful as always.

The other three problems were more severe. Besides Charlie, there were others who were not happy with our impending marriage. I came home from shopping one day and found Nick on the phone. He did not look happy. After managing to complete his conversation, he handed me the phone. If was my sister Lindsey. I got an earful of what she had been telling Nick, and I wasn't happy either. Lindsey thought Nick was all wrong for me.

"He's much too old for you. Because of his wealth and power, you'll lose any self-identification you have. You'll never be Danielle, you'll always be Nick Amonti's wife. Being married to him will kill your career. You'll become dependent on him."

Nothing I could say would change her mind. After I hung up with Lindsey, I tried to talk to Nick about her feelings. His attitude didn't help the situation.

"The problem is, Danielle, I'm afraid she might be right. We talked about this in San Antonio, remember."

My best friend, Dan Patrick, felt exactly the same as Lindsey. He was not happy at all with my choice for a husband. He reminded me how devastated I was after my break-up with Jack.

"Trust me, Danielle. This time, it will be worse. Nick has powerful friends. This time, you will not be able to easily walk away from a bad relationship. This will be public and dirty. The tabloids will have a field day."

The other person not happy with our union was Nick's daughter Janice. This was a problem I had to solve. I could deal with Dan, and Lindsey would come around eventually, but I had to get Nick's daughter to be okay with our wedding.

I invited Janice and her husband to brunch at my apartment on Sunday. When they arrived, I sent Nick and his son-in-law on an errand. With just Janice and me in the apartment, I put it directly to her.

"Why are you unhappy with your father and me? Don't you believe I love him? Don't you think I want to make him happy?"

Janice didn't expect this, but she did have an answer.

"I wish it were that simple. Danielle, you have no idea what you're getting involved in. You are a beautiful woman. You get hit on all the time."

"I've always been able to handle that. Your father and I have talked about it."

"This is not that! You have no idea. The men who will be hitting on you will not be the kind who are only interested in getting you into bed. These will be rich, powerful men. Men who are used to getting what they want. They will try to use you to gain an advantage over my father. It's not only what you might do, but the perception of what you might do."

"I don't understand, don't all women married to rich, powerful men have the same problem?"

"True, but when an older rich man marries younger, beautiful women, the perception changes."

"Do you want me to call off the wedding?"

Janice shook her head.

"I wish Daddy had done what he went to Houston to do. Now it's too late. If you walked out on him now, it would more than devastate him. He thought you were out of his reach. Now he believes it's not only possible but about to happen. I don't think he could deal with losing you now."

"Janice, I love your father totally and completely. I will do whatever is necessary to be a good wife to him, a perfect wife. I know I'm not marrying an ordinary man. I understand that we will face problems that other couples don't have to think about. I will never do anything to put our love in jeopardy."

I looked at Janice for a reaction. Seeing none, I continued.

"I know I'm in uncharted waters. I know I have a lot to learn about being associated with your father. I know I will need help to understand this. Janice, will you be there to help me do what I have to do? Will you help me be a good wife to your father?"

Nick and his son-in-law walked returned, and I never got an answer.

The following weeks were busy. Colleen and I were running around trying to find a place classy enough for Nick and big enough for six hundred people. I had invited about fifty people which included family, a few friends, and some business associates. Nick had invited about the same number. The rest were all NAS Financial Group guests.

As Nick tried to explain it, "A has to be invited. If you invite A, then B will be insulted if he isn't invited. And, that means C has to be also invited. I told you being rich wasn't always fun."

I knew Nick liked to surprise me, and so I prepared a surprise of my own. It took a lot of time, and I had Colleen and Stacy cover for me while I was working on it.

Having the dresses designed by Stacy saved the time necessary to go shopping. Nick asked his son to be best man, and I ask Colleen and Lindsey both to be my matrons of honor.

We had the church, found a hotel that had a big enough banquet hall, arranged for the music, food, favors all the standard stuff. Nick arranged for the limos and naturally paid all the bills. It was hectic but fun.

Nick wouldn't tell me where we were going on our honeymoon. He said we had use of the BBJ for the entire time. He said he had a plan for our first destination, and when we got bored, we'd fly off to somewhere else.

There weren't going to be bridesmaids or groomsmen. I did ask if we could have the kids involved in some way. I had two nephews and one great-nephew. Nick had seven grandchildren. Nick said he'd try to figure something out, but by the night of rehearsal, nothing was done. It would be the only thing he hadn't managed to accomplish.

My older sister Lindsey arrived three days before the wedding. Nick had sent Jerry and John to Montana in the BBJ to get them. She was still not happy with my choice for a husband and made no bones about letting everyone know it. Lindsey, who is usually so sweet, and was such a great big sister to Colleen and me, was not in a party mood. I tried to talk to her.

"Lindsey, I seduced him, and he almost turned me down."

"Jumping into bed with him was one thing, but marriage to this man is insane."

"I love him."

"You're just infatuated with his charm."

I asked her to be nice to Nick, and she grudgingly agreed to keep her mouth shut. Luckily, they didn't get to see each other much until the rehearsal dinner.

We stayed at the Hyatt, all except Nick. He camped out in my apartment or his house in Tamarac. He had given up his apartment in Fort Lauderdale and spent most of his nights with me since our return from Houston.

Nick and I didn't see much of each other during those last three days. It was just as well. I was very busy, and my surprise was taking longer to prepare than I had imagined. But, it was lonely at night without him in my bed.

Chapter 23 – The Big Day

When Nick came to the hotel to pick me up for rehearsal, I was busy with Stacy and some of Nick's girls. I caught a glimpse of him in the corner of the suite talking to Bob, Colleen, Joe, Lindsey and Anna Lee. It seemed like Lindsey wasn't keeping her promise and was giving Nick an earful and it looked pretty heated.

Not the night before my wedding.

The gathering broke up before I could get over there, and Lindsey seemed perturbed. When everyone headed out for the rehearsal, I asked Anna Lee to stay behind, and I told Nick I'd meet him in the lobby. I asked Anna Lee what was going on in the corner.

"Momma told Mr. Nick that he should be ashamed of himself. Just because he was rich didn't give him the right to take advantage of a young, gullible girl. She said if he were twenty years younger, he'd be in jail for what he was doing. Mr. Nick listened until Momma had said her piece, and told her, he had listened to her, and now she should listen to him.

"He told Momma Danielle is not fifteen years old, as she would have been twenty years ago. Your sister is young, but by no stretch could you call her gullible. She is probably the most intelligent women I have ever met.

"Momma was going to walk away, but Mr. Nick stopped her. He said to let him finish what he had to say. Momma said there was nothing he could say that would change her mind. Mr. Nick said he didn't want to change her mind.

"Mr. Nick said, "Lindsey, I love your sister. I don't care if you believe me. I don't care what you think of me. But, tomorrow is your sister's wedding. It's supposed to be the happiest day of her life. It will be if you don't spoil it. You are the only one who can ruin this day for her. It must be obvious to you that your sister is in love with me. You are not going to stop this wedding, but if you persist in making a scene and continue to harass her about me, you will most definitely spoil it for her. And, after the way Danielle talked about her big sister, I assumed that was the last thing you'd want to do."

"Then Mr. Nick walked away. That made Momma even madder. Auntie Colleen told Momma Mr. Nick was right. That if she continued to put down Mr. Nick to you, it would spoil your perfect day."

When I reached the lobby, everyone was gone but Nick. He seemed to be in a good mood. I knew Lindsey's insults bothered him, but he wasn't going to let me know about it. We took Anna Lee with us and went to the church.

Even though there weren't going to be bridesmaids or groomsmen, we were going to have the families enter the church in a precise sequence, and that had to be arranged. The organ player and the lady who would sing Ava Maria were at the rehearsal. We ran through everything a couple of times to get it all right. It's wasn't very complicated, but Mr. Detail had to have it perfect.

After we had finished, he sent me back to the hotel to change for the rehearsal dinner. He said he would meet me in the banquet hall. He was still fussing with details, even after we were through.

Dinner was pleasant. Even Lindsey seemed to be in a better mood. Maybe Nick had gotten through to her. If she would only give him a chance, I thought, she'd understand. Even though they weren't part of the wedding party, we invited my team from Deltron Motors, Stacy and Terry and Dan and his girl Cindy.

Nick's son, the best man, got up to offer a toast. It was meant just for me.

"Danielle, you haven't had time to get to know us yet. I think you will like us. We're a bunch of varied personalities, but there is one thing we all share in common. We all respect, admire and love this man. For the past ten years, we have hoped he would find someone to make his life whole again. Someone who would love him and understand him like we do. We believe he finally has. I cannot tell you the change in this man since he came home from Houston. We didn't know why, but we knew it had to be good. Now that we know the reason, we are overjoyed. So, Ms. Danielle Palmer, on behalf of both the Amontis and the Kennedys, welcome to our family."

All of Nick's family stood and toasted me, even Janice, although she wasn't smiling. I really did feel like family. Then

Nick Jr. turned to his father and raised his glass.

"Ya did good old man!"

This made Nick smile and brought cheers from his family.

Nick had hired a DJ for the dinner, and we were having a party. Nick reminded everyone that we all had an early day tomorrow, so not too late, and easy on the booze. Then Nick pulled a package from under the table and handed it to me. It was wrapped in lovely wedding gift paper.

"What's this?"

"It's your wedding present."

It felt like a picture frame. I didn't remember any pictures being taken of us. I tore open the wrapping and was confused. It was some kind of newspaper inside the frame. It looked like a front page with a headline and a story.

What's this, did he have our wedding plans placed on the front page of a newspaper?

I started to read the story. Suddenly I understood what it was saying. I looked at Nick, and with the picture frame clutched tightly in my hand, I bolted from the room. I was followed by Colleen, Lindsey, and Anna Lee. I found a bench in the corridor outside the banquet hall, put my hands, still holding the picture frame, to my face and bawled. Colleen sat beside me, and Anna Lee knelt at my feet.

"It's okay Auntie Danielle, everything is going to be okay from now on."

Lindsey, probably still burning from the dressing down she had gotten from Nick said, "What did he do to you?"

I lifted my head to look at her. I practically threw the picture frame at her.

"This is what he did **for** me!"

She read the article aloud:

"Ms. Mary Ann Cauldwell, President of Cauldwell Industries in Cauldwell, Georgia, announced today that Ms. Danielle Palmer of Fort Lauderdale, Florida has purchased fifty percent of Cauldwell Industries. Ms. Cauldwell said Ms. Palmer, a former resident of Cauldwell will invest approximately two million dollars into the plant to modernize and revitalize the facility. Ms. Cauldwell further states the modernization will allow the plant to compete with other manufacturers, and full employment should return before Thanksgiving."

She finished reading before I stopped crying.

"So, he's rich. He likes to throw money at you. What is there to cry about?"

Colleen tried to soothe me. Anna Lee was patting my hands.

"Yes Lindsey, he's rich. He's filthy rich. He could have bought me a mansion on the Inter Coastal. He could have bought me a villa in Spain. He could have taken me on a year-long cruise around the world. Damm, he could have bought me my own yacht."

"Danielle, I don't understand."

Starting to gain some control of myself, I tried to explain.

"Lindsey, don't you see how much this man loves me. He could have used his money to do so many things for me. To him, Lindsey, two million dollars is nothing. It's not the cost. He knows I don't care about his money. It's what he did with the money. He did the one thing he knew I wanted. Lindsey, he gave us our home back. He knows how important Cauldwell is to me, obviously as important as I am to him, and he found a way to save our home."

I turned to my younger sister.

"Oh Colleen, how do I tell him how much I love him? There's nothing I can give to him to show my love for him like he's shown his for me."

"Of course, there is Sis. Tomorrow when the preacher says do you take this man, you say I DO! Danielle, that's what he wants most from you. More than anything in the world, he wants you to be his wife."

Anna Lee got off the floor and returned to the banquet hall. My eyes followed her, and I noticed Janice standing by the door taking it all in. A minute later Anna Lee was back with Nick.

"I'm sorry Danielle. Me and my stupid surprises. I shouldn't have sprung this on you. I should have waited until we were alone. I'm sorry!"

He lifted my chin and forced me to look into his eyes. I could see the concern. I got myself together as much as I could.

"Nick do you know how much I am in love with you? Do you really know?"

"Danielle, that's what this is all about, who loves who more?"

"You've shown me love in so many ways, how can I show you how deeply I love you?"

"Danielle, baby. Do you remember the night we got engaged? Do you remember I was going to end our relationship? Do you remember asking what changed my mind?"

"I remember every detail."

"Do you remember I said it was in your eyes?"

"Yes, you did say that,"

Nick looked deep into my eyes.

"Baby, I knew I was wrong for you. I knew marrying me would be bad for you, but when I looked into your eyes and saw all the love that was there, all that love aimed directly at me, I was too selfish to walk away from it. I do know how much you love me, and I promise to spend the rest of my life trying to earn that love."

He kissed my hands, stood up, helped me up and wrapped his arms around me.

"You're my girl because you love me, and I'm your guy because I love you. DEAL?"

I nodded.

"DEAL!"

"Pretty up that face and come say goodnight to our guests."

I did as I was told. When I got back to the banquet hall, Janice was gone. Nick said he had explained that in the rush to plan the wedding in such a short time frame I just got overwhelmed for a moment. I made my way around the hall, and thanked everyone for coming, promised I would be in better shape tomorrow and went upstairs to my room. Lindsey stopped by to say she was sorry.

"Baby Girl, I still think he's all wrong for you. I don't think you will be happy with him, but he's your choice, and unless I see something definite, I'll keep my mouth shut."

It was an absolutely beautiful day, unusually cool and dry for August in South Florida. I had a light breakfast, just coffee and toast, I was much too nervous for anything else. I just sat and contemplated what I was about to do.

Marry the mostest man I had ever met. I can do that.

Nick's girls, Colleen, Anna Lee, Lindsey, and Judy arrived practically all at once. I was just getting out of the shower when the barrage started. The dress Stacy had designed was a simple white strapless sheath that stopped at mid-thigh. That was my party dress. Over that, I wore a jacket of lace and a long flowing skirt with a train attached. Altogether, it was a beautiful wedding dress, maybe the most beautiful wedding dress I had ever seen. Stacy was a genius, and the pieces were put together so that it looked like one dress and you wouldn't have guessed that it was three dresses in one. The complete set was for the ceremony. For our first dance together, a waltz my man insisted, the jacket and train came off, and it was a ball gown. After that, the skirt came off, and it was a party dress. I had been to Stacy's shop for fittings but had never had the entire ensemble on at the same time. When Stacy arrived and made some adjustments, I checked myself out in the full-length mirror. I could hardly take my eyes off the dress.

I felt like a princess.

The girls, all done up in Stacy Geer Originals, were all stunning. Stacy was the hottest designer around because every woman looked good in one of her dresses. We all made it to the lobby where Dwayne was waiting. Nick had hired Dwayne as a sort of coordinator to ensure everything ran smoothly. Everything was planned by Nick and me, and he just wanted to ensure it all went as planned. Almost went as planned.

I'm sure Nick will have a surprise or two waiting for me somewhere along the way.

The guys were all in the lobby waiting for us, all except Nick and his son. Dwayne rounded us up and sent the couples out to the limos while Charlie and I waited. Dwayne informed us, "Mr. Amonti's plan is for Mr. O'Rielly to exit before you and wait by your limo. Mr. Amonti wants you to exit the hotel alone."

While everyone was following Dwayne's instructions, I thought back to Atlanta and waking up cuddled up against Nick.

That's what I have to look forward to.

When my turn finally came, Dwayne said, "You exit the main door and wait at the top of the steps while the photographer and videographer do their thing. When they're done, I'll come over and give you my arm to assist you down the steps. You walk alone to the limo, where Mr. O'Rielly will be waiting for you."

The time came, the bellmen opened the doors, and I could see all the way to the curb where Charlie was waiting by the open door of a white limo. I stepped outside and was surprised to see everyone was still there. They hadn't left in their limos as planned. They were lined up in two rows with a pathway between the rows. Couples faced each other with boy, girl alternating all the way to Charlie. Behind the two rows of family were two groups of young men in medieval dress holding long silver trumpets.

When the photographer was satisfied, Dwayne climbed the four steps and assisted me to the pathway. He stepped aside, and I walked toward Charlie. The trumpets blared while I passed my court as the men bowed and the ladies curtsied. No real princess had ever felt this royal, I was sure. I was about ten feet from Charlie when he closed the limo door, and the car drove away.

The first miscue of the day.

But I should have known better. There would be no mistakes today, my man wouldn't allow it. As the limo departed, I heard, clop, clop, clop and six white stallions pranced past Charlie pulling a beautiful white coach. There were two men seated in front, and two young coachmen sitting high in back, all in medieval dress. The coachmen climbed down from their perch and assisted first me, then Lindsey, Colleen and finally Charlie into the carriage. While we were boarding, the trumpeters lined up in front of the carriage. As we pulled away from the curb, the trumpets blared again.

Charlie was seated next to me facing forward while Lindsey and Colleen sat opposite us facing the rear. The smiles on my sisters' faces told me they had been privy to all of this, and they were really enjoying my reaction.

The trumpeters stayed with us for a couple of blocks and then moved aside in two rows while the carriage passed between them. As we continued toward the church, I could see one limo after the other pass us by with the rest of our families.

After the trumpets had stopped, I heard Nick's voice. It was coming from a hidden speaker in the side wall of the carriage. As soon as I heard his voice, all of the tension left my body. At that moment, I was probably the most relaxed person in either family.

"Good morning, Danielle," the voice said, "I know tradition

dictates I'm not allowed to see my bride the morning of our wedding, but no one told me I wasn't permitted to talk to her. Danielle today is our sunrise and the day we start on the journey toward the horizon I showed you in Galveston. We will never get there sweetheart, but I promise you it will be a great ride. Now, get that cute little butt of yours to the church, I'm here waiting for you!"

There must have been additional speakers on the outside of the carriage because suddenly there was music coming from right outside. It was loud, and it was Beth Midler singing, 'Going to the Chapel.' It was glorious, and all four of us started singing, and so were the people we were passing on the street. It must have been quite a show. I was afraid we were going to scare the horses we were so loud. And I was going to the chapel to marry the mostest man I had ever met!

The limousines arrived at the church before the carriage, and as the coachmen assisted me from the carriage, I saw my court had lined up just as they did at the hotel, with the trumpeters lined up behind them. Again, the gentlemen bowed, and the ladies curtsied and the trumpets blared as I passed them.

With my hand on Charlie's arm and Lindsey and Colleen trailing us, we went into the church. In the vestibule, off to the side, were two wide benches; one for Charlie, Myrtle O'Reilly and me and one for Colleen and Lindsey. We sat while Nick's family and Anna Lee entered the church in couples.

Nick's daughter-in-law was escorted by my brother-in-law Bob, and Anna Lee was escorted by her father. The organ was playing as the family entered, then Nick's son appeared to escort Myrtle to her seat. Then, he rejoined his father on the altar, and it was my turn.

Dwayne directed Charlie to enter first. I was to stay behind the doors until the music started again. Charlie would be waiting for me just inside the doors. Dwayne told us, "Mr. Amonti wants you to enter the church alone."

When I heard the music, it was not the organ, but violins. I waited, but the doors didn't open. I looked at Dwayne.

"Mr. Amonti told me to let them wait. He said you were worth waiting for!"

Just like him.

I hoped the violin recording was long enough to cover the

delay. It was twenty or thirty seconds before the doors opened. As I stepped through into the church, Charlie appeared at my side and offered me his arm. I glanced over to where it sounded like the music was coming from, and it wasn't a recording, it was an orchestra with eight or ten violins. And the aisle I was to walk down was covered with rose petals. Not a bunch of rose petals dropped by a flower girl but pew to pew and front to back, every inch of the aisle was covered.

And, standing against the pews, evenly spaced out down the entire length of the aisle were the children Nick couldn't find a way to include in the ceremony. And as Charlie and I passed them, each boy bowed, and each girl curtsied. The church was packed. Every pew was occupied, mostly by people I didn't know, or hardly knew. The orchestra was playing: Here comes the bride, and as Charlie and I reached the front of the aisle, Nick stepped down from the altar to greet me.

The preacher did the Who Gives This Woman speech, and Charlie answered with tears in his eyes. As he placed my hand in Nick's, I heard him say, "Take good care of her!"

"A gentleman's promise," Nick replied, sincerely.

The ceremony itself was beautiful.

Nick and I each wrote our own vows, and although the priest had copies for us to read from, neither of us needed them. We both in different words promised the usual love, honor, fidelity and so forth, but we also vowed openness, honesty, trust, never to break a promise, eternal love and we both promised each other the last dance. The exchange of the rings was also moving, with unique words Nick had made up.

The orchestra played Ava Maria, and instead of the lady who sang at the rehearsal, it was Janice's daughter who mounted the pulpit and sang. And she sang beautifully.

And, finally, the moment came.

"By the power invested in me by the State of Florida, and in the sight of God..."

Nick suddenly put up his hand.

"Father wait! Something is not right."

He looked at me.

"Danielle, something is missing."

I was at a loss. I didn't know where he was going, but I knew my man had something special prepared for me. He turned to the congregation.

"Guys, can you help me out here?"

All of Nick's grandchildren, Colleen's two boys, and Johnny left their seats and formed a semi-circle at the foot of the altar. These were the children Nick couldn't manage to fit into the ceremony, so he had said. When they had assembled, Nick asked them, "What are we missing?"

Nick's youngest grandson said, "The rules, Grandpa. You have to have rules."

And I fell in love all over again.

Two of Nick's granddaughters handed Nick and I each a glass of champagne. Each of the boys had a question for us.

"Grandpa, Rule Number One, it starts?"

Nick looked into my eyes.

"Rule Number One: It starts the moment Father Pascal pronounces us husband and wife."

"Aunt Danielle, Rule Number Two, it ends?"

Gazing longingly into Nick's eyes, I said, "Rule Number Two: Never, ... it never ends!"

"Grandpa, deal?"

"Deal."

"Aunt Danielle, deal?"

And still looking into those beautiful brown eyes, I said, "Deal."

While Nick and I clinked our glasses and sipped the champagne, Johnny wheeled a fifty-five-gallon drum to the foot of the altar. It was painted white with rings of gold, the same color as that beautiful nightgown I wore in Galveston. It was completely empty except for a few large rocks nestled at the bottom.

Johnny said, almost entirely without stuttering, "Having used these glasses for this important toast, they may never be used again!"

Nick and I threw our glasses into the drum and heard them shatter against the rocks.

Nick turned to the kids gathered around us, "Is that it guys?"

One of Nick's granddaughters said, "Just one more question!"

And in unison, they all asked, "Till the death?"

Nick and I said together, "Till the death!"

Then one of the boys said, "You can finish now, Father."

And Father Pascal said, "I now pronounce you husband and wife. You may kiss your bride!"

And just before our lips met, I heard Nick whisper, "Gotcha!"

Chapter 24 – The Reception

The orchestra played the Wedding March as we left the church. The reception line was very long, and Nick had provided stools for Lindsey, Colleen, and me to use. I'm sure Nick's hand hurt from all the handshakes, and both of my cheeks were red from all the kisses, but it was glorious.

We left the church in the carriage, but only rode it about five blocks. Nick explained it would take two days for us to get to the reception in the carriage, so switched to a white limo.

We had a private room prepared for the family and us while our guests arrived and enjoyed the cocktail hour.

Of course, Stacy and Terry, my Deltron team and Dan and Cindy were there, all being considered family by Nick and me.

Nick, watching Stacy and Terry whispered in my ear, "Do you know what's going on with those two?"

"Just a little prospecting!"

"And just what are they prospecting for?"

"Something we already found. Maybe it will rub off!"

And my man smiled because he could wish his two friends nothing more beautiful than what he and I had found.

The conversation ended when Stacy came over to us. As she was removing the train from my dress, Janice stopped by.

"Remember that question you asked at brunch last Sunday?"

I nodded.

"Front of the line," Janice said, and then hugged me.

She turned to her father.

"Nick's right Daddy. Ya did good!"

Nick and I both smiled. One down, two to go.

After everyone but the wedding party had entered the hall, we lined up for the traditional introductions. Charlie and Myrtle were introduced followed by Colleen and Bob and Lindsey and Joe. Then Nick, Jr., and Karen moved into the room.

When it was our turn, Nick asked me to wait for a moment. He pushed through the doors. The MC sounded surprised Nick had entered alone.

Nick must have taken the microphone because I heard him say, "Ladies and gentlemen, family and friends. Today, I break with tradition. Today, I reserve to myself the honor of presenting to you my bride. Mrs. Danielle Grace Palmer Amonti."

The ballroom doors opened, and I walked into the hall. Nick walked up to me and offered me his arm. We walked to the center of the dance floor. Colleen and Lindsey came to us and took my bouquet and the lace jacket. And, now I was wearing my beautiful ball gown.

The MC announced the couple will dance for the first time as husband and wife to Waves of the Danube by Ivanovic. I looked at Nick with alarm. He smiled and whispered, "You've heard it before, My Lady!"

When the music started, I realized it was the beautiful song that Nick had played for Mike and Agnes at the Keynote in Atlanta. And, we waltzed.

After the band had gone through the verse once, the lyrics began, just like in Atlanta and were being sung by a voice I was sure I recognized. It was Roger from the Keynote. Nick had flown him to Florida so he could sing this song at our wedding.

Quite a romantic, my man!

After the dance, Nick took me over to the table where Roger was sitting. We were introduced to Roger's wife, and Roger said he knew that first night there was something special between us. Also at that table were our pilots, Jerry, and John. Nick made introductions and then asked Jerry if all was set.

"Ready to fly whenever you are, Boss!" And he winked at me.

We moved to the head table, Nick Jr. made a beautiful toast, Nick thanked everyone for sharing this celebration with us, and the party began. Stacy helped me remove the skirt, and now, I was in my party dress.

There were nearly six hundred people in the hall, sitting at over sixty tables. Nick's sense of manners dictated we make the rounds and say hello to everyone, and even at a minute or two per table, it took a while. And, of course, some tables got more than a minute of our time.

We did manage to dance once or twice, but most of our time

was spent going from table to table.

Nick had put on the invitations in lieu of gifts to the Bride and Groom, we suggested a donation to the Wounded Warriors Foundation.

Nick had lost a grandson to Post Traumatic Stress Disorder, and he felt this organization was worthwhile. He had pre-addressed envelopes at every place setting as a reminder. My man was very generous with his good fortune, but this was his favorite charity.

There was one table with Nick's friends. They were also business associates. These were the first five companies he had invested in when he started NAS. Stacy and Terry were the first two. Then there was Marc Antonelli, Harry Combs, and Tony Marchetti.

When Terry and Stacy decided to come as a couple, there were two seats open at the table, and Nick suggested, "Why don't we move Dan Patrick and his girlfriend there? My closest friends and your closest friend should get to know each other."

I totally agreed, and it seemed like they were all getting along.
Although I had become very close to Stacy and Terry, I had only met one other of Nick's friends. Marc Antonelli had escorted Pam to the announcement dinner, and we met briefly. I moved around the table to thank everyone for attending our wedding.

When I reached Marc, who might have been the best-looking man I had ever laid eyes on besides Jack, he said very quietly, "Danielle, six people at this table love and respect your husband. Not only because of what he did for us financially but because of the man he is, the friend he is to us. We are so pleased he has found someone special to share his life with. We will always be there for him, and now, it means we will always be there for you. Please, don't ever hesitate to come to us for anything."

I could feel the sincerity in his words, and I knew we would all be good friends. Knowing Nick is loving him. I could understand how these people felt about him.

This is the man I have chosen to spend the rest of my life with.

When I got around the table to Dan and Cindy, I asked Dan to dance with me. Besides Nick and Charlie, Dan was the only other man I danced with at my wedding. I wanted to tell Dan thanks for almost fifteen years of friendship and also let him know I didn't want anything to change between us. I also wanted to tell him I was sure Nick understood our relationship and wouldn't have any problem with it continuing.

When I asked Dan to dance, Nick, being the gentleman, he is, asked Dan's date, Cindy to dance. Dan looked over at Nick and Cindy.

"Danielle, you know I wasn't too happy when you told me about your decision to marry that man, but I've changed my mind. I think you got a good one. I think he will take good care of you and make you happy, and I don't believe we 'll have any trouble remaining good friends."

That earned Dan a kiss, and I wrapped my arms around his neck for a more than a friendly hug. I wondered what changed Dan's mind, but I wasn't going to worry about it. Two down and now only Lindsey still had objections.

When Dan and I returned to the table, Dan had my lipstick on his check. Nick took his hankie and wiped it off. He looked at his hankie and said it looked like a familiar shade.

I smiled wickedly, "It's my wedding day, I can kiss whomever I want!"

Nick laughed.

"So, it is My Lady, so it is!"

I glanced at Dan and Cindy. Dan was smiling, but Cindy was looking at us with a serious expression as if she was deep in thought.

The rest of the party was fun, even though we had the responsibility of making the rounds. When we got to the two tables where the government people were sitting with their wives and dates, we spent a little more time. While Nick was trading stories with some of the guys, one of them asked me if I knew what Nick had done for his country. He introduced himself as John Casivetis. I recognized the name from the day the Broward County Detective stopped at our table while Nick, Gene and I were having lunch.

I responded that I knew he had done something, but Nick wouldn't talk about the details. The man whispered he couldn't tell me either, but he wanted me to know it was very, very important, and that his country was grateful!

We also spent quite a bit of time at the table with my friends from Cauldwell. Nick had sent his son's 'G' to Georgia to bring them to the wedding. Mary Ann told me the new equipment was already on order, and she thought full employment could start much earlier than originally planned. It was a perfect wedding present. She also said teasingly, "I'll never forgive you for getting to Nick first."

Then, we arrived at the tables where the people who didn't like the government people were seated. Just as Nick had said, he sat them at two tables, adjacent to each other. The two Dons were sitting as far apart as possible, and if it weren't so important to Nick, it would have been comical. Nick grabbed one of the younger men.

"Danielle, this is Sal Chassy. The Dons' English isn't very good, and I asked Sal to translate for you."

He told Sal he wanted me to know every word, word for word. We approached the head of one of the families, and Nick introduced me to Don Chassy. The Don was a very pleasant man.

"Nicko, you are a lucky man to have won the heart of such a beautiful woman."

"Signora, Nick is a great man, and there is nothing the family wouldn't do for him. Nick is considered a part of the family, and now you would be too. There is nothing the family would not do for you."

Of course, this was all second hand, as it had to pass through Sal first. Then a thought struck me. It was silly. It was probably stupid, but I did it anyway.

I whispered to Sal to please repeat everything I say. When Sal acknowledged my request, I looked directly into Don Chassy's eyes.

"Don Chassy, would you honor a bride's wish on her wedding day?"

"Of course, Signora, if it is within my power."

Nick looked at me warningly. I plunged on anyway.

"Don Chassy, would you consider honoring me on this my wedding day by making peace with Don Vito?"

You would think I had asked him to murder his firstborn. He exploded and called me some names Sal refused to translate. That angered Nick, and Sal did tell me what Nick was saying to

Don Chassy.

"That is my wife you are talking about, my woman," Nick shouted at the old man, "and as much as I respect you, Sir, I will not allow you to talk to her in that manner."

Nick was really pissed. I can only guess what the old man had said.

Damn, now I have screwed everything up for my husband, and we've only been married a few hours.

Don Chassy looked at Nick with wide eyes.

"Nicko, my apologies. I did not mean to insult your lady. I am sorry Nicko, I would never insult you in that way, but I was surprised by her request."

That seemed to mollify Nick a bit. The old man looked back at me.

"Signora, please forgive me for my outburst. You caught me completely by surprise. Please Signora, why would you make such a request of me? You don't even know me."

Well, you started this. You better find a way to fix it.

I crouched down so I could look the old man directly in the eyes. Sal crouched down next to me. I said, "Sal, every word!" He nodded.

"Don Chassy, today I have married the most wonderful man in the entire world. The mostest man I have ever met."

Sal had a problem with translating mostest. Don Chassy replied.

"I know this man Signora, he is a good man, a very good man."

"Yes, Don Chassy, a magnificent man, and last night as a wedding present he gave me back my childhood, my memories, my hometown."

There was confusion in the old man's eyes, but I pressed on.

"Don Chassy, the little town where I was born and raised was dying. The factory where everyone in the town worked was closing, and all the people in the town were going to move away. This man I married is wealthy. For a wedding present, he could have given me anything. He could have spent millions and millions of dollars.

"But, this man loves me as no woman has a right to be loved, and because he loves me, he bought the factory, brought it back to life and saved my hometown."

"I know he is a good man, Signora, and he obviously loves you dearly, but what does that have to do with me?"

"Don Chassy, this man is very wealthy. What can I give him in return for what he has given me? How can I show him the love he has shown me? This man needs nothing, this man wants for nothing. But, there is one thing he doesn't have. One thing he hasn't been able to get for himself. One thing no one else can get for him. That is peace between you and Don Vito. I know how important this is to him. I know it is the only thing he desires that he cannot have. This silly girl thought if I can give this one thing to him, maybe he will understand how deeply I love him."

The old man looked up at Nick and then back at me. I kept my eyes locked on him.

"Signora, I understand what you are seeking, and I understand why, but I am not in a position to grant your wish. That old goat sitting over there does not have a romantic soul such as I do. I am sure he will never agree to your proposal."

Nick was looking at me, and I've never seen such an impassive expression on his face. I continued to look in Don Chassy eyes and pleaded.

"Don Chassy, if I can convince Don Vito to meet you halfway, no apology given, no apology needed, just an end to this feud, would you meet him halfway?"

After a very long pause, Don Chassy very quietly agreed.

"Si Signora, for a woman so much in love, I would do this!"

"Grazie, Don Chassy," I whispered, "Grazie, Grazie," in what little Italian I knew.

I stood up and asked Sal to come with us to see Don Vito. Sal hesitated.

"Signora Amonti, I'm not exactly welcome over there!"

"Please Sal, you know where I'm going with this, I need you."

Sal looked at Nick and Nick nodded. When we got to Don Vito's table, Nick introduced me and told the Don that I spoke no Italian, and he had asked Sal to translate for me. The old man wasn't pleased, but he accepted Sal's presence.

This time, I started with the Cauldwell story, and then what

Nick had done, emphasizing how much love he had put into that gift to me. Then I gave him the speech about how much Nick wanted the feud ended and how much it would mean to me if I could be the agent that ended the dispute.

Don Vito said, "The face of an angel and the soul of a witch."

Nick smiled at him.

"True Don Vito, but a very loving witch with a beautiful heart."

"This means so much to you, Signora?"

"It means that much to my husband, so it means that much to me."

He shook his head, looked first at Nick and then at his wife who was Don Chassy's sister.

"This man means so much to this family, Signora, and for his woman, I will do this."

Don Vito stood up. Nick said something to Sal in Italian. Sal went back to the other table, helped Don Chassy to his feet and escorted him to the space between the two tables.

Don Vito was already there. The two men glared at each other. No one said a word. Nick and I were also facing each other. I took Don Chassy's right hand and held it out in front of him. Nick seeing what I had done held Don Vito's hand out.

They touched, shook hands and suddenly wrapped their arms around each other like long-lost brothers, and both men had tears in their eyes.

I didn't understand a word they were saying, and Sal couldn't keep up with both men, but he did manage to tell me it was good. Finally, Don Vito said, "Come say hello to your sister."

As the two men walked over to Don Vito's table, his wife shouted out something in Italian that made Sal smile.

"What did she say?" I asked.

"Donna Vito said, "Mary Mother of God, Bless this woman!""

Nick was still looking at me with an impassive stare. After a minute of watching the two men, he grabbed me by the wrist and pulled me toward the nearest exit. I didn't know what was going on.

Was he angry with me?

Chapter 25 – The Honeymoon

Once we were outside the hall in the corridor, he spun me around to face him.

"Twenty-five years, Danielle," he screamed. "Twenty-five years! Do you know what you have done?"

I didn't know what to say to him. Suddenly he pulled me to him and kissed me so passionately he took my breath away completely. When he finally let me up for air, he looked into my eyes.

"What have I ever done in my life to deserve so much love?"

I looked back into those beautiful brown eyes of his.

"You reap what you sow, my love!"

That got me another kiss, this one much gentler and sweeter. Nick wouldn't let me go for a long time, and when we finally reentered the hall, we walked directly over to Terry's table.

"What's going on you two?" Stacy asked.

"How long have the Dons been feuding?" Nick asked.

"About twenty-five years," Terry answered.

"Well, I introduce my wife to them, she bats those beautiful brown eyes at them and says, guys, how about ending your feud as a wedding present to me? And they both say, sure Signora, anything for such a beautiful lady!"

Stacy just stared at me, mouth open. Terry said, "I don't believe it."

"Look for yourself."

Terry stood up, looked over at Don Vito's table, shook his head in disbelief and sat down.

Stacy, regaining her composure looked at Nick.

"Is there such a thing as a Made Woman?"

Everyone else at the table hadn't the faintest idea of what the four of us were talking about, but I didn't care.

My husband was happy, and I was responsible.

After finally getting around to all of the tables, we had a

chance to sit down with the family. Nick Jr. had noticed the two Dons sitting together and asked what was going on. Nick said I'd have to explain, and I told them what I had done. They all knew how much Nick wanted the feud ended, and they all were so pleased.

Nick Jr. in a low and conspiratorial voice said, "You now have friends in low places, and you could probably get anything you wanted from those two."

That put another idea in my head. After a while, I told Nick I wanted to see how the two Dons were getting along. On my way over, I asked Sal to come with me and translate. The two old gentlemen were thrilled with me. It was obvious they wanted the feud to end, but they needed an excuse. I gave them that excuse. I was gold in their eyes, and they both told me if I ever wanted anything, and they emphasized anything, all I had to do was ask. So, I did!

I asked for one more favor and explained what and why. They argued over it for a few minutes, both men having different opinions as to how to grant my wish, and for a minute I thought the feud was going to start all over again. But Sal explained it was just friendly banter, and finally they came to an agreement.

Don Chassy instructed Sal to take care of it. Sal asked, "How do I get in touch with you?"

"You'll have to work through Jerry, our pilot. Nick can't know anything about this."

Sal knew Jerry, and that was that. Before I had a chance to leave, Sal had something to say.

"Donna Amonti, both families will remember you forever. If you ever need anything, all you have to do is ask, and, I mean anything!"

"First thing, my name is Danielle, and second, those two old men have allowed me to give my husband a present he wanted very badly and couldn't get anywhere else. It's me who owes them."

"Just remember Danielle, anything, anytime, anywhere. All you have to do is ask!"

I thanked Sal and headed back to my table. On my way back to Nick, a young woman approached me.

"What is your name, Mrs. Amonti?" she asked.

"My name is Danielle," I told her.

"That is a beautiful name. That will be the name of our first child unless it's a boy, and then we'll call him Daniel."

I thanked her and went back to my husband. I pointed the young woman out to him and asked who she was. He told me her name was Francine, and she was Don Chassy's granddaughter. I told Nick what she had said.

"Danielle, do you know what a great honor it is to have a first child named after you in an Italian family?"

"Why would she do that?"

"She is in love with one of Don Vito's grandsons, and there couldn't be any wedding until both Dons were dead. Thanks to you, my love, that's all changed now."

Could it get any better than this?

We stayed at the reception for about six hours. We did the garter and bouquet toss and cut the wedding cake. We managed to stop at every table and say hello to everyone. We even managed to dance a little.

When it was time to go, Roger sat down at the piano and played Loveliest Night of the year just as he did at the Keynote. Nick and I waltzed around the dance floor a couple of times, stopped by the main exit door, waved to our guests and ran out the door.

The limo was waiting to take us to Fort Lauderdale/Hollywood International Airport. Jerry and John were already there pre-flighting the BBJ. Nick took his place in the left seat with John on the right. Jerry stayed in the cabin. Just before engine start, John told Nick he had a hatch indicator light and left the flight deck to check the main cabin door. I slipped into the right seat, and Jerry strapped into the jump seat. Nick looked over at me and then glanced at Jerry. Nick got a nod from Jerry, smiled and called the ground man to check engine clearance.

"Clear left turn one." I hit the respective switch, and when the engine was turning at seventy percent, I hit the fuel switch. The engine came alive, and I watched the engine temperature indicator. When both engines were running and stable, we were ready to taxi.

Nick said, "This isn't legal."

Jerry replied, "I won't tell if you don't."

Jerry and John had been working with me for weeks. With all the wedding planning Colleen and I were doing, it wasn't easy to find enough time and hide my absence from Nick. I was hoping he wouldn't deny me this chance to do this with him.

"And just how far are we going to take this?"

"Until we can fly off together without these two as company."

"Okay wife get us out of here."

I contacted Ground Control and announced my second surprise.

Instead of requesting taxi instructions for NAS One as was usual, I announced:

"Ground, 'HONEYMOON ONE' ready to taxi from TR three for departure."

The Ground Controller gave us our instructions, and I repeated them.

It's not an easy process to change the Call Sign of an aircraft, but Jerry managed to get it done for us. I could see the great big smile on my husband's face as he advanced the throttles and taxied us to the runway. I ran down the various checklists with him as professionally as I could manage and when we were close to the runway, I was instructed to change frequencies to the Tower. The tower instructed us to move up and hold short of Runway Ten. Coming from the Executive Parking Area rather than the Terminal, we approached the runway from the opposite side than the commercial jets did. I could see four commercial aircraft waiting for their turn to take off.

The Tower Controller called, "Jet Blue 442 continue to hold short, we have a priority departure ahead of you."

The Jet Blue pilot acknowledged the order and the Tower Controller called, "Honeymoon One, Position, and hold."

As Nick moved us onto the runway, he asked, "Priority Departure? How did you manage that?"

My answer was simple.

"I know people!"

This only broadened Nick's smile. We were given clearance to take off, and as both of our hands advanced the throttles, I felt a thrill right down to my toes.

The strange voice called V-ONE and Nick said, "Are you ready to fly, Danielle?"

"I'm always ready to fly with you, my love!"

"Then let's fly!" he shouted.

The voice called V-R and Nick said, "Rotate."

The nose came up, I could feel the lift, and I thought I was on my way to heaven.

Nick wouldn't tell me where we were going on our honeymoon. He just said he had our first stop set and after that, we would go where the mood took us.

But, before we turned the aircraft over to Jerry and John, I heard the Center Controller call, "Honeymoon One, direct now Bermuda."

I had never been there, and the only thing I knew about it was Nick had once said that it was the most romantic place he had ever been.

On my 'Wedding Night,' I wore my Sunrise Night Gown. My new husband appreciated the gesture. For three days we rode around the island on motorbikes (no car rentals in Bermuda), swam in the ocean and the outdoor pool, and got pampered in the spa. It really is a very romantic place. At night, we dressed for dinner and dancing. We stayed in the Penthouse Suite at the Southampton Princess Resort. I didn't want to leave, but my second surprise was waiting.

Thursday, I insisted we do some very exhausting things. I wanted my hubby tired that night. After dinner, we returned to our suite, and I started to pack.

"Going somewhere?"

"Yep," I replied.

"Am I invited?"

"Wouldn't go anywhere without you."

"Can I know where?"

"It's a surprise."

"How are we going to get there?"

"It's covered," I told him.

That brought a smile, and he dutifully packed his things. We traveled by taxi to the airport where Jerry and John had the BBJ fueled, pre-flighted and ready to go. Nick asked Jerry what was going on and was told he was under the Lady's orders not to tell Nick anything. When Nick tried to take his usual place at the controls, Jerry told him he was not allowed on the flight deck.

Nick walked back into the cabin where I had champagne chilled and ready.

Nick asked, "What are we supposed to do during the flight?"

"I have something in mind," I told him.

All the window shades were drawn, and once Jerry and John had closed the door between the flight deck and the cabin, I went into the bedroom and put on my Sunrise Nightie again.

The boys had very strict orders not to open the cockpit door until we were in the bedroom. By that time, we were ready for takeoff and Nick, and I sat down and belted ourselves in.

As we accelerated down the runway, Nick noticed the unusually long take-off roll.

"Heavy tonight must be a long flight."

"Long enough for what I have in mind."

"Exactly what do you have in mind, my love?"

"I thought it was about time I joined the Mile-High Club."

His grin turned into a wicked smile, and he said very seductively, "I think I can help you with that, My Lady! But My Lady, it's not very fair of you to put that outfit on while I'm strapped into this seat!"

"A little anticipation won't hurt, I'm worth waiting for."

"I've been waiting for you all of my life," he said sweetly.

Once the seatbelt sign went off, we moved into the bedroom. All the shades were drawn in there also, but these were blackout shades so the NAS people could get some sleep even in daylight. I had disconnected the alarm clock so Nick wouldn't be able to figure out how long we were flying.

There's a lot to be said for the Mile-High Club. Although most people join it in rather cramped quarters, mostly the lavatory on commercial jets, I had a queen size bed in a private bedroom for my initiation. Afterward, I slept against Nick, with my head cradled on his shoulder and my arm across his chest.

It was still dark in the room when we started our descent. I wouldn't allow Nick to touch the shades. I'm sure he had some idea of how long we had been flying, but he couldn't be sure. Unfortunately, the bathroom was outside the bedroom, and the shades in the cabin let in enough light to give away the fact it was daytime. I estimated it was around early afternoon. We dressed quickly, no time for a shower before we had to belt in for the landing.

On the ground and parked, John came back and opened the door and let down the stairs. A man in a uniform climbed into the aircraft, talked to Jerry and John and then stepped over to Nick and me.

"Passports please," the man said in Italian. Nick produced them, and while they were being stamped, Nick gave me a weird look.

After the Official was satisfied, he handed Nick the passports and said, "Welcome to Napoli!"

The drive to the villa was in silence. Nick seemed genuinely surprised and pleased. It was everything I had hoped for.

A beautiful view of the bay, a magnificent veranda to watch the sunset from and a picture-perfect bedroom to make love in.

I knew Nick was pleased when I did something or said something showed I had paid attention to what he had said to me. And, I remembered what else he had told me that morning in Galveston, and I vowed to myself to talk to his security people and seriously pay attention to what they tell me. I didn't want to give Nick any reason to worry about me unnecessarily.

We stayed there three days, and Nick seemed relaxed and content. He mentioned he had never been to Europe before.

"Just never got around to it."

We spent those three days talking and being intimate. Nick wanted to talk a little about our finances. I said I'd leave everything up to him. He insisted he wanted me to know how everything was going to work and where I stood regarding it all.

"I asked Colleen's husband, Bob, to open an investment account in your name only. It will be completely under your control. The Cauldwell stock was the first part of the account, and when Cauldwell starts paying dividends, you should leave the money in the account for Bob to invest for you. Also, I suggest you take your 401K money from Deltron Motors and transfer it to that account, along with your salary from Peterson and anything else you might have, including your checking and savings accounts. I had Bob checked out, and he is an excellent broker, and his clients do very well. When I started with Deltron and realized what a big deal the LNG/Diesel thing was going to be, I purchased some Deltron stock, and that will go into your account also."

"What am I supposed to do with that money?"

"It has two purposes. First, it would be your bequest account. I suggested you make out a will to cover everything that is in your account, just in case."

Knowing that Nick had lost his wife five years after they were married, I understood his concern.

"Second reason is you need access to money that I have no knowledge of, sort of a Mad Money account."

"That's not necessary," I argued.

"You'll probably never use it, but I want you to have a security blanket, so you don't feel dependent on me. My money is going to split into two pieces.

"Half is going to stay with my current broker, and we are going to live off of that account. The other half is being transferred to Bob to invest for me, and that will be my bequest account. The kids helped make NAS what it is, and I'm going to leave that to them. Lindsey, Colleen, and Anna Lee are part of my bequest account, but you're not."

That didn't surprise me. I figured the account Bob was setting up for me would be sufficient for me if anything happened to Nick. I still would be making good money at Peterson.

"The dividends we receive from NAS will go into our Living Account. That account will be in both of our names. Equal control while we both were alive, and either-or survivor if one of us passed away."

Nick had given me access to everything he has except the bequests. I tried to tell him I didn't want access to his money. That resulted in a very lengthy discussion, at the conclusion of which he said, "Danielle, everything I am is yours. Not only the money and physical things, but all my love, all my caring, and all my desires are tied up in a pretty bow for you. Take any part of it, and you have to take it all. I believe we love each other so much

233

we can overcome the burden of our money. It will take time, my love, but you will eventually deal with it."

What he said next did surprise me. Nick told me how much was in the account that we were going to live off. I couldn't comprehend the number. I went all spacey for a moment. I had no idea.

Maybe I just never had the time or desire to think about how much he was worth. His worth to me was not in dollars!

Considering he was splitting his money in two, this was only half his net worth. I had assumed he was worth fifty or sixty million dollars, not more than a half billion.

I knew I could get anything I wanted from this man, and I could have changed his plans for our financial future, but it wasn't worth the effort. I would get used to being rich, because that's what he wanted, and it was a small price to pay for his love. I also knew it would be okay to use some of that money to help out Lindsey, Colleen, and Anna Lee.

After Naples, we went to Rome and Venus. Nick remarked, "As long as we're here, why not!"

He was right about what he had told Bill on the morning I signed my contract. It was the most fabulous Honeymoon a girl could hope for!

Chapter 26 - Destiny

If I go back to Nick's original concept of Before and After, I'd say our three-month courtship was the Before, our Wedding and Honeymoon was the Doing, and married life was the After.

And, the After was all a girl could ever ask for! We traveled quite a bit. It was nice sharing the excitement of visiting new places together, and Nick enjoyed showing me the places he had been before we met. My flight to Houston on that fateful night Nick proposed was the last time I ever flew commercial. The BBJ or Nick's son's 'G' was always available to me.

The week after we returned from our honeymoon, while I was busy putting together my team for Peterson Enterprises, Nick was reconnecting with his office at NAS Financial Group. That Thursday evening at dinner he mentioned he had run into my friend Dan Patrick.

"We had lunch together and had a nice talk. I like Dan, and I'm sure we could be friends."

Of course, that pleased me.

The next night, Friday, again at dinner, Nick mentioned he wanted to have a little party.

"Sort of a Welcome Back party. We were away for almost a month, and we can share our adventure."

Knowing the gleam in my husband's eye, I knew there was more to the idea than he was telling me, but also knowing he loved to surprise me, I didn't press for the real reason, just went along with his plan. Being very busy getting my team together at work, I didn't take part in any of the party plans, so when we arrived at the Hyatt ballroom the following Friday evening, I didn't know what to expect. There were over forty people there. This was my husband's idea of a small intimate party.

My entire team from Deltron, Nick's family, my two sisters and their husbands, Anna Lee, Terry and Stacy, Marc and Tony, plus their dates, Harry and Angie, Dan and Cindy, Bill Peterson and his wife, Crystal, and her boyfriend. Also, a couple of members of the team I was putting together at Peterson.

This was the second time I had met Marc, Tony, and the Combs. I did get to spend more time with them that night, and I was sure we would all be good friends. After everyone had been seated, Nick stood.

"Thank you all for coming. Gathered here are the people closest to Danielle and me, and we wanted to share our happiness with you, and, give you all the details of our wonderful honeymoon."

Dinner was pleasant, and Nick had arranged the tables so there were two empty chairs at each table. This allowed Nick and me to sit at each table for a while and talk with our guests.

Before dessert, Nick stood again and asked our guests for patience while he said thank you to some people who made it possible for us to be here to celebrate this occasion. He started with the Deltron team.

"Because you were such a great team, and I enjoyed working with you so much I extended my stay at Deltron from one or two weeks to almost six months. The hours we spent putting the Paterson proposal together in San Antonio were some of the most exciting and thrilling hours I have ever spent in a business environment. My extended stay at Deltron gave me time to get to know Danielle and fall madly in love with the lady."

Then he turned to Colleen and Bob.

"Thank you, both for the month of hell we put you through while we were trying to decide where we were going in our relationship. Thanks Bob for the advice you gave me the night before I left for Houston. Colleen, you don't know what an important part your panties played in my asking this lady to marry me."

Of course, that got questioning looks from everyone, but Nick, being the tease, he is, was not going to elaborate.

"Stacy, you know how much I love you and how important your advice was in helping me make the decision to propose. You were the first person I told that I was in love with Danielle."

Next, he turned to his family. His words were full of love and emotion.

"I am so grateful you had allowed me the time to work at Deltron, even though you didn't know what I was doing. I had complete confidence in your ability to run NAS Financial Group in my absence, and that made it easier for me to devote myself to the Deltron team."

Then, after looking at each member of his family individually, he said, "You know how important you all are to me. And, I've always felt love and respect from all of you. But the way you reacted to my announcement that I had met someone and had intentions of marrying her within thirty days, surprised me. Here was a woman you had never met. You didn't know anything about her. But because she was my choice, you took her in and made her a part of our family. You showed her love and respect. I will never forget that."

Then, he got to the reason for this party.

"As most of you know, I do not believe in destiny. When I tell people how Danielle and I got together, many say it was meant to be and would have happened no matter what the circumstances. I don't believe that! I believe just the opposite. For Danielle and I to be here today required a particular set of events to take place in a specific order.

"For instance, the bank rejecting the Deltron loan just before Dan mentioned NAS Financial Group. Then, there was the timing of Chester quitting without notice the very day Janice had an important meeting with Danielle. Think about Charley's grandson having his soccer game switched from an afternoon to an evening event. If that didn't happen, I would never have had the pleasure of escorting the beautiful Ms. Palmer to that charity dinner.

"Our trip to Cauldwell. My contacts with the Navy Seals. If Robbie had been in any other branch of service, I couldn't have helped explain what had happened. Billy Harris being such an ass. Danielle's decision to leave a day early. Anna Lee, your gesture at Carl's Place and your phone call to your Aunt Danielle were all critical events that led us in this direction.

"If one less person had taken a cup of coffee in Deltron's break room Thursday morning, Danielle wouldn't have heard me talk about Atlanta. If any one of these events had not taken place, chances are we wouldn't be here today."

After looking around the room, he continued.

"I've thought about this chain of events many times, and I always come back to the same question. What was the catalyst? What started the ball rolling, the spark that ignited the fuse? The answer was simple, it was lunch! Then the question is why did Dan call Danielle for lunch on that particular Tuesday morning? It wasn't unusual for the two of them to have lunch together. They had met for lunch many times over the last fifteen years. But, why that particular Tuesday? If they had lunch on Monday, Danielle wouldn't have known about the bank turning her down. If they had lunch on Wednesday, Danielle would have already moved on in pursuit of other financial options."

Nick turned his attention to me.

"I don't think I've mentioned this to you Danielle, but while I was waiting for you to arrive at the church on our wedding day, I went out into the congregation to welcome our guests. While there, I noticed Dan walk in with his date. Being the curious fellow I am, I wanted to know what prompted that lunch invitation. I asked the lady to excuse us, and I took Dan over to a corner and asked him why he had invited you to lunch on that particular Tuesday."

Now I had an idea where my husband was going with this story. Still looking at me, he continued.

"I'm sure you remember the reason, and I know that Dan does! But, before I reveal it, I have to clarify something. Women and men are very different in many ways. One of the significant differences is women have no problem telling their most intimate secrets to their girlfriends. They will tell them the details of their lives, their loves, their relationships. It's how girls are.

"Men, on the other hand, hold everything much closer. Oh, I know some men will brag about their conquests and even some that will talk about the intimacy with their girlfriend and wives. But, for most of us men, we tend to keep things to ourselves, and that is always a source of trouble between men and women. Women always want to know what we men are thinking, and men are always wondering how she could tell a co-worker about the most intimate details of our life?

"But, there is one-person we men will tell almost everything to. We feel safe telling our most intimate secrets to our BEST friend. So, it was with Dan Parker. He had a secret he could only tell to his best friend, and he invited her to lunch to reveal it."

Dan had been watching Nick intently while this was going on, and he seemed nervous. Nick started to say something else, but stopped himself and looked directly at Dan.

"I don't think it is my place to tell you all what that lunch date was about. Dan, I think you should tell us!"

Dan stood and looked around the room. He really seemed nervous now.

"Okay Nick, I'll tell you. On that Tuesday morning, I wanted to tell my best friend that the previous weekend I had met the most wonderful woman I had ever known. She was everything I could hope to find in a woman, and I was sure that I was hopelessly in love with her."

Cindy was blushing now and looking at Dan with wide eyes. She had no idea where Nick was going with his story, and now, suddenly she knew it was all about her. Looking at Cindy now, Dan continued.

"And to satisfy your curiosity, Mr. Amonti, this is the catalyst. This beautiful lady is the spark that ignited the chain of events you mentioned. And this lady has also ignited another chain of events that has led to this…"

Suddenly, Dan got down on his knee and said as sweetly as he could, "Cindy Mae Mason, would you do me the honor of becoming my wife?"

Cindy was in shock, but recovered quickly and whispered, "Yes, Dan, yes!"

Dan slipped a ring on her finger, and now we really had a reason to party!

Nick sat down, all smug with himself.

"Happy?"

"You rat. You could have told me!"

"And ruin the surprise?"

"When did you two set this up?"

"I told you we ran into each other last week and had lunch. Dan said he was ready to propose, but he wanted it to be dramatic, something that Cindy would always remember.

"We met for lunch a couple of times after that and cooked up this little playette! You didn't answer my question. Happy?"

I looked over at Dan and Cindy. They were being inundated with congratulations and best wishes. Dan seemed happier than I had ever known him to be.

"Yes! Extremely happy, he deserves a good woman in his

life."

Then, looking into Nick's eyes, I said sincerely, "Mr. Amonti, every time I am convinced I love you as much as a woman can love a man, you find a way to make me love you even more!"

"Get used to it Mrs. Amonti, because I never intend to stop."

After everyone else had their turn with the happy couple, Nick and I wandered over to give them our best wishes. Nick shook Dan's hand, and I saw the two of them look into each other's eyes. There was more than friendship there. It made me feel good.

I gave Dan a hug and a kiss, and Cindy put her arms around Nick's neck and gave him a big kiss. The hug lingered, and she whispered something into his ear that neither Dan nor I heard. And, Nick whispered something to her. There was something special going on there. I didn't know what it was, but I knew I would eventually find out. Nick and I had no secrets!

The list of women who adored my husband was growing, and two of them were related to me. I think most women would have been jealous of the attention their man got from other women, but it just made me love him more. Maybe because there was never any doubt that he was all mine!

After the party broke up, Nick asked Terry, Stacy, Dan, and Cindy to join us for a nightcap. Nick, being in an excellent mood, glanced around the table.

"The six musketeers!"

We all laughed and then he added, "It must be obvious to all of you, we have something special here. We're not friends, we're more like family. I like that, and I'd like us to stay as close as possible forever."

The laughs turned to genuine smiles and nods of agreement, and I knew the six of us would be just that, family. It was a pleasant feeling. We could never find better people to be close to.

Not another word was spoken until it was time to say goodnight. Nick had booked a suite for us, but not the Penthouse Suite as usual. That one he reserved for Dan and Cindy. Nick and I didn't say anything on the way to our room, but that night, in his bedroom it was very, very special.

About a month later, I got a call from Cindy. She said she and Dan had set a date and wanted us to celebrate with them. I called

Nick, and he suggested we have a small dinner party at the apartment, just the four of us. We hadn't had anyone over for dinner since the Pre-Nup debate. That was fine by me, and when I called her back, Cindy said it would be perfect. We set a date for the coming Friday evening. Nick had some outstanding wine he saved for really special occasions, and he said he'd decanter a couple of bottles for the celebration.

Friday, I left work early, and when I arrived at the apartment, Nick was already there setting up. Nick's not much of a cook, but he's a great organizer, and he sets a great table, probably a leftover from his restaurant days. I, on the other hand, was a pretty good cook, and we managed to distribute the chores so that each of us contributed equally. My husband believed if I were to work, he should take on some of the responsibility for running the household.

When Dan and Cindy arrived, they were very excited about their announcement. They had planned a June wedding, which was only eight months away. Nick and I offered them whatever help they needed, and the dinner was pleasant and comfortable. Nick and I both felt private dinners with good friends were always a joy. After Cindy and I had cleared the table, and we were on our second decanter of wine, Dan and Cindy got serious.

Cindy said, "Dan and I made a deal. We would each write our top three choices for Best Man and Maid of Honor on a piece of paper, and if any of the choices matched, that's who we would pick."

I knew Dan had two brothers and Cindy had three sisters. Cindy told us, "When we compared notes, only one name was listed for each, and they matched exactly."

Dan looked first at me and then at Nick.

"Would you two do us the honor of standing up for us at our wedding?"

I was flattered. Nick was overwhelmed.

"Why?" Nick stammered.

"Many, many reasons. Hopefully, some of what you two have will rub off on us."

Cindy looked directly at Nick. "We probably wouldn't be talking about marriage if it wasn't for you."

Dan got serious.

"Danielle, do you remember Nick saying he and I spoke the morning of your wedding?"

"Yes, he asked you why you invited me to lunch on that Tuesday."

"That's not all Nick, and I talked about that morning."

Nick told Dan, "That's not necessary!"

"Maybe not, but I'm going to say it anyway. When I told Nick why I had asked you to lunch, he asked me how Cindy felt about it. I told him I wasn't sure because I hadn't told her. Nick suggested I bring it all into the open and tell her exactly how I feel. He said Colleen had given you that same advice about your feelings for Nick and that led to the two of you admitting your love for each other for the first time. So, that night after your Wedding Reception I told Cindy I was hoping for more in our relationship. I told her I wanted to see if we had a real future together, and she said she wanted the same thing."

Dan looked at Nick, and they both smiled. Cindy gave Nick a long endearing look, as she squeezed Dan's hand and I was sure that there was more to this story.

"He also said something else."

This time, Nick said, "Definitely not necessary!"

Dan ignored Nick and went on.

"Danielle, Nick said he understood your relationship with me. He told me everyone needs that special friend they trust, and he knew you trusted me. He said he hoped I would remain your best friend because he thought you might need someone to confide in if his concerns about your relationship with him proved to be true."

Dan paused and looked at Nick before he continued.

"Danielle, you know I had doubts about your marriage. My concerns mirrored Nick's almost exactly. I was afraid being connected to him would hurt you and your career. But, after our talk that morning, I knew you had picked the right man. I knew whatever happened he would be there to protect you, and if not stop the hurts, he would make them better. I do love you Danielle Amonti, and I will always be there for you, just as I trust you will always be there for me! Be there for Cindy and me on our wedding day."

That's why Nick asked about my relationship with Dan. He wasn't jealous. He wanted to know if I could depend on Dan to be there for me if things got rough. And, that's why Dan changed his mind about Nick.

Then Cindy told me, "Thanks to your husband, I know what your relationship with Dan is all about, and I can't think of anyone I'd want to stand by me on my wedding day than someone who really cares about and respects my man. Nick, I don't have to tell you why I picked you, and I'm sure Dan doesn't either."

Dan added, "We took a chapter from your wedding manual. No secrets. I know about the conversation you had with Cindy while I danced with your bride. And, I know what you whispered to her on the night of our engagement."

"Nothing but the truth," Nick smiled.

"And that's why I need you at my side when I take this beautiful woman as my wife."

Nick looked at me. I nodded. He nodded, and it was settled.

While Cindy helped with the dishes, she told me the whole story of her conversation with Nick on my wedding day, and what passed between them at her engagement.

Cindy had her doubts about the relationship between Dan and me, and Nick put them to rest. If it wasn't for that, they might not be together today.

And, on the night of their engagement, when she wrapped her arms around his neck and told him thank you and that she loved him, he told her, "He's a good man, Cindy. Be good to him. I know he'll be good to you!"

That's the man I'm married to. That's the man I love!

So, on a beautiful Sunday morning in June, Nick and I stood up for Cindy and Dan.

Cindy was beautiful in a Stacy Geer Designs Original Wedding Dress. Nick managed to get the carriage and six white stallions for her ride to the church, and for a wedding present, Nick gave them the use of the BBJ and Jerry and John for their entire honeymoon.

Chapter 27 – Married Life

Nick liked to hold impromptu parties with our family and friends, and we always had a big party to celebrate our anniversary. But, the day of our anniversary was always private. It didn't matter where we were, on the evening of our anniversary, we would have a romantic dinner at a very nice restaurant. Nick would order the exact same meal we had in Atlanta and Houston. After dinner, he would take me to a local Piano Bar, and we would party late. Our favorite place in Fort Lauderdale was the 88's on Las Olas Boulevard. After that, we retired to a suite at the local Hyatt and used his bedroom. Because Nick had such a romantic soul, I always felt our honeymoon had never ended, just interrupted occasionally while I was at work.

We were in Fort Lauderdale for our first anniversary. On the way to the restaurant, Nick asked Thomas to stop at the airport. When we arrived, I could see there was a stanchion leaning against the BBJ's nose. There was a patch below the window and just behind the nose cone. My heart sank.

What had happened to our beautiful airplane?

As Nick and I walked toward NAS One, Jerry approached us.

"All done?" Nick asked.

"Let's see!" Jerry answered.

Jerry climbed the ladder to reach the patch. I looked at Nick.

He must be heartbroken.

When Jerry reached the top of the stanchion, he pulled off the patch.

Under the patch, something had been added to the nose of the ship. In big, beautiful script was a name:

Danielle

And above the name was a caricature of a sexy lady wearing my vamp outfit, in a cheesecake pose. A month earlier, Nick had asked me to wear that outfit, so he could take some pictures. When I asked him why, he said he was keeping a special album just for himself, and he wanted that day included. Now, I knew what those pictures were for. The sexy lady sitting above the name was me.

"Happy Anniversary," Nick whispered.

I couldn't say anything. I just squeezed his hand, and after we had received best wishes on our anniversary from the crew, we went back to the limo and continued on to our anniversary dinner.

Nick took me to La Chez, the fanciest restaurant in South Florida. It was beautiful and classy. I commented on how elegant the restaurant was, and Nick said it could be better. I knew he had been in the restaurant business before he started NAS but topping this place would be a stretch.

For our second anniversary dinner, Nick said he wanted to try a brand-new restaurant that had just opened. When Thomas dropped us off, I was impressed. The exterior of the building and the grounds were exquisite. Inside was, even more, beautiful, definitely better than La Chez, but there were no customers there. We were approached by a very distinguished looking man in a tuxedo. He introduced himself as Andrei, the maitre'd.

He told us, "The restaurant isn't due to officially open for a couple of days, but your table is ready."

I looked at Nick.

"One of the perks of being rich!"

That brought a smile from me, and I assumed NAS had financed this place, and they were allowing Nick and me to have a private dinner here before they opened. My husband has a very romantic soul, and this is just the type of thing he would do for me.

The service was old world captain's service. It was elegant. The captain, Chad, who was to serve us tonight, was a handsome younger man who seemed to be well trained in the art of fine dining service. His dress, manners, and style were impeccable. He informed Nick his instructions had been attended to with care and if there were no changes, he would begin our service. Nick nodded.

Chad left us, and a very pretty young girl brought us our drinks, margaritas, just like in Atlanta. Our ribeye steaks were done to perfection, and the creamed spinach had a spicy tang. Between courses, I took the time to look around the room.

It was exquisite. This place made La Chez look like a slum. Someone had put a lot of care into this, and the results were beautiful. I asked Nick if he knew what the owners were going to call this fantastic restaurant. Nick summoned Chad over and requested a menu for me.

Chad placed an open menu in my hands, and the first thing I noticed was there were no prices listed. When I inquired as to the reason, Chad explained this was the owner's idea. It was how things were done in a classier time. Upon request, only the host's menu would have prices so no one in his party need worry about what their host would be spending. I liked it. I closed the menu, looked at the name of the restaurant printed on the front. Nick smiled.

"Happy Anniversary, Mrs. Amonti."

On the front of the menu, in beautiful script was the name of the restaurant:

Danielle's Kitchen

What could I possibly say?

"I've been working on this since our first anniversary dinner. Terry, Marc, and Tony were involved in the design and building of the restaurant. Dan handled the legal stuff: permits, licenses and all. I gave them each ten percent of the place as a reward for doing such an excellent job. I also guaranteed they would be able to get a table without reservations any time they wished."

Then he handed me an envelope. In it was sixty percent of the restaurant's corporate stock in my name. I was sure my life couldn't be any better, and this would be the best present Nick ever gave me, but I was wrong on both accounts.

A little over a year later, I finally was certified to fly the BBJ. The day I brought home the news, Nick suggested we visit Colleen and Bob. Nick did the walk around while I got our clearances, and then it was just him and I. For the first time, we could leave Jerry and John behind.

We went through the startup and taxi procedures as usual. I had been flying right seat even though it wasn't legal on most of the flights we took together unless there were other people on board. Nick felt as long as Jerry was in the jump seat in case of an emergency we'd be okay.

We were given clearance to position and hold. Nick set the

nose wheel on the center line and locked it. Then he reached over his head, flipped a switch and said, "Your airplane!"

Before I had a chance to say anything, we were given clearance to take off.

Nick acknowledged the Tower Controller, and I called, "Take off power!"

During more than three years of training, I had made dozens of takeoffs, both in simulators and on actual flights. It had almost become second nature. But, this time, it was different. As our hands connected on the throttles, I got that thrill again. The voice called V-ONE.

I asked, "Ready to fly, Nick?"

"I'd fly anywhere with you, Danielle!"

When the voice called V-R, I pulled back on the yoke, saw the nose come up and felt the lift of the wings.

I am in control of this big beautiful bird and sitting next to me is the mostest man I have ever met! Could my life be any better?

Nick knew how much Cauldwell meant to me, and he managed to include my hometown in some of my anniversary surprises. One year, it was a baseball field for the kids he called Palmer Field. Another year it was a stadium for the high school football team. He named it Palmer Stadium. After that, I asked him not to name everything after me.

"It's beginning to make me feel self-conscious when we visit."

So, the library was named Cauldwell Library and the new Sheriff's office, jail, and courthouse had no name at all. When he had the rec-center built, we decided to call it the Bandwagon. It was a free-standing structure on the edge of town, and it could be used for dances, parties, weddings and other types of functions.

Nick also set up a non-profit foundation to cover the cost of maintenance for all these facilities and also award scholarships to the Cauldwell High School graduates. The foundation would also pay the salary of Charlotte Anders, a friend of Mommy Palmers and a lady I had known since my teenage years. Charlotte would be responsible for renting out the rec-center for various functions, planning parties and keeping the books. Charlotte held raffles and fundraisers and rented the center for local parties. Mary Ann Cauldwell and I contributed to the foundation to cover any shortfall and help with the scholarship fund.

Even though Nick and I lived a simple life, not in line with his wealth, being the wife of a very wealthy man did have some very nice benefits. I did eventually get used to being rich. We continued to live in the two-bedroom apartment I had when we met. But, when we traveled, it was first class all the way. Whenever Colleen's boys or Anna Lee's Johnny were with us, Nick let them ride the jump seat in *Danielle*. The three of them got the bug, and they all eventually became qualified pilots and certified to fly the BBJ.

Robbie's Secret Missions were finally declassified, and we flew Anna Lee, Johnny, Colleen, Bob, Lindsey and Joe to Washington to accept Robbie's medal. The entire Seal Team was there, including those who had retired. The seven whose lives Robbie had saved brought their families.

When the citation was read, it was almost word for word what Nick had told us in Anna Lee's kitchen. Mary Ann Cauldwell and I shut the plant down for three days, and we all flew from Washington to Cauldwell for the big celebration in Robbie's honor. Because Robbie was awarded the Medal of Honor, Johnny had an automatic appointment to the Naval Academy.

I have a closet full of Stacy Geer Designs clothes now, some I bought, and some were gifts from Stacy. It was never necessary to help out Lindsey or Colleen. Joe was very good at what he did for the oil companies and provided a very comfortable lifestyle for them. When word got out that Nick Amonti of NAS Financial Group had invested over a quarter of a billion dollars with Bob, clients beat a path to his door. Between that and the commissions he made from both bequest accounts, he did very, very well.

We did help Anna Lee and Johnny. It took some convincing, but Nick was good at that. He started another company, NAS Aviation, and leased both his BBJ and his son's 'G' over to the new enterprise. When we weren't using the aircraft, the company would charter them out to other people. He put Anna Lee in charge of the new corporation. She was very conscientious and, of course, Nick paid her very well. The company did so well, they purchased three additional aircraft.

We went to the Keynote in Atlanta at least once a year. It wasn't the same after Roger retired, but he and his wife would often join us there when we visited. Cauldwell was another destination we went to often, sometimes taking Colleen and Bob and/or Lindsey and Joe with us. It was always a blast when we were all together.

Nick never stopped being a tease, but I managed to get him occasionally. The subject of Colleen's panties would come up a couple of times a year, and we never tired of the joke. He also never tired of surprising me, and I never tired of being surprised by him.

We continued to attend the corporate and charity dinners. Bill Peterson tagged me as the go-to gal for most of the events, and Nick's responsibility to NAS kept the invitations coming.

Nick didn't dance as much as the years moved along, but he never minded if I did. Only twice in all those years did my dance partner make a pass at me, and Nick was right about that too. It was insulting. I also found out one night it works both ways.

We were at a very dull event one evening. Nick excused himself to visit the men's room. I asked him to bring me a glass of champagne on his way back to the table. No sooner had he left, then Stacy and Terry came by. Terry complaining about the annoying people at their table suggested we meet Nick at the bar and have a few laughs.

When we got there, there was a very good-looking lady who was just walking away from the bar, apparently pissed at someone or something.

Terry being Terry asked the bartender, "What's her problem?"

The bartender, Tim, told us, "A gentleman stopped at the bar to order a couple of drinks. The lady asked him to buy her a drink. The gentleman, very politely, said it would be a pleasure to buy a pretty lady a drink.

"The woman indicated she was interested in more than a drink. The gentleman lifted his left hand and wiggled his fingers at her. It was obvious he was showing her his wedding ring.

"The lady told him she could show him things that his wife never thought of, and she'd never know.

"The gentleman said he'd know, and that was enough reason. The gentleman paid for all three drinks, and as he was walking away, the lady called after him that he didn't know what he was missing."

Tim, laughing now, said, "The gentleman turned around, walked back to the lady, stood directly in front of her and seeming very annoyed said, "You obviously don't know who my wife is, madam. If you did, you'd realize there is nothing I am missing." And then, he stormed away, angry."

Tim stopped laughing and pointed.

"That's the guy. The gray-haired gentleman with the two champagne glasses."

As Nick approached, the three of us couldn't help but laugh. Nick asked what was so funny, and that made us laugh even more. Stacy cuddled up to my husband and in her sexiest voice said, "Buy a lady a drink, good looking, and I'll show you something special!"

And we laughed all the more. Nick leered at Tim, and the bartender retreated to the other end of the bar.

"That was a good-looking lady. Couldn't you have turned her down without shooting her down?" Terry asked.

Nick started to say something, but I interrupted him.

"It's like this, Terry When someone makes a pass at someone who's obviously married, what they're actually saying is you look like someone who would cheat on your spouse. And, that sir is insulting."

I grabbed Nick's hand and led him onto the dance floor before anything else could be said. I put my arms around his neck and pressed myself closer to him.

Very quietly he whispered, "It seems My Lady does hear what I say!"

"Every word you've ever spoken to me, Kind Sir," I replied just as quietly.

It was true. Nick lived by a code. His own code. I didn't always understand it because it didn't always make sense to me.

But whenever he talked about it, I listened, and I tried to follow it. It never let me down.

Life with my man was as good as I had ever imagined life could be. We had very few spats. I wouldn't call any of them arguments, just minor disagreements. The most significant argument we ever had was about Andrew Lighter. When I understood what Nick was trying to tell me, I had to agree, and I

250

followed his advice.

No man was ever going to think I was available to anyone but Nicholas Amonti!

All the other disagreements usually ended with me wrapped in a bear hug, and Nick saying, "But you still love me, don't ya?"

And, after I melted, and he kissed me, we would quietly discuss the item in question and find a solution. We were very compatible.

I was happy at Peterson Enterprises. I had some successes and one or two failures. My batting average was good enough that Bill never chastised me for those, but always encouraged me to move ahead. Nick was right. Peterson was the place for me.

Nick spent less and less time working, and when I had to go out of town on business, I would usually be able to talk him into coming with me. He would wait patiently at the hotel while I conducted business, and then we would have the night or weekend for us. My forty hours a week in the office was all the time I could tolerate being away from him.

Nick took some of his free time to write a couple of books on finance. They did reasonably well and resulted in his being away for book signings and interviews. He also became a Guest Speaker at many business functions.

When it wasn't possible for me to accompany him on these trips, he always scheduled them, so he would be home that night. Having *Danielle* available made it possible.

There were a couple of things Nick and I did that were a little unconventional. Because Nick didn't want my career to be all about NAS Financial Group, he insisted I use my maiden name for business. I was Danielle Palmer to the corporate world I traveled in.

We attended many corporate and charity banquets together and occasionally, we both would be invited to the same banquet, separately: Nick through NAS and me through Peterson. On those occasions, if we were seated with people we didn't know, we would openly flirt with each other.

The rings on our fingers indicated we were married, but because I was Danielle Palmer, representing Peterson Enterprises and he was Nick Amonti, representing NAS Financial Group, no one realized we were married to each other.

The flirting game got pretty serious at times, and many people at our table were shocked. We always let them know before the night was over that we were married to each other, and they always seemed to take our little game in good humor.

The other game we played was just for us. It started one night about three months after our first anniversary. I was sitting at the bar at the Crown Plaza Hotel on State Route Eighty-Four waiting for Nick. He was flying into Fort Lauderdale/Hollywood Airport and suggested I meet him at the hotel for dinner. I came straight from the office, and I had to wait for him.

Four businessmen came into the bar to wait for a table. One of them started to flirt with me. I don't care how great your husband is, or how much you love him, it's always nice to know that you are attractive to other men, even if you're not interested. I have this move where I brush my hair back with my left hand, obviously showing my wedding ring. Most men will take the hint. This gentleman did, and although the conversation continued, the flirting stopped.

Right after he left with his friends for their table, Nick showed up. He sat down next to me and introduced himself as Nick Amonti. Thinking he was in a flirty mood, I introduced myself as Danielle Palmer.

We talked as two strangers that had just met. When Nick's table was ready, he invited me to join him for dinner. I demurred at first but allowed myself to be talked into having dinner with this stranger. He suggested we have after dinner drinks in his suite. Again, I demurred, and again I allowed him to talk me into it.

Once up in the suite, he tried to seduce me. I coyly let him know that if he played his cards right, I might be available to his charms.

He did, and I was.

Nick and I had retained the two-bedroom concept that we developed in Atlanta. When we traveled, we always had a two-bedroom suite. At home, the bedroom was designated hers or his according to the mood we were in.

In my bedroom, it was fifty percent sex and fifty percent emotion. In his room, it was ten percent sex and ninety percent emotion.

That night at the Crown Plaza it was ninety-five percent sex and almost no emotion. It was an experience we hadn't shared before. Nick treated me entirely differently, and I reacted differently.

It wasn't what we usually had, and I'd never trade our lovemaking for sex, but as an occasional release of energy and excitement, it was awesome.

The practice continues. Once or twice a year, I allow this stranger to pick me up and seduce me. I picked him up on two occasions. There's no set date or time, it's a mood thing. We are both so perceptive to each other that we seem to know when the time is right. Only once did I turn him down. I was in the mood to be made love to that night, and Nick didn't have a problem with that.

We vary the setting and rules. Like I said it's a mood thing. Sometimes I act as if I've had too much to drink. Other times I act lonely. Twice I demanded money for my services. The first time Nick paid me without question. The second time, the bastard bargained with me over the price.

It's always fun, but it wouldn't be possible if our love and trust in each other weren't as strong as it is.

I do love my man!

Chapter 28 - The Dark Days

It happened in our third year of marriage. One morning, while we were having breakfast, Ron, a friend of Nick's who owned an Air Freight Company, called and asked if Nick would fly with him to Freeport in the Bahamas and ferry a plane back to Fort Lauderdale/Hollywood International Airport with one of Ron's younger pilots. Nick looked at me.

"I have no objections. Freeport to Fort Lauderdale will get you home in time for dinner."

Ron was one of NAS's clients, and Nick often helped him out. Ron had a fleet of 737's which was what our BBJ was, and Nick was always current.

When I got to the apartment after work, Nick wasn't there. It was no big worry; flight schedules weren't as precise as everyone wished. Six o'clock came and went, then seven o'clock.

I called Ron's office.

"There was a storm on their route, and they were going around it. That would make them late arriving."

It sounded OK, but I worried because Nick always let me know if his plans changed. Eight o'clock. I called Ron's office again and asked to speak with Ron.

"He can't come to the phone right now, he's talking to the Coast Guard. I'll have Ron call you as soon as he's through with the Coast Guard.

I hung up on Ron's office and called Colleen.

"Nick was flying back from Freeport today, and he's overdue. Ron is talking to the Coast Guard."

"I'm leaving right now. I'll be there as soon as I can."

"I'll send *Danielle* to pick you up."

"The round trip will take too long. I'll call Anna Lee and have her make arrangements for a local charter. It will be quicker."

Twenty minutes later my intercom buzzed. Andy announced Dan and Cindy were in the lobby. When they got to the apartment, Dan was worried.

"Colleen called and told us about Nick. Anything new?"

"I haven't heard anything else since I talked to her."

Dan called Ron's office and insisted they give him more information. When he hung up, he told me what he knew as gently as he could, but it was impossible to soften the news.

"The plane Nick was flying is overdue and presumed down. The departure time and the amount of fuel on board meant it couldn't still be in the air. The Coast Guard was starting a search. That's all they have."

"Nick would never leave me like this. He'll find a way to get home, no matter what he had to do. He wouldn't do this to me."

By the next day, my apartment was crowded. Dan and Cindy, Terry and Stacy, Colleen and Lindsey all were there. Dan and Terry took turns answering the phone and talking to the Coast Guard. The girls looked after me, but I needed to keep busy, so I tried to keep the coffee hot and put out some food for everyone. Marc Antonelli, one of Nick's business partners and a very good friend, came by with his girlfriend and was very encouraging.

"He'd walk across the water if he had to."

Nick's kids came by in shifts. Their grief was as deep as mine, but they didn't want to burden me any more than necessary. They talked to Terry and Dan.

"We'll all camp out at Janice's house and drop by here one at a time. Danielle doesn't need us all here at once."

That afternoon we got some good news. Dan took the call and relayed the information.

"Nick's copilot was picked up by the Coast Guard. They were sure they would have Nick shortly."

That evening, Dan had more news.

"Nick's copilot was in good shape. He told them what happened and why he and Nick were separated. After they had left Freeport, they skirted around a thunderstorm. Suddenly both engines shut down. They couldn't restart them. They were in a glide in heavy weather, and Nick attempted to steer them toward blue sky. The copilot said it was a great piece of airmanship that Nick was able to get them in the water in one piece. The copilot broke his wrist in the landing. Nick put him in a one-man raft and sent him adrift. Nick said he would be right behind him in the other one man raft, but first, he was going to attempt to retrieve the black boxes so the NTSB could pinpoint the cause of the crash. The co-pilot never saw Nick again. The Coast Guard is still looking."

The second day passed with no additional news. Dan and Cindy took turns with Terry and Stacy, one couple staying with me and the other going home for some sleep. Colleen and Lindsey never left my side. When they insisted, I try to get some rest, one of them would lay down with me, and the other would keep the apartment running, coffee, food and such. At least the constant ringing of the apartment phone had stopped. At the end of day three, we got a call from the Coast Guard. Again, Dan took the call and relayed the news.

"The official search has been called off. Nick is presumed lost at sea. No one could survive more than three days in a raft at sea. They will keep an eye out for him and let every ship and plane in the area know a man was missing, but the dedicated search is over."

Everyone was affected by the news. Lindsey and Colleen came over and put their arms around me. Cindy was in tears. I tried to stay calm.

"I refuse to believe it. Nick would never allow this to happen. He would never leave me this way. He is out there alive and trying to get back to me. I can still feel a connection with him."

I hadn't slept for more than thirty minutes at a time since Dan first called Ron's office. I looked in the mirror. I couldn't let Nick see me like this when he got home. He had told me about the time he greeted his son's ship when it returned from a six-month cruise to the Mediterranean.

"Some of the wives and girlfriends were all prettied up, all decked out in their finery, but some of the women looked as if they couldn't take the trouble to comb out their hair. I couldn't understand how they could greet their men, after six months at sea, looking like that."

Well, that wasn't going to happen to my man!

But, there wasn't too much I could do about it. I couldn't sleep, and that was taking a toll. At the end of day four, everyone was pretty convinced Nick was gone. They tried to hide it from me, but they all loved him, and they were all feeling his loss. I knew this couldn't go on forever. They had lives and jobs and responsibilities. I couldn't allow them to continue to hold my hand when all looked so hopeless.

But, I know he's alive. I could still feel him. He's out there trying to get back to me.

Lindsey tried to get me to sleep.

"Every time I close my eyes, I can see Nick floating all alone in a bright yellow raft at sea. I wish I were with him. If he was going to be lost forever, I want to be by his side."

The afternoon of the fifth day, I was keeping busy washing some coffee cups at the kitchen sink. Dan was on his cell phone, and Cindy was alone in the living room, crying. She had a special love for Nick because of what he had done for her and Dan so many years ago.

Lindsey told me, "Joe went to Cauldwell to be with Anna Lee. He's having a tough time keeping her from flying to Florida to be with you."

My family and the Musketeers. Nick would be so happy to know they were all here to support me

Colleen and Lindsey, who stayed awake all night to keep an eye on me, were trying to catch some sleep in the Guest Room. Terry and Stacy were in the dining room cleaning up after lunch.

The cup I was washing slipped from my hand and landed in the soapy water. It sank to the bottom of the sink. I stared at the cup under the water, and I knew Nick was gone. I had suddenly lost the connection. I no longer felt him. I was trying to find the words to tell everyone it was over and that they should get on with their lives. Nick was gone, and I was alone! All the love and caring I felt from these people couldn't change that. I had lost the connection I had with him since our first pinkie touch in Atlanta

The mostest man I had ever met was gone, and I would never see him again!

I felt arms slip around my waist from behind. Holding me tightly, Dan whispered, "They got him, he's alive!"

I tried to spin around, but Dan was holding me so tight I couldn't move. He let up on his grip just enough for me to turn and face him. He smiled and nodded. Then the reason he was holding me so tightly became apparent. My legs gave out, and Dan carried me into my bedroom. When I opened my eyes, I was on my bed, Dan was sitting on the edge of the bed, holding my hand and Cindy was applying cold cloths to my forehead.

When Dan noticed that I had opened my eyes, he immediately said, "It's true, Danielle, he's alive!"

I tried to sit up, but my head felt like it weighed a thousand pounds. Colleen and Lindsey were sitting on the opposite side of the bed.

"Relax Sis, he's on a ship right now, you can't see him or talk to him for a while. He's alive and being taken care of."

I knew it! I knew it! I knew it!

"I told you Nick would never leave me this way. He would find a way back to me."

I tried to get control of myself. It took a while. Dan and Cindy left the bedroom, but Colleen and Lindsey stayed with me.

"Just lay here for a while and collect yourself."

They were right of course. I did have to collect myself before I could fully understand what was happening. When I felt almost human, I went into the dining room and found Dan on the phone. He motioned for me to sit down and when he was finished with his conversation, he gave me the details.

"A Navy aircraft carrier was returning to Norfolk after a workup around Gitmo. When they return to homeport, they fly the planes off the carrier to the Air Squadron's home bases. One of the Hornet pilots thought he saw something in the water and broke formation to check it out.

"He saw a raft with a man inside and notified the carrier. They sent out a helicopter and divers, and while the Hornet pilot and his Wingman circled overhead, they picked Nick out of the raft. They said he refused to leave the raft without the two black boxes."

Dan smiled.

"The Navy man I talked to said when Nick reached the helicopter he was nearly dead and the only thing he said was, "Please call my wife."

"Of course, that took a while, because they didn't know who this man was and had to wait until they contacted the Coast Guard before they were sure of his identity. Nick is onboard the carrier. The ship has full hospital facilities on board and doctors, not just Corpsmen. He's dehydrated, and they are keeping him sedated until they check out all his vital organs to make sure there is no permanent damage. It will take a while, and he'll be doped up most of that time. Once he's stable, they'll move him to a hospital in Pensacola."

"Is the ship going to Pensacola?"

"No, they were going to fly Nick off the ship on something that sounded like a fish."

Remembering what my nephew Johnny said he wanted to fly after he graduated from the academy, I asked, "Do you mean a COD?"

"It could be a codfish," Dan answered.

That made me giggle. I think it was just the release of pressure knowing at least Nick had been found.

"He's going to be so mad."

"Who's going to be mad?" someone asked.

"Nick. He's going to be really angry."

Dan probably worried I wasn't thinking straight, asked why Nick would be angry. That made me giggle again.

"Ever since Nick took a Tiger Cruise aboard his son's ship, he's had a desire to catapult off the deck of an aircraft carrier. He's finally going to get the chance, and he'll be too doped up to realize it."

That brought nervous giggles from everyone. When things quieted down, and everyone was settled, I went to Nick's desk to look for a phone number. I found what I was looking for and asked Terry to make the call for me.

"Terry, this is the number for Nick's Navy Seal friend, the one who taught the Hand to Hand Combat Course. Maybe he can get us some inside information on Nick's condition."

I remembered Nick told me that Commander Becker is the one who put him in touch with Robbie's commanding officer. That's how he got the information about Robbie. It took time, and Terry seemed frustrated.

"I'm sorry it took so long, Danielle, but this number is old. Commander Becker is now Admiral Becker, and it took a while to track him down. I had to use Nick's name to get him to answer the phone."

"Was he cooperative?"

"Very! The Admiral said he will check into the situation and keep us informed as to Nick's condition and when they intend to ship him to a shore hospital."

Nick was on board the carrier for a couple of days, and I never got a chance to talk to him, but the Admiral kept his promise and kept us informed of his progress. The last call we received from the admiral was good news. Again, it was Terry who relayed the message.

"Nick is being transferred the day after tomorrow. They'll fly him off the ship to Pensacola Naval Air Station. The Admiral arranged permission for you to land *Danielle* there. You can be there when the COD arrives from the ship."

The night before we left for Pensacola, Dan, Cindy, Terry, Stacy, Lindsey, Colleen and I had a quiet dinner at the apartment. Now that things had settled down, and I had a chance to think clearly, I had a question.

"I'm surprised that Nick's other friends hadn't bothered to check on Nick's condition. Except for Marc, who stopped in that first day, no else has bothered."

Terry told me why.

"When Cindy called Marc, and told him Nick was missing, he came right over. When he got here, he saw the crowd in the lobby, reporters, television people, well-wishers and the curious. When he finally reached the apartment, he noticed the phone never stopped ringing. He told us he would call Tony and Harry and along with Nick's kids, they would set up an information center at the Hyatt.

"He had the incoming calls to the apartment transferred over there, and while Nick's kids handled the press, Marc, his girlfriend, Harry, Angie, and Tony handled the phones. It was twenty-four hours a day over there, and it won't be over for a couple of days yet while they handle the news of Nick's rescue."

I did remember Marc being here that first day, and I also remember the phone constantly ringing. Then, it suddenly stopped. I also remembered his words of encouragement that morning and what he had said at my wedding. He had told me they would always be there for Nick and me, and when they were needed, they were. Among my husband's many talents is his ability to pick good friends. Nick doesn't have many really close friends, but the ones he has are super.

"I'm glad Catherine was with Marc."

"Hopefully, that's a good sign," Cindy said.

Nick had known Marc for over ten years, and he had confided in me with all the lovely and charming women Marc knew, he never seemed interested in any of them. That was until Catherine came along. But they had recently gone through a very bad time, and Cindy, Angie, Stacy and I tried to help them sort things out. I hoped it was working out for them.

When the Musketeers left that night, there were hugs and kisses all around. I wouldn't see them again until Nick was ready to travel home. I knew there were no words I could say to them that would express my feelings for these four people, or for Marc, Tony, Harry, and Angie. Nick and I were blessed to have such true and loyal people in our lives.

Lindsey and Colleen flew with me to Pensacola. We landed about an hour before the COD arrived. I had to be restrained by a sailor until the propellers came to a complete stop, and then I rushed to the plane just as the ramp was being lowered. I watched as they carried the stretcher down the ramp.

The first sight of my husband was a total shock. He was burned to a crisp: sunburn, not any fire from the plane. He had lost a lot of weight, and when Nick lost weight, it always showed in his face. He looked awful. His last dose of painkiller was wearing off, and he recognized me.

"Hi baby, I'm home!"

I couldn't stop the tears. Luckily, he was still too doped up to see me clearly. He was put in an ambulance and taken to a civilian hospital. For the first time since I married Nick, I was really glad I was rich. I insisted on a private room, and I made them put another bed in the room for me. I stayed with him the entire time he was there. Colleen and Lindsey stayed at a local hotel and came to the hospital every morning.

"Let's go, Sis. He just got another shot. He'll be out for a while. Come to the cafeteria with me. Lindsey will stay with him. You won't do him any good if you run yourself down."

Colleen was right, and I allowed her to lead me away for some food and fresh air. My sisters stayed with me almost a week, and then I shipped them both home to their own husbands.

As they reduced Nick's painkillers, he remained awake for

longer and longer periods at a time. We spent the time talking.

"The other pilot was picked up right away and had said he was alive because of your skill as a pilot."

"Danielle, you know I never blow my own horn, but that was one thrilling ride!"

"Why did you remain behind to get the black boxes? It almost cost your life."

When he answered, he wasn't talking to his wife. He spoke to me as a fellow pilot, which I was. He was precise and technical, and he knew I'd understand.

"It was weird. We lost both engines at the exact same time. Just flamed out, no apparent reason. Up to that point, everything was nominal. Then we couldn't get the APU started. Made no sense! We tried a restart on each engine and got absolutely no response. It's as if we were disconnected from the airplane. Almost like one of those Bermuda Triangle stories."

"Well, you were in the triangle."

"You know I don't believe in that nonsense, there's always an explanation, and I wanted the black boxes to figure it out."

I looked at my husband.

"I don't care why, I'm just glad you survived, even as messed up as you are."

Nick looked directly into my eyes as he always does.

"You really didn't think I would leave you like that, did you?"

I looked back into his eyes and gave him the answer I'm sure he expected.

"No, I knew you'd be back even if it was just to tell me goodbye and say you loved me."

It was true, and we both knew it. But I had a bad feeling. Just before I got the news that he was picked up, I had lost the connection I felt with Nick ever since Atlanta. I was ready to tell everyone he was gone.

But, he was safe now, and I put it out of my mind.

When he was ambulatory, he was sent home. Recovery took almost eight weeks. I went back to work, and Nick busied himself working on his third book. Everything got back to normal around the Amonti house, and our life picked up where we had left it. Knowing I almost lost him, you might think I would appreciate him more. But, I loved this man so much there was no more to give.

The black boxes did turn out to be significant. The NTSB final report indicated poor maintenance on the aircraft and for a while, Ron's entire fleet was grounded. The maintenance company Ron used to maintain his fleet was fined by the FAA and life went on.

Nick never flew for Ron again. It wasn't that he didn't trust Ron's aircraft, or that he didn't want to, but he knew I would be a wreck until I saw him again. The only aircraft Nick flew after that was *Danielle*, our own BBJ.

I spent a lot of time thinking about my life with Nick Amonti. It was impossible to imagine life without him. Of course, if I had never met him, I wouldn't know what I was missing, but having been loved by this man, there was no way I could have a life without him.

I knew I would lose him someday; until then, I wanted our life to be exactly what it had been up to now, so I put the accident behind me, and we moved ahead with our lives.

Chapter 29 - Fifth Anniversary

Even though our anniversaries were private, we did celebrate with our family and friends on the closest weekend. For our fifth anniversary, Nick decided to have a big party. He invited everyone close to us. The party was very large because now my nephews and Nick's grandkids were old enough to join us and our list of close friends kept increasing. The newest member of our group was Brian De Salvo.

Brian had hired Tony's company to do some work for him, and they became friends. They had done a few joint projects together, and I knew they were working on a massive project, and NAS was financing it.

The project was the renovation of an old hotel, and it was supposed to be spectacular. It was almost complete, and the grand opening was set for next week. The hotel would have three restaurants, a Dance Club, a Piano Bar, and all the amenities of the fanciest hotels in Florida.

Nick and I had flown back from Nashville that Thursday morning where I attended a three-day conference. Nick and I had played our flirty game at the conference dinner last night, and we were both in a fantastic mood.

Since today was our actual anniversary, Nick made plans for our private dinner that evening. Ever since our second anniversary, our anniversary dinners were always at *Danielle's Kitchen*, but, Nick had other plans for tonight.

"I thought we'd try one of the restaurants at the hotel Tony and Brian are working on. They say it's very nice."

There were two entrances to the restaurant, one from the hotel lobby and the other directly from outside. We used the outside entrance, and when we walked in, I could swear we were in *Danielle's Kitchen*. This was an exact duplicate.

I looked at Nick, and as he handed me a menu, he said softly, "Happy Anniversary, Danielle."

The name on the menu was:

Danielle's Pantry

One might think after five years, this man couldn't surprise me anymore, but he never stopped finding ways. I looked at Nick for an explanation.

"Hotels usually don't operate restaurants. They lease the space to restaurant operators, and I put in a bid for this space. It was the same deal as *Danielle's Kitchen*. The same five partners with you owning sixty percent."

We were served the same meal we had in Atlanta all those years ago, and then we stopped at the 88's for a while before heading for the Hyatt and a glorious night of lovemaking.

A week later, on Saturday evening, was our anniversary party with family and friends. Everyone was there. Our parties were usually held in one of the smaller ballrooms at the Hyatt on SE 17th Street, here in Fort Lauderdale. I was wearing one of my newest Stacy Geer gowns, and Nick had donned a tux for the occasion. But, we didn't go to the Hyatt. Thomas drove us to the hotel where Nick and I had dinner a week earlier. It had opened for business the previous week and was about twenty-five percent occupied.

Before we entered the ballroom, Tony and Brian introduced me to the other members of their team, "Danielle, this is Bruno Thurman, the architect, and Chase James, the Project Manager."

Bruno offered Nick and me a tour. The rooms were beautifully done. The suites were fabulous, and the penthouse suite was out of this world. The lobby and public areas were spectacular. This place was world class elegant and would definitely be the classiest hotel in all of Florida.

"It's fabulous, what are you going to call it?"

Brian answered.

"We don't own it. My company flips properties. We purchase rundown properties, renovate them and sell them at a profit. The only property I ever kept was the house Caitlyn, and I lived in."

That made me sad because I knew Brian and Caitlyn were in the middle of a divorce. Tony said the owner couldn't decide between two names.

I almost fainted when Nick asked me, "Which sounds better? *Danielle's Nest* or the *Palmer House?*

My mind was reeling. Nick kissed me gently. Tony brought

us over to the front desk and told us we had to check in. Everyone would be staying here after the party.

Tony told the desk clerk, "Mr. and Mrs. Amonti will be staying in the '*Palmer Suite.*'"

The desk clerk picked up the phone and asked the General Manager to come to the front. When the door to the Manager's Office opened, I got another surprise. Out walked Dan and Cindy Patrick.

Over the past ten years, Nick had gotten Dan, and my brothers-in-law involved in a number of projects Nick was sure would be profitable. Dan and Cindy were doing very well financially.

"We couldn't turn down Nick's offer. In addition to an outrageous salary, we would be living here at the hotel in a beautiful three-bedroom apartment Nick had designed to my specifications. But, this is only temporary. Once the hotel is fully operational, I'll be taking over management and Dan will be running a new company for Nick. NAS Hospitality Management will take over operational control of all three Danielle properties."

Before we returned to the ballroom, I pulled my husband into a corner and gave him a kiss. One that promised much more later.

Nick told me, "Tony, Brian, Bruno, and Chase have been working on this project for over a year, and when they came to me for financing, and I saw what they intended, I knew I had to buy the hotel for you."

He handed me an envelope with fifty percent of the stock certificates in my name.

"Happy Anniversary, Mrs. Amonti."

Over the years, Nick's anniversary presents to me were always unique and surprising. Because Cauldwell meant so much to me, they included those improvements to the town and even the scholarship fund for the Cauldwell High School graduates. But, this hotel was by far the most lavish present he had ever given me. I thought back to our second anniversary when I was sure *Danielle's Kitchen* was the best present Nick could ever come up with. I was wrong then, and I didn't want to contemplate what was in our future.

When we entered the ballroom, Roger from Atlanta played the same song that he and Nick played for Mike and Agnes so many years ago.

I always loved to dance with my husband, but this song was special. Roger would also play another special song tonight. This one was a present from me to my husband.

When we were all seated, Nick Jr. stood up to offer a toast. Just as he did at our rehearsal dinner, his toast was meant just for me.

"Danielle, five years ago we didn't know you or anything about you, but we saw the effect you had on Dad, and that was reason enough for us to welcome you to our family. Now, we have all gotten to know you and love you, and now we know why this man loves you. Tonight, I can say for all of us, we are so very happy that you are part of our family."

Nick's entire family stood up and toasted me. In the beginning, my biggest fear was that Nick's family wouldn't accept me. I knew how close he was to them, and I wanted to fit in. They quickly allayed those fears, and I have a super relationship with each of them, especially Janice.

Then Nick Jr. turned his attention to his father.

"Dad, I can only repeat what I said to you five years ago. Ya did good, old man."

That got a rousing round of applause from Nick's family. Then to my surprise, my sister Lindsey stood up. She meant her toast strictly for my husband.

"I am older than Danielle and Colleen. I have always felt a need to watch over them and advise them. I was the one who told them, when they were in high school, that Billy Harris was bad news. I was the one who told Colleen she had found a good man in Bob Rogers. I was the one who told Danielle Jack Reynolds couldn't be trusted. And, I was the one who told Danielle Nick Amonti would cause her nothing but unhappiness."

Lindsey had to pause and wipe away a tear from her eye.

"I am so happy I was wrong about that last part. Nick, I'm sorry for the things I said to you before your wedding. I had no idea of the depth of your love for my sister. Thank you so very much for bringing all this happiness into her life."

My entire family stood and toasted Nick.

Then Lindsey said, "To you Danielle, I can only repeat what Nick's son just said to his father. Ya did good, Baby Girl."

That brought cheers from my family and big smiles from Nick and me.

Then Nick rose. He looked much too serious for this occasion. He turned to his family first.

"I will never be able to thank you guys for the kindness and love you showed toward Danielle. Now that you know her, it's easy to love her. But, in the beginning, when all you knew about her was that I said I had met someone and was going to marry her, you took her into your hearts and made her feel a part of our family. I've always loved you guys, but that made me feel so much closer to all of you. It made it so much easier for Danielle and me to start our life together."

Then he turned his attention to Lindsey.

"Lindsey, you were right about me. I was all wrong for this lady. There were so many reasons I couldn't make her happy. I told you, before the wedding, there was nothing you could say that I didn't agree with. It was only the love of this good woman that has made it possible for us to be here today.

"Don't ever stop being the big sister to these ladies. Don't ever stop advising them. You're still batting a thousand, Sis!"

That brought smiles to all three Palmer girls.

Then Nick looked around the hall.

"We all know it hasn't been all peaches and cream for Danielle and me. We've had a couple of dark days in our life together. It is because of the people here that we managed to get through it and for that, we will be eternally grateful. Part of the reason for our happiness today is due to the people in this room. You have all played a role in our lives, and we thank you."

Then, we partied!

Just before the party was about to break up, I gave Nick my surprise. His granddaughters and I had been working on it for a couple of months, and we even flew to Atlanta twice to coordinate with Roger. With Nick's four granddaughters as back up, I moved over to the bandstand and announced, "It's time I tell my husband exactly what I think of him."

I'm no Celine Dion, but I can carry a tune better than Nick

can, and as I sang those beautiful words to him, I moved toward our table. I completed the last line of the song just as I reached him. Tears were streaming down his checks. There was no doubt Nick knew I meant every word. There also was no doubt we would use his bedroom tonight!

After five years, we were more in love than ever. This was still the mostest man I had ever met, and I was sure there was no one better.

If you had told me in less than a year, Nick would ask me for a divorce, I would have said it was a dreadful joke.

But, eight months after our fifth wedding anniversary, sitting at our dining room table, with my two sisters, Dan, Cindy, and my nephew Johnny around us, Nick slid an envelope containing a petition for a Mutual Consent Divorce across to me. And I couldn't wait to sign it and get this man out of my life forever.

I had another love I wanted to be with, and Nick Amonti was in the way.

Chapter 30 - Lost in Time

It all started simply enough. I was in a parking lot, and I couldn't find my car. After wandering around for a while, the Security Guard came over and asked if I was alright.

"I can't find my car, and I don't recognize this parking lot."

He led me over to an Audi.

"Here it is, Ms. Palmer, parked in your reserved spot as usual."

I didn't own an Audi, I couldn't afford such an expensive car on my salary, but he insisted it was mine. After arguing with him for a while, he spoke into his radio, and an older, distinguished gentleman came over.

"Are you okay, Danielle?"

I didn't know this man; how did he know me? I was getting agitated, and finally, the older man told the Security Guard to call 911 for the Paramedics.

I tried to run away from them, but they held me there until the Paramedics arrived. After talking to the older gentleman, the Paramedics spoke to me. They asked very strange questions.

"What is your name?"

"Danielle Palmer."

"Do you know where you are?"

"It's a parking lot, but I don't recognize it."

"Do you know these two gentlemen?"

"No."

"Where do you live?"

"In Tamarac, off Commercial Blvd."

"Do you own a car?"

"Yes."

"Can we see the keys and your driver's license?"

I handed them the keys to my car and my driver's license. They used the keys to open the door of the Audi.

Then they showed me my driver's license was in the name of

Danielle Palmer Amonti, and my address was downtown, not in Tamarac. After a few more questions they decided I had to go to the hospital for an examination.

"You seem confused, and you need medical attention."

I argued with them, and when the police arrived, they convinced me I had to go, or they would put me in handcuffs and force me to go. I really was confused by everything that was happening, and I finally agreed to go to the Emergency Room.

There, I got a complete examination. They paid particular attention to my head, looking for bumps or bruises. Four or five different doctors examined me, and finally, a Dr. Klein came in to talk to me. He didn't examine me, just asked me a lot of questions. They seemed odd at the time, but I did my best to answer them. I wanted to get out of there and get home to Jack.

"Danielle, how old are you?"

"Twenty-five."

"Are you married?"

"No."

"Do you know what today's date is?"

Just as I was answering, another man, an older gentleman, came into the exam room. He looked very concerned and came over and held my hands. He acted strangely as if he knew me well, but I had never seen him before. Dr. Klein took the man out of the room, and they talked for a while. Then Dr. Klein returned alone.

"Danielle, can you give me the names of people close to you, family or friends?"

"My boyfriend, Jack Reynolds and my sisters, Lindsey, and Colleen."

Dr. Klein left and again talked to the man waiting outside. When he returned, he told me, "Your sisters have been notified, but they both live out of town. Jack Reynolds can't be located at the moment. Do you know a man named Daniel Patrick?"

"Yes, Dan is a good friend."

"Mr. Patrick has been notified, and he'll be here in a few minutes. Right now, I want to start an IV and give you something to help you relax."

"I don't want to be doped up!"

"I promise, you won't be. You're very anxious, understandable under the circumstances. This will just take the edge off. You won't lose any of your faculties, I promise."

I allowed the doctor to start the IV, and it did make me less anxious. Dan arrived ten minutes later. I felt so much better with Dan there. I could trust him, and he would take care of me. I asked him why they wouldn't let me see Jack. Before he could answer, Dr. Klein came back into the room to talk to me.

"Danielle, you've had some type of incident. We're not sure if it's medical or psychological, but it has caused you to lose the last fifteen years of your life. We need you to stay here for a while until we can sort this all out."

I couldn't grasp what he was saying.

"I didn't lose anything. I know who I am and what year it is. I don't know what your problem is, and I'm not going to trust a stranger, even if you are a real doctor. I want to see Jack."

Dan tried to calm me.

"Danielle, you haven't seen Jack in more than fifteen years. You moved out of his place six months after you moved in."

That couldn't be right. I asked him who the older man outside the room was.

"His name is Nick Amonti. He's your husband."

"That's impossible. I couldn't be married to such an old man. He has to be at least twice my age."

Again, Dan tried to calm me.

"Danielle, you're not twenty-five years old, you're forty. Look at me, Danielle! Do I look like I'm twenty-seven?"

He was right, he had aged. He wasn't Dan as I knew him. Dr. Klein brought in a newspaper and showed me the date. I was frightened, but it was gradually sinking in what they were saying was true. I agreed to stay in the hospital for a few days. I received a complete medical exam with all of the machines they had there being used to probe me and take note of every part of my body. Dr. Klein visited me four times a day, and we talked. He asked me a lot of questions. I tried to be as cooperative as I could be. He wanted to know exactly where I was in my life at this moment.

"I'm was twenty-five years old. I live with my boyfriend, Jack Reynolds, and I work at Strollman Associates in Fort Lauderdale."

"What is the first thing you remember about the day this started?"

"I was in a strange parking lot and couldn't find my car."

After four days, they released me from the hospital, but I had to promise Dr. Klein I would be in his office every day for a while. He was sure we could find out what happened to me. Little by little I was getting used to the idea I had lost all that time. I didn't work at Strollman any longer, I was not living with Jack, and I was married to a stranger, an old man. Dan and Colleen took me home from the hospital. They brought me to a very nice, large, upscale apartment that would have been way out of my price range.

"This is where you were living when you met your husband, and after you were married, you decided to stay here. You were working for Deltron Motors at the time, and you developed an idea for an LNG/Diesel thing. That made you a star in the corporate world. You quit Deltron, and now you're a Vice President at Peterson Enterprises."

Everything was so strange. I hadn't seen the man they said I was married to since the first day in the Emergency Room, but he was at the apartment when we arrived. It was obvious the man was very upset, but I had no feeling for him. I figured I had to talk to him, so after I settled in, I sat down with him. I made Dan stay close to me while we talked.

"Danielle, I know you don't remember me. But, you are my wife. I will make sure you have the best of care. I had Dr. Klein checked out, and he's a top man in his field. Since you have no recollection of our relationship, I think it best that I move out of the apartment until you do remember. That will relieve some of the stress you are under. I'll keep in touch with Dan and your sisters. If there is anything you need, let them know, and I'll take care of it."

That pleased me immensely. I hadn't thought about it, but now that it had come up the idea of sharing an apartment with this man was absurd. I thanked him as one would thank a storekeeper. He was trying to be nice, but I didn't like him. In fact, I had a great dislike for him, and I didn't know why.

Colleen and Lindsey took turns staying with me. One would stay at the apartment with me for a week, and when she went home to take care of her husband, the other would stay a week. I asked how they could afford all that air travel.

"Nick is taking care of it, and most of it was on his private jet."

Every time they said something nice about the man, I disliked him more. It went on like this for about a month.

Lindsey, Colleen, and Dan gave me a short version of the lost fifteen years. I had left Strollman and went to work for Deltron. I did very well, and now I was a Vice President at Peterson Enterprises.

"You've been married to Nick Amonti almost six years. He is a very wealthy and powerful man, and he loves you passionately. Because of some work he had done for the government years ago, he had a connection to two Mafia Dons, but he wasn't one of them. You also have a link to these two men because of a big favor you did for them, and you are considered gold in their eyes."

Dan came over early every day and stayed with me until late in the evening. I asked Dan if he wasn't going to be fired for missing so much work.

"Danielle, I work for you. I manage the three properties you own."

That was another shock, but everything was so strange, I didn't question it. After the first week, Dan started bringing his wife over. I was glad he had found someone special. His wife, Cindy, seemed very friendly toward me, and when I asked Dan about it, he explained after his engagement, we became very close.

"You and Nick stood up for us at our wedding."

That really surprised me. Why would Dan ask Nick Amonti to be his Best Man, and why would Cindy want me as her Matron of Honor. I knew there was so much I didn't know about the years I was missing, but this seemed very strange. I wasn't sure I wanted to know why my best friend was so close to that man.

I put it out of my mind and tried to concentrate on my situation. Life was taking on something of a routine. Nick Amonti never came around or called. I saw Dr. Klein three times a week, I was physically okay, and I began to think about my future. Most of all, I wanted to see Jack.

One day, while Colleen was out shopping and before Dan

arrived, I called the number of the apartment Jack, and I shared. The phone had been disconnected. I was still having a difficult time remembering it was fifteen years later than I felt. I tried Strollman, and I got through to him. He was surprised to hear from me. I told him what had happened to me, and I wanted to see him.

"I want to see you too, Danielle, but I have an important business dinner tonight. I can get out of work early and see you before that. I've missed you!"

I gave him the address of the apartment, and he said he'd be here by three. That made me very happy. Jack had been on my mind since all this started. Dan arrived about ten o'clock.

"I saw Nick this morning. He's coming over this afternoon to talk to you."

"I won't be here, and I don't care if I ever speak to Nick Amonti again."

Dan seemed angry but tried not to show it. What is it with these people? Not only Dan but my family too. What kind of hold does this man have on them that they get annoyed when I say I don't want to be around him?

"Why won't you be here?"

"I have a date with Jack."

It was apparent Dan was not pleased.

"I know you don't like Jack, never liked him, but that's no reason for me not to see him."

Dan came over to me and wrapped his arms around me.

"Danielle, am I your friend? Do you trust me?"

"Yes Dan," I answered sincerely, "You're probably the best friend I've ever had."

"Danielle, you believe we have been friends for at least three years, but the truth is, we have been friends for almost twenty years. You are closer to me than family."

"Yes Dan, you have always been my best friend, and I appreciate it."

"Then, do your old friend one favor, please."

"Anything, Dan, anything for you."

"Put off your meeting with Jack for twenty-four hours. Just one day. You haven't seen him in fifteen years; one more day can't hurt."

"Why?"

"As a special favor to an old friend."

I didn't know why it was so important to Dan I put off my meeting with Jack, but I agreed. I called Jack and told him I would have to put off our date.

"But, that's good, because now you won't have to rush off to that business dinner. We'll have more time together."

Jack was annoyed but agreed to meet me the following day instead.

"But it will still have to be in the afternoon. I'm scheduled to have dinner with another client tomorrow."

I didn't give it too much thought. Jack probably had advanced at Strollman in the last fifteen years, and he had a lot more responsibility. Around noon, Lindsey showed up. She wasn't scheduled to be here for a couple of days, and I was surprised. Dan seemed to expect her.

"What brings you to Florida days earlier than expected?"

"Nick has something important to say, and he wanted everyone here."

Now I was really annoyed.

"What right has he to tell you what to do and when to do it?"

"It's not an order, Danielle, it was a suggestion. He has something important to say, and he thought we'd all want to be present."

That didn't help my mood at all.

At one o'clock the phone rang. Colleen answered it and told Lindsey it was her grandson.

"Grandson, Anna Lee is here with the baby?"

Lindsey brought me up to date.

"Johnny isn't a baby anymore. Robbie was killed while serving in the Navy and he was a hero. Anna Lee felt disappointed about his being a hero. Robbie had told her he was a medic and would never hurt anyone. Nick had gotten some information about Robbie and made Anna Lee feel better. He also got Johnny into a program that fixed his stuttering problem."

The more I heard about this man, the more I disliked him. We weren't even married yet, and he was sticking his nose into my family's business.

Lindsey also told me Johnny, and I had a very special relationship. She said since the day Johnny was born, we were extremely close. He was the only one who was allowed to refer to me by anything but my given name. I had always been known as Danielle.

In Cauldwell, my friends and classmates tried to call me Ellie or Dannie, but I always insisted my name was Danielle, and I wouldn't answer to anything else. Except for Colleen who sometimes called me Sis and Lindsey who occasionally called me Baby Girl, Johnny was the only person who was allowed to refer to me by anything other than my name. Johnny sometimes called me Aunt Sissy, and I not only allowed it, but I melted every time he used it, and he used it to his advantage.

Colleen added whenever Johnny wanted something he would give me his sweet little boy look and say, "Please, Aunt Sissy!" and I would always give in. I couldn't wait to meet my nephew.

When Johnny arrived, I was surprised. I expected a little boy. But, Johnny was a good looking young man, all decked out in a Naval Midshipman's uniform. Everyone got hugs, including Uncle Dan and Aunt Cindy, but the best one was for me. I could actually feel the special affection he had for me, and I immediately felt something special toward him.

"Are you ready to go?"

"Go where?"

Johnny laughed and said this was no time for fooling around.

"United States Navy Ships wait for no one!"

Lindsey took Johnny into the bedroom and explained what was going on. He had been at sea for over a month and hadn't heard about my condition. When they came out of the bedroom, Johnny was very sad. He looked directly at me

"Don't worry Aunt Danielle, Uncle Nick will get you better!"

Even Johnny, I thought. What kind of spell does this man have over everyone I care about? Now, I didn't dislike him, now I hated him!

At three o'clock the intercom buzzed, and Andy announced Mr. Amonti was in the lobby. Colleen told Andy to send him up. She seemed very sad.

"The man feels he has to be announced to enter his own home."

As far as I was concerned, if this was his home, I'd move out, and he could have it. I knew I could move in with Jack just as soon as we had a chance to talk.

And then I would be through with Nick Amonti's interference in my life.

When Nick came into the apartment, I was in an awful mood. I didn't want to see him. I hated the way my family and friends catered to him. I hated him for being him.

How did he ever get me to agree to marry him?

Nick greeted everyone and was very apologetic to Johnny. As part of his Academy work, Johnny was assigned to a ship to gain practical experience. It seems Nick, and I were scheduled to board Johnny's ship and sail to Norfolk, Virginia with him. It was something the Navy called a Tiger Cruise.

Well, that wasn't going to happen!

After the greetings were over, Nick sat at the dining room table and asked me to sit opposite him. I obliged only so we could get this over with. Everyone else sat down around us, and when we were all settled, Nick started his speech.

"I've been talking to Dr. Klein."

That really got me angry, and I didn't care who knew it.

"Who gave you the right."

"Technically I am still your husband. I have the legal right and moral obligation."

I was ready to give him an earful, but Lindsey stopped me and suggested we just listen to what he had to say. I must admit he looked sad and haggard, but I had no sympathy for him. He waited until I calmed down before he went on.

"Dr. Klein is convinced there is less than a five percent chance you will ever regain your memory. He said whatever has caused this is buried so deep, he can't get to it. He thinks your condition is permanent, and the therapy from now on will be geared toward helping you cope with your new environment."

He put a large manila envelope on the table between us.

"Danielle, it is clear that you don't want to try to find what we had before this happened. I understand. I've always felt the unique set of experiences that brought us together could never be duplicated. I've asked my attorney to prepare divorce papers for us. It will be a Special Circumstances Divorce. There will be no blame, no responsibility. It will be clean and simple. Please have an attorney look over these papers and if he's satisfied, sign them and send them to my lawyer. If he has any questions, my lawyer can answer them. I'm sure Dan can find you a good attorney."

He looked into my eyes.

"If there's no problem on your end, the divorce can be final within thirty days. I won't give you any trouble on any issue you might have, but I do want to keep my NAS Financial Group stock for my children. I have never put your name on it, and I would like to keep the BBJ, and I'd like your permission to keep the name and caricature on her. You'll have to sign off on both of those. Other than that, I have no other issues."

There were objections all around. Johnny complained loudest.

"You can't do this Uncle Nick!"

"It's the only thing I can do."

I took the envelope and got up from the table.

"I'll have an attorney look these over first thing tomorrow."

And I went into the bedroom without another word. As soon as I was gone, they all started in on Nick. Pleading, practically begging him not to do this. I had left the bedroom door partway open so I could hear what was being said. Nick managed to quiet everyone down.

"It's the only fair thing I can do. It's ninety-five percent sure Danielle will never recover. Dr. Klein is very sure with a little therapy she can lead a normal life. I don't want her looking over her shoulder wondering when I'll come out of the woodwork to bother her or interrupt her new life. This way, she can be happy again, maybe meet someone special, maybe fall in love again."

Johnny was still adamant.

"She'll never meet anyone as good as you. No one could make her as happy as you do."

"DID, Johnny! I did make her happy. That's gone. I made her happy because she loved me. Your Aunt Danielle will never love me again, and, therefore, I can never make her happy again."

Colleen asked, "But what if she does get better?"

Dan answered the question.

"She'll know where to find him, and she'll know what to say to him."

Lindsey added, "She'll know he'll be waiting for her."

I stayed in the bedroom until I was sure Nick was gone. When I came out, everyone was still around the dining room table. I smiled.

"Well, I guess this means there is no reason I can't see Jack tomorrow!"

Lindsey went ballistic. I had never seen her so angry.

"Baby Girl, are you completely crazy or just stupid? Why would you ever consider having anything to do with that cheating no good bastard?"

I wasn't going to be intimidated. I yelled right back at her.

"Don't start that all over again. I know none of you liked him, but it's my life, and I'll see whoever I choose."

Dan stayed quiet, but Colleen joined in the argument.

"WHY?" she shouted, "Why would you want to see the guy who cheated on you with your best girlfriend and broke your heart?"

"That's bull. You're just trying to get me to stay with that old man. I don't know what kind of hold he has over you. I'm your sister, I'm family, why aren't you on my side?"

Dan shouted at my sisters.

"That's enough! Let's just settle down and talk about all of this."

Colleen looked at Dan. She was wide-eyed.

"Dan, how could you? How could you allow her to see that jerk? After what he did to her. He broke her heart, and you were the one who had to put her back together again. You saw what he did to her! How could you let her go through it again?"

"He didn't do anything to me. It was you. You drove him away from me. Because you didn't, like him."

Lindsey shook her head.

"Danielle, no one drove him away from you. You came home one day unexpectedly and found him and Nancy Cummings in bed together."

Dan shouted at them, again.

"Lindsey, Colleen, that's enough, not now, please!"

I looked at Dan.

"Tell them. Tell them it's not true."

Dan glanced at me for a moment and then turned his gaze toward the floor. He couldn't look at me. I yelled at my two sisters.

"No, no, no, it's a lie; it has to be a lie! You don't care about me! You just want me to be with that old man. You're all on his side."

With that, I ran into my bedroom and slammed the door. I threw myself on the bed and wept. I didn't want to believe what they were saying. I was never sure of Jack's feelings for me, but when he asked me to move in with him, I jumped at the chance. But cheat on me? I couldn't allow myself to believe that!

Chapter 31 - Memories

I don't know how long I was in there before there was a gentle knock on the bedroom door.

"Go away. Leave me alone!"

But they didn't go away. The door opened, someone came into the room and gently closed the door. I felt the bed move as whoever it was sat on the edge of the bed.

"It's me, Aunt Danielle."

"Go away, Johnny, I want to be alone."

"You'll never be alone, Aunt Danielle, you have your family."

That started the tears flowing again, and Johnny held my hand and waited for them to stop before he said anything else.

"We're not on his side, Aunt Danielle. We're family, we're all on your side. Even Uncle Dan is family. Everyone is on your side."

"It sure doesn't sound that way."

Then, I found out my young nephew Johnny wasn't a boy, he was a man, a sensitive and caring man. And I could understand the special feelings I was told I had for him.

"Aunt Danielle, you probably don't remember how much I love you. You were always there for Mama and me. Even more than Grandma. When Daddy didn't come home, you were the one who helped Mama deal with it. You were always my favorite. That's why I was so happy when you and Uncle Nick got together. I knew he would be good to you and take care of you."

I sat up next to him on the edge of the bed.

"Johnny, it's so very complicated."

"Aunt Danielle, believe me, we **are** on your side. You don't see it because you don't remember."

"Remember what?"

He hesitated before he answered.

"How much you loved that man. He was your entire life."

He hesitated again, looked at me with sincere eyes, and went on.

"Aunt Danielle, you never wanted to be away from him. In your entire life, you were never as happy as you were the last six years."

"Johnny, I don't even know the man. I have no feeling for him at all."

"I know Aunt Danielle. But if you've lost fifteen years as Grandma said, then you probably don't remember me either, and I swear to you our relationship was very special."

I started to say something, but he put up his hand to stop me.

"Aunt Danielle, we all love you. All we want is for you to be happy. In case the doctor is wrong, we don't want you to do something you'll regret."

He paused again and continued.

"Uncle Nick made you happy because you loved him. You loved him with a passion few people know. If you can't get that love with him back, then we want you to be as happy as you can be, but we know you will never be as happy as you were with Uncle Nick. If you remembered him even a little bit, you could never treat him the way you do. If you do get your memory back, you'll want to be with him again, and we don't want you to do anything to spoil that."

"If I loved him so much and he made me so happy, why am I here like this?"

"I don't know!"

I looked at my young, handsome nephew and I could feel his love for me. I could also see the sincerity in his eyes. He believed what he was telling me, but I still couldn't imagine myself in love with that old man. I had to tell him something to make him understand.

"Johnny, it's obvious everyone likes Nick, maybe even loves him. He's probably a good man. I can accept the fact this man loved the woman he was married to, and maybe she loved him. Maybe even loved him as much as you say she did. But, I'm not that woman. I don't know the man. I have no feeling for him. I can't believe I could love a man that much and not have any feeling for him at all. I can't take everyone else's word that I loved him, I have to feel it myself, I have to know it. I have to understand it, see it for myself."

Johnny looked at me thoughtfully.

"Aunt Danielle, would you do a favor for me, please?"

"What kind of favor?"

He answered in a firm, sure voice.

"Would you let me show you something? It will only take five minutes, maybe less. Please, Aunt Danielle, it's important, and I think you'll understand why you believe that we're on his side."

"Johnny, nothing will help this situation, I don't remember."

His reply was pleading.

"Please, Aunt Sissy, five minutes, that's all I ask, please."

I looked at my handsome nephew.

"That's not fair Johnny, I've been told I never could refuse you anything when you call me Aunt Sissy."

Johnny smiled for the first time since he heard the news. He looked at me with a gleam in his eye.

"I know that Aunt Danielle, I've known it since I was a little boy!"

That earned him a punch in the arm.

"You're a real con artist, aren't you?"

"A guy has to use what's available to him."

That made me laugh, and for the first time since all this started, I felt sane. It was obvious why he was always so special to me. It was also obvious he was hurting, so I told him I would look at what he wanted to show me, but I wanted to talk to Dan first. Before he left, Johnny made me promise I would look at what he wanted to show me, and then he sent Dan in.

Dan was miserable, and I could see the concern for me in his eyes. He sat next to me on the bed.

"Dan, I've always trusted you. You have to be totally honest with me now. I need that more than anything."

"I've always been totally honest with you, Danielle. That's why we've remained friends all these years."

"Please, Dan. Tell me the truth about Jack!"

"Danielle, it will be better it you waited. You have enough to think about right now. The divorce. Starting a new life. Jack can wait. That's why I asked you to put off your meeting."

"Please, Dan. I have to know the truth."

He thought about it for a minute and gave in. What he told me turned my current world upside down.

"I always felt partly responsible for what happened. I advised you to leave the company you, and I worked for and take the job with Strollman Brothers. It was a step up in your career. That's where you met Jack. He was very handsome and charming. He had all the girls crazy about him, even though he was a jerk. But the girls didn't care. A smile from Jack made their day. When Jack came after you, you were elated. With all the girls he had available, he picked you to move in with him."

Dan paused, trying to decide how far to go.

"Jack only did that because you were so gullible. Everyone knew he was a playboy and a bastard, but you refused to see it. I never believed you ever loved Jack. At that time of your life, you were a sweet, shy country girl from South Georgia and you didn't have a lot of self-confidence."

I could tell Dan was picking his words carefully.

"Jack was a salesman at Strollman and would come into the office in the morning and then say he had a client meeting and disappear for the rest of the day. He brought in just enough orders to keep from getting fired. Everyone but you knew his afternoons were spent cruising for women.

"One day, you had a business dinner scheduled with Mr. Strollman and a client. You were going because you had prepared the official proposal that was going to be presented to the client and you could explain it best.

"Jack knew you wouldn't be home until eight or nine o'clock that night. While you were making copies of the proposal for everyone, there was a problem with the copy machine, and you got black carbon all over your skirt. It wouldn't brush out, and Mr. Strollman told you to go home, change and meet them at the restaurant."

Dan paused again. He looked at me for a long time.

"Everything, Dan. I need to know everything before I can think about a new life."

"You called me around five o'clock, crying and out of control. You told me you were at some diner near my apartment. I left my office and went right over. You were a mess, completely distraught, crying. You told me when you got to the apartment everything was quiet as if no one was home. Jack was supposed to be out with a client. When you walked into the bedroom to change your skirt, you found Jack and Nancy Cummings naked and sweaty in bed together. It was apparent they had just finished having sex.

"I was ready to kill Jack, but you wouldn't let me. It took months for you to get over the hurt. You quit your job at Strollman, so you wouldn't have to face Jack and your co-workers. Everyone in the company knew what had happened and had sympathy for you, but Jack thought it was a hoot!"

I listened quietly to Dan's story and believed him completely. Now, from a distance, I could see it all. Jack was beautiful and charming. I did fall under his spell, but now I was sure Dan was right, I never did love him, not real love. Then, Dan said something else, and it surprised me.

"Every dark cloud has a silver lining!"

"What silver lining?"

"The incident with Jack that day changed you. You became more aware of yourself. You became self-assured, having more confidence in yourself and your abilities than I had ever seen in you before. You got a job at Deltron Motors and developed a device that made you a rising star in the corporate world. You went from a simple, sweet country girl to an elegant, self-assured, woman, and that's the woman that had the guts to seduce Nick Amonti."

I smacked him on the arm.

"This is not the time to tease me."

Dan smiled.

"It's the truth, you seduced him, and when he hesitated, you went even further."

I looked at him and was pretty sure he wasn't lying to me, but I didn't want to hear anything about that man. While I was looking into his eyes, I had to ask.

"Dan, why didn't we ever …?"

"You mean get together, romantically?"

I nodded my head. Dan smiled.

"We did!"

"Don't tease me, please."

"I'm not teasing."

"What happened?"

"It's a long story."

"Since I don't have a date with Jack this afternoon, I have time."

Dan thought about it for a minute.

"When we first met, I was attracted to you. We both had a thing about interoffice relationships, so I never did anything about it. When you moved to Strollman, I thought I might give it a shot. But before I had a chance to make a move, Jack came into your life. After you found Jack and Nancy together, you moved in with me. That was not the right time for you, and I went out of my way to avoid any romantic or intimate contact."

That sounded just like the Dan I knew.

"When you started working for Deltron, you were a changed person. You put Jack behind you and seemed to be moving on. You started to date again, and that's when I told you I how much I was interested. We fell into an exclusive relationship for a while. It was very intimate, but we both felt something was missing. We had a serious talk about it and mutually decided that as much as we liked each other, even loved each other, we weren't in love. We began to see other people. We still dated, but not exclusively and eventually the sex stopped, and we evolved into best friends. And that's the way it has been ever since."

"Does Cindy know?"

"There is nothing in my life that Cindy doesn't know. We learned that lesson from you and Nick. We decided if two people can be completely open and honest with each other and be as much in love as you two were, it must be the right thing to do, so that's how it is with us."

"Does that mean Nick knows?"

"Of course, he knows. You told him. That's one of the reasons he and I are such good friends and the primary reason that Cindy and I are together."

"I don't understand."

"Cindy wasn't my wife at the time, just a girlfriend. I wanted more, but I wasn't sure how she felt. The morning of your wedding, Nick and I had a talk before you got to the church. Nick suggested I tell her and after the reception I did.

Cindy said she wanted the same thing, but if she hadn't danced with Nick at your wedding reception, she might have said no."

"I still don't understand."

"Do you really want to know?"

"Yes!"

"It would be better to hear it from Cindy. You and Cindy have gotten very close ever since that day. Are you sure you really want to know?"

After thinking about it, I nodded. Maybe I'd understand why everyone liked this man.

Dan asked Cindy to join us. Cindy came into the bedroom and sat next to Dan. Talking across him, she told me the entire story about her jealousy toward me and how unsure she was about Dan's feelings for me.

"It was apparent Dan had special feelings for you. I didn't understand why you two hadn't gotten together, or maybe you had, and Dan was still carrying a torch for you. I hoped by marrying Nick, Dan would be convinced to move on, but I was also worried he picked me on the rebound. So, I wasn't sure what I was going to do about him.

Cindy smiled. Not a great smile. More of a friendly smile.

"It was obvious there wasn't a lot of time for you to dance at your wedding reception and the only person you danced with other than Nick, and the man who gave you away, was Dan, and you had asked him. When you asked Dan to dance, Nick asked me. I didn't want to, but he was insistent. I didn't want to cause a scene, so I danced with him. As we were walking to the dance floor, I got a glimpse of you and Dan. You had your arms around his neck, and you two were very cozy."

Cindy looked at Dan, and he nodded.

"It's true. You even gave me a kiss on the cheek."

Cindy's smile got brighter.

"As soon as we started dancing, Nick asked if I were worried about Dan and his wife. Before I had a chance to answer, he told me don't be. I really didn't want to talk to him about his wife and my boyfriend, but he has a way of making you listen to him. He's always so sincere and honest. Nick told me to take a good look at them.

""It's obvious neither one of them lacked friends and lovers. Imagine them when they met. Dan is a good-looking guy, and probably had as many girls after him as he could deal with, and you know Danielle never had a problem attracting men. Think fifteen or twenty years. Both of them fresh out of college, new job, strange city, no friends, and no family available. They worked for the same company and became friends. They may have had an intimate relationship along the way, but something happened, and it cemented their relationship forever. They both realized having a true, trusted, best friend was more important at the time than having another temporary lover. And that's the way it's been ever since, and I hope it will remain that way.""

Again, she paused. She looked at her husband before she continued.

"I glanced over at Dan and asked Nick if he wasn't just a little bit jealous. Nick said that at this point in their relationship, Dan has too much respect for you to ever make a pass at you, and both Dan and Nick knew if he ever did, it would break your heart. Nick also said marrying him would probably cause you some pain, and you probably wouldn't tell him about it. He said he was glad you had such a close friend to confide in if things got rough, and he also told me he had said the exact same thing to Dan that morning in the back of the church."

Dan nodded. Cindy continued.

"I asked Nick if he knew what had cemented the relationship so tightly. Nick said he wasn't absolutely sure, but he had an opinion. He told me, "Danielle and I have no secrets, but I'm not sure if she ever actually thought about it. Dan was your best friend, and you never actually examined the reasons. I believe when Danielle had a very devastating breakup with a lousy guy, Dan was there to help her through it. Nick said it would have been easy for Dan to take advantage of the situation, but he knew it would be short term, and then you never could be friends again. Their relationship would be over, and he felt their relationship was more important to him than a roll in the hay with you. Then Nick said, "I know my wife, Cindy. I'll bet right now, she's telling Dan thanks for being one of the good guys in her life.""

Cindy looked directly at me before finishing her story.

"When the four of us got back to the table, Dan had your

lipstick on his check. Nick wiped it off and said the shade looked familiar. You told him it was your wedding day, and you could kiss anyone you wanted. Nick laughed at that. I looked at the three of you and knew that everything Nick said was true.

"Later the evening, when Dan said he wanted to see how far our relationship could go, I agreed."

"If you think about it Danielle, he had us figured out perfectly. At that point in our lives, we both needed a really good friend and not just another temporary lover. Once we figured out that a romantic relationship wasn't in the cards for us, that's the relationship we developed. And, your breakup with Jack was probably the thing that cemented us together like this forever. He had the other part figured out too. I do have too much respect for you and our relationship to ever make a pass at you, and I do believe if I ever did, it would break your heart!"

"You really like him, don't you?" I asked Cindy.

"I love him! It's easy to love that man., I'm sure everyone here loves him."

Dan added his thoughts.

"But, we understand why you don't. You don't know him or anything about him. He's a stranger to you, an old stranger. But the other Danielle loved that man totally and completely."

"Tell me, please. I want to know why that man loved her and how she could love him."

"In time. He's out of your life now, and although I hate to admit it, he's probably right, it's the only way you can have a full and happy life. Nick doesn't believe the person you are now could ever love him like the other Danielle did and he doesn't want you to hesitate moving on with your new life because of what you once had with him."

After talking for a while, the three of us headed back out to the living room. Dan suggested we look over the divorce papers, and everyone went into the dining room and sat around the table. I noticed Johnny sitting alone on the couch, and I told the group I would join them in a minute. I went over to my nephew.

"I'm ready to see what you wanted to show me."

"It's a video, and it will only take five minutes, but you have to promise to watch it all, or it won't mean anything to you."

I promised, and he hit the Play button on the DVD player.

He had cued up the video to the place he wanted me to see. There were four women lined up, all between the ages of twenty to thirty.

"Those ladies are Uncle Nick's granddaughters."

Then another woman walked into the scene. It was obviously me, but I couldn't believe what I was looking at. This was a beautiful, elegant woman wearing a gorgeous gown that must have cost a fortune. The scene widened, and I could see they were on a bandstand, and she had a microphone in her hand. As I watched this unfold, Johnny explained.

"This was taken at your fifth wedding anniversary party at Danielle's Nest Hotel, and everyone you and Uncle Nick loved were there."

That elegant lady nodded her head, and a piano started to play, and this woman began to sing. The words were beautiful, and you could see how much she meant every word. The four other women were her backup singers, and as she sang, she walked over to the table where Nick Amonti was sitting. She reached him just as she got to the last line of the song. The piano stopped and looking right into his eyes, I heard her say to this man, "I'm everything I am because YOU love me!"

At that very point, the camera closed in on a close up of the lady's face, and Johnny paused the video.

"This is what I wanted you to see, Aunt Danielle. Look into her eyes and tell me what you see!"

My tears were flowing so fast I had a difficult time focusing, but his point was clear. I saw love in those eyes. Deep, undying love for that man.

Then Johnny ran the video forward and paused on a close-up of the man's face. I saw the same emotion in his eyes, despite the tears that were streaming down his checks.

Chapter 32 – The Divorce

I finally understood why everyone I knew loved this man. The emotion that passed between these two people was undeniable. As much as that man loved that lady, he was willing to walk out of her life, so she could be happy again. What must it feel like to be loved that deeply? I couldn't look at it any longer. I buried my face in Johnny's chest and cried. Johnny wrapped his arms around me and cooed.

"It's okay Aunt Sissy, we know you don't feel that way about Uncle Nick now. We understand. But, you have to understand why we love him. He was good to you, he made you happy, and he made you love him that much. And even though you can't love him anymore, we just wish you weren't mad at him. He really does love you."

It took some time, but I finally got myself under some kind of control. I apologized to Johnny for getting my makeup and my tears all over his white uniform.

"That's okay, Aunt Sissy, my Navy Whites are available for you to cry on anytime you need them."

I do love that boy.

The rest of the crew had come into the living room when they heard the video. There were tears evident on other faces besides mine. After I had gained control of myself, we all went back into the dining room and sat around the table.

The envelope with the divorce papers was still on the table. Dan said I should make a decision on the terms of the divorce and we all sat around the table while Dan took out the legal papers and told us what they said. I was trying to concentrate, but my thoughts were back on that video. I had absolutely no feeling for that man. But I was so very jealous of that woman!

"It's basically what Nick told you. It will be a no-fault divorce based on special circumstances. Both parties will be held blameless."

Dan read from the document:

"The court having been informed and having verified the claim, that for reasons which could not be foreseen, it has become desirable for Nicholas J. Amonti, Sr. and Danielle Grace Palmer Amonti to dissolve their marriage. Neither party having claimed any wrongdoing by the other and both parties agreeing to the settlement of assets as described herein, the court is inclined to grant the requested divorce for reasons of Special Circumstances.

"It's clean and simple. No blame, no wrongdoing, no other claims. If you agree to the terms of the settlement, this can be finalized within the month."

Then, he moved on to the settlement.

"Nick gets to keep his stock in NAS Financial Group, his Bequest Account, the Boeing Business Jet, his Audi and one-half of the money contained in the account managed by Tyler Brokerage Partners.

"You get to keep your Audi, this apartment, your Bequest Account and one-half of the money held in the account managed by Tyler Brokerage Partners. You also give up the right to demand the name Danielle and the caricature painted on the nose of the BBJ be removed."

After watching the video, I was surprised by the terms of the settlement.

"I get a car, this apartment, and some money, and he gets to keep an airplane and his company? This is the man who loves me so much?"

"It's not that simple. You were always aware he intended his share of NAS Financial Group would go to his kids. You never had a problem with that. The airplane, he had when he met you. It's still owned partly by the finance company, and it's very expensive to operate. It's leased to NAS Aviation and is part of his Bequest Account. You really don't need that kind of expense."

"What's with the name and caricature?"

Johnny took me by the hand and brought me into Nick's den. It was actually an alcove off the living room. There was a desk and some office equipment and two walls full of pictures. I had seen the pictures as I moved around the apartment, but I never paid any attention to them.

Johnny pointed out a collage of photos of a big airplane with the letters NAS painted on the tail. Nick and I were in most of the images. In one, we were standing by the front wheels of the plane pointing at something painted on the nose. Above that picture was one of what we were pointing to. In beautiful script was painted, *Danielle* and a caricature of a sexy lady in a cheesecake pose.

"Who's the girl?"

"It's you, Aunt Danielle."

"I'd never wear an outfit like that, and I certainly wouldn't pose like that for anyone," I bellowed.

"Oh, it's you alright, Baby Girl," Lindsey said, "and you did wear that outfit twice, no, three times. That's the outfit you used to seduce Nick with!"

"That's the second time I've been told I seduced him. Somebody better tell me what you're talking about. I'd never seduce anyone, and definitely not in that outfit."

"Later," Dan said, "Let's finish this up first."

"Wait, Dan! If he wants to keep my name and that picture on his airplane, I want to know why it's there."

Colleen answered.

"Nick had that done for your First Anniversary. He got you to pose for him here in the apartment and he had an artist do the painting from the picture. It was a surprise."

"I actually allowed him to take a picture of me like that."

"It's right here in his scrapbook, Sis. Nick kept a scrapbook of memorable moments you two shared. It contains newspaper articles of the Cauldwell Industries deal, the LNG/Diesel thing you did at Deltron, a copy of your contract with Peterson, and other stuff that marked special moments in your life together. He also kept some special pictures in there, not only your vamp outfit but also your sunrise nightie among others. There wasn't much you wouldn't do for that man if he asked you!"

I wasn't sure I wanted to hear any more. Then, suddenly, Colleen started to cry. Johnny went over to her and wrapped his arms around her.

"What's the matter, Aunt Colleen?"

"It's not here. He must have taken it with him. He must truly believe he's never going to see you again!"

I actually felt very sorry for that man. I still had no personal feelings for him, but the thought of how much he loved this woman, and what it must take to walk away from her, so she could have a good life without him, made me very sad and very jealous of that woman.

Dan broke in, "Okay, let's finish this."

Back into the dining room, we all went, and Dan continued explaining what I would get and what was expected of me. I had no complaints. I would be free to pursue a new life, and that man, as good as everyone thought he was, would be out of my life forever. Colleen suggested we call her husband, Bob.

"He handles most of your financial affairs, and he could explain the financial aspects of the settlement and tell you how much you would wind up with."

After talking to him for a few moments, she put her cell phone on the table and pressed the speaker button. I didn't remember Bob, but he had been to the apartment with Colleen over the past month, and my sister seemed very happy with him. After a few pleasantries, and Bob's hope I would be alright in time, he told us where I stood financially.

"Nick had been talking to me for about a week, setting everything up. Your Bequest Account has always been in your name only. Nick never had any access to it.

"It contains your stock in Cauldwell Industries, the Deltron stock Nick bought while he was working there, your 401K account you transferred when you left Deltron and your entire five-year salary from Peterson Enterprises. Nick set all this up during the two weeks before your wedding.

"Because Nick's children were in NAS from the beginning and were mostly responsible for its success, he wants his shares of NAS Financial Group to go to them.

"You also own sixty percent of two restaurants and fifty percent of a hotel, but those three properties are mortgaged. All three are profitable, and the mortgages are at a very low-interest-rate because NAS Financial Group guaranteed the loans."

"How much money is in each account?"

"Ethically, I can't tell you how much is in Nick's Bequest Account and I can't tell Nick how much is in yours. I'm sure you both were aware of what was in each account because you two never kept anything from each other. I'm not sure exactly how much is in the Living Account because that's handled by another broker. But I can give you an estimate based on the last time Nick, and I talked about it. Nick kept me pretty much updated on his complete financial picture. Nick is closing the Living Account with Tyler and transferring half the money into his Bequest Account and half into yours.

"Since both of you will be single, there was no reason to have separate bequest and living accounts. I can't give you an exact number tonight because everything changes daily, and I'm not sure exactly how much is in the Living Account."

"Can you give me a best guess?"

"Based on everything I know for sure, and some assumptions, I can give you a conservative estimate. You will probably wind up with somewhere between three to five hundred."

I didn't understand. According to what everyone had been telling me about this wonderful man, who was so rich, I couldn't believe he was offering me less than five hundred thousand dollars in total assets. I really didn't want his money, but it didn't fit with the picture everyone was painting of this man.

What was I missing here?

Thinking out loud, I said, "He gets to keep his car, an airplane, and his company, and I get a car, an apartment, and some money. That doesn't sound anything like the man you all have been describing to me. By giving me less than five hundred thousand dollars, he gets me out of his life forever?"

I could hear anger in Bob's voice when he replied to my question.

"Wrong on three accounts, Danielle. In the first place, he's not getting you out of his life. He's giving you the freedom to lead a happy and fulfilling life on your own without his shadow constantly hanging over you. Right now, he's in meetings with his kids. He's turning the entire NAS operation over to them and leaving Florida for good. He doesn't want to take the chance you will run into him. Believe me, Danielle; you will never be out of his life! Once you start a new life, Nick wants you to look toward the future, not the past. He's doing everything he can to stay out of your way."

Before I had a chance to say I was sorry, Bob went on.

"Danielle, he's not giving you anything. Everything but the NAS stock and the Bequest Accounts is in both names. Nick and

I spent weeks before your wedding going over everything and setting everything up. Two days before you married him, he transferred everything he had, except his NAS stock and the BBJ into both names, either/or. Right now, you have access to it all. He's asking you to give him back a part of what he has given you."

"Bob, I'm sorry. I really didn't mean it. It's just all so confusing."

"I know honey, I can't imagine how tough it must be for you. You know I'm with you, Danielle, we all are."

"So, I'm finding out."

"Hang in there, honey, it will work out. This will all be over in less than a month, and then you can go on and build a new life. Many people care for you deeply, and they will be there for you."

"Thanks, Bob, I'm trying to sort it all out."

"While you're sorting everything out, here's one more thing you have to think about. You're not going to wind up with three to five hundred thousand dollars. Your five-year salary from Peterson is worth almost more than double that. Add to that the money transferred from your 401K with Deltron and your Deltron and Cauldwell stock, plus half of the Living Account, and the stock in Danielle's Kitchen, Danielle's Pantry and Danielle's' Nest. When this is finalized, you'll have approximately three to five hundred million dollars in your account!"

"You're joking!

"No, Danielle, I'm not. You are a very wealthy lady, and you will continue to be a very wealthy woman when all this is done with."

I couldn't get my head around it. I had a feeling like this had all happened before. Someone told me I was filthy rich, and I couldn't comprehend what that meant. I lost it for a moment and drifted away somewhere, and when I came back, Dan was looking at me questioningly.

"You okay?"

"I'm not sure. It's like I've lived through this moment before. Someone told me how much money I had access to, and I couldn't understand what they were saying."

I thanked Bob, and I apologized again for my flippant remark. I told him I loved him and appreciated he would be there for me. Colleen took the phone and talked to him for a few minutes, and when she was through, she sat down at the table with the others.

"Sis, I don't know if this means anything, but you told me while you were on your honeymoon, Nick told you about your financial situation. You said you didn't care that you would trust him to take care of all financial matters, but he insisted you understand where you stood, so you listened to him."

After looking at Dan and getting a nod, she continued.

"You said he told you about the three accounts and the NAS stock and when he told you how much you were worth you couldn't get your head around it, and for a minute, you went all dreamy, just like you did when Bob told you it was millions and not thousands."

Colleen looked around the table.

"I think you had a flashback moment or rather a flash forward moment. You remembered something."

Dan looked at me.

"What do you think, a memory?"

"I'm not sure. It just seemed I had lived through the scene before."

"Okay! Let's tell Doctor Klein about it. It may mean something, or not. Any questions about the settlement?"

"No! It's much more than I have a right to expect. He can keep the NAS stock for his children."

"And the BBJ?"

"You might as well let Uncle Nick keep it, Aunt Danielle. They won't let you fly anymore."

"Why not? What has my situation have to do with me flying in an airplane?"

"Not flying in it, I meant flying it."

"I don't understand what you're saying, Johnny!"

"Aunt Danielle, you are, or were, a qualified pilot. You were certified to fly that plane. You've been certified for about two years, and I must admit you're pretty good at it. Your landings are still a little rough, but overall, a pretty good driver. Of course, you're not as good as I am, but you're damn good for a girl."

That earned him another punch in the arm.

"Aw come on, Aunt Sissy," he cried in mock pain, "You know any pilot worth his wings won't admit another pilot might be a better stickman then he is."

"Are you telling me I can fly that great big airplane?"

"No Aunt Danielle, not anymore. Once the FAA finds out about your situation, they'll pull your ticket for sure."

"Why?"

"It took more than three years of intense training to get certified. That's all gone now. You would have to start all over again and get re-certified before you can fly *Danielle* again."

"Why did I want to learn to fly?"

No one wanted to answer. I looked around the table and then looked directly at Johnny. My eyes told him I needed an answer.

"Uncle Nick was a pilot, and when you flew with him, you sat in the jump seat on the flight deck.

"By FAA rules, it takes two people to operate a 737, which is basically what the BBJ is, so one of Uncle Nick's regular pilots, Jerry or John would fly right seat. You wanted to surprise Uncle Nick, so for three weeks before your wedding, you had Jerry teach you enough about the radio procedures and the takeoff and landing procedures, so you could fly right seat with him.

"On your wedding day, when Uncle Nick was getting ready to take off for your honeymoon, you jumped in the right seat and did the entire takeoff procedures just like a pro. Uncle Nick was thrilled. You told Uncle Nick you wanted to fly with him, and he arranged for you to receive training and be certified. Later on, Uncle Nick arranged for Bobby, Hank and me to be certified; we can all fly *Danielle*."

Then Lindsey added a comment.

"Baby Girl, you told me next to your husband the thing you loved most in the whole world was being in control of that beautiful airplane."

Colleen added, "It's true Sis, you loved it."

I was shocked, flabbergasted, amazed. I was a pilot, and I could fly that great big airplane in the pictures. But, Johnny said not anymore, and I knew he was right.

"Might as well let him have it, I probably wouldn't know an

elevator from a rudder anyway."

Johnny grabbed my hand.

"Aunt Danielle, what did you say?"

"I said Nick can have the airplane."

"No Aunt Danielle, what did you say after that?"

"I don't remember, Johnny, something about not knowing what parts are on an airplane."

"You're not thinking, Aunt Danielle, you said you wouldn't know the difference between an elevator and a rudder."

"So?"

"What's an elevator?"

"I don't know what you want me to say. An elevator is a box that moves up and down in a shaft. One brought you up to this floor."

"And a rudder?"

"A rudder steers a ship."

"They're also important parts of an airplane."

"So! What does that mean?"

"I don't know, but I need another favor."

"Johnny, not now," Lindsey told him.

"Grandma, it may be nothing, but it may be important."

"Please, Aunt Sissy. The last favor worked out pretty good didn't it?"

"But what did it prove?"

"That Uncle Nick is a good man, and you don't have any reason to hate him."

"But I don't love him either."

"You don't, but now you know she did."

Chapter 33 – The Locked Box

"That's enough," Lindsey said.

Dan put his hand up to silence her.

"Let's hear what the boy has to say."

"I just want Aunt Danielle to play a little game with me. I promise it will only take a few minutes."

Lindsey started to say something, but Dan stopped her.

"Listen to him, Danielle."

I was confused, but I agreed.

"Okay, Johnny, what do you want me to do?"

"Word association. I say a word, and you say the very first thing that comes into your head."

"Alright, what's the word?"

"ATC."

"I don't know, automatic tiger cage,"

"Aunt Danielle, please be serious!"

"I don't understand what you want me to do."

"Don't think about it. There is no correct answer. If I say white, you would normally say black. But, if the first thing that comes into your head is apples, then you must say apples. There is no right or wrong answer."

I looked at Dan, and he nodded.

"Do what he wants."

I nodded to Johnny, and he said, "Clear your head and say the very first thing that comes to mind, okay?"

I nodded again. Johnny said, "V-One."

"Fly or die," I said.

"VR," Johnny said.

"Rotate," I answered.

"Airfoil."

"Wing."

"Flaps."

"Lift."

"VFR."

"Visual Flight Rules."

"ATC."

"Air Traffic Control."

"ILS."

"Instrument Landing System."

"She knows, Uncle Dan, she remembers," Johnny said excitedly.

"It seems she does," Dan replied.

"Knows what? Remembers what?" Lindsey asked.

"Her pilot training," Johnny said, still excited.

"Those words don't mean anything, I know what most of them are," Lindsey said.

Johnny was sure and firm with his answer.

"You know the words, Grandma, because you have been on the flight deck during takeoff and landing. But you don't know what they mean."

"What are you talking about?"

"Grandma, what does V-One mean? What does VR mean? Why do we use flaps?"

"V-One is what the computer says as you go down the runway, and VR means to take off, and you use the flaps when you take off and land."

"True, Grandma, but that's not what they mean. Aunt Danielle knows what they mean, she remembers her pilot training."

"Nonsense, enough of this.".

Dan again put up his hand for silence.

"Everyone quiet down, Johnny's on to something, let him spell it out."

I didn't know what to make of the conversation. I still didn't understand what Johnny was trying to get at, but Dan seemed to have at least some idea.

"Okay, Johnny, I think I know where you're going. Tell us what you're thinking."

Johnny talked very slowly so we all could understand.

"A lot of people have heard those terms, but not everyone knows what they mean. A pilot knows. V-One is a calculated speed. You consider the type of aircraft, the total gross weight, the wind direction and speed, outside temperature, altitude and length of the runway, the distance required to stop the aircraft, and you calculate that you must be at a given speed before you reach a certain point on the runway. The computer calculates all that and calls out when you reach that speed.

"If you hear the call, V-One before you reach that point, you continue the takeoff roll. If you reach that point on the runway and haven't reached V-One, you have to abort the takeoff, or you might run out of runway before you can stop. Most pilots call it the go - no go point, or Decision Point. But some pilots, my instructor, for instance, call it the fly or die point. Aunt Danielle had the same instructor I had."

He took a breath and continued,

"Grandma said VR was the takeoff point. What it technically means is Velocity of Rotation. We don't take off exactly. We rotate the aircraft using the main gear as a fulcrum. We pick the nose up and drop the tail, we rotate the aircraft over the main gear, and it flies."

He looked around the room to make sure we were all following him and went on.

"The wing of an airplane is an airfoil. It has a precise shape that causes a difference in air pressure under and over the wing. This is what allows an airplane to fly, the difference in pressure caused by the shape of the wing or airfoil."

Johnny finished with, "Grandma said the flaps were used during takeoff and landing. Aunt Danielle knew why. Extending the flaps changes the shape of the airfoil, causing the air below the wing to slow down with respect to the air above the wing. This generates additional lift, which allows the plane to stay airborne at lower speeds, which you want at takeoff and landing."

Johnny looked at Dan, and Dan gave him a smile and a nod. Dan looked around the room, and then at me.

"Danielle, you know what those terms mean. You have a pilot's memory about certain things, and you couldn't have gotten that before your pilot training."

"But I don't know anything about what Johnny just said.

They were just words. He said something, and I said the first thing I thought."

"Exactly! Just random words that are in your head that matched what Johnny said to you. They just came out. You didn't think about them. You instinctively knew what answer to give him. You were thinking like a pilot."

I still don't understand."

"I'm not sure I do either. But I'm going to ask someone who might."

Dan asked Colleen for Dr. Klein's number and went into the living room to call him. The doctor had told them to call at any time, day or night, and Dan wasn't going to wait until morning. The four of us girls just looked at each other. It was evident Johnny had stumbled onto something, but no one knew what it was or how important it might be to my situation.

Johnny had disappeared into Nick's den. When he came back into the dining room, he had the collage of the airplane pictures in his hand. He put it on the table in front of me and pointed to one particular image. It looked like the dashboard of a car, but more complicated, with many more switches and dials.

"Look at this, Aunt Danielle. Can you tell me what any of these dials or switches do?"

I looked at the picture but couldn't make sense of it. It was all so foreign to me. I couldn't tell one dial from another, but there was one that caught my eye. It was very unusual. It didn't look like any of the others. I pointed to it.

"Maybe this one."

That made Johnny smile.

"What?"

"Do you know what it is?"

I looked at it and tried to concentrate. It did seem familiar, but I didn't know why, or what it was.

"It's one of the most important instruments in an airplane. It's one of the first things you learn about."

"It looks familiar, but I can't remember what it is, or what it's used for."

"It indicates if your wings are level and if the nose is pointed up or down. It's called the Artificial Horizon."

That sent me into another dream state. I had this notion in my head I had to go to the horizon, but I wasn't allowed to go there. The others in the room, seeing me go all dreamy again, brought me back to the present and wanted to know what I was thinking. I told them, and both Colleen and Cindy looked at me, oddly.

"What?"

It was Colleen again who told me, "The day Nick proposed, he took you to a hotel in Galveston, Texas. You watched the sunrise together. You said when the sky lightened a bit, Nick pointed to the horizon and said you two were going to head for it, but you would never reach it because it would always be out in front of you."

"But," Cindy added, "He told you it would be one hell of a ride!"

By the time Colleen had finished her explanation, Dan had returned from his conversation with Dr. Klein. Cindy told him I had another flashback. He didn't seem at all pleased at the news. Dan sat down across from me.

"Danielle, I'm going to explain this exactly the way Dr. Klein explained it to me, so please bear with me."

I nodded.

"Dr. Klein said whatever caused you to regress is very traumatic. It is so traumatic you have locked those fifteen years' worth of memories in a box, and the key to the box is buried so far inside you that he can't seem to dig it out. That's why he decided to begin counseling you on accepting what has happened and starting a new life."

Dan looked around the room, making sure everyone understood what he was saying.

"But, it's not uncommon for that box to have cracks in it and for random memories to slip out."

"That's good, isn't it Uncle Dan?"

"Maybe, Johnny! Dr. Klein said if enough memories slip out, and they are strong memories, the box can break open without the key, and everything will come back in a flash. But, that will mean that the original problem is still there, and another trigger can cause you to find a new box, a stronger box, and bury the key even deeper.

"But, the other possibility is this box is pretty strong and that these memories will continue to slip out a little at a time. That will result in you having occasional flashbacks, but not break open the box so everything will come back. In that case, you will start a new life, and while you're trying to cope with that, you will occasionally be reminded of your old life. That prospect, he said, would not be very pleasant."

Dan looked around again to make sure everyone was still following the reasoning.

"That doesn't sound very hopeful."

"Not necessarily. If your memory does come back, Dr. Klein thinks it will be easier to find the key. Once you are faced with the possibility of living with the trauma, he thinks he can dig it out and fix it."

"Where does that leave me?"

Dan looked at me hopefully.

"Danielle, you must know we love you. You know no matter what happens, we will be here for you. You must believe we are on your side."

I looked at all the faces around me, and I did know.

"Yes, I know the other Danielle was very much in love and very happy with that man. After seeing that DVD, no one can deny it. But, you must realize I am not that woman."

After a second, I added, "But, after seeing the love in that woman's eyes, I would really like to be that woman. I would do almost anything to have that much love for a man, and have a man love me that much."

"Okay," Dan said, "Dr. Klein wants to push tomorrow's appointment off to the next day."

"Why?"

"Tomorrow, Dr. Klein wants us all to tell you about the lost years of your life. He wants to see if we can generate as many memory flashbacks as possible. But, it has to be in chronological order. He wants you to know as much about those lost years as possible."

"Why?"

"Two reasons. Maybe, if we generate enough flashbacks, it will break open the box, and everything will come rushing back. If that doesn't happen, he wants you to know as much about those fifteen years as possible, so when you find yourself in a situation that seems familiar, you will understand why you feel the way you do.

"Dr. Klein believes you will definitely run into people who know you and go to places you've been to before and be in situations that you've experienced before. When that happens, you will be better able to cope with those memories if you've heard about them previously."

"What does he mean in chronological order?"

"He said you have to know when each event we tell you about happened, within those twenty years, but we don't have to tell you them in exact order."

"I'm confused."

"What it means, Danielle is I can tell you about your fifth wedding anniversary before I tell you about your second wedding anniversary, but I have to tell you when each event occurred so that you can put them in logical order."

"And, if we do this, how will it help me get better?"

Dan sighed.

"If we generate enough of the right kind of memories, you might get your fifteen years back as if they were never lost."

"And if I don't?"

"In the future, when you run into a situation that generates a memory, you will understand it and be able to cope with it."

"And what are the chances of everything coming back?"

"Pick em," Dan answered, "No odds either way."

I closed my eyes and pictured the look in that woman's eyes. Was I capable of loving that much? Was I worthy of being loved that much? I wanted to know. I wanted to be that woman. I wanted to love and be loved without reservation.

"Let's do it."

"Take off power?" Johnny asked.

"Let's fly!" I answered.

"OK," Dan said, "Let's do it!"

Cindy offered a new idea.

"Dan, I think Stacy and Terry should be included."

Dan gave it some thought.

"Danielle, two people were initially friends of Nick's. They became good friends of yours also. In fact, Cindy and I are very close to them too. They know as much about you and Nick as any of us. I think they should be here for this. Nick called us the six musketeers."

"Why haven't they been here already?"

"Except for Cindy and Johnny, we've restricted the people you've come in contact with to the people you knew fifteen years ago. We didn't want to confuse you any more than you already were, but I think it's time."

"They're terrific people," Cindy added. "Dan or I keep them up to date on what's going on here. They're as concerned about you as we all are."

"Okay. Let's have all the Musketeers back together."

"There'll be one missing," Dan said.

"Would it help?"

"Maybe, but it may cause you to hold back."

"Why would I hold back?"

"Danielle, you don't love Nick, but you don't hate him any longer. You're a good person, I'm sure you don't want to hurt him any more than he's already hurting. You might hold back if you feel what you had to say would affect him the wrong way."

"You're probably right. So, it will be my sisters, Johnny, and the five musketeers."

"Let's get something to eat, and we'll get started tonight," Dan said.

Colleen asked me if I wanted wine or beer with my pizza.

"Since when do I eat pizza?"

"Ever since you married an Italian."

That made everyone laugh, and the atmosphere was starting to lighten up around me. It had only taken a month.

While we were waiting for the pizza delivery, I went into Nick's den and looked at the pictures on the wall. Most of them were collages of different events. There were a couple of my wedding. I looked at those and could see how happy that woman was. Colleen and Cindy were standing there with me. I still couldn't associate the woman in the pictures to me

"Did she have a nice wedding?"

Colleen said it was a wedding to die for.

"It was the best, fanciest, the most romantic wedding I have ever seen. A queen couldn't have had a better one. You looked like a princess that day, and you were treated like one."

Colleen pointed out the single portrait of me in my bridal gown. It was stunning.

"Where did I get such a beautiful dress, and how much did it cost?"

When she told me the details, I was anxious to meet the lady who thought so much of me that she dressed up my entire family and made me a one of a kind Stacy Geer Original Wedding Gown.

Danielle Amonti must really be a special kind of lady... But I still couldn't relate her to me.

While gobbling down pizza and beer, we watched part of the wedding DVD. The lady was a princess that day. The beautiful dress, the trumpeters, her court, bowing and curtseying before her, the beautiful white carriage pulled by six white horses. She must have felt just like the princess she appeared to be. What went wrong?

Johnny was sitting on my left. He hadn't left my side since he arrived. Dan was on my right. Suddenly, I was puzzled.

"Why, Dan?"

He didn't understand. I pointed toward the television.

"Look at her, she has everything. A man who she adores. A man who adores her. Money, prestige, a great job, a comfortable home, great friends, a loving family. Why would anyone give all that up and just walk away?"

"It's more complicated than that."

"No, it's not. It's really simple! This lady turned her back on all of this and just walked away. Whatever the reason was, it must have been so devastating the pain of facing it was far worse than what she was losing."

"Yes, when you put it that way, it is simple. That's basically what Dr. Klein said, but the reason is hidden so deep inside you, he can't dig it out. You may not even know what it is. It's possible only the other Danielle knows, and this Danielle will never know."

"You're wrong," my nephew said.

Chapter 34 - Why

"Wrong about what?" Dan asked.

"Aunt Danielle didn't turn her back and walk away from everything."

Everyone stopped at looked at Johnny for an explanation.

"She still has her family. She still has most of her friends and can get the others back if she wants to. She still has this apartment and a lot of money. She's still a VP at Peterson Enterprises. The only thing Aunt Danielle walked away from was Uncle Nick!"

That brought complete silence to the room. My nephew had not only grown up to be a caring and sensitive man, but he could see things very clearly that other people miss.

"You're right, Johnny. The only difference between this Danielle and that Danielle is Nick Amonti."

The talk changed from bringing me up to date on the lost years of my life to why Danielle would walk away from this man. It was decided very quickly all possibilities had to be explored, no matter how outrageous. We all threw out suggestions and made a list. We would talk about each item in detail later. All the usual stuff came up. Did he cheat on me? Did he lie to me? Did I find out something about his past that was horrible? Was it his connection to the Mafia? The list grew. Did he intend to do something that I couldn't deal with? When we were finally running out of ideas, Johnny came up with another suggestion.

"What if it's the other way around? What if you had done something that you couldn't tell him about, couldn't face him with?"

That started another list. We talked about it until Dan said it was time to stop.

"Enough for one day. I suggest we all get a good night's sleep and start again early in the morning."

The meeting broke up. Dan and Cindy headed home. Colleen and Lindsey shared the guest room, and Johnny used the couch in the living room. I had the master bedroom all to myself, but I hadn't gotten too much sleep in there since I got home from the hospital.

The three of us girls got up early. Johnny was gone. Around eight, Dan and Cindy arrived, and about ten minutes later, another couple showed up. I was introduced to them, and over breakfast, we got acquainted. It was obvious they loved Nick as much as everyone else did, and it seemed they had special feelings for me also. I was starting to believe everything that had been said about Nick and Danielle and how everyone around me felt about them.

Johnny returned around nine. Nick had contacted Admiral Becker, a friend of his, and the Admiral arranged Emergency Leave for Johnny. He had gone back to his ship to gather up his clothes and stuff before it sailed back to Norfolk.

After breakfast, we explained to Stacy and Terry what we were doing, and we all sat around examining the various possibilities. I was the least useful one in the discussion because I really didn't know Nick, ...or Danielle either for that matter.

Every idea we came up with was discarded. Neither Nick nor Danielle would ever consider cheating. They had no secrets, so there was nothing either could find out about the other they didn't already know. Everyone told stories that proved the various theories couldn't be right. They were a happy, honest couple who had everything going for them. Then, Johnny came up with another idea.

"What if we are looking at this all wrong? What if it wasn't something one of them had done, but something one of them could potentially do in the future?"

We explored the same theories again with the same results.

Lunch was ordered from the deli, and we took a break. I used the time to watch some more of the DVD collection we had in the apartment. It seems Nick liked to have parties with all of our families and friends involved and he always had a photographer and videographer there to capture the event.

When everyone was ready to start the discussion again, I hesitated. They waited for me to get my thoughts together, and when I had it straight in my mind, I looked at the four women in the room. My two sisters, my best friend's wife and Nick's best friend. Maybe they knew something I didn't.

"You four have men in your lives you love and respect. Please think! What would be the very worst thing that could

311

happen to you in relation to your man? What could be so bad that it would devastate you to this degree?"

That got a very spirited discussion going. All of the scenarios that were discussed earlier were brought up again, this time, as it related to them. Just as we were running out of ideas, the intercom buzzed. Being the one closest to it, I answered. Andy, the doorman, said a Mr. Jack Reynolds was in the lobby. I had completely forgotten about our date. I told Andy to send him up. Everyone was surprised. Lindsey started to say something, but I stopped her.

"I want to do this, I need to do this! If I'm going to live in this new world, I have to put this episode of my life behind me once and for all."

Johnny wrapped his arms around me.

"Don't worry, Aunt Sissy, we'll be here with you."

I had learned a lot about Nick Amonti over the past month, and I was pretty sure Jack would know who he was. Nick Amonti was a very wealthy and powerful man in the legitimate business world, and for some reason, which was not fully explained to me, he had connections with the underworld, and, thanks to something I did at my wedding so did I.

I had seen enough gangster movies in my life, to know what that meant. Maybe I could frighten Jack. I'd love to knock him down a little, and even if it was only temporary until he realized I was bluffing. I wanted him to know I wasn't that silly, insecure girl he knew.

"I want to see Jack alone. You guys hide in my bedroom. You can keep the door slightly open and listen, but you have to keep quiet and stay out of sight."

It took some convincing, but I finally got them hidden in the bedroom just as the doorbell chimed. I opened the apartment door, and there was Jack, as handsome as ever, maybe even more so. Age had made him distinguished in addition to being the most beautiful man I had ever laid eyes on. But, my heart didn't flutter the way it used to. There was no doubt how I felt.

I am so over you!

Jack immediately made a grab for me, but I managed to wiggle away from him. He took a quick glance around the apartment, probably trying to locate the bedroom. Same old Jack.

I indicated I was as interested in what he was here for as much as he was, but we had to talk for a bit first. I got him to take a seat at the dining room table. He tried to pull me down into his lap, but I wiggled free again and sat opposite him. He glanced at this watch, knowing his time with me was limited. He probably had to be home for supper with his wife, and he didn't want to waste any of it talking. I looked at his ring finger. No wedding band, but there was the telltale ring of skin that seldom saw the sun.

"I knew you'd go far in business. I'm glad you put your beauty to work for you. A girl with your looks could always climb the corporate ladder faster than any man."

I wanted to slap him, but I just smiled. I asked him if he ever married.

"I tried it, but I never got over you, and that got in the way. It didn't last long."

I asked him how long, and he said it was over years ago.

"Jack, why did we break up?"

He thought about it before he answered.

"It was because of Dan Patrick and your sisters. That Patrick guy had been trying to get into your pants ever since you met, and when you moved to Strollman, he was pissed at me for getting to you first. He bad mouthed me to everyone who would listen, even your two sisters. They put so much pressure on you, you couldn't bear it anymore, and you left me. You went straight to Patrick, and he got his way. Then, you married that old goat for his money. I figured you had it pretty good, and I didn't want to ruin it for you, so I stayed away. But, I knew you couldn't stay away from good old Jack forever, and here I am."

"So, basically, I left you for Dan Patrick, and not because I found you and Nancy Cummings naked and sweaty in our bed?"

That hit him right between the eyes. Bang! He jumped up from his chair.

"What's going on here, Danielle? I thought you called me to renew what we had."

"I don't think your wife would approve."

Double hit, bang, bang.

He came around the table and reached for me. I knew how Jack thought. If he could get his hands on me, kiss me, pull me against him, I would succumb to his advances. He was that good,

313

but not this time. I really hated him, not because of what he had done to me years ago, but because he had so little regard for me that knowing what had happened to me, he was here trying to get me in bed again, just for his own ego. What a waste of manhood.

Suddenly, Jack stopped and stared. I glanced to where he was looking, and three angry men were moving toward the dining room. When they got to the table, Johnny put his arms out to stop Dan and Terry.

"I got this!"

A big smile spread across Dan's face. He pulled out a dining room chair and sat down at the table. Dan told Terry to have a seat and enjoy the show. Terry seemed undecided until Dan said, "Nick introduced Danielle's three nephews to Commander Becker."

That brought a smile to Terry's face, and he also sat down at the table. Johnny walked past the table and stood in front of the apartment door.

"I think you owe my Aunt Danielle and Mr. Patrick an apology."

"Don't try anything, kid or I'll have the cops here in no time, and you'll have more trouble than you can imagine."

Dan took his cell phone from his pocket and slid it across the table to Jack.

"Call them Jack, 911. Tell them you are trespassing, uninvited in the apartment of a woman who lives alone and is under physiological stress. Tell them you tried to molest her and her nephew had to pull you off her."

"Bullshit! She told the doorman to send me up."

The four women had followed the men out of the bedroom, and when Cindy heard what Dan said to Jack, she went to the intercom.

"Andy, this is Mrs. Patrick."

The conversation was pure cloak and dagger.

"Andy, there's a strange man in Mrs. Amonti's apartment. How did he manage to get up here without being announced?"

Andy didn't understand at first. Cindy persisted and eventually, Andy got it.

"I'm so sorry, Mrs. Patrick. He must have sneaked in while I was helping Ms. Anderson with her groceries. Is there a problem? Do you need me to come to the apartment? Should I hit the panic button to NAS Security or call the police?"

"No, it's alright, Andy. I think the three men here can handle it. When will the security camera be fixed? You said it has been out all day."

"I've called the repair company Ma'am. It should be fixed in a couple of hours."

"Go ahead, Jack," Dan said, "Make the call."

I watched Jack's arrogance fade, and I had a delicious thought. It started slowly and blossomed into a sumptuous idea. I would use Nick's power and influence to frighten Jack, but I would let him know it was coming directly from me.

"Don't worry about it, Johnny. I don't want an apology from this creature."

I looked squarely into Jack's eyes, so he could see how sincere I was.

"Jack, Johnny will let you go in a minute, but first I have to tell you something."

Jack gave me an exasperated look to show he had no interest in what I had to say.

"You better pay attention, Jack. The lady is serious," Dan advised.

Jack looked in my direction, but not directly at me. I smiled at him.

"Since you already know my husband is rich and old, you probably know who he is and how powerful he is. When he hears you were here in his home trying to screw his wife, he's going to be very upset. But before I tell you what he's liable to do about it, let me ask you a question.

I let that sink in. I had his attention, now.

"Jack, do you know what happens to someone who screws around with a Made Man's woman."

The blood drained from Jack's face, but he tried to bluster past his fear.

"It figures, no one gets that rich legitimately."

"I don't care what you think of him, Jack. The important

thing is you know I can do that. I don't even have to go through my husband. I am gold to these people Jack, I did them a big favor once, and they owe me. You know how that works, don't you Jack? I can fix it, so you never screw anyone ever again. At least not physically screw anyone."

Jack tried to say something, but I cut him off. He was looking directly at me now, his bravado gone. I had him. I moved in for the kill.

"Jack, I don't care about what you did to me fifteen years ago. I was a silly girl and probably deserved what happened. But I do resent you coming here and trying to screw with me at this time in my life with everything that's happened to me. I resent it so much I'm going to make you wish you had never met me."

I had his full attention now, and I let him have both barrels.

"You haven't changed a bit. You're still the same jerk you've always been, and I bet you still bring in just enough orders to keep your job at Strollman. Mr. Strollman has wanted to fire you for years, and after what you did to me, he wanted to beat you. But because you always made your quota, he couldn't let you go without the chance you'd sue him. But that's about to change."

There was no doubt, Jack was listening to me, now.

"That rich, old goat I married knows a lot of people in South Florida, Jack. Those orders that allowed you to keep your job are about to dry up. They are going to go away. You will never make quota again, and with your reputation, finding another job won't be easy."

By the look on Jack's face, I guessed he wasn't sure if I could do that, but the possibility frightened him.

"I'm telling you this, Jack, so that when it does happen, you'll know why. You'll know it was that silly, gullible girl you thought you could walk in on and screw up her life a second time."

I gave him ten seconds to absorb what I said.

"Let him go, Johnny, I want this trash out of my home!"

Johnny opened the door and stepped aside. Jack didn't waste any time. Just before he crossed the threshold, I added the kicker.

"Jack, if I ever see you again, or even hear your name mentioned, I'll drop a dime and revert to the other option I mentioned!"

Johnny stood in the doorway and watched until Jack was in

the elevator. Colleen buzzed Andy and told him to make sure Jack left the premises. She thanked him for the part he had played earlier and assured him all was well. When Johnny closed the apartment door, everyone was looking at me.

"Thanks, Johnny. My hero, always coming to my rescue."

"You didn't need me to come to your rescue, Aunt Danielle. Uncle Nick's security guys said you did really well in your self-defense training."

"Who's Commander Becker?"

"Commander, now Admiral Becker, was the chief instructor at the Navy Seals Training Facility. He taught hand to hand combat to the Seals. He also instructed Nick and your three nephews in the art," Dan answered.

They were all still staring at me.

"What?"

At first, no one said anything, and then Stacy said what they were all thinking.

"That sounded like the Danielle we all know and love!"

"I couldn't help myself. I wanted to put the fear of God into him."

Terry laughed.

"I think you did that. But, calling Sal seems kind of extreme. But, the other option is reasonable."

"What are you talking about? I was just trying to scare him, he probably knows it was a bluff and will have a good laugh over it. But I did love the look on his face when I said those things."

Terry came over to me and wrapped his arms around me.

"Danielle, everything you said to him is doable, and I think you should follow through. He deserves it!"

"Right, I can ask Nick to call the Mafia and have Jack's balls cut off!"

"You could, but you don't have to ask Nick to call. I'm sure you have Sal Chassy's number here somewhere, and you could call him yourself."

I was dumbfounded. That started a conversation about my connection to the mob. They explained in detail about the favor I had done for the two Dons and how important I was to them. That led to the story of our trip to Cauldwell and everything that happened there, our weekend in Atlanta and my vamp outfit. I was slowly getting a picture of a very good man who obviously loved this woman very much, and who this woman loved so completely, but I still couldn't see me as this woman.

But, I was sure I wanted to be her.

While all of this was taking place, we ordered dinner. I asked if we could have pizza again. To my surprise, I had discovered I liked it. Being from South Georgia, pizza had never been a staple of our diet, but it seemed since I married Nick, I had acquired a taste for it. Pizza and beer, I was told had become my favorite fast food meal.

Conversation at dinner was light until Terry brought up Jack's visit.

"I think you should go ahead with what you had threatened. You should get Jack fired from his position at Strollman. Nick could definitely do it."

Dan added, "He deserves it, and Mr. Strollman would love you for doing it."

"Nick has that much power?"

Stacy told me another story.

"Being a beautiful, sensuous woman, you get hit on a lot. Usually, all you had to do was wave your left hand at the guy, and he understood. Occasionally, some jerk would persist, and you had to shoot him down. Nick always had confidence in you to deal with the situation, and he never had to interject himself into it. But one night, at a party, you agreed to dance with a representative of one of your clients at Peterson Enterprises. Because of your business association with him, you thought he was a decent guy, but he made a pass at you. When you told him you weren't interested, he got out of hand and made an improper grab for you. Because of the self-defense training, you were given by the NAS Security team, you almost broke the guy's wrist. You had the guy on his knees before you let go of his fingers. Nick had witnessed the incident, but because it was over so quickly, he didn't have a chance to intercede. When you got back to the table, Nick knew you were pissed. You said something to the effect that you'd like to teach that jerk a lesson.

"The next time you had an appointment with that client, a different representative showed up at your office. When you asked where the other guy was, you were told he was fired. No one knew why. He was called into the CEO's office and terminated. That night, you mentioned to Nick that the guy who got fresh at the party was fired. Nick said, "That should teach him!""

"He really did that?"

"Not only did he have him fired, but he let the guy know through the grapevine that it was him who did it and why. Because of another incident at a charity ball, before you were married, Nick knew you'd be angry when he told you what he had done. He said the guy would get another job, and all he would lose is his seniority and a few bucks a week. It wouldn't hurt too much. When you asked him why he had done that, he told you no one was going to insult his wife with impunity."

"But, if he knew I'd be angry, why did he tell me about it?"

"Because Nick told you everything, he never kept anything from you, good or bad," Colleen said. "That's the way it was with both of you."

"Even if I wanted to do it, I couldn't ask Nick to do that for me, not under these circumstances."

Terry said, "You don't have to ask Nick. I could ask him and tell Nick it was for Dan. Nick would understand that Dan wanted to punish Jack for what he had done to you."

I looked at Dan.

"He'd do that for you?

Dan nodded. "You have to understand the relationship between Nick and me. It's unique, I admit, but it's deep, and it's honest."

"Tell me about it. Please!"

"It's complicated but really simple in a way. You must know how I feel about you Danielle, have always felt about you. Even though I thought Nick was going to cause you pain by marrying him, when I saw how much this man was in love with you and how happy he made you, I gained a whole lot of respect and admiration for him. And, when he told me he wanted us to stay best friends because you might need a really good friend because you were married to him, I couldn't say no. When Cindy told me what he had said when he danced with her, and she might have rejected me if it wasn't for that conversation, our friendship was as cemented as yours and mine are.

"Nick respects me because he feels it would have been so easy for me to take advantage of the situation when you were all broken up about Jack. He said he knew it must have been really tempting, and only a real, true friend would resist the temptation. The fact that I didn't try to have a more intimate relationship with you until after you were completely over Jack allowed Nick to believe that the friendship between you and me was real."

Terry looked at me, and although I don't consider myself a vindictive person, I nodded. It didn't make me happy, but there was satisfaction in knowing Jack would find out that he was all wrong about me.

Chapter 35 – The Event

When that subject was closed, I asked why I had been given self-defense training and what was the NAS Security team. The answer was another indication of what kind of man Nick Amonti was. Terry did most of the talking. He gave me a rundown as to what NAS Security was and why Nick had formed them.

"The limo driver, Thomas, is a member of the security team. Andy and the other doormen here at the apartment have been given special training by the team. There is a direct line from the lobby to NAS Security. Every member of the family has a special cell phone with a Panic Button and special pieces of jewelry that if pressed a certain way would send out a GPS signal through the phone to the security team. NAS Security is friendly with every police department in South Florida, They could have a police car to their location in minutes."

Stacy said the jewelry was probably in my bedroom.

"Does that mean every member of Nick's family is under constant surveillance?"

"No, it only sends out a signal if it is activated."

Stacy must have guessed the meaning of my question.

"No Danielle, you were not being watched. You had the freedom to do as you pleased, and Nick never knew about our secret meetings."

That got my attention, and I had to ask what secret meetings. Stacy explained.

"Nick loved to surprise you, and you loved being surprised, and you also loved to surprise Nick. There would be no way you could set up a surprise for him if he knew your whereabouts at all times. You met with me quite a few times, in secret, to set up something special for his birthday, or your anniversary, and I imagine there must have been meetings with other people also."

Cindy added, "We had a few secret meetings also! You two loved your surprises. And, the song you sang at your fifth anniversary took over two months to get right, and you and Nick's granddaughters met in secret almost every day."

That made me feel better. While we girls were clearing away the dinner stuff, Stacy had a question.

"Danielle, how do you feel about Nick, right now?"

I had to think about it. My answer was complicated.

"When Dan first told me at the hospital he was my husband, I was confused. How could I marry such an old man? He was more than twice my age. I thought I was twenty-five, not forty.

"Then when I saw how everyone close to me loved this man and catered to him, I disliked him. Eventually, I began to hate him."

I took a minute to gather my thoughts.

"Now, listening to all of you, watching the videos, hearing about the divorce and the reason for it, Bob's explanation of what Nick was doing, I've come to respect the man and the love he has for this woman. I might even like him, but I still can't see myself married to him."

Stacy smiled.

"That's because you've learned about him, but you don't actually know him. You've seen him three times for a total of maybe an hour. You don't know the man, just other people's opinion of him."

"What's your point?" Dan asked.

Stacy took a minute before she replied.

"We're trying to generate memories in hopes it breaks open the box the last fifteen years are locked up in. What better way to generate memories than for the two of them to sit down together and talk. Face each other and have a conversation. Let Danielle see the man, not just hear about him. See his manner, the way he moves, the way he talks. They don't have to talk about their life together, just talk about everyday things. Maybe something will break through and widen the crack that's already there."

Dan was thoughtful.

"What do you think, Danielle? We can do it right here. You and Nick can sit here at the table, and we will be in the living room in case you need us."

"I don't know. Wouldn't that just cause him more pain?"

"Probably," Stacy said, "but I know that man, and I can tell you he would suffer anything if there were just a slight chance he could get his wife back, his real wife."

"I'd have to think about it."

We were all silent for a while. Everyone was thinking about what Stacy had suggested.

Dan finally broke the silence. "Let's move on."

It seemed no one had anything to say until Cindy offered,

"Danielle, what you said before, about what Dan could do that would devastate me, I've been thinking about that. I trust Dan completely, and the idea of him cheating on me or doing something awful behind my back seems so impossible I can't relate to it. But, there is one thing that I would have a difficult time dealing with. I would be totally lost if Dan ever left me."

After a moment's thought, Colleen and Lindsey nodded in agreement.

"Great point," Stacy said, "but I can't imagine any situation that would cause Nick to leave her. He'd die first."

And then, clear-headed Johnny said, "But he did!"

Everyone looked at Johnny.

"Uncle Nick did leave Aunt Danielle."

Feeling everyone's eyes on him, he added, "Uncle Nick left Aunt Danielle for five days, and we all thought he was never coming back."

I didn't have the slightest idea of what Johnny was talking about, but everyone else seemed to understand.

Dan said, "That was years ago, why would it affect her now?"

Johnny was ready with the answer.

"You told us Dr. Klein said what happened a month ago could just be a trigger that brought up something that Aunt Danielle was trying to suppress for a long time. It didn't have to be anything that just happened. That's why it was so difficult for him to get at it."

"Possible, but if that's the issue, what could have been the trigger?"

"I think Aunt Danielle knows."

"Keep talking," Dan told him. "Talk it out. Expand it."

Johnny thought for a while.

"If the event Aunt Danielle is trying to suppress happened a long time ago, and it only came out now because it was triggered by something else, then the something else just happened, a month ago. We don't have to look for what she's trying to suppress, we need to find the something else, and Aunt Danielle knows what that is. She's not trying to suppress that. All she has to do is remember what she was doing when the something else happened."

"What are we talking about? What is the event I'm trying to suppress and what is something else?"

Everyone started talking at once. Dan, seeing the confusion, silenced everyone and told Johnny to explain everything to me. Johnny took my hands in his.

"Aunt Danielle, over three years ago Uncle Nick was ferrying a plane from The Bahamas to Florida for a friend of his who owns an airfreight company. He did this often. Uncle Nick loved to fly, and it saved his friend the cost of hiring a pilot for a ferry flight.

On this particular flight, the plane crashed into the ocean. They found the other pilot the same day, but they couldn't find Uncle Nick. After three days, the Coast Guard abandoned the search because three days was the maximum a man could stay alive under those circumstances.

By the middle of the fifth day, we had all given up hope. Everyone was sure he was gone. Everyone but you. You kept saying Uncle Nick would never leave you like this, not without saying goodbye and telling you how much he loved you. You were sure he would come back, even if it were just long enough to say goodbye."

Now Johnny had tears in his eyes.

"You were right. He was found barely alive by a Navy Aircraft Carrier. The first thing he said to them was, "Call my wife!" When he was able to speak, they asked how he had managed to stay alive against all the odds. He told them he couldn't leave his wife like that. He had to see her at least long enough to tell her he loved her one more time."

"I'm not sure I understand what you're saying. You think Nick's plane crash is the reason I lost fifteen years of my life?"

"Just a possibility," Dan said, "It may not have anything to do with what's happened, but Johnny is right about the something else."

"Please, you're losing me!"

Dan looked around the room, and since no one else had anything to say, he tried to explain:

"Dr. Klein said you are suppressing something you feel is so horrible you can't face it. You're hiding this something, not from us, but from yourself. You are protecting yourself. The way you are protecting yourself is by regressing to a time in your life it hadn't happened yet. If it hadn't happened, you don't have to face it. Following me so far?"

I nodded.

"There are only two things that have happened in the last fifteen years that might upset you that much, at least as far as we all know. There may be something that you never told anyone about, but you're such an open person, it's not probable. One is your breakup with Jack. But after what you did this afternoon, I'm sure it can't be what's bothering you. The other is Nick's crash. That was terrible. It could be what you're afraid of, losing him. If you never met him, you couldn't lose him."

"So, you think because Nick crashed a plane and was lost for five days I fear losing him so much that I am hiding in the past?"

"Maybe," Dan said, "It's only a possibility. It could be something else entirely."

"But, Dr. Klein and I talked about Nick having a serious accident, and it didn't mean anything to me."

"I said it was only a possibility. It could be something else entirely, or something that has to do with the crash that isn't evident to us. It could be almost anything, that's why what Johnny said about the something else is important."

"I don't understand that at all."

Johnny explained.

"Dr. Klein said whatever you're hiding is in a locked box, and he can't find the key. Let's just say we know the key, a real key, is here in this apartment. We know it's here, but we don't know exactly where. This is a very large apartment, and the key could be anywhere. Maybe in a dresser drawer, maybe under the carpet, maybe under a floorboard or buried in the plaster on the walls. We don't know where it is, except it's somewhere in this apartment. Got that?"

I nodded.

"Now, let's say we find out there are directions that will lead us to the key, and those directions are somewhere in the kitchen. Does it make more sense for us to search this entire apartment looking for the key, or should we search just the kitchen looking for the directions?"

"I guess it would make more sense to search for the directions in a smaller space."

"That's what the something else is," Dan said. "Instead of looking for the key over fifteen years of your life, maybe we should be looking for whatever caused you to hide it. That something else, or trigger, only happened a little over a month ago. It may be easier to find."

"How do we find it?"

"First, I have to call Dr. Klein," Dan said. "I have an idea."

While the men went into Nick's den to call Dr. Klein, the girls went about setting up for coffee. I glanced into the den a couple of times, and the conversation among the men was intense. It lasted a while before they returned to the dining room. We all settled around the table and waited for Dan to tell us his idea and what Dr. Klein had said about it.

"I talked to Dr. Klein about an idea I got because of Johnny's something else theory. I asked him if it would help if we went back to Peterson's parking lot and tried to retrace your steps back to the point where you got confused. Back to the point where you lost fifteen years of your life. Maybe we can figure out what caused you to hide inside yourself."

"And?" I asked.

"Dr. Klein told me the reason he hadn't suggested that is because there were three possible outcomes. The first is it doesn't help at all, with the possible side effect of making you suffer through all that confusion again.

"The second is if we do discover the trigger, it might enable him to pull the key out of its hiding place and open the box. If we do this, he has to be there.

"The third possibility is a killer. Dr. Klein said if we find the trigger, and he can't get to the key, you may regress even further. The doctor told me if you remember what you are afraid of and he couldn't stop the fear, you might feel you didn't go back far

326

enough."

"How far back?"

"No way to know for sure. But possibly, to a point, you don't remember who you are or anything about your life, you would be completely lost and not even know your sisters. You would be all alone."

"Odds?"

"Same as before, pick em!"

No one had anything else to say. It got very quiet. Johnny came over and put his hands on my shoulders.

"If I decide to do this, Dr. Klein will be there?"

"All the way. But he can't take responsibility for the outcome. He can't advise you either way. He just doesn't know how it will turn out."

"How much time do I have to think about this?"

"No time limit. He wants you to take your time and give it serious thought. The results could be wonderful, disastrous or somewhere in between. You can't rush this."

"Thoughts?"

Everyone was against it. It was too chancy. Dan said even if the odds had been a little in our favor, the chance of losing me entirely was too high. I think Johnny spoke for everyone.

"Aunt Sissy, we all love you. We would love to see you back to your old self. We would love to see you and Uncle Nick together again. You were so happy then. But, we are more than happy to love this lady rather than losing you altogether."

I don't know why, but I wanted to know Nick's opinion.

"What would Nick say?"

I got an immediate response from everyone.

"No way, wouldn't even consider it, would put a stop to it."

"Why? There's a chance we'd be together again. He loves her, he wants her back, doesn't he, why wouldn't he allow it?"

"Because he loves you," Stacy said.

"That answer doesn't make sense."

"It makes perfect sense," Stacy replied, "To this man, loving you means making you happy. He knows the way you are right now, he can't make you happy. But, given a chance, you can find happiness without him in your life. He wants to give you that chance. If this experiment goes wrong, you'll lose that chance. He won't allow that to happen. He'd rather walk away from you completely than take even a thirty percent chance the rest of your life would be miserable."

I wanted to argue with her, but I knew she was probably right. Everything I had been told about Nick Amonti seemed to point in the same direction. My happiness was more important to him than his own. He could never be happy if I weren't, even if it wasn't with him.

Could I do this? Could I take a chance of losing myself completely just to be with a man I didn't know? If we had some sort of relationship, maybe, but the only thing I knew about him was what these people have been telling me about him.

And, as far as I was concerned, I had the chance of a very good life ahead of me. It's not as if I would miss this man. I had some memories of things that passed between us, but nothing that would make me want to be with him. It was crazy to even consider it. The risk was much too great.

Dan, Cindy, Stacy, and Terry headed home around ten. Colleen, Lindsey, and Johnny sat in the living room and tried to bring up more memories. Johnny played some of the DVDs of the parties Nick and Danielle had. Just before eleven, Lindsey and Colleen headed for bed. Johnny and I were alone.

"Please, Aunt Sissy. Don't do this."

"Do what?"

"I know what you're thinking. You think you're so close it would be worth the chance. But, it's not. It's not worth giving up the rest of your life for a short time with Uncle Nick."

I was surprised. Johnny was the most adamant about Nick and Danielle getting together again.

"Johnny, why the change of heart?"

"I haven't changed my opinion. When you were with Uncle Nick, it was the happiest time in your entire life. I still believe that. But this is wrong. You're taking a chance you can get that back, and you're not even sure what that is. Against that, you risk losing everything and everyone you know. You'll be utterly alone."

I had nothing to say to that. But, Johnny did.

"You're forty years old. You have a good thirty or forty years ahead of you to be happy and productive. You're thinking about trading that for maybe twenty years with Uncle Nick. He's fifty-six now, he's not going to be with you forever. Add to that the fact Uncle Nick will never allow you to take a chance on losing yourself entirely."

"He doesn't have to know."

"Do you really believe one of us won't tell him? He'll have a judge issue a temporary injunction before we reached Peterson Enterprises."

"How could he do that?"

"Technically, he's still your husband, and you are not in your right mind, so to speak. The temporary order would be easy. Then there'd be a long court battle to get it overturned."

Johnny was probably right. I had a lot to think about. For a while, Johnny and I watched DVDs.

Chapter 36 - The Cure?

When I opened my eyes, I was stretched out on the couch, and Johnny was asleep on the floor. The noise of Lindsey and Colleen getting breakfast ready woke me. The TV was still on, and the picture of Danielle's face was on the screen. It must have been the close-up of her when she finished singing that song to Nick at their anniversary. I recognized the love and devotion in her eyes.

Lindsey noticed I was awake and brought me a cup of coffee. She shut the television off and sat on the couch next to me.

"Bad night?"

I nodded.

"He been here all night?"

Another nod.

"I'll wake him and send him into the guest room. Why don't you get a shower? The gang will be here shortly."

I did as I was told. When I came out of my bedroom, everyone was sitting around the table drinking coffee and having breakfast. I fixed myself another cup of coffee and went to sit in the living room. The TV was off, but I could still see those eyes. Each member of our gang came into the living room individually to talk to me. Colleen was first.

"I couldn't bear losing you. Even if there were only a ten percent chance this would turn out badly, I couldn't allow you to do it."

One by one, they said their piece. The sentiment was unanimous. They not only didn't think I should do this, but they all seemed to threaten they would try to stop it. But, the decision was mine, and everyone knew it. Terry expanded on the suggestion that came up last night.

"You could meet with Nick here, with everyone around and if you felt comfortable, maybe you could go out for dinner one night and maybe dancing. You two loved to dance. You might fall in love with Nick all over again."

"But, what if I don't? What then? How much more pain can

I put this man through?"

"Nick would endure the pain if there was a chance."

Dan said, "I've seen signs of the old Danielle in you lately. The girl you were fifteen years ago could never talk to Jack that way. There also were signs of a more self-assured Danielle. Your personality of a month ago is in you and the problem with your memory didn't affect it. I think you could lead a very happy life once Dr. Klein helpes you to adjust."

Stacy said Nick was right, a full and happy life as the Danielle I am now was my best option.

"And Nick is always right," I said sarcastically.

"Not always," she replied, "Nick's not perfect. He's made some bad business decisions, and he's not always right in his personal beliefs. For instance, he was absolutely certain a relationship with him could only hurt you, and as much as he loved you, he could never make you truly happy. He was dead wrong about that!"

"Then why did he ask me to marry him?"

"When Nick told me about the engagement, I asked him that very question. He said when he looked into your eyes and saw how much love was there, love aimed directly at him, he couldn't walk away from it. He knew he was being selfish, but he just couldn't walk away from all that love. So, he vowed to make you the happiest woman alive, no matter what was required."

By ten thirty or so, we were all in the living room together. Dan suggested we continue with the memory exercises. Before they had a chance to get started, I put up my hand.

"Wait!"

Everyone looked at me. I looked into each pair of eyes.

"I am so blessed to have you people here with me. The love I have felt from you this past month is overwhelming. I have no right to ask this of you, but I must. I need a tremendous favor."

"No Danielle, absolutely NOT!" Dan immediately yelled.

"Dan, I have to. I have no choice. There will be no happy ever after for me if I don't at least try."

"Why?"

I looked around. I didn't have an answer I could explain. There was nothing I could say that would make them understand. I wasn't even sure of the reason, but I knew I had to try. I looked at the television. The screen was blank, but the DVD was still turned on, and the Pause light was blinking. I remembered the very last image that was on the screen when Lindsey turned the set-off. I grabbed the remote and switched the TV on. The picture of Danielle's face filled the screen, the close up of her right after she had said the last line of that beautiful song.

That woman was me. Could I be thsat woman again! I had to know.

With tears streaming down my checks, I pointed at the tv screen.

"I want to be that woman! I need to be that woman! I need to know how it feels to love someone that much!"

Johnny was seated next to me and gave me his shoulder to cry on, again. Everyone was quiet. I don't know how much time passed before I gained control of myself. With Johnny's handkerchief, I wiped away the tears. Dan was standing directly in front of me.

"Ready? Dr. Klein will meet us at Peterson's parking lot in an hour."

"Nick?"

Dan shook his head and told me to clean up my face. Colleen had called NAS and asked for Thomas to pick us up. Nick had given the gang the use of Thomas and the stretch whenever they needed it.

I had no second thoughts. I had to do this. I had to try anything, everything to make me that woman again. I knew no matter how much I had grown, no matter how good my life could be, this Danielle would never love a man like that Danielle had, and I needed to know what that was like.

Before we left the apartment, I looked around. I didn't know what condition I would be in when I returned. Would I be the same gal who was leaving? Would I be the Danielle who shared so much love here? Or, would I not remember this place or who I was at all?

Dr. Klein met us at the entrance to the parking lot at Peterson Enterprises. He explained what we were going to do, and once again described all the possible outcomes. He made me repeat them a couple of times until he was sure I understood what might happen. I met Bill Peterson. I remembered him from the day this all started. He was very concerned.

"Everyone inside loves you and is rooting for you."

He also told us what he knew about that day.

"You were in a meeting with the Executive Staff and me most of the morning. It was a great meeting. There was nothing that happened that morning that should have upset you. I questioned everyone in the building at the time, and except for Crystal, no one had seen or talked to you after the meeting. Crystal, your Administrative Assistant, told me after the meeting you had stopped in her office and said you were going to the break room for a cup of coffee. She said you seemed to be in good spirits. That's the last time anyone saw you until you ran into the Security Guard in the parking lot. But, a few people said they heard a scream coming from the direction of the break room. They never did find out what it was about."

Mr. Peterson led us through the lobby. It looked familiar. We took the elevator to the tenth floor. He brought us to the break room. When I stepped inside, it also seemed familiar.

Dr. Klein asked if I remembered being here. I told him it did look familiar. He asked me to look around and tell him if anything upset me or made me feel bad. There was nothing. Mr. Peterson shut off the television, so we wouldn't be disturbed. Dr. Klein told me to think back to that day. What did I remember? Look, hear, smell, anything familiar?

I walked around the room.

"This table. I was standing here at this table."

"Anything special about this table?"

I looked at the table and concentrated as hard as I could.

"There was coffee spilled all over it."

Mr. Peterson said, "My people are very conscientious about cleaning up after themselves. If there was coffee spilled on this table, it most probably was Danielle, who spilled it."

"Good," Dr. Klein said.

Dr. Klein told me to sit down at the table. He asked for someone to get me a cup of coffee.

"Danielle, concentrate on this moment. Was there anyone else in the room with you? Did you have anything with you, papers, a report, newspaper? Were you hot? Were you cold? Was there any unusual odor, did you smell something?"

The answer to all his questions was, no. I was trying to concentrate, to bring it back, but this is as far as I could go. I could remember everything back to this point, but no further.

He asked me if I heard any sound.

"Yes, the television was on."

Dan asked, "Is the television tuned to any specific station at any particular time?"

"Yes, it's always tuned to Fox News."

Dan whispered something to Dr. Klein. The doctor nodded, and Dan went into a corner and called someone on his cell phone. The doctor continued to throw questions at me. I didn't have any answers. When Dan was finished with his call, he rejoined the group. Dr. Klein asked him if he had any luck.

"I had to use Nick's name, but it's better news than we hoped."

Dan turned his attention to Mr. Peterson.

"Nick has friends at Fox News. I told them I needed to know what was on the morning this all started. I asked if they could fax me a transcript of the broadcast. They did better. They're sending a streaming video to my e-mail. I need a laptop and a way to hook it up to that television."

Five minutes later, two men from Peterson's IT Department arrived in the break room and set everything up. When everything was ready, Dr. Klein took over again.

"Danielle, think. It was over a month ago. You're sitting here having a cup of coffee after a meeting with your boss and the other executives. You are alone. There is no one else here. The only thing you hear is the television. Concentrate, Danielle, focus on the television."

Everyone moved behind me out of my line of vision. The IT guys switched on the television, and I listened. It was a news broadcast, I couldn't remember the newscaster's name, but it was familiar. It was the usual stuff, politics, scandal, the economy. Suddenly, I jumped up so fast I bumped the table and spilled my coffee.

"NOOOOOOOOOOOOOOO," I screamed.

Dan was behind me now, holding me.

"It's not him, Danielle. Nick's alive. I talked to him an hour ago. It's not him!"

I turned to face Dan.

"I swear, he's okay! That wasn't him!"

When I opened my eyes, I was lying on my back, looking at the ceiling. Dan was kneeling next to me.

"He's okay, Danielle. I promise you, he didn't fly today."

Dr. Klein knelt down next to me and asked if I could sit up. I nodded, and Dan and the doctor helped me into a sitting position. I was on the couch in Bill's office.

"I have to see him. I have to see for myself."

"In a minute. First, we have to get you settled down."

"Please, I have to see him!"

"Danielle! Do you know how much that man is suffering?"

"Yes, yes I do! I have to tell him. I have to let him know. I have to tell him how sorry I am."

"Do you want to cause him more pain?"

"No, no, no! I have to see him, please."

"In a minute, Danielle. Let's make sure you're all the way back. It would be awful for him if he believed you were all right and then found out that you weren't."

Dan intervened.

"Doc, how about if we let her hear his voice, but don't tell him what's going on here."

Dr. Klein nodded. Dan told Colleen, "Call the NAS office and make an excuse to talk to Nick."

Mr. Peterson indicated the speakerphone on his desk. Colleen called and got the switchboard operator. We heard through the speakerphone, "I'm sorry Ma'am, Mr. Amonti is in a closed conference and cannot be disturbed."

"Didn't Mr. Amonti give you a list of names that didn't apply to?"

"Yes, Ma'am."

"This is Mrs. Colleen Rogers, I'm sure I'm on that list."

The girl asked Colleen to hold, and thirty seconds later I heard Nick's voice. It was full of concern.

"Nothing's wrong, Nick. Lindsey staying this week. I'm

headed back home tonight, and I wanted to have dinner with you before I left."

"Of course, Colleen. I'll have them get the BBJ ready for the trip. I can meet you in the lobby of the apartment at six. Will that be okay?"

Hearing his voice made me feel better, and I listened to Dr. Klein. He asked me some questions. What was my name? How old was I? What year was it? Did I know where I was? Did I know the man standing by the desk?

He seemed to be satisfied with my answers. Then he asked me if I remembered the past month. I did! I remembered it all. How horrible I had treated Nick. The divorce papers. Jack's visit. I remembered everything, including the people who stood by me.

Then he asked me if I had an office here. When I said yes, he asked me to take him to it. Bill volunteered to lead the way, but Dr. Klein insisted I show him. I assured the good doctor my memory was completely back and showed him into my office. When we got there, he asked if my computer terminal was password protected. When I said yes, he asked me to log in. While I was doing that, he was talking to the others who were with us. When my desktop came up, he was pleased. Everyone but Dan and Dr. Klein had left my office.

"I sent everyone to the breakroom for coffee. I need to be alone with you."

I glanced at Dan. He was still there.

"I need Mr. Patrick's help."

Dr. Klein had Dan and me sit together on the couch. He pulled up a chair from my desk and sat down directly in front of us, our knees practically touching.

"Danielle, you're back, but the question is, are you back for good?"

"What are you saying, Doctor Klein?"

"I'm sure this has a deeper meaning than you realize. There is much more to this than meets the eye. You are hiding something. Hiding it from yourself. It is so devastating you can't face it, so you buried it. Hearing about the plane crash a month ago brought it to the surface, and that frightened you so much you regressed fifteen years, so you would never have to face it again."

"I don't understand. Wasn't the fear of Nick being in that plane what caused this?"

"No. It just brought back another fear you have, a fear you can't face."

"What fear is that?"

"I don't know. But you do. Right now, it's close to the surface. With each day that passes, you'll begin to bury it again, this time much deeper. The plane crash a month ago was just a trigger. There may be other triggers out there, and if you come across one this can happen again, and next time, the result may be worse."

"What can I do?"

"Help me find out what the real problem is."

"Okay. Let me spend a day or two with my husband, and I'll do whatever is necessary."

"Now, Danielle. Right now!"

"You mean here, today?"

"Right here, right now. With every hour that passes, you'll bury it deeper and deeper. It has to be now."

"Dr. Klein, now you know it was the plane crash almost three years ago, wouldn't you know how to get her back if this happens again."

"It's not that simple, Mr. Patrick. It has something to do with that crash, but it's not the crash that's the issue. It's something else. Something that stems from that accident, but not the accident."

"I'm lost, Dr. Klein."

"Look at it this way. Let's say Nick died in that crash. You would be broken hearted. You would be in pain. You would be devastated."

"That I understand."

"Now, let's say you and Nick had a major argument that morning, and the accident report said the crash was due to pilot error because the pilot wasn't paying as much attention to the task at hand as he should have been. How would you feel then?"

"I couldn't live with that guilt."

"So, because you couldn't live with that guilt, you'd bury it, way down deep inside, where it couldn't get to you."

"You think I'm harboring some sort of guilt about that accident?"

"Not necessarily about the crash itself, but something that is involved with the circumstances of the time period."

"And if I don't find out what it is, I can regress again?"

"Possibly, and possibly even worse."

"How do we find out?"

"You let me dig down into your gut and pull it out of you."

"That sounds painful."

"It will probably be very painful, but not physically painful."

"When?"

"The sooner, the better. Right here and now would be best!"

"What are the chances another trigger will bring this on again?" Dan asked.

"No way to know. May happen tomorrow, may never happen. What we don't know about the human mind would fill volumes. But it is possible, and I'd very much like to eliminate that possibility."

"Okay, Doc. What do I have to do?"

"Just talk to me. Answer my questions."

"That's it? Sounds simple enough."

"Yes, simple. But I guarantee it will be painful."

I agreed, and Dr. Klein explained what he was going to do.

"I'm going to start an IV and introduce a drug that will put you in a hypnotic state. I need your friend to hold your hand and keep your arm steady so you don't break off the needle if you get excited. I also think it will help if you have someone you trust close by."

When the IV was in place, and I was as comfortable as I could get, he started the drug flowing into the solution.

"Count with me Danielle, backward from one hundred to zero."

Immediately I got very dreamy. I heard him talking to me, but he seemed far away. The first questions were very personal, and if I hadn't been drugged, I would have been annoyed.

"Danielle, have you ever cheated on Nick. Have you ever lied to him about anything serious that could affect your relationship? Have you ever done anything behind his back, deceived him in any way? "

Of course, the answer to every question was no.

"Has Nick ever cheated on you? Are you absolutely sure or do you have any suspicions? Has he ever lied to you or deceived you? Do you think the reason he flies for his friend so often is because he wants to get away from you or he has a girlfriend in Freeport? Are you really sure, or do you just hope it was true?"

"Did he ever lie to you, or deceive you, even about unimportant things?"

I tried to make Dr. Klein understand I had complete faith in Nick on all matters. He was the most honorable and honest man I had ever met.

"Danielle were you angry Nick flew for his friend?"

"No, Nick loves to fly, and he was always home for dinner."

"You love to fly also, were you jealous?"

"No!"

"Were you happy he would be away all day? Did you have a reason to want him gone? Did you have a secret meeting with someone that day, maybe a secret lover?"

Even though I could feel the affect of the drug, I was getting angry. These were stupid questions. Nick and I had complete faith in each other. We had no secrets between us, and that's what I told the doctor. Then the questions moved on to the morning of the regression. These questions were rough.

"Danielle, that morning, when you heard the news of a plane crash, did you think Nick had died in that crash?"

"Yes!"

"That's not true, Danielle."

"It is true. He was on that plane, and they said no survivors."

"That's not true, Danielle," Dr. Klein said again in a much sterner voice.

"Nick wasn't going to fly that day, you knew that you said, he never lies to you, he never deceives you. You have no secrets between you. He wasn't on that plane, and you knew it. You knew it!"

"He was. He was on that plane, and it crashed!"

"No Danielle," Dr. Klein continued, now shouting at me.

339

"Nick wasn't going to fly that day. After his accident, he said he'd never fly for anyone else ever again. Nick never deceives you. He never lies to you. You know that you believe that."

"He was. He was on that plane, and the Coast Guard said he could only last three days, he was gone. He left me."

"Not that day, Danielle. You never talked to the Coast Guard that day. They couldn't have told you he could only last three days. You knew it wasn't him on that plane. Admit it. Admit the truth!"

"He was, he was. He was gone for five days, he couldn't be alive. He had to be dead."

"Not that day, Danielle. That day he didn't fly, it was the other crash where you thought he was dead, wasn't it. Admit it, Danielle, tell me the truth."

"No, no, no! I had faith, I knew he'd come back to me."

I was bawling now, the tears gushing out of me. I could feel Dan's hand holding my arm.

Dr. Klein pushed harder.

"When, Danielle, when did you realize he was dead? When did you know? When, Danielle, when did you admit to yourself he was gone?"

"No, No, No," I screamed, "he couldn't be dead, he promised never to leave me. I had to have faith. He would come back. He would find a way."

"But you lost faith," Dr. Klein screamed, sounding very angry now. "You lost your faith, and you thought he was dead. You knew he was dead."

"No, I could still feel him, he couldn't be dead."

"When, Danielle, when did you lose faith?"

"I couldn't lose faith, I couldn't."

"But you did, Danielle. Why did you lose faith, why?"

"I couldn't feel him anymore. He was gone. I couldn't feel him," I finally admitted.

"I'm sorry, I'm sorry, I tried to believe. I wanted to believe, but I couldn't feel you anymore!" I cried out to my man, but he wasn't there.

"Nick, please, don't be disappointed in me," I whispered, "Please, I'm sorry!"

Chapter 37 – Back to Being Me

Dr. Klein's voice was strong and firm.

"Breathe Danielle, breathe. Deep breaths. In and out, deeply. Count with me Danielle, count from one to a hundred."

Dr. Klein was counting with me. I felt the drug starting to wear off. As the dream state dissipated, I felt this overwhelming pain. I buried my face in Dan's chest and cried. It was a long time before I could control myself. Dr. Klein handed me a bottle of water and demanded I drink it all. It was over, but I had no idea what had happened.

When I had some semblance of sanity about me, Dr. Klein asked me some more questions.

"Tell me about when you realized that Nick was dead."

I had to think about that. It was a while ago. I tried to recall that exact moment.

"It was the fifth day after the crash. I was washing coffee cups out at the kitchen sink. One cup slipped out of my hand and fell into the soapy water. It sank to the bottom of the sink, and I knew that Nick was gone."

"You never told Nick that you thought he was dead?"

"The only time we ever talked about it was when they were carrying him to the hospital. He was doped up and said that I should have known that he would come back to me at least long enough to tell me he loved me. I didn't want to upset him, so I just agreed with him. We never talked about it again. I totally forgot about it."

"There were at least six people in your apartment. Didn't you think that one of them would tell Nick that you finally had given up on him being found alive?"

"No one knew. I was standing at the sink trying to decide what I was going to say to them when Dan told me that Nick had been found alive. I never got a chance to tell anyone what I was thinking."

Dr. Klein smiled.

"Simply a matter of timing, amazing!"

"I don't understand."

"If you had said out loud what you were thinking, this never would have happened."

"I'm still not sure what happened."

"The bond between you and your husband was so strong you wouldn't allow yourself to believe he was dead. After five days, even you couldn't avoid the truth. You had given up. But, your faith in Nick's promise that he would never leave you was so strong you felt guilty about losing faith in his ability to come back to you."

"I still don't understand, Doctor Klein."

"You were so worried about your husband's condition, you completely forgot that you had lost faith. You really didn't remember. When you heard about the plane crash a month ago, you would have had a momentary fear, and probably a flashback to Nick's accident. But you would have immediately realized Nick couldn't be involved. It should have ended there. But, it didn't.

"You suddenly remembered that you lost faith and thought Nick was gone. The fact of the lost faith by itself wasn't a big deal, but you also realized that you had kept it from Nick for all those years. You had never kept anything from him before, and you couldn't face him. There was no solution. You couldn't continue to keep your secret from Nick, and you couldn't tell him.

"So, you mind decided to forget that you ever knew him. It only remembered the parts of your life that didn't include him. Your mind decided that was the only way you could live with yourself."

"But I've only known Nick for a little over seven years. Why did I regress fifteen years?"

"I think the reason you went to this particular point in time was because you wanted to go to a place when you were happy. And as long as you were getting rid of the trauma in your life, you might as well avoid the trauma of your breakup with Jack Reynolds and go back to the time before it happened."

"But, wouldn't the fact I was going to break up with Jack affect where I landed in time?"

"No, when you landed at that place in time, you had no recollection of anything in the future, so you didn't know you

342

were going to break up with Jack."

It made some sense, but I was still confused. I didn't want to drag this out. I had someone I needed to see, right now.

"Am I cured? Can I see my husband now?"

"Yes and no and yes," Dr. Klein said with a smile, "You're cured, but we still have work to do. There is another underlying problem, and I think it has to do with your relationship with your husband. I believe we can get to it easier than this one because I don't believe this one is a secret. And yes, you can see your husband now! But, my office, ten o'clock tomorrow morning. You and your husband. Don't put this off, Danielle, it's essential."

"My husband doesn't believe in your kind of medicine, doctor."

Dan hadn't said anything since the doctor started the IV.

"He'll be there, Dr. Klein. Remember what he said that first day at the hospital: whatever it takes, and if it takes him going through therapy, he'll do it for this lady."

"Ten o'clock tomorrow. Now, go get your husband and tell him the news."

We went back to the break room and gave everyone the news. Fully back to myself. I thanked Bill for his patience, and I promised to be back at work soon and make up for my absence. Downstairs and into the limo. Thomas held the door as everyone piled in, with me taking up the rear. When I got to the door, Thomas asked, "Where to Ms. Palmer?"

"What was that you said, Thomas?"

"Sorry, Ma'am. I asked where you want to go."

"It's Mrs. Amonti if you don't mind, and I want to go see my husband."

A broad grin spread across his face.

"My apologies, Mrs. Amonti, it's nice to have you back Ma'am."

I looked at this man and remembered the first time I met him and the first time I rode in this limo. I remembered the drive to my apartment after Nick, and I returned from Atlanta. Thomas and I had a long history together.

"Thomas, have I ever told you how much we appreciate you?"

"Yes, Ma'am. Many, many times Mrs. Amonti., You have always been such an elegant lady."

"Okay, Thomas. Drop me off at the NAS offices, the rest of the group goes to the apartment. And Thomas, do you know where Mr. Amonti has been staying?"

"Yes Ma'am, he's been staying with Mr. Antonelli."

Of course, that's where he'd be. Marc has an apartment in the same complex. Nick would be out of my sight, but close enough to be there if I needed him.

"Good. After you drop this bunch off, I'd like you to pick up Mr. Amonti's stuff and bring it home."

"With pleasure Ma'am!"

That earned him a kiss on the cheek and a warm hug. Thomas dropped me off at the NAS offices and headed for my apartment. I strode through the door as if I owned the place. Technically, I didn't. It was the only thing Nick had not put my name on. NAS was for his children, and I was okay with that.

When I arrived on the executive floor, Sara, the gatekeeper, greeted me warmly, but not as warmly as usual.

"Good afternoon, Mrs. Amon... Ms. Palmer."

"Right the first time," I grinned.

Sara looked at me and seeing the big smile on my face, guessed I was back. Tears started to flow, and that surprised me.

"Oh, Mrs. Amonti, we were all so worried about you. We all love you so much. Does the boss know?"

"I'm on my way to tell him now. Conference room?"

"Should I announce you?"

"Don't you dare!"

Sara understood, and I think she also understood the thank you look I gave her as I breezed toward the conference room. Wiping the smile off my face, I took a deep breath and let myself in. The long end of the conference room table faced the door. Nick was at the other end of the table. His kids were sitting along the sides. When he heard the door open, he looked up. Seeing me, he rushed over to where I was standing, just inside the door.

"Danielle is everything all right?"

"I just need a few minutes, we have a few things to talk about."

"Let's go into my office."

"No need, this won't take long, and there's no reason they can't hear it."

We were facing each other, but not looking at each other.

I didn't want him to see my eyes because he'd know immediately I was back. He didn't want to look in my eyes because he knew he wouldn't see what he wanted to see there.

"Is there a problem?"

"I'll say there's a problem."

"I'm sure we can work it out."

"I'm sure we are going to work it out."

"What is it?"

I could hear the pain in his voice. I couldn't do this much longer, it was hurting him. That wasn't my intention.

"The divorce papers, Nick. Everyone tells me you're an honorable man, you keep your word, and you never break a promise!"

"Tell me what you want, and I'll take care of it."

"I want you to keep your promise."

"Which one? I've made so many to you."

"Rule number two, Nick!"

I turned and looked directly at him. When he heard what I had said, his head snapped up, and he finally looked into my eyes.

"You promised it would never end, never, ever end. You promised."

He didn't say a word. He took the few steps over to me and wrapped his arms around me and held me. I put my head on his chest. He placed his face against mine, and I could feel the tears rolling off his checks onto my neck. I don't know how long we stood like that. It could have been a minute, it could have been an hour.

Finally, he pulled back and looked at me.

"How?"

"Later."

He smiled. I turned to the conference table to see five beaming faces watching us.

"I hope you realize this meeting is adjourned."

They all jumped up at once and came over to give us hugs and kisses. It was awkward hugging everyone with one arm. Nick wouldn't let go of my hand, and I didn't want him to. When it was Nick Junior's turn, he pulled back and looked into my eyes.

"I knew you'd be back. I told Dad that much love had to find a way through whatever barrier was trapping it."

That earned him another kiss and a request.

"Would you drive us home, I'm not sure your father is up to it."

He left to get his car and told me he would be waiting out front. I looked at the other four.

"Gather everyone up. Cookies and milk for all at our apartment."

Since we first broke our embrace, Nick never let go of my hand. On the way out, everyone in the office was waiting to see us. No applause, no big deal, just happy smiling faces watching us walk by. When we were settled in the back seat of Nick Junior's car, Nick asked again, "How?"

"It's a long story, and so many people had a hand in it. We have great people in our life. Lindsey, Colleen, Johnny, Dan, Cindy, Terry, Stacy, they were all there for us, for me."

"How do we ever thank them?"

"By being the loving couple, they know we are. That's all the thanks they want."

When we reached the apartment, Andy was so pleased to see us together. Upstairs, Nick finally let my hand go, just long enough to get a hug from everyone. Almost everyone. Dan got a handshake and a long look. It always amazed me how men have this secret language. They can say so much with a look when words aren't enough. There were no words to express what we felt for Dan and the others. Words could never be enough.

Nick and I went into the living room, and he made me sit on his lap, with my legs across the arm of the chair. I wrapped my arm around his neck and felt happy for the first time in over a month. We all talked about the past month and what we were doing here in the apartment. I told Cindy and Johnny their idea of Nick leaving was the key to everything.

I told Nick, while everyone else listened, what I was hiding and why it affected me the way it did.

"I'm sorry I put so much pressure on you to believe everything I said."

But, he was wrong. Our belief in each other was the basis of our entire relationship. It's what made us special. It's why our love was so strong because we did believe in each other.

Nick's kids and grandkids stopped over for a while. Everyone was in town for the meetings at NAS. Nick asked his son to arrange a dinner party at the *Nest*, for the following night.

Everyone was in a great mood. Nick finally let me go, and I wandered into the kitchen to mingle with our friends and family. When I went back into the living room, Nick was gone. Johnny said Uncle Nick was in the bedroom. I opened the door and saw Nick and Cindy sitting on the edge of the bed.

I closed the door to give them some privacy, but when I thought about what could be going on in there, I opened the door again and walked in.

"No Nick! Don't do it!"

"What?" he said, surprised by my sudden appearance.

"Whatever you're thinking about, don't do it."

"I've been trying to tell him it would be insulting," Cindy said.

"He doesn't want anything. He doesn't need anything. Just leave it be, please," I begged.

"But," Nick stammered.

"No buts! That's his wife, don't you think she would know what's best?"

Cindy added, "Please Nick, a handshake is all he needs."

Nick looked at Cindy and then at me.

With a shrug of the shoulders, he finally gave in.

"I yield to the two beautiful ladies!"

Back in the living room, the party was breaking up. Everyone was leaving to give Nick and me some time alone. Colleen, Lindsey, and Johnny were going to *Danielle's Nest* for the night. Dan and Cindy were the last to leave. When we were all at the door, I was sure Nick was going to say something, but he behaved himself and just shook Dan's hand again, and they had another one of those looks pass between them.

Dan looked at his wife and said to Nick, "Even?"

Nick looked at me and after a pause smiled and said, "Even!"

And that was it. Nick had a hand in getting Dan and Cindy together, and Dan had a hand in getting Nick and me back together. I guess Even was all that had to be said.

That night in our bedroom, all we wanted to do was cuddle together. We talked for a while and then fell asleep with me pressed up against him, my arm around his chest and his arm around my shoulder. I slept soundly for the first time in over a month.

My man was home!

Chapter 38 - Back to Normal

The next day, Colleen, Lindsey, and Johnny were back. Nick took Johnny aside for a private conversation. When it was over, they both were sporting great big smiles. Then Johnny came over to me.

"Are you angry with me for the Aunt Sissy thing?"

"Johnny, you can call me anything that pleases you, and after the past couple of days, you can have anything you want from me."

Nick's son called to ask who should be invited, and Nick told him the usual suspects. That meant thirty-five to fifty people. Bob flew in from San Antonio, and Joe came in from Montana. Colleen's boys were in college and couldn't make the party, but Anna Lee would be there.

Nick and I spent the morning talking.

"Nick, I'm sorry for the pain I caused you."

"We have a rule about saying we're sorry, remember. You only have to say you're sorry if you meant to hurt someone."

I had to remind him of the rule later on when he tried to apologize for putting so much pressure on me. During a lull in our conversation, Nick said, "Danielle, I got an unusual request from Terry the other day."

"I'm sorry about that. I just wanted to show Jack I wasn't that stupid, simple girl he always thought I was. I wanted him to know I was somebody."

Nick knew about my relationship with Jack. During our early years together, we had talked about our lives before we met. I didn't think there was anything he didn't know about me and I didn't know about him. Except exactly what he had done for the government, way back when and exactly what his connection was to the two Dons.

"Not a problem. It's already in the works, and I just wanted to make sure you approved. I remember how angry you were the last time."

That made me think. Did I really want to do this? Did I really want to hurt Jack that badly?

"It's not a big deal. It's easy enough. I just want to make sure you can live with the results. There's no question he deserves it."

"I never considered myself a vengeful person."

"It's not vengeance. It's like you said, just letting him know who you are, and he screwed with the wrong woman. Tell you what. It's been started already. Think about it and let me know if you want me to stop it."

At ten o'clock, we were in Dr. Klein's office. The doctor talked to us together. He told us about what had happened to me in more detail and said he didn't think it would be repeated.

He said I had a lot of courage to take the chance I did, and that our love must truly be something special. That got me a look from Nick, and I knew I'd have to tell him about the possibilities.

"Was there anything in particular that caused you to finally lose hope? It's not vital to your condition, but every piece of information I get would help me to better understand exactly what happened."

I didn't have to think about it, I knew exactly what had happened, but it was very personal, and I wanted Nick's approval before I said anything. Nick understood I was hesitating because he was there.

"Whatever it takes, Danielle."

"The very first time Nick and I made love was in Atlanta. After the very first time we had sex, we were side by side on the bed, on our backs and Nick slid his hand over to mine, and our pinkies touched. I know it sounds strange, but ever since that touch, I've always felt a real connection to Nick. Even when we weren't together, I could feel him. That afternoon, while I was washing out the coffee cups, I lost that connection, and that's why I thought he was gone."

"Did that connection ever came back?"

"When we were in *Danielle*, on our way to Pensacola, I felt the connection return."

Nick asked me what time that happened.

"Around one in the afternoon, just about the time, Dan was talking to the Coast Guard. They called and said you were found alive."

"Dr. Klein, do you believe in the paranormal?" Nick asked.

"I neither believe nor disbelieve. Why do you ask?"

"The Hornet pilot found me around ten in the morning. I begged them to call my wife. They told me they would have to go through the Coast Guard. I wouldn't let them give me anything to knock me out until they said she had been notified. Around one o'clock a Corpsman told me the Coast Guard was in the process of calling Danielle, and he gave me an injection that knocked me completely out. The next thing I remember was when they were moving me onto a stretcher for the trip to Pensacola, two days later."

Dr. Klein shook his head.

"Unbelievable. Knowing what shape you were in, I'd assume they put you in a medically induced coma. They'd want to slow down all of your organs until they had a chance to find out if there was any permanent damage. Your brain would still work to keep you alive, but your mind would be shut off. If you believe in that sort of thing, I'd have to say because of the coma, the connection you felt was technically broken."

"I do believe in it, Dr. Klein. And, I feel better knowing there was a reason I felt like the connection was lost."

The doctor did have one more question he said was bothering him.

"Why is it you have no fear when Nick flies *Danielle*, but you worry when he flies anything else?"

I had the answer ready.

"Dr. Klein, if I have any competition for my husband's affection, if I have a rival, it's that airplane. He loves her almost as much as he loves me."

"I don't understand."

"Maintenance, Doc," Nick answered, "I take better care of that girl than I take care of myself. When she's not in the air, she's well taken care of. No commercial airfreight company could afford to look after their aircraft so well."

I added, "I never have any fear when we're flying her, and I never have any fear when Nick is flying her. That *Danielle* would never let her man down."

That night, the party was cheery and fun. Afterward, Nick

and I returned to the apartment instead of staying at the hotel as we usually did after parties. We made love in our own bed. It was the gentle, tender, romantic kind, and afterward, I slept the sleep of angels.

The next morning Nick asked me if I wanted to do anything special. My answer was immediate.

"FLY," I said.

After about a half dozen phone calls, Nick announced, "We'll drop Anna Lee off in Albany, Johnny off at Norfolk and take Joe & Lindsey home. We'll all spend the night in Montana and then take Colleen and Bob back to San Antonio. We can spend the night there and return to Fort Lauderdale the next day. We'll take Jerry and John with us, so we can spend the flight time in the cabin with our guests. Sound okay?"

"It sounds wonderful!"

Life with my man was back to normal. At least as normal as life with this man could be. About two months after I started work again, Crystal buzzed me.

"There's a Jack Reynolds on the phone. He's very nasty and demands to speak to you."

Nick and I never talked about Jack again after our initial conversation, and I had to assume Nick had gone ahead with my threat.

I picked up the phone, and in a very uninterested voice said,

"What do you want Jack?"

Jack was full of venom. He called me every name he could think of. Threatened to sue Nick, me, NAS, Strollman, the world. I let him rant. He finally left room for me to get in a word.

"Jack, I told you what was going to happen. It's not my fault you didn't believe me."

I had the knife in, and I was ready to twist it.

"You could have avoided this. All you had to do was put in an honest forty hours a week, and you still could have made quota. But, you choose to be the same old Jack, doing just enough to get by so you could spend your afternoons finding women to screw over. Sorry, Jack, you should have quit while you were ahead."

I took a breath and continued to twist.

"I got over what happened twenty years ago, but when you found out about my condition, and you decided to screw me over the second time, I thought it was time to let you know you were fucking with the wrong gal."

That brought on more threats and abuse. When I had enough, I interrupted him.

"Jack, when you came to my apartment, and I told you what was going to happen, you didn't believe me. But, it did happen, didn't it Jack, just the way I said it would. Jack, I also told you I had another option. Remember Jack?"

"Don't think you can screw around with me."

"But I did Jack. You know I did. And Jack, if I ever hear from you again, or if I ever hear about you, or if anyone I know is bothered by you, I'll exercise that other option and your screwing days will be over."

"Bullshit!"

"You didn't believe I would do what I did, Jack," I said, as I plunged the knife all the way.

"Don't believe me now at your own risk. Oh, and Jack," I concluded with as much sweetness in my voice as I could muster.

"If I were you, I would get my financial files in order. I have a strange feeling the IRS is about to pay you a visit."

And I hung up.

I never heard from Jack again. I know I'm not a vengeful person, I'm really not, but Jack's phone call made me feel so good I wanted to celebrate. I never wanted to mention Jack's phone call to Nick. I was afraid he would take additional action, but the no secrets rule meant he would have to know. After listening to my account of the conversation, he smiled.

"Feel good?"

I thought about it before I answered.

"I shouldn't, but I really do!"

That earned me a kiss and a smile.

"It's nice to be rich, isn't it?"

"It has its moments," I replied, and that got me a kiss and a hug.

"I do know people at the IRS."

"You wouldn't?"

"Wouldn't I? If anyone deserves it, it's him,"

I know it was a silly question. I knew the kind of man I was married to, but I had to ask.

"Do you often use your money and power in this way?"

He was quick to answer.

"It's difficult not to take advantage of what you have available to you. Do you remember when I got Paterson to cover for you in San Antonio? Also, when I got to the hospital, I made some calls and had Dr. Klein checked out. It's handy, and I've made use of it on other occasions.

But, this type of thing I've only done twice before. You do remember the second charity ball I escorted you to? And the client rep that was fired without notice?"

I did remember, and I knew both had to do with me also. No one is going to screw around with Nick Amonti's woman!

"Should I make the call?"

I never did answer him, ...and Jack never called me again.

Everyone attended Johnny's graduation at the Naval Academy. He graduated in the top twenty-five percent of his class. Not bad for a stupid kid that stuttered. After flight school, his was assigned to the Aircraft Carrier, Theodore Roosevelt. He called it the 'Big Stick' and Nick called it 'TR.' Johnny got his wish, and true to his promise to Anna Lee, he didn't fly fighters or bombers, he flew a cargo plane that he called a COD and Nick, and Colleen's younger son called a trash hauler.

Nick and I finally got a chance to take the Tiger Cruise that was canceled because of my regression. And during that cruise, thanks to Admiral Becker, Nick finally got his wish to Cat & Trap a Super Hornet. He said he would have preferred a Tomcat, but he wasn't complaining. The only bad part about those four days was that Nick and I had to sleep apart.

Some things changed over the years, and some things never changed. Sometimes, I think back to that two-week trip to Cauldwell. If I had never asked Nick to help me with the numbers. If he had never met Anna Lee and Johnny. If Billy hadn't been such an ass, would Nick and I have ever gotten together?

Nick almost never went against his instincts, and they told him a relationship between us was impossible. But, he asked me to marry him in spite of his better judgment. It was the right decision for me, and I believe he always felt the same.

I always wanted to believe we were meant to be together, and nothing was going to keep us apart. Nick didn't believe that. He always believed a strict set of circumstances were necessary for us to find each other, that's why he was willing to divorce me and give me the freedom to be happy without him. He didn't think we could create the magic again.

And it was magic. I can't imagine my life being any other way. If I hadn't regained those lost years, where would I be today? I'm not sure Nick would have agreed to Terry's idea of us dating and getting to know each other all over again. Could I survive if I lost my mostest man?

Epilogue

After our tenth anniversary party, Nick wanted to go back to our apartment instead of staying at *Danielle's Nest*. He had something he wanted to tell me. It was unusual, but I didn't mind. I knew we would definitely use his bedroom that night. It took him a while to get started.

"Danielle, over the years, I have told you everything about my life before we met. All except for one instance."

"I know Nick. I remember you mentioned it and I'm okay with not knowing."

"But, I want you to know everything. I've written a book. It's about those eight months. I can't release it because I have signed a Non-Disclosure Agreement. It explains everything, including why I was given thirty million dollars."

"If you can't disclose it, why did you write about it?"

"I want you to know. My attorney has a key to a safety deposit box. He will give you that key when I'm gone. I will leave it up to you to decide if you want to read it. If you do, it will also be your decision who to share it with. Keep it to yourself. Allow our family and friends see it or publish it. Once I'm gone, the agreement has no force in law."

"Nick, you are an honorable man. Whatever is in that book will never change my opinion of you or my love for the man I know."

Nick smiled and led me into the bedroom. Before we made love, I had something I wanted to say.

"I have had many good men in my life. I was only ten when I lost my father, but from what I remember and what I've been told, he was a good man. Daddy Palmer took two orphaned young girls, brought them into his home, adopted us and made us feel as if we were born to his family.

"Both of my brothers-in-law are good men, and my sisters are extremely happy with them.

"I can't imagine what my life would be like today if it weren't for Dan Patrick. A friend who was there for me at the most crucial times of my life.

"Charlie and the guys at Deltron were always encouraging me to push ahead, and they were always there with whatever I needed. Bob Peterson gave me a chance to shine, and never lost faith in me when one of my projects didn't go as planned."

I looked into Nick's eyes, and in the sincerest voice I had, I told him exactly how I felt.

"But, you my love, are still the mostest man I have ever met, and I will always love you!"

Need I tell you what happened next?

####

Books by: Nick J Mercorella

Danielle and Friends Series

The Mostest Man
The Last Dance
The Front Porch
The Lieutenant Commander
The Cauldwell Incident
The Promotion – In Progress
A Better Man – In Progress
Sadie's Dream – In Progress

The Adventures of Riley Series

Murder One
Finding A Killer
Deception – In Progress

In the Works

Eight Months in Hell - A Terror Thriller - Available 2018

If you have comments for me, please e-mail me at:
NAS_Books@yahoo.com

Or, visit my website:
https://NAS-Books.com

From the Author

I hope you enjoyed this story. I enjoyed writing it. If you did, please take a minute to write a review. Reviews are the lifeblood of authors. They are the way other readers make decisions on what they will read. At this stage of my writing career, reviews are more important than sales.

If you did enjoy this story, I urge you to check out the 'Danielle and Friends Series'. Each book is about a different couple, but they are all connected to each other in some way. They are each about true love overcoming obstacles to the relationship, each in its own way.

At present, there are five romance stories in the Danielle and Friends Series. Three additional books are in progress. The original story in the series is The Mostest Man. It sets the tone for all the others, and Nick and Danielle appear in each story.

I am also working on the story of what Nick Amonti did for the government that earned him the $30,000,000 stake that started NAS Financial Group. It's a Terrorist Thriller.

The Adventures of Riley series is based on one of the secondary characters in The Front Porch. Murder One is the first book in that series.

Thank you for taking the time to read my stories. I hope you continue to check out my work. If you have comments for me, please e-mail me at:

NAS_Books@yahoo.com

Or, visit my website: https://www.NAS-Books.com

Nick J Mercorella

About the Author

Born and raised in Brooklyn, New York, I have had a interesting if not profitable life. Married twice, divorced once, widowed once. Two wonderful children of my own and five more I inherited when I married for the second time.

I worked in management most of my life when I wasn't operating my own business. Had the opportunity to travel a great deal throughout our beautiful country, parts of Canada and Mexico and some of the islands of the Caribbean. I've visited 40 states and uncountable cities. Never been to Europe, Asia or Africa. Don't feel like I've missed much. Might like to visit Australia, though.

Coldest I've ever been was in Halifax, Nova Scotia in February. Hottest I've ever been was in Phoenix, Arizona in July. I've been in Salt Lake City in June when the sun didn't set until after nine o'clock at night. I've seen the Sierra Mountains from the observation car of a train. Sailed aboard a United Sates Nuclear powered aircraft carrier, twice. Never been in the military, but I respect all those who serve. Flown hundreds and hundreds of thousands of miles. Love to fly, but poor eyesight prevents me from qualifying for a pilot's license.

Now, I sit in Fort Lauderdale Florida thinking about love and writing Romance Novels. Not a bad way to spend my retirement years